Michelle,

Thank you for sharing light with me. Without the confidence of love emanating from you & Rob, I couldn't do this writer thing.

The Broken Veil

A Dragon Bitten Novel

By Rayna L. Stiner

Thank You!

Rayna L. Stiner

Tagorbi Publishing, LLC

The Broken Veil, A Dragon Bitten Novel

Printed in the United States of America

ISBN-10:099679591X

ISBN-13:978-0-9967959-1-3

Cover Design: Lynn Mackey

Visit raynalstiner.com to learn more about the author and her other works.

Join the conversation at facebook.com/raynalstiner or tweet the author with @rlstiner.

ACKNOWLEDGMENTS

Writing a book requires a tribe effort. I cannot do this without the amazing support of my wonderful family – and the word 'family' extends to friends. My partner is truly that: a partner. He has given me time, patience, love, support and also shared his incomparable imagination with me. He is my inspiration and my rock.

To Danny and Anthony: for being an inspiration of love and evolvement to become better people, and for your kindness in reading my work in all its roughness.

To Fran, Dan and Penney for their continued moral support and exceptional beta-reading skills: there are not enough cookies in the world to make up for your support.

To my best friend, Rachel: for not only provided caring encouragement, but a sense of belonging in sharing our common craziness and love for life.

To all the other friends, coworkers, family members and Twitter friends: THANK YOU! Every ounce of cheerleading has made a difference.

To my kickstarter backers, thank you for your support!

Fran & Dan, Danny & Anthony, Josh, Gerry, Matthew, Michelle, Leanne, Sharon, David, Jannine, Penney, Randy, Susie, Anne, Heather, Dave & Noelle, Donna, Kara, Matt & Brandi, Louise, Lynn, Jesse, Shelley, Monika, Chris, Sue, Dave, Allyson, Lyndon, Stephanie, Brian, Caryn and Kimmi!

ONE ~ RORI - HIKING, APRIL 2004

It was hard to say which emotion would win the wrestling match in my gut: disappointment or embarrassment. I needed that job and now it was gone for good. I bit back the mixture of terror, shame and sorrow building into tears and growled instead. Nobody would hear it out here in my North Carolina woods except for my twin, Andy, who was behind me on the path. Maybe some of the more exotic residents could hear me, but they wouldn't care.

I reached the top of a grueling hill and waited for Andy. His auburn crown peered back at me from where he was still climbing. Wuffers, my black wolf Labrador, or Wolador, trotted past him and to me, panting far less than my brother. I ruffled the fur on the top of her head and scratched behind her ear. She peered up at me with orange eyes, smiling to reveal her wolfy canines.

Spring had sprung and the vegetation was budding with new life. The air smelled like sunshine and leaf litter and empty acorn shells. I sucked in a long, deep breath and let it soothe my mood. Andy finished the climb, stood beside me and wiped at his glistening brow.

"Whoo," he managed. His head shook in a slow back and forth motion that said to me, "no, this is so not fun." Wuffers whined and bumped my hand with her head. I scratched at her fur absently.

"Okay, bro'?"

"Oh yeah, just, ya know, trying to not die." He emphasized the word "die". I chuckled and slapped his arm. He clapped a hand to the spot and made an "ow" face.

"Maybe you need to get out more," I said and stretched a quad. The warm pull was delicious.

"Well. Med school," he explained with a shrug. He was visiting me for spring break. I switched to the other leg. "So, now quit trying to kill me with mountainous hills and talk to me. What's going on? Why did they let you go?" He pursed his lips, tilting his head down so I could catch the full effect of his mismatched stare. Our eyes were the same: one an animal gold color, the other sea-green.

"Just couldn't do it," I said, unwilling to say more. I crossed my arms. He looked confused for a moment and I thought I'd have to explain. My thumbnail found its way to my mouth and I chewed. Understanding dawned on his face and he nodded.

"I can understand that." The last time I'd been at work was months ago and I'd lost my baby there. Walking in today had been... an experience. I'd barely made it through the door before I started hyperventilating. The memories slapped me in the face. I couldn't take it. I'd simply walked out again. The owner had called me on my cell an hour later and apologized that he'd have to take me off the schedule. So, here I was: hiking, working my other job, instead of whipping clients into shape.

"I'm sorry, sis. It'll be okay though. You'll find another job." He took out the water from the waist pack I'd loaned him. The bottle made a glug-glug noise as he slurped down the cold liquid, his eyes watering after a few seconds.

"Jameson wants me to stay home," I said experimentally before sticking my thumbnail back into my mouth. My husband had recommended that reducing the workout routine by staying home might be the trick to our pregnancy issue. An issue I'd flat avoided after the last miscarriage. "I can't afford the fancy fertility specialist if I don't have a job though."

"It might be worth a shot to take it easy while you try again," Andy said way too casually for my taste. He looked down, his eyebrows arched as he flicked an invisible particle of dust from his college sweatshirt – which coordinated with his black athletic pants striped with purple.

"I can't do it," I breathed, my cheeks burning. I crossed my arms over my torso and gripped my shoulder. I rocked from left to right and back again. "Do you have any idea what it's like to have something living inside of you and then see its spirit leave?" My heart trilled in a collection of staccato percussions that obeyed no metronome. Meanwhile my brain flipped through the images of that day.

"Oh, sis," he said and wrapped me in a hug. "I'm sorry. It's going to be okay."

"How can you say that? You don't know. I have no proof that it will be. I'm a failure at this."

"Rori," Andy took my shoulders and looked me in the face. "It's going to be okay. You'll see. Take a deep, slow breath." I obeyed, shaking away the embarrassment creeping up in me.

"Okay, okay. I'm okay." He released me. I righted myself, pulling my body into a straight line and shaking back my hair.

"Good," he drawled. "Glad you're back with us." He opened his mouth to say something else, but then, his eyes went out of focus and his eyebrows nettled. I knew that look. I jerked my head around, looking, listening and smelling.

"What is it?" I asked. Wuffers whined and trotted off trail. Whatever had triggered Andy's abilities was upwind so my nose gave me nothing. I can smell about half as good as my wolador, which is really something compared to most humans. I couldn't do what Andy was doing right now: listening with another set of ears to the thoughts of creatures.

"Well, I'd say it's something smaller and it feels... hurt. It's in pain. She's in pain," Andy explained to me after a while.

I closed the door on the ache in my soul and was rewarded with a numb curiosity for the creature's danger. Oh sure, being a personal trainer might have been my day job, but this was my real job and I loved it. I was made for it. Unlike being made for making babies. I guessed I wasn't made for that.

I wiped hastily at my face and headed into the trees. Andy strode forward, silent as a snake through the leaves. He had grace where I had strength. He reached the skirting trees of a small clearing and paused. From behind him, I could see his head tilt before he looked back and pointed to a moss-covered log.

I opened my mouth and pulled air softly over my tongue, using the acute sensors to gather chemicals floating around me, and then pressed it to the roof of my mouth. The taste filtered up, transferring as scent to my nose.

I shuffled through the leaf litter, stepping carefully over a collection of spindly tree roots to stand next to my twin. "Dreamcatcher," I whispered to Andy. He nodded. The air didn't just smell like dreamcatcher. It also smelled like blood. I closed my left eye and looked into the forest with the right one – the one that could see the kind of creatures whose protection was my charge.

Wuffers stalked the opposite side of the clearing. The soft huff of the creature's breath pricked my ears. Guided by the sound, I caught sight of the telltale black fluff of the dreamcatcher peeking from under the felled tree. The creature wasn't much smaller than my wolador.

My left sea-green eye opened and nausea washed over me. I let the rolling of my stomach subside, slightly put off by its intensity. My mundane eye saw nothing near the log. It slid over the spot, refusing to focus on what the right golden eye knew was there.

Andy put a hand on my shoulder and followed suit, closing his right, mundane sea-green eye, watching the dreamcatcher scrabble for a moment before opening it again. After a pause, in which I felt his body sway, he released me and moved softly into the clearing, whispering soothing words to the animal.

He was always better with approaching creatures. They were drawn to him in a way I hadn't inherited through the passing of our very unique genetic makeup. Wuffers approached slowly at the sound of Andy's deep, quieting whispers of comfort. She lay down near the dreamcatcher, lowering her head to her paws. Andy knelt near the log and the injured dreamcatcher. I shuffled into the clearing and stood behind Andy, giving him the closest proximity to the creature. In the patch of sunshine leaking into the forest, the air warmed. I hiked up the sleeves of my black workout jacket and unzipped it partway to cool the skin on my neck and chest.

The dreamcatcher had wedged itself in a dip in the ground under the fallen tree. Andy looked up at me. "Little help?"

"You betchya." I knelt down next to the log. Pressing my hands into the rough bark, I pushed against it. My muscles strained against the effort. The log rolled slowly back, groaning for having been woken from its slumber. The moist underside wriggled in a collection of worms and beetles. Andy backed away from it until the bugs had scurried.

The creature nestled in the earth looked from me to Andy. The two largest of its eight blue eyes glinted like sapphires dropped in a well. The eyes took up most of the soft, rounded square head that hovered between two of its many legs. It had a set of antennae perched above its eyes that looked like an expanse of overly long and curled eyelashes.

The dreamcatcher was flat on its thorax and head, its legs pushed close to its body as if it were trying to make itself smaller. Anyone with arachnophobia would probably have a full on panic attack with the sight of a dreamcatcher because of its size. Smaller than Wuffers, but bigger than a house cat. Luckily, the veil spell kept them hidden from those who could misunderstand them.

If normal people could hear them, they would be comforted by the hush of its breath. Its exhalations sounded exactly like the lull and crash of an ocean tide. It looked up at Andy through its antennae, its two front appendages covered in black fur wiped at the side of its reddish orange head.

"Aren't you just the cutest?" Andy crooned, hunched forward and surveying the animal with calculating eyes.

I peered at it closer from over Andy's shoulder. A long, gaping wound opened the creature's head and sliced through the eye to the right of the biggest set. An injury to a dreamcatcher seemed odd. They usually found a place to gather the dreams of the sleeping and stayed there. It was a mutually agreeable arrangement. The sleeper was protected from nightmares and the dreamcatcher captured the dreams in their web, stored them and fed from the dream energy.

"What do you think happened?" I asked. Andy pulled out his second, full water bottle and poured a bit of it into a cupped hand. He shut his eyes and closed his fingers on the liquid. He inhaled and exhaled slowly. His champagne skin, owing to our very old Native American roots mixed with Irish, soaked in the sunshine.

"It's not a natural wound," Andy said. I waited while he continued his slow inhale and exhale. "Someone did this. A person."

"Why? Who could see - ?" I stood, looking around for the perpetrator, as if he was there and I'd simply overlooked him.

"Whoever it was is gone now, Rori," Andy said. I slowly crouched back down. Andy's eyebrows nettled. "Okay, now be quiet so I can focus."

"Yeah, yeah. Do that thing you do," I said and settled into trying to be quiet and not impatient. Who would hurt a dreamcatcher purposefully? And how? The only people who could see them were me, Andy and Mom. Mom wouldn't hurt a creature. She was as much a protector as me. I shifted in the dirt. Andy's hand glowed with a soft blue light that pulsed, escaping the chinks of his closed hand.

He opened his eyes and reached toward the dreamcatcher. She shifted away. I scooted closer on my knees and captured her by the abdomen. She didn't fight, but her breath wheezed a little quicker under my fingers.

Andy shuffled closer, his knees swish-swishing through the dirt and dead leaves. He reached forward and opened his hand over the wound. The light bathing his palm dripped into the wound, the blue hue sparkling and iridescent as it nestled into the open flesh. The dreamcatcher tried jerking away, but with my firm grip she didn't move. "Shh…" Andy whispered, "this will be all better in just a moment." Before he could even finish his sentence the gap soaked in the blue light and began to fill with flesh and eye material. The goop and blood mixed and mashed until it was completely reconstructed and the dreamcatcher stopped wriggling and stilled.

I crab crawled to the front of the creature and took a look at my brother's handiwork. It was as if nothing had happened. "Nice," I said, and held up my knuckles to him, which he bumped with his own.

"Thanks," he said shyly. "You know, I think it helps having an understanding of anatomy."

"I wish you'd consider coming back when you're done with med school." I just couldn't heal creatures the same way. If he were here, he could help with that. He didn't answer, but the sudden chill to my left gave me a clear indication of his thoughts about moving back home. "I know you have good reasons to stay in Washington." I dropped it. He didn't need pressure from me.

"Rori, are you paying attention?" I wasn't. I looked at him and he gestured to the dreamcatcher. It reached a furry leg toward me, its big, deeply sapphire eyes wide and glinting. The dreamcatcher purred like the trill of a bird and the hum of crickets. It half-closed its eyes and almost seemed to smile. Then, it relaxed until it was lying down and retracted its leg.

"What was that?" I asked, looking to Andy for creature reading abilities.

"Sorry, sis, the healing leaves me fuzzy for a bit afterwards. I couldn't catch it."

"Well, can I pass that good juju on to you? Because you're the one that did the healing."

"Maybe it wasn't about that."

"What then?" I asked. Andy shrugged, his eyebrows rising before they rested and he smiled at me. "What's that look for?"

"You seem different today." He crossed his arms over his sweatshirt and cocked his head to one side.

"Could it be the depression and disappointment shining through? Mixed with a little unemployment?" I tried to keep the hurt out of my voice, but I don't think it worked. Andy ignored it though.

"No," he said and huffed. He looked me over with a dissecting mismatched gaze. "It's something, though."

I shrugged. "Been a weird day so far. It's probably just that. Let's walk a little ways more up the trail. I want to check out the rest of the property." Was it possible to hike this day away? I wasn't sure, but I'd try.

We traveled northwest on the trail cutting through the trees for another half mile before it took a dive south and closer to the lake. As the trail began to dip, Wuffers trotted past me. Her ears strained forward, nose weaving back and forth, head extended.

"What's she got up her nose?" I wondered out loud. Andy watched her as she wended up the dirt path.

"She smells something new," he told me.

Ahead of us, Wuffers stopped in the path. She padded forward and with each step her hackles sprang to life. "What's going on?" I asked, never tearing my gaze from my wolador.

"I think there might be someone on your property." My hand reached for the knife strapped to my thigh.

"Hunters?" I asked aloud, but the wounded dreamcatcher popped into my head. I ran down the trail, climbing the slight incline with ease. The trees whipped by me until I skidded to a halt by Wuffers. She growled as she looked into the peeling trunks of yellow birch and bare, twiggy legs of hemlock. The hair on my arms and legs sprang to attention. My spine tingled.

"Rori, wait!" Andy's voice jostled as he ran toward me. I barreled into the woods, readying myself for a confrontation. Undergrowth clawed at my black workout pants. I had no subtlety; the crunching of twigs and pinecones under my feet gave me away.

I followed the direction of my wolador's trained gaze. The air cooled with each step. Mist caressed my skin. The scent of water and wintergreen from the birch washed over me. Of course, even charging in I knew where I was. If a hunter were on this part of my property he would soon become the hunted.

It wasn't just my job to protect creatures hidden by the veil to normal people. It was our job to protect the normal people from stumbling into (and possibly getting eaten by) the creatures that had resided in the Appalachian Mountains since before the first people started populating this end of the earth. Whoever was on my property was in for a surprise.

I raised my nose to the air, picking through scents to identify who was out there. A whiff of the trespasser stopped me dead in my tracks. Recognition caught up to my blind charge.

That was no ordinary hunter.

TWO ~ RORI - NEWS

The pull of a bowstring interrupted my frantic search through the claws of barren tree limbs. Adrenaline burst through my system. I dove over a thicket of bare blackberry bushes as an arrow whizzed toward me. A blaze of pain tore through my back muscle. Rolling through leaf litter, acorn shells bit into the now burning skin on my back.

Staying low to the ground, I scrambled to the trunk of a nearby oak, tucking myself behind it for cover. After one drawn out breath, my heart rate slowed back to something that didn't feel like a caged animal trying to break itself free. When I trusted my voice to not waiver with nerves, I shouted to my dog: "Wuffers, stay!" Fear crawled on spindly legs across every inch of my skin. "Andy, you stay too!" The smell of our trespasser triggered a parade of unwelcome memories. I knew who had injured the dreamcatcher and chided myself for missing the obvious. There was one other person we knew who could see past the veil. See past it and intended harm to the creatures protected by it. Andy couldn't be faring much better than me with the recognition of the trespasser. I couldn't sense his mood, but I knew my brother well enough.

"Staying!" Andy shouted. "Rori, he's Ani'Kutani." Of course, he would have sensed the Ani'Kutani's power. I had to use my nose. His voice broke and I knew he was seeing the same memories as me, only from a far worse perspective. Dragon venom exploded through my blood stream, ignited by the anger called up from days long gone.

"What are you doing here?" Dragon voice laced my words, expanded over the afternoon air, cut through the weak sunshine angling into the trees. The question was rhetorical. It didn't really matter what he wanted with the power he'd gain from killing one of the most powerful creatures of myth. Silence teased at my anxiety. I risked a look over my shoulder. His camo might have hidden him, but he couldn't hide his aura from my Sighted, golden eye. The murky red and black pulsed in a man-shaped blob of color, perched in a tree some twenty feet away. The color blob shifted and I ducked behind the oak again.

"I should have known." My ears perked, taking in the drawl of his words. It was a different southern accent than we had in North Carolina. Georgian, I was pretty sure. We all had a slightly different twang. He also sounded tired. I wondered how long he'd been up in that tree. "Of course there would be a Bitten near the Velith."

"You haven't answered my question." I rose out of my crouched position and sidled to the other side of the tree trunk. I searched the ground for something I could toss at him to get him out of that tree. A largish rock protruded from the earth, but it was some five feet away and well out of my reach. Taking in the rest of my surroundings, I tilted my head up. Turning, I judged the distance, crouched and leapt. My outstretched hand latched onto a tree branch hanging by a few splinters. On the fall, I yanked, straining my muscles, feeling the fibers expand with dragon venom. The tree groaned and snapped as the limb came free.

I hefted it experimentally. It was as big around as my arm and about as long and probably twenty pounds. My shoulder muscles tensed as I raised the limb up to chin level. Air moved in slow and steady through my nose. It glided down my throat, filling my lungs with life, calming my emotions.

Wuffers whined then yipped. I opened my mouth to the air. It smelled like the Ani'Kutani had accomplished what he'd set out to do. He'd called the creature living in the nearby lake to him. The scent gave me a good indication of where the Velith, or underwater panther was. She wouldn't attack me. Whether she understood I was her protector or not, she understood I was dominant because of the Uktena's venom in my veins.

Still, I thanked all the powers in the universe that she was in front of me and not stalking up my backside.

"Oh... Um, Rori?" Andy warned. Biting back the desire to hiss away his warning, I looked through the trees to the path where Andy knelt next to Wuffers, peering out from behind a boulder. Our eyes met and I pressed a finger to my lips. He made an 'oh' face then nodded his understanding. Andy could sense creatures and I could smell and hear them. An Ani'Kutani could call them, but their senses weren't like mine and Andy's. Paul Burning, son of the man that had abducted Andy and me when we were eight, wouldn't know the Velith had come ashore.

"She's sick," Paul said, his voice cracking with desperation, anger hardening his words. "We need that Velith's copper." The underwater panther had a tail barbed in copper and it could heal almost anything. Maybe an underwater panther could choose to heal someone, but ol' Burning wasn't going to ask the Velith nicely if she would be so kind as to make better whoever it was that was ill.

"You're breakin' my heart. So, take one life to save another? Why don't you go to a doctor? Like a normal person." The Velith was getting closer to Paul. If I could keep him distracted long enough I could throw the branch, knock him out of the tree and let the Velith do the rest. It seemed like a very tidy plan to me.

"You spoiled bitch. It's so easy being you, isn't it?" *That's it,* I thought, *just a little closer.* My acute hearing could make out the gentle stealth of the panther's movement through the bracken, although she wasn't in my line of sight.

"Easy?" I baited. "Yeah, let's talk about easy when you've been nearly sacrificed at the age of eight." I stayed my anger, so close to the surface. I wouldn't speak of Andy's horrors. They were his and not mine to share. Speaking them or not, they ripped away at my insides, leaving a hollow, trembling need to avenge him, even though I had killed his assailant. The feel of the man's neck muscles giving way to my teeth, filling him up with venom, surged through my memory banks and made my mouth water. Never had such a horrible thing thrilled me, yet left me drenched in shadow.

"Nearly. Too bad my father didn't succeed. Too bad I was orphaned that day. And yet, your mother survived."

"Excuse me," I had him off-guard. The Velith was in a perfect position. "My father was killed too that day."

"Tit for tat," he said tightly. I stepped to one side, pulled back the branch and launched it forward. It sailed through the air, perfectly aimed. Burning's dark eyes widened over a set of high cheekbones. His mouth opened like a goldfish, revealing a mouthful of jumbled teeth. He looked a lot like his father. The branch landed neatly in the center of his chest. He'd pulled the bowstring, an arrow nocked. Released from the impact, it sailed impotently through the air, landing without so much as burying the head into the moist earth.

Burning fell from the tree. The yowl of the underwater panther reverberated through the woods, the sound a mix between a cat's cry and a whale's call. I could see it through the bracken. That is, my right eye could see it. I pressed a hand to the trunk of the oak and let the wash of nausea sweep over me. The tree proved not to be enough.

Caught off guard by the sudden rush of vertigo, I leaned over and puked into the bushes, my stomach muscles contracted to empty it of the protein shake I'd slurped down earlier. I tried splitting my attention, listening to what was going on with Burning and the panther. A cold sweat broke over me as I fought to regain control of my body.

"Rori, are you okay?" Andy called. I coughed and spat out the rest of my curdled smoothie. Using my red workout jacket, I wiped at my mouth.

"That's new," I said. Why the split vision was causing so much of an issue today, I didn't know. Stress, maybe?

I turned to catch up on the action and found myself face to face with the Ani'Kutani. The knife in his hand, held at arm-length sliced out at me. Unsteady still, I dodged away, faltered on a branch and tumbled to the ground. Air whooshed out of me. Stars flitted in my periphery. I looked up from where I'd landed, fighting to engage my empty lungs. Burning turned his back to me and moved toward the panther. Feet shushed over the forest floor. Andy knelt down beside me, helping to pull me up into a crouching position.

"I thought I told you to stay." I said.

"You looked like you needed a hand." He grunted as he finished helping me up. I swayed, but managed to push him behind the girth of the oak tree. He huffed at me, but stayed.

The Velith stood in the small clearing, her black fur glistening with moisture from the lake. Her neon green eyes locked onto the Ani'Kutani. Beside me, Andy peered around the tree and covered his mundane eye.

Wuffers paced behind us and whined. I didn't blame her. The underwater panther was a predator and she adored the blood of mammals, wolfdogs included. She was three times the size of my wolador and had three sets of muscular legs that made her fast and graceful.

The Velith padded a couple of steps to the right, the full length of her overly long body stretched out in front of us, a show of how big and bad she was. Behind her, a tail as long as her body whipped back and forth, the copper reflecting sunshine. She had no ears, but ear holes. Her head lifted, the flaps of her nostrils opening and closing around the air scented with the odor of Ani'Kutani, wolador and Dragon Bitten. Her head shifted to the side and she peered around Burning and into my eyes. Her gaze widened as she took half a step forward. Behind me Andy's breath hitched, making a soft noise of surprise.

Seeing the Velith distracted, Paul lifted a hand encompassed in a living shadow. He squeezed the squirming darkness, raised his fist to shoulder level and flung it toward the panther. Her gaze on me broke and darted toward the Ani'Kutani. She tried to dodge, but her reaction was too late. The shadow caught her in the middle, wrapping her up in a darkness only distinguishable against her black hide by the way it sucked away light, instead of reflecting it. Inky fingers spread from the main shadow toward the ground, latching into the earth and yanking the giant creature of myth and legend to prostration. She howled, the warbling frustration echoing away from the clearing.

Snarling, I pushed myself up from the crouched position and launched toward Paul Burning. My feet touched down twice, right then left. My right hand flexed into a fist, short fingernails biting into my palm. Paul turned in time to catch the blow to his jaw. He fell hard to the ground and skidded through dead leaves and dirt and broken twigs. I stepped toward him while he pushed his upper body up and spat blood. I pulled the knife from my thigh holster and held it ready.

"You're trespassing here. Leave now, or I'll kill you where you stand." And I would, I realized. It was only the leftover stain from my first murder that stayed my hand. To take a life, even in defense of someone you love, scars the soul. I didn't want that.

"You keep me from this Velith and you can count on me evening the score." The underwater panther's copper-barbed tail flicked in my periphery. Paul gestured with his own knife toward me. "Starting with that babe in your belly."

"I'm not pregnant," I hissed, but inside my thoughts raged. I mentally scoured the calendar for my last period. My insides trembled at the thought. Elation, but mostly fear sank into my bones. No. Not again. I couldn't lose another baby.

"Oh, that's great," he said and pushed himself to standing. I readied my stance, but my arms were more like wet noodles. "You don't know. Well, you can save your money on an EPT now, darlin'. I can see her aura even at such an early stage." Then, it kicked in. The fierceness that made me Dragon Bitten, the need to protect those weaker than me, the whole purpose of my being sparked, caught fire and blazed. He dared threaten me. He dared threaten my child.

"Pregnant or not, I'm gonna kick your ass back to Georgia." Dragon voice rattled through the air. The trees and ground rumbled from the thunder of my yell. Paul lashed out at me with his knife. I blocked with my own knife hand and delivered a powerful blow to the center of his gut. His body lifted from the ground, the sound of air flying from him hissed into my ear.

He smelled of earth and liquor and that other odor I couldn't quite place. The same odor of his father. The only thing I could identify it with was charred flesh. It burned my nose and made me recoil. I pulled back for another blow. He grasped at something under the neckline of his mud green shirt. As my fist plunged toward him he muttered a single word and vanished in a blur of blackened aura. My hand went through nothing and I tumbled off balance, catching myself before falling.

I twisted right then left, searching the trees for the Ani'Kutani, but he was long gone. My breath heaved in frustration and confusion. In front of me the underwater panther lifted from the ground, released from the power Paul Burning had bound her with. My gaze swiveled toward her and I grit my teeth from the nausea from my disjointed vision.

She fixed me with her neon eyes, padded slowly toward me, her head low in submission. "What's going on, Andy?" I asked him, hoping his creature senses were back in play after the healing he'd done on the dreamcatcher. The panther had never approached me before.

"Well, sis. It appears that the Ani'Kutani was right." I tried to let that sink in. It didn't. It couldn't be. I wasn't ready for that. Tears were bubbling somewhere inside me, but the lid was firmly in place. I danced from foot to foot.

"Okay, but why is the panther coming toward me?" I asked a little desperately.

"As far as I can tell," he began, coming a little closer, Wuffers tucked behind him. "It's a blessing of sorts. Like a – " he cut his eyes away while he thought. I looked back to the oncoming panther. She was five feet from me, her head bowed, her eyes closing. She reached out one giant webbed paw and lowered inch by inch until her long body was resting on all three pair of her muscular legs and belly to the ground. "Like paying homage to the next Bitten, who I would say, appears to be pretty special." I looked at Andy. He smirked with one side of his mouth and crossed his arms over his UW sweatshirt. "So, now I know what's different about you today." It was just too much to take in. My body trembled as I holstered the knife.

The panther rose, closed the gap between us, sniffed at me a couple of times then gently butted her ginormous head into my belly and purred. The sound rumbled through me, rattling my bones and pushing away the nervous jitters that shook me. I stood for a long moment like that, unmoving, letting the purr soothe me like a glass of wine warms the cold of a bad day.

Tentatively, I lifted my hand. I would never get this opportunity again. I touched her fur. My fingers slid over it like silk. It was the softest thing I'd ever felt. When she didn't move, I stroked her head with the full length of my hand and nearly giggled when her purr deepened.

After a moment, she pulled away from me, turned and sauntered toward her underwater home. I watched her go, the muscles undulating under her ebony fur, legs moving in rhythm with each other, tail trailing behind, the copper bobbing on its end. My body and head felt empty of anything but the lasting effects of the purr's vibrations through me.

I waited until my sensitive ears heard the splash of her paws on the nearby lakeshore before I sank onto a nearby fallen log. Wuffers trotted up to me, tongue lolling before she shoved her nose under my hands and into my lap. Orange eyes peered expectantly at me. I patted her and she wagged. Andy sat down beside me and wrapped an arm around my shoulders.

"Well. Congratulations, sis," he said a little uncertainly.

I didn't bother trying to feel happy. I couldn't feel anything except dread. Miscarriage after miscarriage played through my mind in a hiccupping succession of sorrow. Not only was I not ready for try number four, but finding out from my mortal enemy was just too much. "So, now that blood-thirsty jerk has it out for my embryo?" My mouth felt like a mushy mess around the word "embryo". My last child's spirit hovered in my mind's eye, a happy, bouncing bubble of rainbows that drifted away. I couldn't do it again. My mind wouldn't accept it. "What am I going to do?"

"Hey," he said. "It's going to be okay. He comes back for you, you'll just kick his ass again, right?" He missed the point. I wasn't afraid of Paul Burning.

I wondered how many months this pregnancy would last. Would it progress to delivering stillborn? In my mind, I picked a name that would be etched on a gravestone and chose the color of an infant-sized casket.

THREE ~ RORI - CATALOOCHEE, OCTOBER 2004

The phone sang out in a series of electronic beats. I walked – okay, I waddled - around the four poster bed to the base where the cordless sat charging. Sunlight spilled in through the sliding glass door that led to the balcony. I pushed the green button on the phone. It answered with a short beep as I pressed it to my ear.

"Hello?" I asked.

"Hi Rori," came a man's voice on the other end.

"Hi Josh." A smile crept across my face. I eased back against the bed to relieve the pressure aching in my lower back. Dragon Bitten or not, being nine months pregnant was no picnic. I looked out the glass door crested with more windows, which afforded us impressive views of the Smoky Mountains.

Josh Mooney was one of those people that lit up a room when he walked in. He was also one of the few people that knew the same secrets I did. "How's my favorite Medicine Man?"

"You can't see it, but I'm blushing now. Your favorite? D'ya mean it?"

"Absolutely!" I returned. "The best, the brightest, the youngest – "

"The buffest and most handsome and charming –"

"Whoa now. Let's not get carried away." He spluttered in indignant surprise.

"Ouch!"

"So, what do you want? You need me or Jameson?" I brushed away some lint on the black bedspread and fussed with the blue maternity shirt draping the bulge that housed my daughter. Josh and Jameson were buds. I had grown up with Josh, but when I had met Jameson and brought him around to the people I know and love, they had immediately bonded.

"Today, I need you," he answered and the tone of his voice dropped all the silly playfulness it carried moments earlier. I sobered, the smile on my face falling. I stroked my belly as the familiar tickling of anxiety's fingers tapped my nerves.

"What's up?" I asked.

"The stone is acting up. There's a disturbance in the force." I half smiled. Josh just couldn't be serious for any length of time.

"What do you think it is?" I skipped past the joking part, not wanting to get him sidetracked.

"I dunno," he said and I could see in my mind his wide blue eyes going wider as his shoulders shrugged and slumped again, probably clad in a flannel, unbuttoned to reveal a worn undershirt. "It's sort of glowing white and the red stripe is pulsing from dull to bright."

"Well, you're a lot of help."

"It's not like a mood ring. I can't check the convenient chart it came with to tell me if it's angry, sad or in love." The Ulunsuti had to be kept by someone other than a Bitten. It was like a checks and balances. The stone, being a piece of the original Uktena that had changed us forever, enhanced the venom that coursed through us. It was power overload. Being near the stone had a profound impact on our ability to make sound decisions. It was like being drunk off a liquor that gave you the ability to sprout wings and level buildings. The Ani'Kutani had not restrained themselves from its use. And the Bitten were their ancestors as much as we were the ancestors of the daughter who had rebelled against them.

I sighed. "Alright, but what do you sense?" The Ulunsuti stone in the hands of our Medicine Man heightened his ability for premonition. I knew he was holding the stone, but even if it was stored away in his double-wide tucked back in the Smoky Mountain forests, its constant presence around him enhanced his other senses.

There was silence on the other end of the line. I let the quiet stretch, waiting while Josh listened with his other ears, watched with his other eyes.

"I see a darkness and caught up in the shadow is another darkness. One fuels the other with rage. It smells for its prey." Josh was pretty miserable at most things when it came to actually being a Medicine Man and the Ulunsuti Keeper. His intuition was a different matter and had proven to be intensely right.

"Cryptic," I told him.

"That's what I got." I mulled the words over in my mind, deciphering the code of Josh's brain coating the truth. "Hey, I'm your favorite, still though, right? Bestest, smartest, handsomest..." Josh trailed off.

"Yup, yup. Sure are," I responded, taking down notes in my head of the exact words of my friendly idiot savant. "Okay, well, keep the stone safe. If anything funky starts happening let me know. You got spells up this time?"

"Oh..." his voice trailed. "Um yeah, good idea. I better go do that."

"Ya think?"

"Okay, gotta go Rori! Uh – be careful, 'kay?"

"No. You be careful Josh." He hung up the phone. I sat there for a moment, worrying. Something was hunting for something else and the stone was flashing like a warning red light at a fire station. And my poor scatter-brained Medicine Man was like a trailer home in a wide-open field in Kansas with a homing beacon for tornados.

After a deep sigh, I looked around the room. What the hell was I doing in here in the first place? Ha... pregnant brain. Casting about, I saw the tennis shoes lying on the hardwood. Oh yes! I smiled as I remembered my original purpose and then immediately frowned. Man, that was a long way down there. I inhaled deeply and let it out in a splutter. Everything is harder when you're nine months pregnant.

Jameson's whistle echoed down the hall. I stuck a toe into the shoe and was pulling it toward me when he walked in the door. He stopped whistling as he rounded the end of the bed and watched me struggle.

"Doin' okay there, love?" he asked.

"Mmph..." The shoe slid on the hardwood toward me then flipped the wrong direction. I toed it back to the right position and looked up at him. He touched my face with warm, calloused fingers, and then stroked my swollen belly.

"Hi baby," he said to Aubry. She kicked his hand. Little bubbles of relief swept over me every time she kicked. Nothing could wipe out my anxiety except to feel her movement. "Little love. Little lovy, love. Daddy loves his lovy love, forever and forever," he sang to her. His voice rumbled as he continued humming to our baby.

Everything in life for Jameson was framed in a tune. After he had graduated college with a masters in music education in Florida, he'd come to Western Carolina University to fill the position of Professor of Jazz and Music Production. There is something magical in music. I think it's why we clicked. My whole world was seeped in magic of one form or another. Although, the word "magic" never quite summed up my own gritty reality. For instance, wrestling a wayward lesser dragon in a foreign habitat being destroyed by its acidic breath was far less glamorous a prospect than any soft magic-believer might imagine.

I looked past Jameson's wavy mop of brown hair into a corridor of the mansion of memories within my mind. The scene of the lesser dragon hunt played out in my head until Jameson looked up at me. "Are you ready to go?" he asked. My eyes sprang back to focus, seeing my blue-swathed swollen belly, and Jameson looking up at me expectantly. I shook away the memory of claws lashing out at my exposed neck, the silvery shine of dragon wings, the fiery explosions of acidic breath that burned my skin.

"As soon as I get these damn shoes on my feet, I'll be good to go."

"You know, you're going to have to work on your swearing before Aubry gets here," he said.

"I know," I said guiltily. Was I really mom material? I wasn't sure, but here she was and this fierce love for her had grown in me as much as she had. The love was even stronger than the fear and paranoia of losing my baby girl. Even that, I had learned to control for her sake. I could cut out the cursing for her. I could do anything for her. If I could only keep her alive.

"Here," Jameson said, "let me help." He sat onto the floor, his legs splayed out in a V around my feet and began untying the tennis shoes, bought a size larger than normal for my swelling feet.

"You don't have to do that. I can figure it out." But he was already slipping the shoe onto my foot. "I feel like a toddler."

He looked up at me and gripped my thigh with his big hand. "You'll be back to normal before you know. You're carrying her, doing all the work. Let me help." I wondered if it bugged him to have a woman so insistent on taking care of herself, never really needing the same level of physical protection some women crave. Maybe I could put my own shoes on and maybe it didn't hurt to let him put them on for me.

We made it onto Cataloochee trail before noon. For a pregnant woman, I felt I was doing pretty good. The sunshine leaked through the dust of the rock road lingering in the air. Autumn was in full splendor. Every tree was alive with fire. I inhaled deeply. I love autumn. I loved that my daughter would be born in autumn. It was beautiful and perfect in every way.

Jameson hummed. I watched him looking past the wheel, over the winding rock road and into a world made of harmonies and rhythm. I wondered if Aubry would inherit his musical talent. Is talent inherited? What Andy and I had, that was genetics. Or a curse. It depended on who you asked.

As the SUV trundled along, Jameson's music filled the air, while my thoughts left me silent. The music stopped and I looked over to find him catching a glimpse at me. "You're so beautiful, you know it?"

"Me?" I asked, with mock incredulity. "Not me."

"Mm-hmm," he confirmed with a nod. "Gorgeous."

"Well," I began. "You're not so bad yourself, handsome." He looked over the wheel and then back to me again. His mouth parted, a small inhale before speaking. His eyes met mine. So, he didn't see the twisted wolf figure when it lurched from the columns of fiery red trees toward our SUV.

Paul Burning's eyes stared out from the jagged face of the Ganagi. Time slowed as I watched him leap toward us. A seam along the bottom jaw of the wolf skin revealed a bloodied dark complexion and black hair. Its forearms were a matted combination of rotting gray wolf skin, streaked with blood and bits of ripped camo. They were stretched too long for Paul's body.

The dormant venom mingling in my blood exploded through my system. The contact lens burned away under the touch of dragon blood. I blinked once to rid my vision of the shrinking material. My muscles bunched, my jaw clenched, my body braced for the impact of the oncoming Ganagi.

Josh's words tumbled back into my brain and I cursed myself for being a fool. The prey was me. Paul Burning couldn't sniff me out on his own. He had to employ the Ganagi for that. At no other time in my life had I ever been afraid of my foe. The child in my womb screamed for protection. And the man who adored me was no match for this creature.

The Ani'Kutani encapsulated by the demon wolf skin roared, its voice a mix of human screeching and wolf and something else so unearthly that it could only have escaped from the gates of Hell.

Jameson's head swung around as the sound of scraping metal rang through the SUV. The impact of the creature wearing the human inside shoved the car across the dirt road. Jameson's head snapped toward me, his dark waves bouncing in my direction. He screamed.

"What the hell -!" he managed. The animal grappled for footing with feet morphed of the Ani'Kutani's hands and its own leftover claws. It was missing a whole ear. Its mangy hide was a collection of pieced together rotting wolf skin. Its mouth was curled back with decay and age. The yellowing canines smiled in blackened gums. It clambered onto the car. I reached over the middle console and yanked hard on the wheel. The engine revved. Rocks rattled underneath us, the wheels sliding as if we were on ice.

The Ani'Kutani-wearing demon grabbed the ledge of the hood by the windshield. Its claws screeched against the metal. Dirt and trees whipped around us. Jameson threw his arm over my chest. "Rori!" he shouted.

The SUV dove off the side of a steep incline. My stomach lurched into my throat as the vehicle caught air. Jameson's strong arm over me registered as incompetent to our fall. I wrapped my arms around my child and prayed. A giant pine hurtled toward us, the details of the bark growing. The Ani'Kutani scrambled to pull himself from the front of the vehicle. The wild scratching and labored growling echoed through the crash of trees.

My eyes burned. I could have sworn someone had dumped sand in them and rubbed real hard. Sand wasn't right. I wasn't at a beach. I tried blinking, which hurt like hell. I gasped for air against a heaviness pressing on my chest. Something was holding me against the pull of gravity. *Seatbelt,* I concluded.

My nose recoiled from an acrid odor that clung to the air. There was something else too. Another smell I couldn't quite pick up through the haze that reminded me of burnt pennies. My hair hung forward and tickled my nose and cheeks. I shook it. Something was pressed against Aubry and my face. I lifted a hand blindly, wiggling against the binding of my seatbelt. My stomach tightened at my movement. The tightness turned to pain as I pressed my hands against my belly turned to rock. I grunted as the searing pain squeezed my middle with insistent fingers.

Not good. I breathed in slow and deep to quiet the workings of my body. Car wrecks at nine months pregnant couldn't be a positive thing. Panic spread through me. The poison of the anxiety filled the muscles of my neck and jaws while my heart pounded on my eardrums. My stomach hardened in response. If Aubry was coming now, we had to get out of this car.

I tried my eyes again, working to blink away the grit and glass. Tears poured into them, washing away at least some of the debris. I pushed aside the deflated airbag with a soft crinkle of plastic and a white puff of powder. I coughed away the dust. The light from high afternoon poured into the car, tinged with the color of dying leaves. I hadn't been out for long.

"Jameson?" I asked as the powder cleared the air. I wiped at my face, trying to get rid of the powder that seemed to have gotten everywhere. "Are you okay?" I tilted my head to my left. He was probably knocked unconscious with the impact too. When I looked, his eyes were open though. At first that didn't make sense and my sluggish, anxiety driven brain fought to puzzle what I was looking at.

When the reality hit me, I squeezed my eyes against the sight. *No.* I thought in earnest. *This is a dream brought on by the car crash. This isn't real.* My body shook. I lost the innate ability to breathe. Something white hot wrapped callous fingers around my heart and squeezed, catching my lungs on fire and spreading into every fiber.

At last I inhaled, the sound rattling through me. Hot tears poured down my face. I opened my eyes again and saw my dead husband through a scratchy blur.

The sound that ripped out of my throat thundered around me, filling the broken SUV with impossible volume. The car shook from the power of my sorrow. Metal groaned in protest as my guts caved in. Jameson's vacant hazel eyes stared at me as if he were surprised. His white face was spattered in his own blood. That had been the smell I couldn't recognize. His blood. The scent of it was covered by burnt talc from the airbag. A tree branch from the giant pine impaled him and the driver's seat from its entrance through the windshield. His body slumped to the right. His arm reaching over the console toward me. My throat burned with my mourning cries and the flood of guilt.

This was my fault. I should have just stayed home instead of insisting to go for a drive. I should have known I might be in danger from the Ani'Kutani. I should have been more careful with him and Aubry.

"I'm so sorry. I'm so sorry," I cried. I wrapped my hands around his, brought his knuckles to my lips and caressed the cooling, graying skin. I pressed the back of his hand to my cheek and wept as if the hot tears would send life back into him and take away the horror of my actions. Straining, I reached out and ran fingers through his hair then let my hand fall to his face, over his dark eyebrows. Agony clutched my shoulders as his eyelashes tickled the skin on the palm of my hand. Memories of butterfly kisses whispered through me. I paused, my hand trembling. Then, I closed his eyes.

A contraction stole away my mourning. The clutch of the birthing process overwhelmed every piece of my energy. I gritted my teeth, clutching Jameson's limp hand and fought to breathe in the steady hissing they taught us in class. Mid-contraction, the car tottered, the shocks squeaking. The contraction died down after what seemed an eternity.

"Oh god," I whispered, sniffling and panting. I looked around the cabin of the SUV. Glass and powder covered everything. I'd had my purse somewhere. I looked into the floorboard at my feet, but it wasn't there. I looked behind Jameson's seat. It wasn't there. Had I left it at home? I needed my phone. The car jostled again, interrupting the quiet of death. "Jameson, we have to get out of this car."

The pine had caught it, impaled it, and saved it from falling down a sheer cliff. But, the SUV was cattywampus, the ass end higher up on the hill was tilted and all that autumn leaf litter and dry dirt weren't keeping it in place. It would fall. It was just a matter of time. The limb wouldn't hold it in place and the SUV was situated off center to the tree.

And I was in labor. There was no question as to what I had to do. I had to leave my husband's body and escape the vehicle to save Aubry. If I could.

The windshield was an angry web of cracked glass spreading out from the entry of the tree limb. The top half of the Ani'Kutani lay sprawled on the front of the SUV. His grizzly, black hair was tousled around his face. His arms were a mess of ripped camo jacket, blood and tissue. I even saw bone peeking out from the flesh. His bottom half was pinned between the hood of the SUV and the pine. But the Ganagi had abandoned him. It was nowhere in sight. And now, there was no one upon whom I could exact the revenge I desperately craved.

Gravity gripped the heavy car and pulled. The car rattled and groaned. The dead man on the hood shifted limply. The crushing car rotated his body so that his face was visible. His empty, dark eyes stared at me as if accusing me of his death.

The band tightened around Aubry. I breathed through the contraction. The car slid an inch, shaking the frame. Talc puffed up in little plumes of white smoke. Glass shifted on the dashboard, scratching against the vinyl. Jameson's head and shoulders shifted around the impaling length of the tree branch. I fought back my horror. I wanted to die in that moment. I wanted nothingness to consume me and swallow my shame along with it.

There was one more life I would die trying to protect. I could not say that I would succeed, but to sit in this car and let death take us was no choice. The burn to live was not for me, but for my daughter.

Pushing the air bag out of the way, I braced my upper body with one hand against the dashboard around the air bag's ejection site. I felt around with my feet and planted them as firmly as I could on the floorboard, against the odd angle of the car. I had a moment to be incredibly grateful for my strong body and habit of wearing tennis shoes instead of a more stylish choice before pain gripped me. Not just the tightness of squeezing muscles. Real pain. I screamed against it. If Jameson were with me, he would hold my hand and whisper soothing words. That was the plan. My scream stuttered into tears as the pain abated.

The car shifted. Tree branches crackled. The body of the Ani'Kutani, pinned between the pine and the car, fell away, the thump, thump, thump of his rolling body fading away. It was just the passenger side of the bumper that held us. The back of the car slid slowly. I had to get out. Now.

I reached for the seatbelt and pushed the release button. With my weight pressing against its constriction, it fought my attempts. I stood against the floorboard, pushing my butt further into the seat and felt the belt give way with a satisfying click. My body lurched forward into the plastic airbag and dashboard. I caught myself, but the sudden shift sent the car sliding, ass-end, further into the incline of the hill.

There was no stopping it now. My luck and time was out. My fingers found the door handle of their own accord. I pushed it open with all my might. Pivoting on my right foot, my left foot found the frame of the door. I pulled my weight out of the car as it began its rolling descent. Tree branches snapped, glass cracked and shattered, metal groaned as I jumped away from the green SUV onto the forest floor.

The door clipped my ankle on my ejection. I landed hard on my knees and hands. I screamed as the pain from the next contraction washed over me. The bouncing crash of the rolling SUV echoed up the hill.

I stayed on my knees as I breathed through the pain, horror and grief that consumed me, gripping my fingers into the dirt and leaf litter. Twigs and pine cones dug into my legs and knees. Tears slid down my hot cheeks and fell with soft splats onto the dead leaves. Once the contraction was over and I could breathe, I looked up the hillside, ignoring the dead and contorted body of Paul Burning, ten feet from me.

I had to get up that hill. Then, I had to get into town. Or I had to find someone to call an ambulance and my doctor. If I sat here, and calmed myself, would the contractions stop? Or would labor continue? I looked around at the red ash and golden oak trees. Would I bear my child on the forest floor? Life was dying in the forest today. I couldn't stand the thought of Aubry being born where Jameson had been killed.

I pushed myself off the ground and turned away from the wreckage below. The next contraction came minutes after I started up the hill. I dropped to a knee. I imagined Jameson by my side, holding my hand and crooning in his velvet bass, *"Breathe in. One. Two. Three. Four. Five. Now, out. One. Two. Three. Four. Five. Good job, honey."* Six minutes apart.

I finished breathing holding on to a tree root as if it were his hand then stood and stared up the incline. There was at least another two hundred feet. And then what?

Nowhere in any lore of the Bitten had there been instruction on magic to stop a birth that came at an inopportune time.

I placed one tennis shoe in front of the other and climbed the damn hill. Sometimes, in life, that's the only choice you get. Right foot, left foot, right foot. The going was steep, but my body was strong, I was accustomed to scrambling, and I would not give up. Every muscle in my body ached from the crash and my heart was even sorer. I could feel the purpling bruises blooming across my chest. The hitch in my left side was probably a bruised rib. I still had sandpaper eyes from the air bag. I'd lost my gray sweater about three hundred feet ago and the pretty blue maternity shirt I wore was smudged and ripped in one place.

Left foot, right foot, left foot... I stopped as the cramping spasms of labor overwhelmed me. I hunched down until my knees touched the ground and breathed through the scorching pain. Was labor supposed to hurt this much? Was this normal? The forest around me danced and swayed. A cold sweat rushed over me. My stomach lurched. I vomited on the ground and fought to keep my knees firmly planted. I could not fall.

Head down, I wiped my forearm across my mouth. The chill coursing over me was blotted by a sudden rush of wetness between my thighs. *No.* Not here. I checked the fluid. My white hand was stained red. The world rocked around me. I had to make it to the top. I had to save my daughter. Even if I died, maybe a passerby could save my child in time. If there was time. I fought back the wave of voices in my head that said I would be impotent to save her, as much as I had been to save my brother from the horrible harm of our childhood. As unable as I was to save three babies prior to this pregnancy. As unable as I was to save my husband.

I gritted my teeth and hauled my body, hand over hand, one painful, nauseating grasp at a time. My hardening belly dragged through dirt. The smell of wormy earth, dead leaves and trailing blood wafted up to my acutely sensitive nose. The light from high afternoon speared my eyes as the world spun and tilted. I focused; the top was only inches from me. The world grew lighter, washing out detail. A gush between my legs sent me into a spasm of pain and fear for my baby. Tears slid from my eyes as desperation fueled me onward.

I hauled myself over the ridge, the dirt road grinding underneath me, tearing away at my already chewed up fingernails. I lay on my back and heaved for air, rocks digging into my spine and skin, dust filling my mouth with grit. My heart thumped rapidly into the bed of white rock. This wasn't right. None of it. And here I lay, without a soul to rescue my baby.

I let the rush of dragon blood spur through my system, praying that it would help to heal the hurts of a childbirth gone wrong. Praying that my child had not died in the crash. It was as if I was on a top, the blue sky and canopy of reds and ochers spinning overhead. I closed my eyes, inhaled deeply and tried the last trick I had up my sleeve. I howled with the dragon voice. Louder and more desperately I'd ever needed to howl before. Would my mother hear me? I couldn't know.

I howled again. Long, low, deep, mournful. Every ounce of energy I didn't have left coursed through me and fueled the scream. I put into it my agony, my mourning, my desperation. My guts hardened around another contraction, but somehow it felt different. As if it was just too much to bother feeling any more. I howled a third time, weaker and more pitiful. Tears poured from my eyes, down my temples and into my hair. *Please,* I prayed. *I can't lose anyone else today.*

It was Josh's face I saw first. His blue eyes peered down at me, much of the white showing around the irises. Something pressed against my face and a cool, slightly sweet, dryness filled my mouth. Things I couldn't see rattled and bumped. The world jostled around me. And the world was currently made of close walls covered in sterilely stacked drawers of medical supplies and equipment. A siren whined and then cut out. A horn filled my ears with a cacophony that raged in my confused and groggy brain. My legs were stretched wide and propped up. Between them peeked a woman's blond head.

Pain sliced through my middle and the lower parts of me. I screamed out, shocked, having forgotten what was happening before the world had gone dark. I was being ripped. The white- hot tearing sensation consumed me in a wash of reds and blacks. My body arced off the gurney, my mouth stretching wide, my eyes squeezing so hard flashes of absent light danced across the blackness.

When the pain lessened and I could inhale once more, another face swam into my visual scope. I knew him, I thought. Had seen him somewhere. He spoke and interrupted my thought process. His thin lips were pinched in a grim line before it opened to reveal a set of off-white teeth that looked as though they had been put into his mouth half an inch off-center. I opened my mouth, meaning to ask what was so wrong with me. Instead a strained growlish whimper leaked out as my jaws snapped shut.

"Rori?" His voice was tinny and thick with southern accent. His hair was very trimmed, as if he had just been to the barber that very day. His white, muscled neck rose out of a tightly buttoned white shirt covered in a variety of brightly colored patches. I looked at him, my eyes darting from his face to his blue-gloved hands and bare muscled forearms. The blue gloves were smeared in vivid red. "We're going to need you to push now."

Push. Push meant it was time to have my baby. Why was I in an ambulance and where was Jameson? Something tugged at my memory and then flitted away. I looked to Josh, my confusion boiling up and steaming away with the need to slip back into the place of quiet sleep, away from the unfathomable pain. Exhaustion stole over me. I blinked heavily. Josh looked back at me. His dark hair formed a soft curly frame around his face. The sweet, cool air from the plastic strapped to my face forced its way into my nostrils and mouth.

"It's Aubry's time," he said to me. His dark blue eyes were still scared and I thought there were tears gathering in them. "I'm here. We're going to do this together." And then the forgotten truth slammed into me. Memories sprang through the haze of pain and exhaustion. The words he'd used finally wakened me from a temporary and blissful amnesia and I knew. Jameson would not be here to utter those words to me.

My insides crumpled. My heart squeezed. Josh grabbed at my shoulder, his strong, steady hands warming me. And that might have comforted me, except the next contraction clamped down and stole away comfort.

The blond paramedic lifted her face. "Okay, it's time!"

"Push, Rori! Push for your baby!" The well-trimmed paramedic at my left side yelled at me above the scream that forced its way out of me.

"Come on, Rori," Josh spoke directly into my ear, squeezing my hand. He pushed his hand further behind me, scooping up both shoulders with his muscled arm. My head jostled with the movement. "You got this." He continued to whisper into my ear. "I know you climbed up that damn hill. By yourself, while in labor. You did that. You can do this. You're one tough bitch, Rori Cantrell."

He was right. I was one tough bitch. I had made it too far to save Aubry to give up now. Even if it was the last thing I would ever do, I would bring my daughter into the world. I gritted my teeth, hunched forward, his arm helping me with the movement, and pushed for all I was worth.

FOUR ~ RORI - FEBRUARY 2014, A CRACK

In my sleep, I wandered through a wasteland painted in grays and blacks. Shapes to which I had no name shifted, beady eyes peered out at me as I walked along a dead road of caked and cracking mud the color of concrete. A blackened tree snapped, groaned then shattered, shards of its remains showering me like broken glass. When the pieces fell against my exposed skin, blood welled out of long cuts that stretched over my arms like a suicide victim's battle with a razorblade.

The road pitched suddenly upward, the creatures flitting nervously, their breath fouling the gray mists with vibrant colors of greens and purples. I tilted forward even as I clasped onto the wounds that wept scarlet. Wake up, *I told myself.* This is just a dream. *I grasped my pregnant belly, the blood from my wounded arms suddenly spilling from between my legs. I clawed into the gray, crumbling road, but it tilted steeper, until my legs dangled above nothing, the world having gone sideways.*

I screamed, "My baby! My baby! Please! My baby!" But the road granted me no mercy, and gave way under my gripping fingers.

I fell.

And I screamed. The black and gray world whipped past me. On their own plane of unreal, the creatures charged at my falling body, mouths gaping, teeth glinting. Vertigo consumed me like one of the many monsters that chased me. I yanked my head sideways. The horizon fell away underneath me, but something yawned darker than the blackness of shadow. A hawk cried. The sound keening away so loudly that I clapped my hands over my ears. The sound rattled inside my skull. Claws reached out, grabbing my shoulders with giant, tearing nails.

"Mama!" My eyes sprang open. Pale light of early morning leaked into my bedroom from the expanse of windows. I flung the bedspread and sheets aside, jumped from the bed and beat a path to Aubry's room. I hurried through the threshold of my nine-year-old's room of pinks and purples, stepping carefully past a litter of dolls. I nestled myself onto her bed.

"Shh...," I whispered. I swept a hand over her forehead, under the damp hairline of her deep auburn hair and down her round cheek. Unseen hands clenched my heart. She was safe. She lived. My baby. "It's okay, Sweetpea. Mama's here."

Her eyes fluttered opened, dark lashes dotted with tears. At first, I could see she only saw the dream images still. Then her golden eyes fell on me. She pushed herself up and threw her arms around my neck. I wrapped her in an embrace, our shared warmth giving us each comfort. "It was just a dream," I mumbled into her hair, to me and to her.

I heard the clacking of nails over hardwood and then felt the warm weight of Wuffers's head resting on my leg. Aubry looked down at her, removing an arm from my neck to pet Wuffers's soft, black fur. She peered up at us with her orange eyes, past her whitening muzzle.

I opened my mouth to ask Aubry about her nightmare, but the phone sang out. I considered ignoring it. Aubry turned her head at the second round of the electronic harmony. "I'll get it!" she said. She jumped up from my lap and ran out of the room, Wuffers on her heels. Her giggle accompanied the percussion of her stomping feet, Wuffers's clacking nails keeping time.

I surveyed the stuffed animals strewn across the floor and puzzled over the dream. Had we both had the same dream? Or was it a coincidence that we both had nightmares? An electric current of anxiety tingled along my spine, as if something or someone were plucking at the veil.

After another minute, Aubry ran back into the room, stepping carefully over a dark-haired babydoll. She handed me the phone.

"Mama!" she started excitedly, "Grammy had a bad dream too!" Definitely not a coincidence.

"Mom?" I said, rising to my feet as I pressed the phone to my ear.

"Better get dressed. Somethin' ain't right."

"We'll be ready in twenty minutes." I hung up, not waiting for her confirmation. I looked at Aubry, who had sat on the floor, cross-legged, and hugged the babydoll. Wuffers laid down next to her on the hardwood, her head resting on her forelegs.

I took one step toward the door before the phone rang again. I looked at the caller id. Josh Mooney. I pressed the button on the phone. "Don't tell me you had a bad dream too?" I asked without preamble.

"What?" he said, thrown off.

"Sorry. There seems to be a rash of nightmares going around." I explained.

"Oh. Well, I think I might know why."

"What's up?" Darkness tickled through me.

"It's pretty hard to explain. Best come out to Cataloochee."

"We're already headed out there." I had assumed Cataloochee since that was where I'd almost lost Aubry. The dream seemed to be pointing us in that direction.

"Oh." He paused. I could hear him mentally catching up. "Well, good. I'll meet you out on Boogerman Trail."

"Okee doke." I hung up and looked at the phone. "Anybody else?" I half expected my twin Andy to call, but the phone was quiet. "Alright, baby girl. Let's get dressed to go hiking." Her auburn hair yanked up to me.

"Really?" She smiled and then clapped, dropping the babydoll and springing to her feet. She was pulling clothes out of her closet as I headed to my own bedroom to get dressed. Energy coiled through me, feeding me a healthy dose of dragon venom. It was hard to say who was more excited: me or Aubry.

After Mom got to the house, we headed out. The cab of the truck was charged with the anticipation of three generations of Dragon Bitten. We pulled up in her beaten up pick-up to the footbridge near the trailhead for Caldwell that would lead to Boogerman. I pulled out my cell. A text message flashed at me. Andy. I shook my head as I typed out a reply letting him know we were checking on the reason for the odd dream.

"Who's that?" Mom asked.

"Andy, of course." My tone reflected the annoyance at her prying question.

"What does he want?" she asked, trying to sound interested and innocent instead nosy. It didn't work.

"What's it matter to you, Mom?"

"I do care about your brother, Rori Anne," she snapped.

"You have a funny way of showing it." I finished typing my message, tapped the send button then dialed Josh.

"Where you at?" I asked once he'd answered.

"Behind the old homestead, about a mile east off-trail." I turned to Mom, my nerves prickling. I knew where he was. If he was looking at what I thought he was looking at, there was indeed something wrong. Mom looked back at me, her golden eyes sharp in the softness of olive skin. Still annoyed with me, she slammed the driver's side door and headed to the truck bed.

"Okay, we just parked, so we'll be there in maybe twenty."

"I'll be here," Josh replied.

I tapped the end button on the screen of the cell and headed to the tailgate. The gate groaned as I lowered it. Wuffers leapt out. She looked up at me and wagged. "You keep an extra watch on Aubry, 'kay?" She tilted her head, her tongue hanging out then trotted over to Aubry who'd wandered across the small rock parking lot to stand near the footbridge that marked the trailhead.

Mom came around the truck, throwing her old, beat-up mute green backpack over her small shoulders. Her dark hair was pulled back in a short pony. She pulled a knit cap on over her head, tucking away the stray strands of hair. Her thick, sage green winter coat made crinkling noises with her movement. She had that closed-off look on her face that said she was really pissed and didn't want to talk about it. Which was good. I didn't want to talk to her either.

I zipped up my gray coat, grateful for the fleece lining to keep me warm against the nearly freezing temperatures. The sky was leaden gray and promised no sunshine. I pulled my own pack on, cinching up the straps so that it rested comfortably on my shoulders.

I stood over Mom, a whole head taller. The thought crossed my mind, not for the first time, at how little we looked to be kin. Her skin was dark olive where mine was champagne. She was five foot two where I was five foot seven. Her hair was dark brown, mine dark auburn. The only similarity was the golden eyes (in my case just the one eye), and the shape of them: rounded on the insides and then squeezed into upward curving lines on the outside.

She said I got the rest of my looks from my father. I could barely recall his face and when I did, my memory showed me the last moment I had seen him when I was eight, with an arrow in his back. At least Aubry had been spared seeing her father killed.

I rolled my shoulders under the weight of the backpack and the weighing absence of my husband, giving up on the idea of the burden getting any lighter. He might have had a hefty life insurance plan that covered me and Aubry for the rest of our lives financially, but it didn't make up for not feeling his touch, not hearing a constant song on the air, not having his warm kindness around me or kisses on my hairline when I laid on his muscular chest.

I shook my head, fighting back the sorrow and annoyance turning in my stomach. "Let's do this," I said to my mom. She nodded, her jaw clenching to one side, and made her booted way to where Aubry swung on a post of the footbridge.

We hiked through the rhododendron-laden North Carolina forest, the morning still chilly and wet with heavy mist. It clung to my face with eager fingers. The old-growth hemlocks towered around us, silent and watchful in the blanket of fog. The birds were silent. That was never a good sign. Aubry walked next to Wuffers and kept touching the black fur on her neck, as if to reassure herself. Or maybe to reassure Wuffers. She'd put on jeans and her rainproof winter coat that was the color of buttercups.

The trail was hard in parts from freezing and muddy in some patches, but blessedly abandoned. We had the place to ourselves. After turning onto Boogerman from the Caldwell Creek trail, we came upon the old settlement of Robert "Booger" Palmer, the hermit who'd built his home in the middle of the old-growth forest to keep nature close around him.

We exited the trail at the stone wall Mr. Palmer had built around his homestead and headed east, not needing to check the compass buried in my backpack. These were our regular stomping grounds. We knew it better than we knew our own faces, Aubry included. She skipped through evenly spread poplars, stopping here and there to touch a tree, stare up into its empty branches, her head tilted.

After a mile of tromping through the woods, away from the trail, our journey led us to an open meadow, dotted by the imposing presence of several sprawling oaks. They were bare still, their limbs drenched near black with rainwater. The image of the black tree from my dream struck me so hard I stopped in my tracks. Mom inhaled sharply behind me before she bumped into me. "Honey?" She came to stand beside me in the field and caught her breath. "Oh my."

Aubry skipped along toward the tree, Wuffers bounding next to her. "Wait!" I screamed at Aubry. Josh rounded the tree, scooping Aubry up into his outstretched arms. My momentary anxiety died at the sight of our medicine man. Wuffers jumped around him, tail wagging.

"You're smiling," my mom said, beside me. I looked down at her, surprised.

"What?" I asked. She was grinning, smile wrinkles gathering around the corners of her eyes. Her anger with me forgotten. She raised her eyebrows and shook her head.

"Oh honey," she began, "he's good, you know. A good man."

"Mom, please." How many times could I have the same conversation? "You know how I feel. It just wouldn't be fair to him." Even after nine years, I couldn't be disloyal to my husband's memory. Plus, romance would just complicate life for Aubry and me. We didn't need that. She turned fully toward me, her mouth hanging open, her eyes wide. She perched her fists on her hips.

"Now, doesn't he get a say in this?" I fidgeted with my backpack strap and watched as Josh carried Aubry toward us, still well outside of earshot.

"Well, he's the stone keeper, anyway." As if this ended the argument. Because a Dragon Bitten couldn't be around the Ulunsuti stone, the gem that had once been embedded in the forehead of the ancient Uktena dragon that had changed we Bitten forever. It was a power source and had a way of going to our heads. Like a drug, kind of. If drugs gave you crazy powerful energy to do things like fly and spit acid and heal the near dead. But the stone needed guarding and it had long been the responsibility of the Cherokee medicine people to do that. Without protection, the stone could be used by any entity looking for a boost to their mystical power. Even Josh was affected by it. His healing and intuitive abilities and sight for the future were all amped up from being around the stone so much.

"You know and I know he'd hand it off to someone else if it meant he'd get to be with you. You don't seriously think he keeps the stone for any other reason than to be close to you, do you?" I stared at her, nonplussed. I hadn't considered that. He really was a terrible stone-keeper. I crossed my arms and worked on an intelligent reply, but came up with nothing, so I turned on my heel and stalked away from her.

"We have stuff to figure out, Mom," I told her over my shoulder. Without looking at her, I knew she was rolling her eyes and smiling away my discomfort.

"Life's lonely without someone to live it with, sweetheart," she whispered, startling me with how much heartache hung in her words. "I just hate to see you make the same mistake I did." Coward that I was, I didn't turn to look at her, afraid her face would mirror the loss I felt for my husband, Jameson. And the same loneliness of being a single mother. I let the silence stretch as we crunched our way on semi-frozen blades of grass toward Josh.

I caught glimpses of his familiar blue eyes first, framed in dark lashes. He had his longish mop of dark, wavy hair tucked into a tacky fur-lined cap with ear flaps, which hung loose around his head like halfway raised wings about to take off in flight.

"Hey," I said.

"Good to see you," he said. He set Aubry onto the ground and opened his arms up to me. "You've been keeping away way too long." The sight of his outstretched arms sent a warm buzz through my head. I took that one more step and fell into his embrace. He squeezed me as if he wanted to become part of me. My head fell into that perfect position on his shoulder and chest. His familiar scent washed over me: a mixture of soap and sage and sweetgrass, mingled with that other something that was no more explicable than to just call it 'him'. The earthy odors of outside clung to his clothes and skin. I soaked in the smell with relish, but pulled away before I wanted to, conscious of my mother standing behind me, and probably reading my mind. He planted a kiss on my face with warm, soft lips before I pulled away, and despite my thirty-four years of life experience, I felt the rush of blood rise to my cheeks.

When he pulled away, he held me by my arms and looked me up and down, his blue eyes growing concerned even though his mouth stayed curved in a playful smile. "Tough night, huh?"

"You could say that." Truth be told, the darkness that pulled at me all morning was dissipating in Josh's presence. As though the dawn were finally rising in my night.

Mom walked up to us and Josh turned to her. "Mrs. Ferrish. Good to see you." He wrapped my mom up, her tiny frame enveloped by him. When she pulled away she smiled, the infection of Josh's kindness traveling through us like a breeze that springs up in a meadow.

"Josh," she began, "how've you been?"

"Busy," he told her.

"Busy is good. Means you're outta trouble," she said.

"Well. I didn't say that." He gave her a sly smile. "Life's no fun without a little trouble." He winked at me. Something swelled inside of me. I didn't care for it. If he was talking about ladies, I didn't want to know. Mom was saying something, but I turned away and stomped toward the black tree, thinking green thoughts about some imaginary chick.

My coat swished with the purpose as I headed toward the oak. The tree's giant branches stretched wide and many of them had dived into the earth, forming an arched gate that shimmered against the morning gray. I heard Mama and Josh chatting behind me, and then the light hops of Aubry as she bounded through the field. Wuffers sidled up next to me, barely making a noise. The first sign of her presence was the warmth on my leg. I reached down to ruffle her fur when she growled. Behind me, all in company froze, except for Josh.

Behind the gate a giant dog stalked past the opening, his red eyes glowing as he peered out. The demon dog of Valle Crucis was easily eight feet tall, hairless and muscular, its mouth curled back in a permanent scowl around lower canines that jutted over his upper lip. Aubry caught her breath. Her little feet pounded up behind me. I looked down to see her peering past me at the creature beyond the gate.

The dog wasn't what startled me. This was the gatekeeper. He was there to keep all the things past the gate in and all the things not past the gate out. In short, he was a guard dog.

No, his presence was normal, expected, comforting. It was the gate itself that was wrong. In the top corner, the shimmering portal sparked out of a glistening crack the length of my arm. The gate was a piece of the whole veil and having a crack in it was a bad sign. Left unhealed, the gate would weaken and the veil would break. And I didn't even want to think about healing a broken veil. The sacrifice involved... I glanced at Aubry, barely resisting the need to wrap her in an embrace and keep her safe in my arms forever.

Josh however, didn't seem to be bothered by the beast or the crack. He waltzed right up to the gate, perching a hand on his hip and leaning forward until his nose was nearly touching it. "Dude!" I said. "Get the hell away from the gate!" Wuffers whined. Josh turned.

"What?" He swung his flapped head back to the gate. "This is one of them, isn't it? A gate? I can't believe I can see it. It's pretty cool." Pretty cool because our medicine man saw the other side of the veil only in the presence of the Ulunsuti. The fact that he was seeing the gate now at the same time the gate had a huge crack in it set my nerves on edge. What else could he and others with a slight gift of Sight see?

He turned to look at me, his smile wide and sweet on his handsome face. "I've always wondered what they would feel like, if I could see and touch them." He raised a fist.

"No!" I shouted, but too late. He rapped on the shimmering substance. The dog's gigantic head whipped around to fix his burning eyes onto Josh, which Josh didn't see. So, he could see the gate, but not the creatures.

"It's fine," Josh said, his eyes bright, his white smile brilliant against his Native American dark skin. "It didn't hurt m- " he didn't finish his sentence. The towering gray monster dog behind the gate lunged as Josh's knuckles touched the hardened transparency.

"Josh!" Aubry's high-pitch scream tapped a nerve in me.

"It's okay, sweetheart," I told her, grabbing her cheeks between my hands. "Mama will go get him." I turned back to see the dog with a mouthful of Josh's navy winter coat and yanking him through the gate. His legs were still poking through; his blue eyes fixed on me and stretched in fear. The dog chomped again, nudging Josh's body up into the air, making his head yank around. His ridiculous hat fell off, sliding off the dog's ginormous nose and falling to the ground. The monster gave a mighty pull on Josh's coat, his gray legs bunching against the solidity of the gate. He yanked and then shook him back and forth like a chew toy. I could see the nib on the dog's tail wag. Josh looked as if his eyes were still rattling around.

I lunged forward, running toward our idiot medicine man with all I had. Mid-stride I pulled my arms through the backpack and let it fall to the ground with a solid thunk. Everything but Josh's booted feet was through the gate. I grabbed onto his feet and pulled, a groan of effort escaping my mouth.

"Yyyeeouch!" Josh cried out. The giant dog tugged against my efforts.

"Mom!" I cried out. She skidded up next to me, grabbing a hold of Josh's other foot. We yanked again on Josh, but the demon dog wagged some more and pulled again, as if this were the best game in the world. If Josh got all the way through, the chances of me finding him and bringing him back to safety dropped dramatically. This is where we sent the banished creatures. The ones that harmed people. The nasty ones. They were all on the other side of this gate. Josh couldn't fight his way out of a wet paper bag. Surviving past the gate would be impossible for him.

"Now, listen here," Mama shouted. Aubry's voice cut her off.

"Put him down!" she screamed at the dog. The dog stopped wagging and looked down at her, the swirl of his glowing red eyes slowing. I spared a look at Aubry. She stood in her buttercup yellow coat with her hands perched on her hips. She raised an arm, pointed a small finger. "Bad dog! Let go of Josh and leave 'im alone." Her childlike voice thrummed with dragon's voice. The air shimmered around her. Her head was tilted way back to look up at the dog and command his obedience. She was dragon-born and the dog faltered, loosening his grip on Josh's coat.

Mom grasped tighter to Josh's leg and as the dog let go, we yanked, hard and fast. Josh's body hurtled through the gate. He yelped in surprise before he landed with a thud on top of us. "Mph," I said, as Josh's ass landed on my gut. Mom groaned.

"Oh, Josh," she said. I shoved myself up onto my elbows and watched my daughter, anxiety spreading through me like poison. She approached the gate slowly, her head tilted and arm outstretched. My legs were tangled into Josh's. I kicked and pulled to get them free as Aubry got closer to the gate. Flashes of my dream hurtled back to me. Was it a warning Aubry wasn't safe?

No way was I going to wait and see. I yanked myself free from the pile of Josh and my mother and rolled to a crouch. The demon dog of Valle Crucis lowered itself slowly to the ground in front of the gate, its wide head sideways as Aubry kept her eyes locked onto his. I jumped over Mama and Josh and darted toward my daughter.

The dog had laid itself completely down. Aubry reached toward the gate. Her hand was the level to the dog's mouth, but as she got closer, the dog lowered its head to its massive paws. My arms were around her in an instant, my heart thudding triple time. She ignored me, pushing her body away from mine to reach into the gate.

Her hand pushed through the gate and rubbed the top of the dog's nose. I grabbed her arm, wanting more than anything to pull her away from the danger, but the dog lay still. "It's okay, Mama. I'm safe," she said. I wasn't so sure. So I kept a loose grip on her arm. The dog's swirling red eyes fell from open, to half-lidded, to closed at Aubry's touch.

Aubry smiled at the dog then and after a few pats on his massive nose, I pulled her away. "Okee dokee. I think that's enough petting of the demon dog for one day," I said.

The dog's eyes sprang open. He looked at her and whined. Or at least it sort of sounded like a whine. It was deep and garbled and menacing, but Aubry was unafraid. "Good boy," she told the dog. It wagged slightly. "You be good and watch the gate, 'kay?" The dog barked. Aubry jumped in my arms and giggled.

She wriggled against my grasp and realizing the danger had passed, I loosened my grip and let her go, recovering from the panic. "I told you I was okay, Mama," she said, sounding confident and annoyed I needed to protect her. She pushed away from me and wandered away from the gate. Something off to the side of the gate caught her eye.

Josh and Mom came up behind me. Mom put a hand on my shoulder. "You have to let her do these things, sweetheart. She's getting bigger and has to learn."

"I know. I just... the dream. And then Josh nearly getting pulled through. I was scared."

"I understand," she said as she rubbed my shoulder. My eyes were still fixed on Aubry. She looked down at the ground near the end of the gate that was cut through with a sparking gash. She bent and picked up a feather. A feather as long as her arm. It glinted an oily black. She turned to the gate with it and the dog growled, low and mean. Then she turned and jogged over to us. "Mama, what's this belong to?" She handed me the feather. My heart dropped into my stomach. The memory of the hawk's cry in my dream rattled around inside my head.

I took the feather from Aubry. My hands tingled, the prickling sensation running up the length of my arm. "That's a big bird," Josh commented.

Mom was at my elbow, looking at the feather with a stern and knowing gaze. "That looks like a whole lot of trouble," she said. She took the feather from my hand and walked over to Josh. "Alright, young man. Come on over here." With her free hand she led Josh close to the gate and held him there. He looked down at her like a child waiting for instruction. She was looking at the feather, a frown on her small, rounded face, her gold eyes glittering under pinched eyebrows. She peered up at Josh, surprised to see him still standing there. "Well. Sit down," she said impatiently.

Josh's eyes were wide as he quickly perched himself on the frozen ground, legs folded into themselves. My mother extended the feather toward him, looking at it as though she were studying a complex algebra formula. He reached up for it, his eyes darting between it and my mom's face. He paused before touching it. My scalp prickled. I pulled my coat tighter into me and pulled Aubry into my side. Wuffers whined.

Josh's thumb and pointer finger closed on the feather. A gust of wind sprung from nowhere, blasting Josh's dark hair. His eyes immediately sparked, the blue irises blazing like a flame. He inhaled sharply. The guard dog on the other side of veil gate threw back its massive head and howled. The sound of it on the fog-laden morning stretched away from us like the shadow of a ghost.

Mom beckoned me with a flick of her hand and raised eyebrows. I obediently jogged toward her, Aubry at my heel. She clapped on to my hand and in her other hand she held Aubry's. I grabbed Aubry's other hand. We stood surrounding Josh on the verge of the gate that led to the other side of what is real for most. Mist began to gather as my mother began to sway, her eyes closed, head tilted toward the leaden sky of February. She inhaled deep and rhythmically, in time with the steady shift of weight from one foot to the next. I followed her, and closing my eyes I could feel her steady rhythm with the gentle push and pull of her hand in mine.

In the darkness of the dance, under the cover of the red gray of dull light penetrating my closed eyelids, images sprang forward, soft and subtle. For my mother and Aubry, the images would be more acute than real life. Each image would cut into the darkness, spring from beyond the veil into their consciousness. Aubry was not as practiced, so the images would come fast and furious, or so I was told by my twin Andy.

I squeezed Aubry's hand as my mother began to lead. "Imagine the crack in the gate," she instructed us. "Imagine the venom coursing through your veins. Picture the magical properties of the venom floating to the surface of your skin, pushing past the barrier and into the air around us."

The image in my mind, after a disturbing parade of monster after monster from beyond the gate, shimmered in a gentle cloud of ruby red. It hung around the image I had in my mind of my body. I tried collecting it and adding it to the center of the three of us, but it hung there resolutely ignoring my command.

"Good, Aubry," my mother said, a smile in her voice. "Rori?" In response I growled. This, this… spiritual stuff, was too abstract for me. Andy and I had split the genetic passing of being Dragon Bitten. The first set of twins in centuries, we were a major anomaly.

Andy had gotten all the intuitive abilities. I had just gotten the physical aspects being born with dragon venom in my veins. I was a better guardian of the veil when Andy and I were together. But, my mother had made it impossible for him to stay here. Her prejudice against a male being born with our heredity had pushed him all the way to Washington state. She insisted on trying to force my own intuitive abilities, which was asinine. I had none.

I shifted at the wrong moment, throwing myself out of the rhythm then huffed loudly at my frustration. "Focus, Rori," I heard my mother say. The red shimmering cloud around my imaginary body in my head faltered, glowed, darkened then went out like a candle in the fog.

"Shit," I muttered.

"Language!" My mother reprimanded me. She fought to keep the rhythm of her swaying steps even while I was totally off. She was quiet for a moment while I fought to rebuild the image in my mind of my aura. No luck. It wouldn't come. Pretty soon, I couldn't even keep my eyes closed, I was so flustered. My eyelids rose despite my commanding they stay shut.

Mom's face squinched up, her eyes still closed. She inhaled and exhaled slowly. "That's okay, Rori. Aubry's energy is ginormous. It should be enough to heal the gate."

I watched the coalescing energy in the center of us, relieved I wouldn't have to fight my way through seeing the imaginary auras. I could rely on my right, golden eye to see them with my eyes open. Aubry's aura glittered with white and gold, shot through with prismatic rainbows. I found myself simply staring at its loveliness. It bounced around, shifting left then right, jumping up and down. Wuffers came and laid at her leg and the aura slowed to a steady swirl.

My mother's aura was deeply emerald. Strong and comforting to look at. When their energies coalesced, Josh's own earth tones and yellow rose up to meet them. He raised the feather into the air, his fiery eyes staring into nothing. He waved the feather into the ball of swirling colors, like stirring a spoon in a pot. The swirling motion marbled the collection of energy. When all the colors were evenly distributed, Josh held his hand still and slowly let go of the feather.

It hovered in the sphere of colorful energy: whites, greens, browns, yellows, little shots of rainbows and gold. We separated our grasps and raised our arms to cup the globe with gentle hands. Aubry raised her hands, staring at the globe with wide golden eyes. We moved carefully around Josh and approached the gate. I listened, waiting for the screech of a hawk to fill the air.

We raised the globe up. As it neared the gate it floated to the crack in the gate. The feather inside twisted, sparking, smoking and then was sucked back through the gate. The globe of energy spread, filling the crack like ethereal glue. It shimmered, glowed and then rested, leaving the gate whole again. I breathed a sigh of relief, gripping Aubry's hand a little tighter. The veil was safe. Aubry was safe.

But no hawk came to the call of its feather being returned to the place it belonged. My mother turned from the gate and looked out over the barren fog-heavy field. Black and empty tree skeletons drooped like sleeping guardians under the oppressing blanket of gray.

Silence echoed itself with more silence.

"Hey," Josh said, breaking the spell. "I don't suppose someone could get my hat back for me?"

"Thankfully," I started, "no." The Demon Dog of Valle Crucis held the cap between his teeth, taking turns chewing and sniffing it.

FIVE ~ HAELYN - THE TURNER RESIDENCE, FEBRUARY 2014

"Haelyn Turner! Get your butt down here, right now!" Her voice echoed up to my attic bedroom. My shoulders hunched and my heart sped. I jumped up from my plastic tea set and ran. Devon came out of his room at the sound of my pounding feet as I flew down the stairs. The music blared before he closed the door on it.

"Where ya headed, squirt?" he asked.

"Mom's mad," I hissed. The stairs creaked under my feet. Devon huffed and then his footsteps resounded behind me. I sprinted over the old hardwood floor and nearly ran into my mom by the dining table. "Yes, ma'am?"

I put my hands behind my back and squeezed them into knots. She had on a pink sweater and a bunch of gold bracelets. Her light brown hair was curled and pulled into a pony that lay across her shoulder. Her lips were shiny with lip gloss and her green eyes looked heavy with makeup.

"Uckh, look at you. Do you ever take a bath?" She crossed her arms over her stomach. Chinks of light shone through little triangles of space between the crook of her elbows and her body. "What are you looking at?" My eyes yanked up to hers.

"Noth - ," I started to say.

"It doesn't matter. What matters is why you left the milk on the counter."

"I didn't," I said, knowing she wouldn't believe me. It was always the same. Something went undone, and I was blamed for it.

"I left it, Mom. Gah... chill." Devon brushed past her, knocking into her shoulder with his. He grabbed the milk off the counter, disappeared from my view. There was a suctioned slurp of the refrigerator door opening, the clunk as it shut and then the stomp of his feet before he reappeared. "Happy?"

"You're just covering for her, like you always do." She walked toward me, the click of her high heels against the hardwood echoing like a warning. I backed up, but she swooped down and grabbed my arm with her shiny, red nails. Her bony hand wrapped around my arm and squeezed. The overly sweet smell of makeup and perfume enveloped me. It was not comforting. Fear twisted inside me. I wondered if all children were afraid of their mothers the way I was. She shook my arm and my body followed suit. "I'm sick of you leaving a mess wherever you go. I work so hard to give you a clean home. The least you could do is show a little gratitude. You're ten years old. Old enough to pick up after yourself."

"But, I didn't - !" I began. Thwack! Her hand whipped across my face so fast that I hadn't been prepared for it. I grabbed the cheek she smacked with my free hand, my mouth falling open. Tears sprang to my eyes and I whimpered.

"You want me to smack you again? No? Then stop crying!" She raised her hand as more sobs bubbled out of my mouth. I couldn't help it. "I said stop – " She jerked her hand back.

"Leave her alone." Devon held her arm on the upward swing she meant for my face.

"Devon. Let go of me. You stay out of it."

"No. I'm not going to stay out of it. You're abusing her!"

"No, I'm not. I'm disciplining her!"

"You're hitting her. You never once hit me, but her, your own blood, you smack her around all the time. And I'm sick of it! Get off of her!" He pulled her arm. She yanked as she was drawn away, scratching the skin of my upper arm. I hissed and grabbed it. Mom fought to maintain her footing then fell to the floor. Devon shouted at her some more, his words lost to me in the ringing of my ears, the pounding of my heart. Why did my mother hate me?

I ran from the room, out the back door as her voice echoed behind me. I slid the glass door closed and ambled down the deck stairs and into the dead yard. The chill nibbled at my bare arms as I stood on the wooden deck and breathed, listening to the shouting inside, muffled through the walls.

The flapping of wings broke in on the yells from inside. On the top of the old shed, perched a giant hawk with black and white wings. I rubbed my arms at a sudden chill as I looked at the monster-sized bird. It cocked its head toward me, peering down with big, black eyes. Its hooked beak was black with a bit of yellow. There was something else to the bird. Something that surrounded it. I looked around to see if anyone was watching me from the neighbors to our left and right. Everything was quiet.

The dead trees on the other side of the fence swayed in a light breeze. The yard under my feet was cracked and dry, the grass gone. My shoulders hunched up to my ears, my arms crossed over the hand-me-down black t-shirt from Devon. The bird stared at me, unmoving. I stared back, curious, even though an insistent fear. The shadow wrapped around the bird shifted like smoke. As I got closer I could see behind the bird's eyes, and in them burned a red flame.

The glass door slid open. I whirled around, ready to see Mom coming after me, but it was Devon. He stomped across the empty yard toward me, his arms bowed out as if he were ready to fight someone else. Once he was standing beside me, he sighed, ran his hands through his sandy hair then crouched down, covering his face with his forearms. I put my hand on his back then glanced up expecting to see the bird had flown. It looked back at me with its black and fiery eyes. The shadow around it grew as the bird's gaze snapped to Devon.

I inched in front of him, but the bird shifted its head to peer around my skinny form. Its head cocked one direction, then the next, its neck extending out. He was making the same face and movements as the robins I'd watched pecking worms out of the ground.

"Devon." My voice rattled. Sharpened talons of panic gripped my gut. "I think we need to go inside."

"What?" Devon's voice came from behind me.

"Let's go in the house." I reached behind me for my brother. The bird shifted from one foot to the next, stretched its wings and opened its beak, its eyes still focused on Devon like laser beams.

"I'm not going back in there, Haelyn. Mom's unbearable." He rose behind me, my hand falling away from where it had rested on his shoulder. The inky blackness around the bird expanded, and as if it had been made of gasoline, it caught fire by the flames dancing behind those beady black eyes. The crown of feathers on the hawk's head fluffed up on end. Its mouth burst open and from the black and yellow beak came an unearthly cry – like a growl and bird and the voices of tortured people all tripping over each other. I covered my ears, dropping to the ground as the bird's scream stretched away.

Devon made a startled noise behind me. Something brushed against my hair. I turned to look at Devon but could only see the giant hawk as it swooped toward Devon's face. The shadow surrounding the animal wrapped around Devon as the hawk clawed into his shoulders. Devon screamed, stumbled and fell backward to the barren ground. The bird's cry ceased. The shadow disappeared and the hawk fell dead to the ground beside Devon, its black eyes no longer burning, but staring at the clouded sky above.

SIX ~ RORI - HAUNTING, MARCH 2014

The smell of popcorn filled the living room as the TV buzzed to life. Aubry was tucked into bed and fast asleep. I fiddled with the remote control, turning to the video-streaming station that had the ghost hunter show. Darkness spilled in from the windows. I had a small table lamp on next to the beige sofa, and light leaked in from the kitchen directly behind the living area. Everything faced the eastern view of the pine-ridged Smoky Mountains, which was lost in the darkness of night.

"It's starting!"

"Almost done," said Josh. The sound of popcorn being shook from the bag into a bowl hushed through the scene playing on the TV of the stalking ghost hunter. He was in near-darkness and the camera bounced lightly as he tiptoed across bare wooden floors in his typical sandal-covered feet. The nightvision on the camera made everything slightly green. Tom, the ghost hunter, pressed his forearm to his beard-covered face, bumping his thick glasses with the back of his hand.

"Whoa. The smell is intense in here." He coughed against the apparent odor.

I curled my legs underneath me as Josh settled into the cushion beside me. I pushed my cold feet into his warm legs, feeling the wiry muscles under his jeans. "Where are they at today?" he asked. I exited the full screen and scrolled down to read the description and date. The blurb indicated the ghost hunter was investigating an old house in the deep parts of Georgia, after people in the area had reported hearing screams and seeing eerie flashing lights and smoke coming from the abandoned house.

The ghost hunter show was one means of investigation for me. While most normal people couldn't see past the veil, sometimes the creatures could affect their surroundings. If something had indeed escaped, I needed to retrieve it and return it to the gated area for dangerous creatures.

So, I kept a close eye on the papers, watched the blogs on ghost hunters and paranormal activity, and tuned in to my favorite ghost hunter shows through the internet. I couldn't count on the TV; it took too long to get the info. This guy was pretty good. He had a sense about him. Perhaps being one of those people that could see past the veil to the other side of things. Most people like that went crazy, had a lot of secrets or tried to prove it to everyone else.

I reached over and grabbed a handful of popcorn, popping a few kernels into my mouth and chomping. Josh's hand touched my feet. The ghost hunter was rounding a corner to peer into an antiquated and empty kitchen area. I jerked my head to Josh, distracted by the touch of his warm hands. "Your feet are freezing," he said.

"I should probably put some socks on," I said, turning back to the screen.

"I'll warm 'em up." He left his big hand over my feet, pressing them further into his leg. A little thrill shot through my middle. It burned dangerously inside of me and as I turned my head to look at Josh, I caught his smell.

Warm, fresh, clean. He was looking at my feet as he rubbed his hands slowly back and forth over them, sending shivers up my legs. He smiled as the warmth returned to my icy toes. I watched his mouth, the curve of his lips inviting.

When he looked up, his blue eyes went wide. "What?" he asked startled. I yanked my body off the couch in one swift movement.

"I'm going to grab some socks." I stomped out of the living room and didn't turn back to see the startled look on Josh's face. When I got to my bedroom I shook my hands free of the shuddering waves of longing coursing through me.

My socks were piled in a small wicker basket. I hate folding socks. Dropping to my knees on the hardwood, I picked through the basket until I came up with two green and blue fuzzy socks. They totally didn't match what I was wearing. I did not care.

Flipping around to sit on my butt, I wiggled my now-warm feet into the soft garments then sat there rubbing the material, as if they would comfort me. As if they would soothe away the guilt dropping in my belly. It wasn't as if I were cheating on anyone. Jameson's face still flashed through my memory, along with Aubry's. *I don't need a man around,* I thought to myself. *We're doing just fine on our own.* It was the same chant I'd been saying the last nine years. And while I believed it, while it was true, there was also a piece of me that was just plain lonely. I stomped my green and blue sock into the hardwood. The thought of walking back into the living room after abruptly walking out filled me with a leaden embarrassment that coated the guilt already spreading through my limbs. I groaned and let my head sink to my knees.

"Rori," Josh's voice rose, drawing out my name. "Better come look at this." Jumping up, I dashed down the hall, skidding into the living room on my socked feet. I faced the TV as I backed into the love seat opposite the couch where I had been sitting. Opposite from Josh.

The green and black image on the screen showed a scene like one out of a horror movie. Tom, the ghost hunter, coughed then covered his mouth and nose. Dark stains smudged the shadows like paint splashed haphazardly on a wall. In the center of the room an irregular lump lay unmoving. What the video didn't show was the smell, which I suspected reeked of blood and death and rotting things.

Tom swiveled, first into the camera and then away from it. Out of sight of the camera his breathing ratcheted through the speaker. In his absence, the green light picked up an empty pit carved out in the middle of the floor, like someone had hacked away a fire pit. There were bits of things here and there on the hardwood. The camera jiggled then the room became illuminated in the yellow glow of a flashlight. Tom came back into view.

"Excuse me folks," he began, "that took me by surprise. Keep filming, Gary. He nudged his thick glasses with a knuckle then wiped at his reddish-blond bearded mouth with a t-shirt-clad shoulder. He pinched the bridge of his nose, breathing slowly, clearly focusing on not puking. He groaned. "As you can see," on cue Gary, the cameraman turned his focus from Tom, the ghost hunter, to the room in front of them, its four walls spattered in dark red, "this appears to have been the scene of a –"

"Sacrifice," I said.

"- sacrificial offering, or something," Tom said. Josh looked at me, mouth pinched in a grim line.

"What do you think? A lesser?" Josh asked. There's all sorts of nastiness in the world. A lesser, or Raven Mocker, was a witch who stole the hearts of other creatures, animals and even people in order to live past the normal life expectancy. They were all over the country. If we heard about them, we dispatched them. I hadn't seen one in years, but that didn't mean they weren't still out there.

"Maybe," I said, turning back to the TV, but my mind was on the hawk feather we'd found at the gate. The small circle of light cast by the flashlight on the camera arced around the room slowly then came to rest on the fire pit and irregular lump on the floor. Josh set the bowl of popcorn on the coffee table in front of him, his face turning green. A big buck was stretched out, flies swarming its bloated body and vacant eyes. It had been slit open, its guts spilling out in front of the fire pit. I thanked my lucky stars no one had invented smell-e-vision. Tom, the ghost hunter gagged. His heavy breathing filled the eerie darkness.

"Well, now we know the source of the smell in here," said Tom. The cameraman swiveled around. Tom knelt on the floor a good distance away from the buck and fire pit. "This is so wrong. I've never in my life seen anything like this. This isn't a ghost. This is just sick." The camera image panned over the room in the abandoned Georgia homestead.

"Come on. Get closer," I said. I was on the edge of my seat. The bits on the floor were still too obscured for me to get a good look at them. Tom rose and pushed himself closer, his face half-turned away from the mayhem, as if this would help him get through the encounter. I could see his horror vying with his curiosity.

"There's some stuff on the floor, here." He coughed as he knelt down, close to two fragments. "Gary, get in here and get a look at this. I'm not sure what this is." He picked up one of the small pieces, tossing it up and down in his meaty hands, as if weighing it. A nervous shot ran through me.

"Hey, be careful with that," I told the TV.

"Zoom in on this," Tom told Gary. As the flashlight wobbled and then took focus, the two pieces Tom held in his hand grew larger on the screen.

"What is that, Rori?" asked Josh.

"This is a little out of my realm," Tom was saying. Shivers ran along my arms and back. He turned the pieces so that they were lined up to connect where a crack had separated them. "I don't know if you can see this, folks, but this appears to be some very ancient artifact. It's made of a very lightweight stone. As you can see it's taking up most of the palm of my hand, so let's call that four inches high and maybe three and a half inches wide.

Sort of a rounded rectangle. The image on it looks like a man in a feathered costume, like a bird."

"The Birdman of Cahokia," I corrected and answered Josh.

"Yeah, but, what is it? I mean - the Birdman of Cohokia, but who's that?"

I turned and faced Josh. "How much do you know of the history of the Bitten and Ani'Kutani?"

"Well," he began, "I know the Ani'Kutani were powerful magic workers and oppressed the Cherokee with it. And I know the original Uktena Bitten was an Ani'Kutani daughter who rebelled against their oppression."

"Particularly, the parts where they sacrificed innocent people to fuel their power," I said.

"Right. As payment for her revolt, the Ani'Kutani tossed her in with the Uktena dragon they'd captured. When the Uktena saw her pure heart and intention to overthrow the priests, she bit her to infuse her with dragon-ish power." He swirled his hands in front of him in a gesture of mystic dragon magic.

"And then the original Bitten led the Cherokee nation to overthrow the Ani'Kutani," I finished.

"Yes. That's what I know."

I inhaled deeply, leaning back into the couch. "We believe the Cahokia Mounds was where it all happened," I explained. "The birdman burial, the tablets of the birdman, the pits and live burials all point to the Ani'Kutani. Because the hawk was the Ani'Kutani's totem. It gave them power, even fed on their sacrifices and fueled their magic. And what our history tells us, as fuzzy as it is, is that the Birdman had joined with the hawk in the final battle between the Ani'Kutani and Cherokee."

"Like possessed it with his spirit?"

"They formed a sort of symbiotic relationship. That sort of screwed the Birdman, because once he joined, he couldn't return to his own body."

"None too bright," Josh assessed.

"I'm thinking he was pretty desperate at that point." I pulled my feet up onto the couch, tucking them underneath me, cross-legged. "While still in the hawk form, the Bitten battled the Birdman. Apparently, she couldn't kill him while he was joined with the hawk. And the hawk he joined with – it was like a monster size hawk," I clarified.

Josh reached for the popcorn and began munching, his eyes fixed on me.

"So, instead, she banished him, forming the lesser gate with a scale from the Uktena." Josh stopped chewing, his mouth frozen mid-chew.

"And *that's* what's escaped the lesser gate?" he asked, incredulous. "An ancient Ani'Kutani priest possessed giant hawk?"

I shrugged and waved at the TV. "That's what it looks like. The question is now, what does it want, and who helped him get here." I reached for my cell phone on the end table and started scrolling through the recent contacts.

"Well, what it wants is pretty easy isn't it?" Josh asked. I looked at him, willing him to speak, while my mind churned at the possible consequences of the birdman's escape from his prison behind the lesser gate. I found mom's number and pulled up the contact to dial her. "World domination, right? Like, 'to watch the world burn' and all that."

"What am I, Batman?"

"Well," he crossed his arms over his blue fleece sweatshirt, cocked his head to one side and appraised me. It made me squirm. "You'd be a sexier Catwoman, but Batman works."

My cheeks simmered and Josh grinned at me. I touched the call button on the phone and pressed it to my ear.

SEVEN ~ HAELYN - HUNTING

"Why do I have to listen to you?"

"Because I'm your big brother."

"No. You're not," I whispered. I watched dust motes dance on afternoon sunbeams coming into the window.

"Look at me, Haelyn." His voice caught on my name. I peered up into his eyes from where I sat on my bed, my favorite doll in my hand. He put his hand gently on my chin and tilted it up. He smiled at me. The emerald in his eyes shone brightly. His rounded nose and chin were pink with warmth. But there were heavy, gray bags under his eyes.

"Devon?"

"Yeah, squirt," he said. I threw my arms around his neck and hugged him. He smelled like laundry soap. The gray t-shirt he wore was soft against my arm and the firmness of his shoulders underneath comforted me. This was Devon. He wouldn't let anything happen to me. "Now, you gotta do me this favor, okay?"

"We have to?" I asked into his shoulder.

"Yeah, squirt. If we don't, well…" his voice cracked, "we just have to. Otherwise, I'm going to get in some bad trouble. Okay?"

"Okay," I agreed. He pulled me up from my bed. I laid the doll down and followed Devon down the stairs and out to the back yard, moths of worry flitting through the middle of me. The sky had a thin cover of gray so the afternoon was muted. Devon veered away from the shed and to the rickety gate on the fence. He fiddled with the metal latch then pulled at the gate until it creaked open enough to let us through.

Mom was out. Probably at the bar. I hoped she didn't bring some guy home again. She left Devon in charge. It had been a few weeks since the hawk and Devon was different. Some days he didn't say anything at all. Just went into his room and locked the door. He had that smoky red look in his eyes sometimes and didn't go to school for a week. Last week, he'd gone to school, but I heard Mom talking on the phone once. The principal had called her. Devon was getting into a lot of trouble. His grades fell and his friends stopped coming over. His girlfriend broke up with him. She'd come to the door, yelled at him and then left. All while Devon stood rooted at the door, looking like she was an alien.

The forest behind our house wasn't our property. It was a green belt, but we could go into it if we wanted. Devon and I were the only kids in the neighborhood, so we were the only ones that came back here. It was a nice place to go to get away from mom. At least when it wasn't raining or really cold out.

I tromped over the wet leaves and mud until we came to a little clearing I liked to play in. The air was cold and wet. I huffed and a cloud of steam hung in the air in front of me. I wrapped my skinny arms around my body. My sweatshirt was old and scratched at the skin on my arms, which were covered in goosebumps. "Why are we here?"

Devon slid into the clearing beside me. He rubbed his hands and looked down at me. His eyes flashed the color of lava. "There's a certain animal we need to look for," he instructed. "It's…" Devon looked away from me, peering into the gray sky, like the animal would be waiting there. "It's not something we've ever seen before. I keep telling – " Devon doubled over. Air whooshed out of him, like someone had punched him in the gut.

"Devon!" I leaned by him. My breath was heaving. I reached out my hand then yanked it away at the feel of fiery electricity pulsing around Devon's body. He wobbled, fell to his knees and at last gulped at the spring air.

"It's okay," he said, gasping. "It's okay. I'll be fine. That was just the wrong thing to say." He stood straight again, rubbing at his belly. "And we need to get this animal. I'm going to die, Haelyn, unless we get this animal, this creature."

I sobbed. My stomach hurt and I shook all over. "Okay, okay, I'll do whatever you need!" I promised. Tears streamed down my cheeks.

"Listen," Devon's voice hitched on the word. I knew without looking that the red would be back in his eyes. "Look out into the woods. Sit. Take this." Devon handed me a big, black and white spotted feather. I recognized it immediately as a feather from the hawk that had flown down on Devon. Shaking, I took the thing and slumped into a sitting position on the leaf-littered ground, wiping my tears away with the sleeve of my gray sweatshirt. The dead trees around me, interspersed with a few evergreens swayed in a gentle wind.

"Now what?" I asked.

"Call them."

"Who? How?" I looked up out of instinct. I wished I hadn't. Devon looked down at me and all the emerald was gone. His face was slack and lost all sign of the love he had for me.

He frowned. "You do not know these things?"

"What things?" Devon kept saying stuff like this and I didn't understand it.

"Your blood," he said, pushing a finger in to my forehead, "is sacred. And. Capable." He sounded out the last word slowly. "I smell it?" He scrunched his eyebrows down together and down over his eyes. "Sense it." He nodded slowly with a flat mouth.

My blood was sacred and capable? What did that mean?

"Someone broke the tablet and released me from my prison, but it was you who brought me here. Your blood and my blood are the same." He pointed to himself.

"Well, I wish I hadn't brought you here. I wish you'd leave my brother alone."

"Quiet. I will teach you the ways of your blood. My blood. So that we may be strong again. So that we may be powerful." His eyes burned. I pulled away from him. My insides squeezed around the freezing feeling of fear. Yet, a part of me wondered. I wanted to know what he meant as much as I wanted my brother back. "Now, think. Hard."

"Concentrate," I interpreted. I breathed slow and steady, twirling the giant feather in my hand by its quill.

"Think about a small creature. With fur all over. You know this creature?" he asked.

"That could be any animal. Fox? Raccoon? Cat? Dog?"

"No," he said and made a slicing gesture with his hand. "This is *creature*, not *animal*."

"Creature?" I asked. I knew what he meant but I didn't want to believe that they were real. Those other things that stalked around that no one could see except me.

"The name is yunwi. Think this name and focus."

I twirled the feather over and over and thought of a small creature covered in fur. I said the name inside my head over and over, until it became a rhythm. *Yunwi, yunwi, yunwi...* The forest fell away from me and I was encompassed by a darkness littered with lights. *Yunwi, yunwi, yunwi...*

My heart flapped in my chest. Under the stony calm and rhythmic song beat a fear that without my focus would consume me. And under that was a swiftly growing desire to see what would happen. Would I really call out a creature that I had never seen before? My curiosity overpowered the fear as the chant grew too loud for my head and I began to utter it out loud.

"Yun-wi, yun-wi yun-wi..." I beat my hand on my leg in time to the rhythm. A light in the blackness grew. I twirled the feather in my right hand. Faster. Louder. The light grew brighter. A shuffle in the leaf litter snapped me out of the place of blackness. As the forest swirled back into my vision Devon launched forward. He moved faster than I had ever seen him move. He lurched at the opposite edge of the clearing onto a waiting shadow. A high-pitched scream pierced the cool spring afternoon air. I had done it. I had called the creature he'd told me to call. Excitement shivered around nervousness. That was magic, wasn't it? My mind raced as an eager rush to learn and do more filled me.

Devon struggled with the thing he held in his hands. It was fur covered and half the size of my brother. I couldn't make out the color of it. Every time it shifted and fought against Devon's pinning arms its fur changed. It was like someone was clicking from one station to the next. One second it was brown then it was moss green and then the next moment it was the raspy color of dead leaves.

Another rustle in the brush nearby drew my gaze. In the bare shrubs and bracken a smaller fur-covered creature crouched frozen and wide-eyed, staring at Devon. Devon smelled the air, his head jerking in the direction of the smaller creature, even as he wrestled the larger one. Faster than lightning, Devon drew a small blade from his belt and launched it into the undergrowth. The thing in the brush yelped, stumbled backward and then bolted away on hobbling steps. I watched its retreat, still puzzling out what sort of animal ran upright on two legs and had a hair swoop like those plastic troll dolls. But, it was out of sight before I could get a good look at it.

Devon struggled with the other, bigger thing he held to the ground. I took a few steps toward them. Devon fought to hold the thing still. "Come," he commanded. His eyes glowed red. I jumped and ran to him. "Help hold." I hesitated. Devon's eyes yanked from the creature to me. "Hold or your brother dies!" His eyes cleared and the emerald shone through. "Haelyn, you have to help."

I grabbed onto the creature's muscular hair-covered legs, fascinated as the fur around my hands changed to my skin color. The legs bucked wildly and my hands were thrown off, slipping into the dirt of the forest floor. I squealed in terror as Devon's ember eyes pinned me with anger. Scrabbling over the constant moving legs, I finally managed to get on top of them and dig my knees in, pressing all my scrawny weight onto the thing. The warmth from the creature leaked through my jeans into my skin. I could feel the silk of its fur and how long it was. More like hair than animal fur. The muscles were strong underneath me, but I worked to pin the thing with all my might, fear making my heart whoosh-whoosh-whoosh against my ears. "Good," Devon said, his breath hitching.

Devon had his back to me. He was on the top half of the creature and I was holding its legs. His gray t-shirt had one spot of sweat in the upper middle of his back. The air in the clearing choked in a sudden stillness, as if the trees were holding their breath. From over his shoulder, I could just see the yunwi's eyes. Nothing else. Devon grunted, fighting to hold the yunwi down with one arm and work at something on his belt with the other. I couldn't see what he was grabbing at until it was too late.

"What are you going to do?" I screamed. Metal glinted in the afternoon light. He answered my question with a downward swing into the creature's struggling chest. Blood spattered my face. My mouth opened and a scream ripped out of me as the second stab jerked into the creature's body. The legs underneath me jerked. The creature sucked in a gust of air, its glittering eyes full of Devon's reflection and the glint of burning eyes. Horror filled me as I watched the creature's fight turn to terror and then to nothing. Its legs went still, but it was still warm and the hair was still soft. The eyes still glittered, but something in them had gone out.

I was still screaming. Devon jumped on top of me. My body felt like jelly under his knees. And jelly doesn't feel. His hand clasped my screaming mouth.

"Shut. Up!" His right hand was slicked red with blood, the knife raised above his head. His face was contorted, lips twisted, eyebrows squeezed low over his eyes, nose quirked on one side. I stopped screaming. If I didn't, maybe he would stab me with my mom's butcher knife.

He climbed off of me, stood above me heaving, his face glistening with sweat. The butcher knife clutched in his hand dripped dark and red. He moved toward me and I squeaked, closing my eyes. I felt the nearness of his body, but he hadn't stabbed me or hit me. I opened my eyes again and stared at the hawk feather Devon had picked up and held in front of me.

"You must call forth one more," he said. I took the feather, fear choking out the words I meant to say to protest killing any living animal or creature or whatever. Tears rolled down my face. He smiled at me. Smile was really not the right word. It was a smile made of sharp edges and shadows. Fire danced in his eyes. The smell of blood wafted over us through the plucking of a spring breeze. "One more that you will give life in exchange for the one we have taken."

EIGHT ~ AUBRY - NEW FRIENDS

"Okay, class. Are we ready?" Mrs. Dott asked. Some of us nodded. Some weren't paying attention. Mrs. Dott turned. She wore brown pants and a red shirt with long sleeves. My fourth grade teacher had a funny name because on her face was a big brown dot. A mole, Andy had told me. Mrs. Dott's mole was on her left cheek. She had sharpish blue eyes and short blonde hair that she curled under all around her neck and face. It sort of looked like plastic because it was so shiny and perfect, especially under the midmorning sun. She waved toward the forest. "Let's go then."

She marched ahead and we followed. There were seventeen of us. I knew how many because Valentine's Day was last month and I'd had to get just the right number of valentine cards for everyone. I didn't get one for Hunter though. He'd noticed. It was a bad day. I rubbed my stomach thinking about how he'd punched me.

I didn't tell Mama because I knew what she'd say to me. She'd tell me to punch him back. I didn't know if I was as strong as Mama believed. And I didn't want to find out that I wasn't and have him hit me more. If I just stayed away, maybe he'd leave me alone.

I watched the heads in front of me bumping up and down on the uneven ground of the kickball field. Mia stumbled a little in her stylish oversized boots. The line behind her had to slow. We picked up our speed to close the gap as we got to the trailhead. Mrs. Dott turned to count us, to make sure we were all there. I saw her eyes touch each face, smiling when she looked at Mia and shifting to a cold flatness when she looked at me. I shrugged away from her, hurrying past her dislike of me.

The trees today were chatty. They seemed excited and happy. Even though they were still mostly bare, I could feel the spring coming. They were getting ready to bloom. Working up the energy. It's like something inside of me wakes up after a long nap when I go into the woods. And it's super happy to be there.

When we reached the big opening by the creek, Mrs. Dott stopped us and let us rest. I thought the rest was really for Mrs. Dott. I sat down on one of the four big log benches with Mia and Ella.

The sound of the creek was loud today. Mom said it was because all the snow at the top of the mountains was melting and running down into the rivers and creeks. I looked over my shoulder, through a couple of small trees at the creek. The bed sloped away from the platform of ground where we sat. There were a lot of rocks and tree limbs, but the water rushed around the obstacles. I turned around and draped myself over the gigantic log. Ella copied me, but Mia looked at us and frowned.

"What are you doing?" she asked. She flipped her pretty, long brown hair around her shoulders. She looked at her red sweater, frowned then brushed something off of it.

"Looking at the creek," I told her.

"Looking at the bugs," Ella said at the same time. I looked down at where Ella was staring. A small trail of ants climbed through the wet leaves and dirt. Mia looked down at us.

"You're going to get your pants all dirty sitting in the mud like that," she said.

"So?" I asked, not sure what it mattered. "I wore hiking clothes so I didn't get my pretty clothes dirty."

"What pretty clothes?" Mia asked. One of her dark eyebrows rose over her bright blue eyes. I had always thought they were pretty until that moment. I looked at Mia's outfit and remembered something Andy had said once. I stood up and gestured to my outfit.

"It's called dressing for the occasion. Something you clearly don't have a grasp on." I mimicked Andy's gesture and put my fists on my hips. Mia's mouth opened like an 'O' then closed again as her cheeks turned red. Then she stood up. Ella turned around, her almost-white hair framing the surprised look on her face. Mia took one step in her stupid oversized boots and tights and shoved me.

I stumbled back. Heat flashed through me. When I looked at her, I saw her through a red haze. Everyone and everything dissolved in my anger. My stomach clamped down, like when Hunter had punched me. As soon as I regained my footing, I shoved her back. My mouth opened and words rushed out of me. Words I didn't expect or even feel past the surging red anger that shoved aside my meekness. "Don't ever touch me again."

Mia flew back and down. She landed in the legs of some of our classmates. Something warm closed around my upper arm. I yanked my arm away, fighting to clear my ears of the thump, thump, thump of my heartbeat. When I turned to see what was grabbing at me, I saw Mrs. Dott's flushed face. My throat tightened and my belly squeezed. I went from angry to scared in a second.

"Aubry Cantrell," she started. Mia was crying. The kids that she'd landed in front of looked from her to me. I looked up at Mrs. Dott. Her blue eyes were like shards of ice under her drawn on eyebrows.

"Mrs. Dott, she pushed me first," I protested.

"Really?" she asked. "Because it looks like you're in pretty good shape for being pushed." She marched me past the open spot. All the kids watched me. Some of them made 'ooo' sounds. Ella still looked surprised.

Mrs. Dott sat me on a stump away from everybody else. She perched her hands on her khaki hips and looked down at me. The forest around me held its breath. I breathed in slowly and looked at my teacher. Now that I was away from Mia, I felt bad for what I'd done. I shouldn't have shoved her.

"I am very disappointed in you, Aubry. I would never guess that you would be capable of such meanness." She didn't have to say that. I didn't think I was capable either. Or mean.

"Sorry," I said, fighting back the urge to burst into tears.

"Well, you can just sit here by yourself and think about what you did while the rest of us have a snack. When we are done, you stay there until the back of the line passes and then you can join us. I'm calling your mother when we get back to the school and you can tell her what you did." I swallowed down a knot. When the knot hit my stomach it burned. Mom wasn't going to be happy with me.

I sat on the stump and looked out into the forest, finally letting the tears free, since nobody was looking. When there were no more tears obstructing my sight, I watched the forest. A cool breeze sifted through the trees. I caught a smell of something. Mama was teaching me to use my nose. She said it was much stronger than most people's noses because of the dragon blood.

I lifted my nose into the air and sniffed, trying to recognize the smell on the breeze. I had smelled it before. The musky aroma was sweet and strong like when Mama brought home flowers and left them sitting there after they died.

Focusing my eyes, I peered into the columns of empty oaks and ash. Not much could hide in the forest right now. Not with all the naked trees. I leaned forward on the tree stump that was my naughty chair and adjusted the backpack strapped to my back. The sound of the straps scraping over my burgundy sweatshirt hissed loudly in my ears. Something shifted in the trees. Its movement sent a shiver of new scent on the wind.

The next movement gave me a clear view of the creature. I fought back an inhale as it moved to another tree. It looked injured. The way he walked was all cattywampus. I stood from the tree trunk and shuffled over the trail two steps before I heard Mrs. Dott's voice and the other kids laughing and chatting.

I hurried back to my time-out seat and waited, holding my breath as I watched the little guy scramble in the leaf litter, pulling himself along the forest floor, to the safety of a burrow in a big oak.

I shifted on my seat, pulled a strand of hair and began twisting a curl. Mrs. Dott's khaki and red shone brightly through the shade of the forest. The line of students followed up the hill and round a bend. When Mrs. Dott got to me, she slowed long enough to give me a stern look and shake of her glossy blonde hair then passed on.

Mia was second in line, and then Ella. Ella was still staring at me with an open mouth, as if her face had frozen when I pushed Mia. Mia tossed her long brown hair over her shoulder and stuck her tongue out at me.

When the last of my class shuffled past I darted over the path, stepping carefully through the bracken. I stopped several feet away from the yunwi and spoke softly, "Hey now." He was so small. Like the size of a baby doll. The yunwi looked up at me with his round face all covered in long hair. His big, black twinkling eyes were wide and scared. I bent to my knees, listening hard to the class as they continued along the trail, trying to hear how far they'd gone and how quickly I would have to move to catch up to them.

The little yunwi was breathing hard. His mouth trembled around his flat teeth. His round nose twitched as my scent gathered around him. His right hand covered a big, ugly gash on his right leg. The leaves in the path where he'd crawled were all spotted in dark red.

"Aw," I soothed, "You're hurt." He looked down at his leg. I hummed as I got closer. Just something I made up in my head to soothe him, since yunwis love music. The yunwi's breath slowed, his eyes softened a little. If he were well, he'd sing along. But that gash in his leg was pretty bad. It even smelled bad. I slowly pulled the backpack from my back and reached in for the paper towel I had left over from lunch yesterday. It wasn't much, but maybe it would help until I could get him to Mama. I folded the thick paper towel as I hummed and reached toward the yunwi. He looked from it to me and back again. "If you let me, I'll help you with that." I gestured toward his wound with the paper towel. He flinched away from it a little then settled again when I didn't move. "You're going to have to come home with me."

A noise behind me made me turn on my knees on the forest floor. I stood up, standing wide, like I'd seen Mama do to defend a hurt creature. If a fox or a coyote or bobcat was out there, it would eat him. No way was I going to let that happen. Normally, if the yunwi was well, it could hide itself. They lived on this side of the veil, not hidden automatically, but they had magic to either show themselves or hide.

Hunter stood there staring at me. I didn't move. If he saw the creature, we'd both be in trouble. There were things Mama knew how to do to hide the yunwi if they were hurt and needed it, but I hadn't been through the Joining yet and didn't know any of those.

"What are you doing?" he asked. "The class is way ahead now."

"I – I dropped something," I fibbed. "I'm trying to find it." Hunter moved toward me. He had a weird grin on his face. My heart sped. Anytime Hunter moved toward me, I wanted to move away. The yunwi was behind me, though. I wouldn't move if that meant not protecting the hurt creature.

Hunter got right up to me, towering over me. If I weren't craning my neck to look up at his dark brown eyes and rusty cheeks, I'd be looking at his chest. This close, I could smell him. His clothes had that sour smell from when they sit in the washer too long. He looked me up and down. He raised a hand and poked my shoulder. My tennis shoes slipped backward. I hoped I wasn't stepping on the yunwi. I hoped he didn't try to move. "Yeah," he began. "What'd you drop, weirdo?"

"It's – nothing, it's just – " I searched around the forest floor then looked at the paper towel in my hand. I held it up. "This," I said. "I dropped this, but I have it now."

"Yeah, well, why don't you get lost then?" He pushed me again, harder. I saw it coming, so I dug my heels in and this time he didn't move me much. His big, pointy fingers poked hard. I hissed through my teeth at the pain, even though I didn't mean to.

"Ow," I said then regretted it.

"Aw, did the poor, wittle giwl get huwt?" he said in a baby voice. He pushed me again with both hands. I slipped some more. I glanced backward before I could stop myself then whipped my head back. "Oh, is there something back here?" Hunter tried to sidestep me. In a panic, I shuffled to my right to block his movement.

He looked at me with his yellow eyebrows high. "Move. Or I'll make you." My breath jagged in and out of my heaving lungs, my heart thumped away in my ears. Any other time, I would have run. I couldn't leave the yunwi to defend himself alone. So, I jutted out my chin and shook my head.

His fist rose. My arms went up to block, but they weren't high enough for how tall he was. His clenched hand crashed into my face. My eye exploded in pain. I screamed. I fell on the ground, against my right side. Tears burst from my eyes. I looked to the yunwi, but he wasn't lying on the ground anymore. He stood in front of the tree, tiny compared to the giant that was Hunter.

"What the - ?" I could see Hunter staring down at the little furry creature in front of him. He stepped away. The yunwi raised his short bare hands, dark, round nubs of fingers spread out. He spoke in short choppy words that I didn't recognize. A blue haze spread from his hands. His face looked stern despite the swoop of hair rising from his head. I decided I never wanted a yunwi to look at me like that.

Hunter turned then froze as a bluish fog rolled over him. His arms and legs went stiff as his brown eyes stretched in fear. His mouth hung open and the fog gathered, twisting into itself and coiled down Hunter's throat. He gurgled and gasped, his shoulders twitching.

When all the fog was gone, his eyes rolled back in his head and he fell like a chopped tree.

NINE ~ AUBRY - WITNESS

The rest of the day, I worried about whether Hunter would say something to somebody, and how the yunwi was doing, nestled in my backpack. I also had a bad headache and my eye hurt so bad. I didn't want to go to the nurse and have somebody else not believe the lies I was forced to tell.

When the release bell rang, I rushed to my cubby and checked inside. My head throbbed as I looked through the swollen eye into the darkness. The yunwi looked up at me and purred, glittering eyes half-closed. He looked really tired. It was probably because he had used his magic.

I pulled the backpack carefully on my arms and hustled to the door. After we marched outside, I stood in line for the parent pick-up. It was even warmer now and the air smelled like things about to grow. Kids ran around the fenced play area where the parent pick-up was. One duty was watching one end of the group of kids, and the other duty was watching the gate we had to exit to get to our parents' cars.

I knelt in the grass and took the backpack off of my shoulders. Mama said I was really strong for a nine-year-old, but the yunwi was still really heavy, and in the sunshine, my head and eye hurt so bad my stomach joined in too. Placing the backpack in front of my knees, I unzipped it. The yunwi looked up at me then wiggled his round nose in the air. He grabbed the edge of the backpack and started to pull himself up. I put my hand on his spiky hair to push him back down as gently as I could.

"No, you can't come out yet," I told him.

"Who are you talking to?"

My head whipped up. There was a blob of a shadow in the sunlight shining down on us. I pushed and zipped at the same time, catching my wrist in the zipper. The yunwi growled in the backpack. *Crap!* I thought.

"What do you have in there? Is that – no, it wouldn't be that." The black blob knelt down beside me. She was older than me. Her skin was dark brown, her hair black and her eyes as dark as her hair. Her face was round, her cheekbones high. She had thin lips which curled into a smile at me. She looked me straight in the eyes and said, "Let me see."

Something about her words made me want to run away, even though she was smiling. "No." I told her. "It's my pet and it's not feeling well and doesn't like other kids." She frowned at me. I was telling so many lies today.

"What happened to your face?" she asked. She studied my face between darting glances to my backpack.

"Nothing," I said and drew out the word. I stood up and pulled the backpack close to me.

"Aubry!" the duty called me and I ran, looking over my shoulder at the girl in the grass. She stared at me, frowning with bunched up eyebrows. Even after I turned and got in the car, I could feel her eyes on me.

TEN ~ RORI - HOMEWORK

"Yes, Mrs. Dott," I began, fighting the urge to hang up the phone, hop in the car, drive down and kick this woman's ass. "I know what Aubry said, but do you believe for one minute that bully did not hit my daughter? And even if he didn't, I would like to understand your reasoning for *not* calling me immediately, as well as *not* sending her to the nurse to be seen. Do you even know what kind of pain she is in?"

Wuffers whined at me. I stood up from the couch and paced in front of the big windows. Aubry tugged on my sleeve as I walked near her. Mrs. Dott was talking, I could hear the fear and chagrin in her voice mingling with her utter pride in not wanting to be wrong. "Mrs. Cantrell, if a child is unhurt, refuses the nurse's attention and says she's fine to return to class then that is what we do. As for Hunter, he's in far worse of a state than your daughter –"

"Stop right there," I cut her off. "I don't give a rat's ass what the boy looked like or why he was sick. His state has nothing, I repeat, nothing to do with my daughter. When my daughter comes home with a shiner, I expect to have been told about it." Aubry tugged at my sleeve again. I held out my hand to her to signal I needed just one more second.

"Mama!" she whispered urgently.

"Well, I expect we'll have to agree to disagree, Mrs. Cantrell," Mrs. Dott was saying on the other end of my smart phone.

"No," I said, "I expect you'll do exactly as I say or I will report your negligence to the school board and have you relieved of your duties as a teacher."

"Are you threatening me?" she asked, incredulous.

"No, ma'am. I'm simply stating the consequences if you should choose the route you've just outlined to me."

Aubry yanked on my arm. Luckily, it wasn't the one holding the phone. Even so, my shoulders and head followed where my arm went and when my head sprang back, it smacked against the cell phone. I looked at Aubry, wondering if she'd lost her mind completely. My stern gaze disappeared when I saw her cradling a yunwi.

"Gotta go, Mrs. Dott." I hung up the phone. "Aubry Cantrell! Why didn't you say something?" She gave me a look, lips pursed and eyebrows drawn together. It said, without her having to say it, 'that's what I've been trying to do.' I knelt down to her and took the wounded yunwi. A girl. She had a gash the whole length of her thigh. It looked old. The swollen mass of it and the gawd-awful smell told me it had been approximately two weeks.

"Can you help him, Mama?" she said, her eyes full of concern. Sweet girl.

"Well," I started, and stood up, "first of all, this is a girl yunwi." I walked to the kitchen counter. The warmth of the creature spread across belly and chest. She was feverish. The counter was a big, wide slab of marble. It made an excellent worktable. I laid the yunwi down carefully, cradling her head in my hand to soften the transition to the hard surface.

"A girl?" Aubry asked. I looked at her expression. Puzzled and happy. I guess some animals you just assume a gender. Like dogs are always boys and cats are always girls.

"Flip on the big light, baby," I said.

That girl was so quiet. Here we'd driven all the way home and she hadn't said anything about the black eye or the yunwi she'd somehow managed to stow away. I heard her scuttle away, the flick of the switch then her soft footsteps back.

"Is she going to be okay, Mama?" she asked.

Wuffers nudged my elbow as I peered down at the yunwi. I moved a step aside for her to take a sniff.

She was tall enough that her nose reached over the counter. She nudged the yunwi with her shiny black nose, sniffing loudly. Then she lowered her head and sneezed. She looked up at me with her bright orange eyes and wagged her tail.

"Wuffers thinks so," I said. Aubry's shoulders slumped and her face relaxed. "It's going to take some doing. This is an old wound. It's infected. Mama's going to need her kit."

"I'll get it!" She was gone, Wuffers on her heels, the clack-clack-clack of Wuffers's nails against the hardwood fading down the hall. While she was gone, the little one sighed. Unconscious, for the most part, I watched as she shook her round head in a gentle back and forth against the black and grey marble counter top. All of the little one's natural brown in the fur began to darken. First just turning black then gathering the detail of the counter. I touched the soft hair sticking up in big long swoops off of her head. By the time Aubry returned you couldn't see the difference between the yunwi's fur and the counter top, except for the shape, bulging against the flat surface.

Aubry grunted as she hefted the leather case onto the counter. When she turned and faced me, her mouth fell open as her left eye grew bigger. Of course, the right eye was nearly swollen shut. She'd never seen a yunwi change to so utterly an invisible camouflage. I bit back a laugh, but a mutter rolled through my closed lips.

"She's still there?" she asked, guessing at the reason for my laugh.

"Come over here." I gestured with my head. The counter was at her shoulder level. I pulled her long, dark auburn hair away from her shoulders, running my hand down the length of the silky strands. She peered at the mass that was the hidden yunwi. "Go ahead, touch her hair."

"Is it really hair, Mama? Isn't it fur?" she asked, looking up at me with that shiner that was likely to be all shades of purple by tomorrow. I considered calling Josh. He was better with kids than adults. And Aubry loved him.

"It's hair, because it keeps growing," I explained. "Fur stays the same length. Like Wuffer's. A yunwi's hair just keeps growing. When they're old, their hair is their prize. You can tell the age of a yunwi by the length of their hair. When they are born, they are covered with a fine, soft fuzz. By the time they are one year old, the hair is around one inch long. So, knowing that, touch this girl's hair and you tell me how old you think she might be."

She reached a hand out and touched the yunwi's hair, pulling her fingers centimeter by centimeter through the now black and grey speckled strands. It was about three inches. She looked back at me. "Three years?"

"I'd say so," I confirmed. She smiled; a rare treat. I bent down and squeezed her. I was rewarded with a return hug around my neck. "Now, shall we see what we can do with this leg?" She nodded and dragged the big black leather case over the countertop, closer to us.

Mom is a vet. It was important to have someone in the family to keep up on the latest information. I opened my big, leather case and pulled out the alcohol, saline, antibiotics and materials to stitch the wound. This was not my favorite part of being a Bitten. I followed the steps Mom had taught me, even though I lacked that extra sense Andy had and the healing touch he possessed. If it was any more difficult than a stitching and administering antibiotics, I'd have to call Mom. I administered a sedative to keep the yunwi from waking in the middle of everything. I went to work and prayed the infection hadn't gone to the bone.

Not wanting to lose focus, I kept our conversation about Aubry's day until we had tucked the yunwi carefully into the loveseat, covered in blankets. After I washed up and put away the supplies, I found Aubry sitting on the floor, watching the yunwi shift to the cream color of the couch. I sat down on the matching sofa, facing the big windows looking out onto the rolling hills and dense forest. From here I could see the pond and the trailhead. The sun was setting, the eastern horizon view from our living room turning shades of blue and purple

I turned my gaze onto Aubry. She touched her swollen cheek and winced. I fished my phone out of my pocket and dialed Josh. He picked up with a "Hello?" His warm voice on the other end eased the tension out of my shoulders.

"Hey, how's it going?"

"Another day in paradise." I heard the smile in his voice.

"I was wondering if you'd do me a favor?"

"Anything for you, O Bitten One." Whenever he said things like that I knew he meant it. But he meant it so much that sometimes I felt uncomfortable. That little twinge of Jameson still lodged in my heart kept me from allowing him too close.

"Aubry got punched by a bully at school today. Could you come work some magic on her?"

"What?" his voice crawled octaves. Yeah, I knew he'd be as perturbed as I was. "Someone hit our girl? Boy, I'm likely to work some magic on that kid. What's his name?"

"Well, someone else came to her rescue. It's a bit of a story. You come over and I'll fill you in. Shoot, I'll even feed you." Not that he needed the bribe to agree, but a single guy likes a home cooked meal every now and again.

"Dinner plus the company of the two most loveliest ladies in all Waynesville? I'm there."

I hung up and regarded Aubry. “Josh is on his way to help with your eye.” She smiled. “Now then. Come on over here and you tell me about that,” I said.

ELEVEN ~ HAELYN - STRONGER

My tennis shoes touched the sidewalk as I climbed out of the bus. The smell of old leather and the laughter of other kids washed away in a gust of exhaust as the bus pulled from the curb. I climbed the short hill to the house, passing the neighbor's yard with the insistent barking of the bulldog behind the fence. The house was old, like the rest in the neighborhood.

I stopped and bent down to Macy, the bulldog. She whined, her short stubbly tail wagging furiously. I reached my hand through a gap in the chained link fence and patted Macy's broad head while she licked at my arm, snuffing and snorting in her excitement. "Hi Macy, hi! Who's a good girl? Is it Macy?" She wagged more and leaned into the scratch I put on her ear.

Macy had a bad habit of digging out of the yard. I spotted a hole near the gate and knew I'd be helping Dr. Sorenson track her down again. Usually, Devon helped me, but not lately. Not since the hawk spirit had entered him.

"Okay, girl, better get home. No more digging," I scolded, shaking a finger at her smushed up face. She panted at me, smiling and wagging. I stood and dusted myself off then continued on home. There were six houses in the neighborhood and all of them were older, but well taken care of. Some of the houses I imagined had the best cooked meals and the kindest grandmothers. Despite my house's fresh coat of white paint and new windows that Mom had had installed last summer, it never felt welcoming to me.

My shoes scuffed against the sidewalk. I watched my toes cross over the cracks. Thinking of the rhyme, I stomped on the next break in the cement.

After reaching our yard, I hopped from one cobblestone to the next until I reached the stairs to the front porch. The boards creaked under my feet. At the door, I twisted the knob, but it was locked. Pulling off the old black backpack that had been Devon's several years ago, I made to reach for the key hooked to a small plastic circle stitched into the front pouch. A hand closed around my arm. I yanked away, thinking of stranger danger that they taught in school. I opened my mouth to scream, but Devon – or more likely, the other guy inside of Devon – clamped a clammy hand over my mouth. My teeth touched the skin of his hand and I tasted saltiness. I pulled away and he let go of my face. His eyes glowed the color of old coals behind the natural emerald.

"Let's go," he said and pulled on my arm. I left my backpack where it was and followed him down the stairs and around the house. He led, walking straight-backed and stiff. We wandered past the line of our property, which was ungated, and into the copse of trees behind our small neighborhood. We got to the clearing where we had been practicing magic. Where many animals had died while one had lived.

Devon handed me the giant hawk's feather I used for summoning. I plucked it from his fingers and twisted it around, staring at the quill and all the fine hairs that formed the whole feather and its speckled pattern. Once he was in the center of the clearing, he turned to me and then gestured over his shoulder. I froze, not sure what the gesture meant or if he would require me to do something based on the gesture. A rustle in the leaves drew my attention. A skinny woman stepped into the open space of sunlight and dead leaves from the ring of trees surrounding us. A breeze picked its way through the trees and fingered through my short, dark hair.

The woman and Devon both inhaled at the same time, their eyes closing to the offering the wind brought to them. It was like someone ran a stick up my spine.

"Who is the friend you hung out with at school today?" My foot moved back a step in the leaf litter before I had time to command it to stay or move. Their eyes on me sent shivers down my arms.

"I don't have friends." Devon cocked his head to the side. It had been about a month since the shadow from the hawk had gotten sucked into Devon. I could see the battle between the two inhabiting one body. The other guy was winning. Every once in a while I saw them merging. Like Devon was confused as to who he used to be. And then, there were other times when he was my big brother again.

"Why don't you have friends, squirt?" he asked. That was my big brother. I perked up at his appearance. Without thinking I began chatting with him.

"I'm not pretty and all my clothes are ugly. The girls think I'm gross and they don't want to –"

"Silence!" A flame burst into the clearing and Devon was gone. The old woman cowered at the sudden fire floating in mid-air. It was bigger this time than the last few times. The other guy was getting stronger. "Tell me whose smell you wear."

What? What a weird question. I sniffed myself. I didn't smell anything. The only person who I'd even been close to was – "I- I don't know her name," I stuttered, fear wedging into my throat. "She's in a grade below me."

"Listen to me."

When the hawk spirit spoke these words it meant he was giving me an order or that he was going to show me how to do something. His English got better within a few weeks. It made me think he was really smart. And he showed me magic. Magic that I could do. So, when he said, 'listen to me', I did. My body leaned forward, eager for the new lesson, hoping that's what it was.

"Make friends with this one whose scent you wear. Bring her to me."

I had no idea how to make friends with someone. The question must have been in my eyes. He read it. "I will help you. Later." I nodded, and lifted my fingers to my mouth. I bit the nail of my pointer finger as he turned back to the old woman. He pressed a hand to her chest and closed his eyes. He gestured for me to come over to him.

I made my way past a tree stump and came to a halt next to him. The woman wore a big pink sweatshirt with cats on the front. Her face seemed stretched in the skin, like it had been pulled tight over her thin bones.

Peeking out over the bulge of a heavy hooked nose, the blackness of overly large irises skidded across the clearing to me. One corner of her small mouth hitched. Her hair was odd. It came down close to black eyebrows, was sleek and shiny blue-black and seemed too thick to be called hair. Her too-skinny body shook and her breath wheezed in and out as she danced from foot to foot. She seemed familiar in a way, but I knew I had never met this woman before.

Devon took my hand and pressed it into the woman's chest. I didn't fight him, I knew better, but my skin crawled at the thought of touching this dirty, smelly woman. I nearly jerked my hand away once I touched her chest. Under my fingertips I felt the beating of too many hearts. I swung my head to Devon. "This is what we created with all those creatures? But, the thing we called looked like a bird." A really weird-looking bird. The kind of thing you'd have nightmares about.

"She is Raven Mocker. We first created them long ago, to help in the hunt. They are helpful in finding the magical. They need hearts. The more hearts, the stronger they are."

My nose wrinkled. And then the thought struck me. He wanted to find more hearts for this woman. I peered up to find him looking at me, the shiny red glowing behind the emerald irises. "Count how many."

I listened carefully, trying to pick out the individual rhythms and where they were coming from. My pinky felt one, my pointer finger another, and then there was a smaller one under my thumb. "Three?"

"Four," the woman croaked. The breath she used to speak rattled through her chest. Devon looked back at me.

"Practice will make you stronger. Summon another."

"What should I summon?" I asked. My heart trilled at the thought of using magic, and then I felt guilty for what would happen to whatever it was I was meant to summon.

"Dog first," he instructed, still feeling the chest of the Raven Mocker. "And then we will summon a distraction for your new friend."

I sat on the forest floor, the dirt beneath me cold and lightly damp. I twisted the feather in my hand and fell into the black universe of stars where I found the things we needed. Dog. I needed to find a dog for the Raven Mocker. I silenced all my worries and the nagging thing in my head that said I was going to kill a dog today. I shoved it aside and focused on the magic. I was doing magic. I could call things to me. I let the wash of power course through me as the feather twisted over and over in my fingers.

The blackness consumed me as I pulled the word dog into my searching consciousness. The first image that popped into my head was Macy, the bulldog. A light in the darkness twinkled like a winking star. *No,* I thought. *Not Macy.* I tried to take it back, to think of another dog, but before I could picture any other kind of dog, Macy's insistent and happy barking broke through the air of the breeze-rustled clearing.

"Good," the Hawkman said. Macy came right up to me. Tears slid down my face and she licked them away. Hawkman snatched her up and before Macy could turn to see who'd picked her up, the knife went quickly across her throat. My stomach fell in on itself. He handed Macy's body to the Raven Mocker who had knelt at his feet, crowing incessantly, hungry eyes glittering.

Hawkman turned his back on her and I closed my eyes and ears and feelings to what the Raven Mocker was doing to the dog. "Now, again and this time we will call something from a place deep in the water."

TWELVE ~ AUBRY - STRANGE GIRL

When I saw the strange girl again, I was on the playground at recess. Since I'd pushed Mia, and then the stuff with Hunter, no one would play with me. Hunter was still not back at school and all the kids whispered behind their hands about me. I could see them. What they didn't know is that I could hear them too.

"I bet she pushed him and he hit his head," Victoria said. She was talking to Mia. Mia crossed her arms over her rainbow shirt and frowned at me. I passed by them sitting at the picnic table. I didn't turn or say anything. I just headed for the tunnel. Mia got up, dusted off her black skirt and followed. I ducked behind a crowd of boys tossing a ball in the air and around the tube slide. After a boy flew out the end, I jumped past the front and over to the tunnel. It was facing the other way, so that Mia wouldn't be able to see in as she walked past. I watched the opening with my back to the cool air of the shadows to make sure she wouldn't come over.

"Why are you hiding?" The girl's voice made me jump. I whirled around to find the tunnel was already taken by the girl that had been so interested to find out what was in my backpack.

"Sorry," I said, "I didn't see you there." I started to back up.

"No, wait," she said and held a hand up from where she clasped them around her twiggy legs. "It's okay, I mean. Uh – you can stay in here."

I looked behind me and saw that Mia was searching for me still. I ducked into the shadows out of her line of sight. Finally she walked away. I turned to the girl. "Thanks," I said.

"Who are you hiding from?" she asked. Her voice was barely more than a whisper and squeaked, like her throat was sore. Her scraggly dark hair hung around her face. Her eyes were as black as the shadows around her. She had wrapped her arms around her skinny legs and rocked forward and back. There was something about her that I couldn't see or smell or hear. The sense made me curious about the girl, so I stayed in the tunnel.

"Mia," I said.

"What'd she do?" She stopped rocking and looked at me with big, round eyes.

"Well, it's more what I did to her." I looked down at the cement tunnel and picked up a pebble. I scratched at the tunnel as I spoke, "I pushed her 'cause she was talkin' crap -" Mama would slap my mouth if she heard me say 'crap'. I felt guilty for uttering the word. "-meanness," I amended. "I think she's mad now. What's your name?" I asked.

"Haelyn," she said. She ducked her head toward her knee and used it to move a strand of hair off her face.

"How old are you?"

"Ten," Haelyn said.

"What grade are you in?"

"Fifth. You?"

I paused, looking at her. I stuck out my hand. "Aubry Cantrell. I'm nine and in fourth grade. Pleasure to meet ya." I smiled at her. Her hand darted forward then pulled back. "I don't bite," I told her. "You don't have to be afraid of a handshake." She put her hand in mine, barely squeezing. I shivered at the touch. It was like I'd plunged my arms into cold water. I pulled my hand away and watched her, trying to figure her out. She wrapped her arm back around the other one and continued rocking.

"So, who are *you* hiding from?" I asked. She pointed. "Those kids over there?" She shook her head and jerked her hand again, her head nodded away from the playground. I looked past the monkey bars and the jungle gym. On the edge of the kickball field, lingering in the brush along the fence, something moved. I focused as much as I could. It shifted. I gasped and clapped my hands over my mouth.

THIRTEEN ~ RORI - MOCKERY

I stretched in front of the TV while I watched the latest ghost hunting show through the web video app. Tom, who had found the hawkman tablet, was back on and walking into a dark cemetery. They were looking for the reported demon dog of Valle Crucis. Which of course, wouldn't be at the cemetery any more, since it was guarding the lesser gate.

"Here, pooch," the guy said, trying to be funny, I suppose. I considered turning off the TV since I knew what I would see, which was a whole lot of nothing. Changing the channel required me getting up to grab the remote, which was on the sofa. So, I sat on the big plush carpet and pushed the coffee table aside with a shove.

The little yunwi was sleeping a ton. I'd gotten her up and fed her several bites of gritts and cream. She whined after the food was in her belly, pointing to the bandaged leg. I'd given her children's advil for pain and tucked her into the playpen I had from when Aubry was a baby. She would heal, I suspected, but with time.

I pulled my feet together, soles pressing into each other, and pushed my knees toward the floor with my elbows as I held my toes. I looked into the carpet, the green strands depicting vines creeping over the beige background. The shuffle of feet through grass hushed through the TV set.

"What was that?" Tom said. The shushing of feet stopped and was replaced by the sawing of nervous breath. I pulled my left leg out and pressed my chest into my thigh and knee. A low rumble leaked out of the speakers. I jerked my head to look at the TV.

"Holy crap!" Tom said. The camera jostled, a whirl of darkness and green light played to the sound of screaming. There was a faint bark, like a dog calling out from a neighborhood away, just background noise. The camera cut out.

I pulled out of my stretch so fast I nearly pulled a hamstring. I crawled to the couch, grabbed the remote and turned on the info button. The blue bar appeared at the bottom of the screen as the camera turned back on. The info read the episode was filmed in February 2014. "What the fuck?"

Tom's face was distorted with the fisheye lens; his nose looking far too wide for the rest of his features. He was in a van. The sound of crickets and tree frogs had disappeared and there was no echo around his voice.

"We've just been visited –" he stopped and gasped for air, "by the demon dog of Valle Crucis." He breathed hard, looking from side to side, the fish lens distorting first his nose then his cheeks and back again. His thick glasses obscured small dark eyes and the scraggly beard he wore dominated the camera lens. "We are going to call that a win for tonight and head back to headquarters. It's been an amazing trip. Full of the paranormal. None more than our visit tonight. Getting chased by the ghost dog. That's something truly special."

"And how the hell did that happen?" I turned from the TV and searched for my phone. He was pretty lucky. If the dog had gotten a nip at him, the bite would fester and likely poison his blood. He'd die within a week without good medicine to pull back the poison. And normal antibiotics wouldn't work on crossed veil wounds.

My phone was nowhere in the living room, so I stomped into my bedroom, fuming the whole time. My phone was on the charger on the nightstand by the bed. I grabbed it, yanking off the charge cord and immediately scrolling to Mom's number in the list of recent contacts. Tapping the call button on the screen I pressed the phone to my ear and paced in front of the windows. Sunlight was weakened by an oncoming storm.

"Doctor Ferrish speaking," my mother said.

"Mom."

"Oh, hi hon'. Listen, I'm a little bit busy. Can I call you back?"

"Mom," I repeated, "the demon dog is on the loose."

"Shit." Something in the way she cursed sounded to me like she was disappointed I knew this.

"Wait. Did you know?"

"Rori Anne. I am a bit busy right now and cannot have this conversation with you at the moment."

"Mom. Why didn't you tell me? Did you at least warn Josh? You know that damn dog's going to go sniffing around his house. You know that right? After he got a good mouthful of him with the taste of Ulunsuti stone all over him."

"Rori. You are blowing this way out of proportion. Josh is fine."

"You don't even get how clueless he is, do you? You just – God!"

"Watch your language with me, young lady."

"Oh, you're going to reprimand me? Do you even give a shit about Josh? I mean, do you really even care? I thought you wanted me to marry him. I can't marry a dead guy, Mom."

"Rori Anne! I just discovered it a few days ago. The crack came back. I'm working on capturing the dog and returning it. Literally, as we speak."

"Yeah, well in the meantime, do you think it might be a good idea to let anyone else know?"

"Why don't you focus on keeping Aubry safe and let me worry about the dog."

"What the hell is that supposed to mean?"

"Nothing." She huffed into the phone. "Look. I'm just worried is all. The gate is cracked. The veil is strained. People are starting to go a little crazy, saying they're seeing things. Like the Demon Dog of Valle Crucis." She sounded exasperated.

"You're keeping things from me," I accused.

"Rori. The hawk is the totem of the Ani'Kutani. Look. All I can think of is what our ancestor had to do to put the veil up in the first place. And why. Everything is just off. And then I keep thinking about when you were a child and that horrible ordeal you went through."

"'Horrible ordeal' *I* went through? As I recall, I wasn't the only one there. And I didn't suffer a tenth of what Andy went through. Or had you forgotten?"

"The most important thing is that I don't want a repeat. And I certainly don't want the veil needing to be re-lifted. You know what that might mean, don't you? " I stopped in front of the bed, turned and looked into the gray sky outside my windows. I knew what that might mean. Fear gripped the part of my mind that would allow me to accept the idea. So I ignored it.

"Why do you do this? Why do you ignore what he went through? And why are you excluding me from protecting the people I love?"

"I'm not!" she shouted. "Focus on Aubry. I'll take care of the rest."

"Just like that? Like I'm not a Bitten with the same responsibilities? Like this is just your fight?"

"Why can't you just trust me?"

"Right. Because that worked out in the past." The words flew out of my mouth before I thought about them. The silence on the other end of the line stung my ears. I didn't want to hear what excuse she'd give me. Knots in my stomach crawled up and clasped my throat. The images of the dream I'd had when the gate had cracked splintered through my mind. "I'm going to check in with Josh."

"That's just fine. You do that." I hung up the phone, considered flinging it across the room, thought better of it, and instead, tapped on the contacts until I found Josh's number. It rang four times then went to voicemail. I cursed long and loud, growled, looked out the window at the gathering clouds trying to decide what to do next.

I called the next number on Josh's list of contacts: his work. A young girl's voice drawled out, "Smoky Adventure Center."

"Hi, is Josh working today?"

"And... who is this?" she said sweetly, if not a little bit smugly.

"An adoring fan," I said sarcastically.

"No," she said, her voice dripping with dislike. "He's been out for the last two days. When you see him, you might want to tell him if he wants to keep his job, he'd better show up." I bit back the comments building on the back of my tongue and hung up on her. I was dancing from foot to foot, worry grabbing my heart with clumsy fingers. When I dialed Josh on his third contact and got no answer, I ran to the door, cell phone shoved into the handy side pocket of my black workout pants.

I peeked at the clock. Nine oh five. I had until two forty-five when Aubry was done at school. Plenty of time to drive out to his house for a look-around. I grabbed my small purse and the keys dangling from the hook I'd hung on the wall. Wuffers met me at the door. She sat on the doormat and stared with her bright orange eyes as I shoved my feet into red sneakers. "Well, someone sure wants to get out, huh?" I asked her. She lifted her butt off the ground enough to wag her long tail. "Alright, girl. Let's go."

Then I remembered there was a sleeping patient in the house. "Hell," I muttered. What was I going to do with the yunwi? I chewed on a fingernail for a second before deciding. I rushed into the laundry room. The basket that didn't have broken handles was full. I dumped it on the floor, spilling dirty clothes on to the linoleum, and rushed to the spare bedroom. Out of the closet I grabbed a big, soft blanket and shoved it into the basket. The yunwi was sound asleep. I felt awful, but I couldn't leave her here alone.

I wrapped her up carefully in the blanket she slept on. Her fur had shifted to white, dotted with pink flowers. She only stirred a little as I transferred her into the laundry basket and carried her out to the SUV. Once she was snug in her makeshift laundry basket bed in the floorboard behind my seat, Wuffers jumped into the passenger side and we jetted out.

I followed 74 south and west out of Waynesville. It would take us all the way to Cherokee and then on to Bryson. About halfway to our destination, the sky shook its gray canopy and the rain fell. I turned up the music – I had one of my favorite metal bands playing from my phone through the auxiliary jack in the SUV – and flipped on the windshield wipers to high. There was barely time for the wipers to keep up with the downpour and my lead foot.

Like many western NC permanent residents, Josh earned his living off the tourists. Being an avid outdoorsman and almost full Cherokee, he'd immediately fallen into the comfortable niche of nature guide. Of course, his duties as the stone keeper were uncompensated. He'd simply been handed the responsibility when his father had gotten too elderly for the job.

I had always recommended there be tryouts for the position, but that idea failed with a lack of competition for the role. I can't imagine why more people weren't beating down Josh's door to keep the stone. I mean, the non-monetary perks should have been enough: working with the Bitten, seeing the occasional magical creature, having your intuition boosted by proximity to the stone. On the flip side, it was hard to sell the attraction of nasty magic to the stone, being at the beckon call of other Cherokee medicine people, the constant nagging of the Bitten, and all the responsibility of caring for the stone itself.

Josh was the guy. End of story. And while his pure heart kept him from corruption by the stone, his pure heart kept him fairly oblivious to the amount of danger the stone put him in. The demon dog would like nothing better than to tote the delicious smelling Josh off to beyond the veil gate and make him his own personal chew toy. Mom not telling anyone about the crack was a major negligence. Because she was the matriarch she considered herself above the check of the younger generation. Not warning Josh was just plain thoughtless. I wondered as I drove if my mom was losing her touch.

Before I reached the Smoky Adventure Center where I already knew he wasn't working, thanks to the friendly office jockey, I turned off 74 onto Wesser Creek Road and then again onto Gassaway. Josh had a trailer on some property away from the highway.

I pulled into the long drive, the car bumping over potholes now filling with fresh rainwater. The open area where the trailer sat was surrounded by trees. For a trailer, it wasn't so bad. A little single wide that Josh had kept well-maintained. It had white siding and green trim. There was a covered porch with a couple of plastic lawn chairs. He'd built it on after he'd moved out here. Jameson and I had helped him. The memory pushed a knife in my gut and twisted.

After I put the SUV in park, Wuffers reached over and nudged my elbow. She always knew when I was sad. I smiled and rubbed her soft lopsided ears. "Alright, girl, let's go say hi to Josh." She tilted her head one way and then the other.

I hopped out and pulled the handle of the passenger side door. Wuffers leapt from the car and immediately froze. Her hackles rose. She stepped slow and careful over the dirt driveway, turned muddy in the steady rain. I turned my head in her direction and smelled the air. Wuffers growled, low and menacing. I smelled it too. Something rotten with evil was visiting Josh today.

"Shit," I cursed. Stupid. Here I'd just rolled right up without a thought in my stupid head. Whoever was in the trailer with Josh would no doubt have seen me. Or sensed me. Or seen me coming before I even pulled up. *Whatever, dammit.* I slammed the door. No sense in playing sneaky now. I pulled the contact out of my eye and tossed it into the muddying driveway.

I reached inside my soul to the piece of me that had been joined with the dragon and called on it. The dragon blood rushed through my system. My already lean muscles bunched with the effect of the venom. My sight and hearing amped up another level. The rain drummed in my sensitive ears. I said a little thank you to the Uktena for sending rain. I focused on the rain around me, drawing in its life-giving energy. The world around me took on a shimmer of silver that even my mundane eye could see. I peered at the house with my right golden eye.

Most people have a sixth sense, that other something that guides you. Intuition, many people call it. Moms know what I mean.

I didn't really have that.

When the Uktena was handing out gifts, I got the physical side of the dragon gift and Andy got the intuitive abilities. Luckily for me, the golden eye could literally see magical energy. Keenly, in fact. That required no intuition. Just sight.

The structure of the double wide melted away in my vision. Under the physical layer of reality, the energies of the living came to life with my focused concentration. Trees sprang into my vision with a glowing green light. The rain fell in sparkling streams of blue. The air even had a subtle golden glow. In the way far distance I saw a dreamcatcher huddled under the tree of a sleeping owl. Even the owl's dreams gave off a subtle golden sheen that twisted and flowed from the owl to the dreamcatcher's web.

In the place of Josh's front room, the white energy of the Ulunsuti stone throbbed against a smear of darker energy. "What the hell?" The darker smudge of energy had a center that fluttered in a collection of what looked like pulsing gems, all different colors. The little gems were so bright and cheery, their colors familiar and yet wrong collected and caught in the darker shadow. My stomach twisted on disgust. I knew what was in there.

I focused harder, letting the sight in my golden eye consume my attention. The shadow with the pulsing gems grew more defined, coming clear like a camera lens twisting into focus. Above the little lights in the torso, a dark face peered back at me. Her skin stretched over the skeletal structure of her face. Her eyes were ebony marbles and her hair looked like she'd stolen it from a crow. Bony hands lifted and in them she held the stone, its bright white and glittering surface marred with the one streak of blood red. Power lust surged through me.

She was so powerful. The lesser witch should not have this much power. Not without an Ani'Kutani around to supply a boost to their magic. And the last one had committed suicide by Ganagi. And killed my husband. *Fucker.* The venom in me pulsed at the thought of Paul Burning.

The Raven Mocker's energy throbbed. I cursed, but didn't dodge in time. A pang of searing heat cracked across my face. I went down hard, the world made of energy springing back into the mud and muck of a world drenched in spring rain. Water and mud slapped up around my legs as my knees squelched into the driveway. I reached a hand to my face. Welts sprang up across my cheek bone and burned like sin. The Raven Mocker inside the trailer laughed. Wuffers yelped then growled, a relentless bark bursting out of her mouth.

Anger swelled within me. Red swarmed my vision like wasps protecting a nest. My skin was on fire. Bitch had to go and make it personal. She was going to pay for that. I stood out of the mud from where I had been knocked to my knees. My black and red tennis shoes squelched. My tee shirt was soaked through. I pulled my hair off of my throbbing face and headed back to the car. My knife was under the passenger seat. After I belted it in its holster onto my thigh, the angry red haze moved me to the screen door that led to the covered porch. Wuffers was on my heels.

As soon as I touched the white handle, pain shot through my body, as if I'd stuck a fork in a toaster. The smack in the back of my head resonated down my arms. I yelped and drew my hand away. I snarled at the house, shaking my hand where tingles of electricity lingered. Wuffers whined. The woman's laugh croaked through the barrier of walls and the drumming downpour. "Yeah, you won't be laughing soon," I muttered, feeling ridiculously inept to deal with something whose strong suit was magic spells. It was my own damn fault. I should have thought she'd throw a protection spell to keep me out. Duh.

I took a deep breath and let it still my throbbing nerves. It had been a while since I'd had to deal with a Raven Mocker. And I'd had Mom there to help me. And it hadn't been given the massive umph from the Ulunsuti stone. There was no telling what kind of shape Josh was going to be in by the time I got into the house. To cast such an effective protection spell, she'd be drawing on some larger energy source. That energy source typically involved something with a pulse. That meant it was most likely Josh. Or his dog. I shivered.

Raven Mockers, Ani'Kutani: they needed a source to perform their magic. Where I had power inside of me from the dragon venom, they had nothing but their hereditary blood line. The thinner it got, the less innate magic lingered, the more they had to depend on other life sources to perform their magic.

I wished for the umpteenth time in ten years for Andy to be here. We weren't meant to do this alone. He would have a counter spell for the hulking shocky wall of protection. Grumbling and shaking my arms of the lingering electricity, I braced myself for what I needed to do. It would not be pleasant. I took a few short cleansing breaths and reached for the door.

Screams tumbled out of me. Spasms of pain broke over me in waves, but I didn't let go of the handle. The shock traveled in a sparking blue line into the palm of my hand, up my arm, into my chest and followed a circuit to my feet and up the other side of my body. NOT. PLEASANT.

Blue lights flashed like lightning behind my closed eyelids. When the pain was at its worst, filling me up with sparking sensations that would kill most people, I yanked on the door. It burst from the hinges and the frame. White painted wood showered me in slivers. I worked hard to release the doorknob from my clenched fist. When I threw it into the grass the knob was completely crunched into itself. "Ha!" I shouted at the Raven Mocker inside.

Wuffers was right beside me. I flew – okay, I teetered – over creaking boards and skidded to a halt in front of the front door. Wuffers barked at the door. I looked at her. She smiled at me and barked again, as if saying, 'Let's do this!'. "You're right. Let's get 'er, Wuff."

I stopped first and made sure there wasn't another barrier. My nose told me no. I pulled my knife from its sheath with my left hand, and laid my back and shoulder against the door. I listened through the aluminum. The crow-haired woman, so full of magic, groaned lightly. Good.

Resting my right hand on the door handle I waited a second. There was nothing else I could do to prepare for going inside. I twisted the knob, pushed the door ajar and kept the metal at my back as a shield. Peering around with my right eye, I saw the woman crouched on the floor, a mess of overly large clothes on her rail thin body and mass of matted black hair.

She smelled bad too. Like she'd never looked at a bar of soap in kindness. I could just barely make out Josh, hog-tied and lying on that tacky brown sofa I always told him to get rid of. It looked like he was in hiking gear. His red and black flannel was smudged in dirt. His mouth was taped shut. He tilted his face toward me. His blue eyes were half-lidded as he regarded me with a flat gaze. He was completely drained. A little more and he'd be dead. I wondered how long she'd taken up residence. Judging from Josh's thin cheeks, I'd say at least a day.

The Ulunsuti stone lay on the berber brown and beige carpet, shining bright and beautiful. It felt like an eye that I'd plucked out, given as a gift and then forgotten about, until I was standing next to it. The venom of Uktena thrashed wildly inside of me. The blood recognized the piece of itself, the magic that was imparted on me. I fought the urge to run in, scoop up the stone and press it close to my heart. I took a steadying breath and planned out my next move.

I gripped my knife and readied my body. I lurched around the door, took two steps and dove for the Lesser. Mid-dive, she decided to pull a fast one on me, moving away in a blur. I rolled, tucking my knife safely away from my body and pulled into a crouch. She was crouched too. Her skinny forearms extended past the sleeves of her baby pink sweatshirt as she dug her bony claws into the carpet.

She opened her mouth and hissed. She grasped at something behind her. It whined. Wuffers snarled from where she stood near Josh. Dragon voice burst from my throat. I lurched forward, my knife high. A black streak flew past me. The Lesser's eyes locked on to my wolfdog. "Wuff!" The cacophony of snarls and screeching ripped through the little single wide's living room. Wuffers snapped at the woman's arms. Blood spritzed the wall behind her. The woman went down screaming. Wuffers found an opening and clamped down on her scrawny neck.

The woman returned the favor, wrapping her bony fingers around Wuffers's neck. She yelped and choked, a sound so startling I was on top of them both before I knew I'd moved. The Lesser shoved as I arrived. Wuffers was thrown at me. I went down with my arms around my dog, scared to death to see what state she'd be in. I laid her beside me and turned to Josh's uninvited guest.

"What do you want here?" I said, holding my knife. The woman stood, matted hair nearly covering her black eyes. Her pink shirt and faded jeans sagged against her hunched frame. The dog behind her wasn't moving. I recognized her as Josh's chocolate lab.

The woman shifted from foot to foot, lightly, on the balls of her feet. Her beady eyes flicked around the room until they at last betrayed her and rested on the Ulunsuti stone. "You know better. You'd have that thing for a day and be dead. What's the point?"

She looked at me then. Her face falling from fierce to confused. Shocked, I'd say. Then she smiled, which was much worse. Her blackened mouth gaped in the absence of teeth and her eyes widened over the gaunt hollows of her cheeks. Fear is for the unknown, so it gripped me when she began to laugh.

She could laugh all the way to hell for all I cared. Still twitchy from breaking through the protection spell with nothing but physical force, I vaulted all of my one-hundred thirty-five pounds at the woman. Her face when my red and black sneakers landed on her chest was priceless. I nearly giggled. The excitement of the hunt thrilled through my bones. It wasn't often I got to do this. It scared me just a little that I liked what was going to happen next. No, I wouldn't kill her, but I'd take back what she'd stolen.

She landed on her back, her hand flailing and smacking hard against Josh's TV tray holder. It clattered to the floor as I got my knees onto her outstretched arms. She kicked her legs and growled. "Oh dear Lord! Haven't you ever heard of a toothbrush?" She thrashed underneath me. I let her until she tired enough to not wiggle around so much for what I was going to do next.

"You left it exposed," I told her. I ran my knife over the pulse at her collar bone. Some Lessers had the good sense to cover their major arteries. Not this one. She was either careless or stupid. I felt her stolen hearts beating through the blade I held at her neck. I listened, my ears strained to pick out the very weakest of them humming quietly in rhythm with each other. They didn't all match pace, but they beat to the same metronome. At least two were cat hearts, or raccoons, I supposed. Another was a dog. And that just made me shudder. Why dogs got more compassion in my book, I didn't know.

There was one other. It struggled and while the rest beat in quarter or eighth notes, this one stuttered in triplets. It was a bad match. Like humans when the body rejects a transplant, this heart fought its new owner. I listened to it, feeling my way along the rhythm of her life blood, pumped by a half a dozen hearts or more, to the source of the off rhythm tucked in the empty husk of the Lesser. Once I found the heart, I studied it, listened.

"A yunwi." I looked at the woman. Her face fell from fight to fear. And for good reason. Lessers know me. They know my legacy and they know my wrath. I was going to relish this. I laid my knife to one side and prepared to make the cut. Magic thrummed through the blade. Oh no. I could not perform magic. That was Andy's gift. And he'd used it on my knife, blessing it in a way that would sever the ties a Raven Mocker had with the stolen hearts.

My eyes blazed as I pushed the knife into the carotid artery. Red dust swarmed from the blade and into the slit I made in her neck. The Raven Mocker wailed. The crooning of her wordless cry like the screeching of the bird of her namesake rose. The red glow of the sandy essence of the blade's magic fell from its gathering cloud into the woman's slit neck. She gagged and choked, her body convulsing under me as her eyes rolled back into her head. Her head shook faster and faster, her feet banging against the floor behind me. The rhythm of the hearts imprisoned in her chest sped. At the crescendo, the hearts abruptly ceased.

The woman stilled. Breath eased its way out of her lungs, the energy of all the animals and creatures she'd stolen floating on the back of the magic from the knife. They took form as little lights, like fireflies. I could feel Wuffers's breath on my elbow. "Lead the way, Wuff," I told her. She limped to the door and nudged it open with her nose. She looked behind her at the little lights and whined. They followed her, bobbing against the cool breeze wending into the trailer from the spring rain outside. I shuffled behind Wuffers over the plastic grass carpeting and pushed open the next screen door of the covered porch.

The little golden lights danced through the doorway and out into the rain. Wuffers hobbled down the stairs and stood in the mud and rocks of Josh's driveway. Five of the golden orbs ascended quickly, but one hovered near the SUV. It circled the vehicle once then came to rest near the back window - near the little yunwi nestled safely behind the driver's seat. The glow of the light expanded, sparking into rainbows, shimmering to blues and purples and finally to bright white as it touched against the window.

A little hand extended from inside the SUV. A soft whine echoed from the car as the yunwi touched the glass separating her from the golden light. Sparks shivered through the glass. The little yunwi cried out, shaking her hand as little splinters of golden light soaked into her fingers. Her cries quieted, the hand disappeared and then the little light at the window eased its way up, following the others to wherever it is souls go after death.

FOURTEEN ~ RORI - STONE

Back inside the trailer, the woman's body shifted, shriveled and turned back into its original form before my eyes. The bird was a sad thing. As sad as the woman had been. After I hauled the Raven Mocker's body out of the house to clear the energy in the living room of her dark magic, I gathered Josh's dog's body tenderly. She was a chocolate lab. She'd been sweet and reliable. Josh had picked her up at the PetSmart in Waynesville on adoption day. It hadn't been that long ago.

The dog's body was still warm to the touch. My arms lifted her easily, but my heart hung heavy for Josh. Once I placed her outside in a safe place for Josh to bury her later, I rushed to Josh's limp form lying on the couch. I ran my hand across his face. His skin was cool. I touched his chest, felt the reassuring rhythm of his heart and the slow wheeze of his breath. Something akin to panic buzzed inside of me. "You're not going to die on me, you hear me?"

He didn't respond. I crawled over the dark carpet and stared down at the Ulunsuti stone. It glimmered against the pale light of a floor lamp, the red stripe vivid. My mouth watered against the seductive pull of its power. I could feel the venom of the Uktena dragon throbbing through my veins. This was the closest I'd ever been to the stone. The only time I'd been closer to an Ulunsuti was when I was between the teeth of the Uktena dragon.

I glanced over my shoulder. With my right golden eye I could see the shifting gold of Josh's spirit hovering above his body. His chest wasn't moving.

I grabbed at the Ulunsuti stone, shoving aside the insistent dread of being overwhelmed by its power. The vibration of magic pulled us together, like long lost lovers caught in an embrace. Power sprang through me like a dam bursting, spurring my senses into hyperawareness. Magic breathed around me. Magic that I normally did not have access to.

My left eye could see it as well as my right with the Ulunsuti stone gripped to my chest. Josh's soul hovered around him. Not good. It should be firmly inside of him. He was on death's doorstep. I inhaled slow and deep, fighting to calm the excitement from the sheer power of the stone in my hand.

My soul swam in the current of throbbing power. I pressed my hand over Josh's heart, just under the ribs prominent against my fingers. Thud, thud. It beat slowly, but it still beat. I focused my intention to transfer the magic to make him strong again, to bring him back from where he traipsed in the shadows. The magic from the stone leapt from my fingertips through the skin of my friend and into his heart.

He gulped in air, his eyes flying open. The stormy afternoon light washed his gaunt features in soothing gray. His heart sped from the touch of the magic. His bloodshot eyes and blue irises stared at the golden soul hovering too far from his body. The stone's power would make him see. At first his eyes were blank then they widened.

"Call it back to you," I told him. His head swiveled limply my direction. Recognition was slow. His mouth fought for a smile.

"Ro-," he began.

"Shh...," I instructed. "Call it back to you before it leaves." Fear twisted inside me as the golden spirit inched slowly toward the ceiling.

His chin dipped a bare centimeter. He closed his eyes. He was still for far too long. I worried, darting glances from the shimmering soul and his physical body. I chewed my lip, fighting the fear of losing him to death, fighting the power that wanted to eat me up while the anxiety of what the stone was doing to me crawled up my spine. I didn't dare move or speak. If he was finding the attachment that still existed between his body and his spirit, he would need all of the concentration his weak body could muster.

Saliva pooled in my mouth. The venom surging through me mingled with the raw power of the Ulunsuti stone and ignited a bonfire of need. *Josh needs me.* The thought waged a war between duty and lust. I closed my eyes to the consuming fire. My body was restless, aching to release the pressure building along my nerves. My thighs burned. My skin crawled, amazingly alive and dancing with desire. My heart sped and breath quickened. I needed. The mantra that kept me from falling in love, kept me from giving in to lust failed to come to mind. What was it? I don't need a man. In the moment of consuming fire, the statement fell dead inside my mind, having no more power than a moth's wings can move the wind. It was a lie. I was nothing but need.

A hand wrapped around my arm. My eyes flew open. The touch exploded across my awareness. Josh stared at me, sitting up on the couch, his body returning to normal in the wake of the Ulunsuti's power. I saw the same hunger I felt reflected in his eyes. The same need radiated off of him in tangible waves. A need we'd always had and ignored in the presence of Jameson's ghost lingering between us. I needed to be strong, to care for my child without complicating my already complicated life. And yet nothing could be more simple than his touch against my skin. There was no need for logic in the cloud of magic wrapping around us. There was no need to plan, to think, to worry. There was only the carnal need to be one with a man I loved and nearly lost to death.

He pulled the stone from my grasp as his mouth melted against mine. My hand gave it up so that I could wrap my fingers into his dark curls. I heard the soft clunk of the stone against the berber carpet, followed by the sound of my own body being eased on the floor next to it. His fingers danced across my bare arms. Every touch inspired visions of color and shapes.

"Are you okay?" he asked between kisses.

For an answer, I pulled his flannel to remove the shirt and heard the resounding rip of fabric. "No," I said. "I'm not okay." I tossed the two pieces of his shirt to either side of us as his head roamed down my body. He pulled away from me and looked with deep concern into my eyes. "I can't do this anymore. I can't resist. So, I'm not okay." He sighed in relief. He pushed my shirt up and placed careful kisses along the muscles of my stomach. His back muscles under my fingertips flexed and relaxed as he found my neck, my collarbone, my chest.

I pressed my hands on either side of his face, drawing his head up to me so I could feel his mouth against mine, soft lips strong, tongue darting out to taste our kisses. My fingers twisted in his hair. He pulled away and I whimpered. Raising his thin and muscled body up, he yanked off my workout pants. My shoes fought and lost. I fumbled with the button and zipper of his jeans. His scent washed over me. Warm sage, the faint smell of sweetgrass, the lingering perfume of the outdoors and that other something that could only be described as 'him'. I growled as the zipper finally stuttered down. With one easy movement, I rolled him onto his back and pulled the pants that obstructed what I wanted.

He gasped a little with the quick movements that rendered him exposed to my longing. I pulled the red and soaking wet shirt from my body, baring myself to him. Pressing my naked breasts against his bare chest, I hovered over him, legs straddling him. My body ached as I let the anticipation build our desire. His hands wrapped around my hips and I gave in to the pull that joined us. I moaned. The current of lust swept me away. I was nothing but sensation as I rocked and swayed, touching him, bending over to kiss, to taste. Our bodies matched rhythm, growing warmer and more insistent. The pace quickened and slowed in intervals. I relished in the feel of him inside me, smiling when little noises of pleasure escaped him.

The warm fire of lust stoked higher, building between my hip bones above my pubic bone. The heat gathered, concentrated as my nipples hardened like stone. I grasped them between my thumb and finger, twisting the sensitive skin as the sensation closed out everything in the world except for it.

The passion launched me into a world of color as light exploded through me. Every fiber of my being cried in joy. My head jerked back as a scream of triumph shrilled from me. Josh cried out, his hand pressing my hip bones into his, thrusting as deeply as was possible. I felt his orgasm inside of me. Felt his body jerk and spasm as the fires of my own orgasm faded. Rolling my hips to intensify his pleasure, the last of his need finally subsided.

We lay panting on the floor, our bodies warm and moist. I shook the last of the muzziness from the stone out of my head and pushed myself onto my elbows. With the magic clearing, I looked at Josh with serious eyes. That much activity after being near death's embrace could push a man over the edge. "You okay?" I reached a hand over and felt for his pulse, listened to his breathing. All seemed well.

"Mmm..." was all he said. He lay naked, his dark curls sweeping over his forearm from where he stretched out on his belly. His angular features were still too pronounced to be called healthy. He needed food and water or he'd be back where he was. I stood and grabbed my wad of damp clothes. He had a drier I could throw them in.

I walked through the little kitchen and dining area and down the hall. To the right was his guest bathroom and laundry room. I pulled the clothes that were in the dryer out, pushing them into an empty laundry basket and tossed my own clothes inside. The dryer made a series of soft beeps as I set the timer, before it whirred to life.

Josh's pantry was pretty sad. There were two boxes of Lucky Charms and a solid row of Denty Moore stew. After searching through assorted canned vegetables, I found some deviled ham. He kept his bread in the fridge to keep it from molding or getting eaten by bugs. After putting together three sandwiches and pouring a big glass of orange juice, I walked back into the living room. Josh regarded me from where he'd pulled himself into a sitting position on the floor against the couch.

"Wow," he said. It was good to see that shit-eating grin plastered on his face again. "Sandwiches even."

I stopped in the middle of the living room and glared at him. Naked. Carrying sandwiches. My glare didn't do much given my current state. I huffed. "Shut up and eat something," I said, walking the last five steps and thrusting the plate of sandwiches into his face. He raised his arms in surrender and took the plate. "You're lucky you were almost dead a half hour ago, or I'd pound you for that."

He chuckled, showing his straight white teeth. I could see bags under his eyes. I turned and sat on the couch opposite from him. After he'd munched his way through most of the sandwiches, he sighed. I gave him his glass of orange juice to wash it down.

"Okay, you've had sustenance. Now, talk." He looked up at me through long, dark lashes. Lashes too much like Jameson's. I swallowed against a surge of guilt. I'd slept with no one since his death. It'd been just me and BOB (battery-operated boyfriend) for a long time. Shivers ran down my spine as I relived our moments of pleasure. That didn't help the guilt.

"She was kind of hot," he started. I shook my head.

"Huh? Who?"

"The Raven Mocker. She had some enchantment. She showed up here a couple of evenings ago. Said she was lost. I offered to take her where she needed to go. I turned to grab my keys and she attacked me."

"You're an idiot, you know it?" He looked at me, his eyes wide, mouth slack. "You're like a flashing beacon for trouble." I emphasized my point by making flashing gestures with my fingers. "You *have* to be more careful."

"I know. I guess I'm not the greatest person for this whole stone keeper thing." His head and shoulders drooped.

"It's not that, it's just you think the best of people. And that's great, but the stone draws the evil that seeks greater power. You have to be on your guard. And speaking of which," I began.

"Don't tell me. There's something else out there that wants the stone."

"Always. Our favorite ghost hunter just posted on the web an encounter with the Demon Dog of Valle Crucis."

"Wait. That's the thing that tried using me as a chew toy, right?"

"Yes. We banished him to the gate because he kept mauling people. So, when he gets out, he goes right back to where he came from."

"So, he's out? But, how?"

"The gate didn't stay healed. There's another crack and it has to be bigger than before for the Demon Dog to be out."

"So, we go heal it again," he said, looking at me with his beautiful guileless eyes. I sighed.

"But, why does it keep breaking? That's the thing. Sure, we go heal it again, and then it breaks again only worse than before. How many times can the veil take a compromise to a gate before *it* breaks?" I pushed myself up from the couch and paced the length of the living room. "The veil cannot break," I said, slicing my hand through the air with finality, while real panic contrasted my gesture by making my voice crack.

"Why? That can be fixed too, can't it?" I stopped midstride and turned to my ultra-innocent medicine man. I didn't even want to think about it. I didn't want to consider fixing a broken veil. Or even a broken veil in the first place. All those creatures hiding in plain sight and then the veil breaks and bam! Creature genocide.

"If the veil breaks, fixing it requires a very specific sacrifice," I told him. The knowledge made my insides quiver.

"What is it, Rori? What's the sacrifice?" Josh rose as he spoke, my anxiety rolling through the room to him. My lips wouldn't move. He made his slow way toward me then reached a tentative hand up to my bare arm. Fear exposed me more completely than my bare skin. As he drew close to me, his warmth wrapped around me, easing my anxiety a little. He placed an arm around my shoulders and I finally found the strength to speak.

"Our ancestor many generations ago cast the veil spell when the Europeans began infiltrating this country. She saw the horrors they imposed on our people and knew their prejudice would most certainly extend to the creatures. To do it though, she had to sacrifice her daughter, an unbitten Dragon Born. An innocent."

"That's very Ani'Kutani-ish," Josh said as he stroked my hair.

"We are related," I said, shrugging. "There's no other magic we've done that's required a human sacrifice. But, there's no other magic that's so powerful it has to hide the entire existence of thousands of creatures." I was just rambling now, looking at nothing, trying to see the past as the past and not some inevitable future. "I guess it makes sense it would require that much of a sacrifice. One life for many. Still. I don't want to be the mom choosing."

"You won't have to," Josh reassured. "We're going to figure this out and keep the veil from breaking." I looked up at him. His dark eyebrows were drawn down over his brilliant blue eyes. It was the fiercest look I'd ever seen on him. My lovable goof of a medicine man was quicker to laugh than to fight. "We won't let anything happen to our Aubry."

I tried to feel confident. After everything I'd been through to not only bring Aubry into the world, but then protect her... Surely, God wouldn't put this on me.

Surely not.

FIFTEEN ~ AUBRY - POND SCUM

I climbed into the SUV with Mama. There was something in the other floorboard. I peeked over. The yunwi was a blur of white and pink flowers, propped into a laundry basket and fast asleep. She was so cute. I wondered why Mama had brought her and not left her at the house. “How’s the yunwi?” I asked.

“She’s sleeping a ton. She needs extra rest to heal. I don’t imagine she’ll be up much at all for the next few days.” I nodded while I watched the yunwi breathe slow and steady.

“Hi Wuffers,” I said. She looked back at me from the front seat and smiled. Something smelled funny. Like rainwater, dirt and something old and sad. I hadn’t ever smelled anything like it before. “What’s that smell, Mama?”

“We went out to visit Josh today and found a Lesser, or Raven Mocker. Wuff and I got rid of her.” She sat very straight. It was different for her. She had both hands on the wheel and she looked only at the road ahead.

“Mama?”

“Yes, baby girl?”

“Is there any way someone who’s not a Bitten can see critters?” I asked. I could see her face in the rearview mirror. Her eyebrows pinched together.

“Why do you ask?”

“Well, I think one of my friends can see the yunwi that are behind the school.” Her face softened.

"Oh okay," she said. "The yunwi do that, especially with kids. They like children a lot."

I don't think they like Haelyn, I thought, but for some reason, I didn't think I should tell Mama that.

"Mama?"

"Yes, sweatpea?"

"Can Haelyn come over to play?"

"Who's Haelyn?" she asked.

"A friend from school."

"Sure, baby. You have her number?" She ran a hand through her hair. It looked like it was damp. Wuffers looked wet too. She smelled wet too. Pew.

"Yes, ma'am."

"When we get home, give me a minute to put the yunwi back to bed, bathe Wuff and shower and change and then we'll have her come over. Okay?"

"Okay," I said.

Mom talked to Haelyn's mom at the door when they arrived. The usual stuff moms say to each other. Do you have any other children? I perked up to hear that Haelyn actually had an older brother. Are there any allergies or big deal health issues. I let the conversation wash over me. Haelyn's mom's name was Edythe. *Funny name,* I thought. Edythe Turner. I watched my mom shake hands with her, saw her rake the woman over with critical eyes.

"Are you married, Edythe?" My mom asked. The woman pulled her hand away and tucked it into her other hand. Her fingernails were a shiny red and her wrists were heavy with bracelets. They jingled as she twisted her hands. She smoothed out the front of her polka dot blouse, pulled the navy cardigan closer around her skinny waist. She smiled at Mom with gloss-laden lips. Her face was thick with make-up and I wondered what she looked like for real. She tucked her curled sandy hair behind an ear pegged with a gold hoop.

"He passed. God rest his soul. Died in an oil rig accident five years ago. That's when we moved here. My late sister left me her house – well, that was a long, long time ago –" Mrs. Turner rambled, fidgeting with a heavy gold ring on her skinny ring finger. "It's just me and the kids now."

Mom's hand slid down the door from her grip on the frame. I couldn't see her face from where I stood, but her shoulders slumped a little. "I'm so sorry to hear that. Being a single mom is... hard." Mrs. Turner nodded, looking down into the door jam. "I'm widowed as well. My husband –"

"Car crash." Mrs. Turner interrupted. She looked up at Mom then with her big, emerald eyes, looking surprised at herself. "Oh. I'm sorry," she said. I couldn't see Mom's face, but she got quiet and her head had cocked to one side. "Someone on the PTA. They mentioned it to me." She smiled, but it wasn't the sort of smile that made sense. Wrinkles on the outsides of her eyes appeared as she half-laughed in a way that caught, like she was in pain. "Busy bodies." She waved away the nosy PTA members in her head.

"I see," my mom said. Haelyn poked her head around her mother's legs. "Ah! This must be Haelyn."

I waved at Haelyn to come inside. Wuffers was behind me. I took a step back and leaned against Wuffers, combing through her now-clean fur on her head, that soft spot between her lopsided ears. As soon as Haelyn got into the entryway, Wuffers growled. The noise rumbled into me. She'd never growled at a person before. It sounded mean. I spun to face her. "No, Wuff," I said, deep, like Mama did. Wuffers cocked her head to one side and whined. Her eyes darted between me and Haelyn. She didn't growl, but her ears shifted forward and her nose wiggled as she sniffed the air.

"Right, well then, what time would you like Haelyn back home?" Mom asked Edythe.

"How about seven? Haelyn needs to do her chores before she goes to bed. Don't you Haelyn?" Mrs. Turner leaned around Mom and gave Haelyn a look that was shot through with threats.

"Yes, ma'am," Haelyn muttered. Haelyn lowered her eyes to her old shoes and twisted her hands into the overly big shirt she wore. Mama looked at Haelyn for a moment, her eyes narrowed. She was watching Haelyn, trying to figure out her body language. Edythe wasn't a very nice woman, I decided. And she didn't like Haelyn. The thing I couldn't figure out is why I felt like Haelyn and Edythe didn't fit. I guessed maybe some moms and daughters didn't mesh like Mom and I.

"We'll have her home on time," Mom said as she turned back from analyzing Haelyn to face Mrs. Turner.

"Alright. Be good, Haelyn." She turned from the door as Mom closed it. We heard the car pull out as Mama turned to us.

"You girls want to go out and play in the yard?" Mama suggested. I looked at Haelyn. She was wearing baggy jeans and a t-shirt that looked like it had belonged to a boy. She twisted the shirttail and looked at me with her big, dark eyes. She nodded, but didn't speak. Her thin lips barely smiled. "Take Wuff with you, Bry-baby."

"Okay, Mama." Mama went into the kitchen from the entryway and pulled a pan from the overhead pot-hanger. I went to the door. Haelyn shuffled out of the way. I pulled it open and smiled at her. "Ready?"

"Mm-hmm," she said.

"C'mon, Wuffers," I called. We walked onto the porch that had exactly eight stairs to the bottom. The sun was shining, but everything was still wet. I looked at Haelyn's shoes. "Are those good shoes?"

"Nah," she said. "Mom made me change into some old clothes of my brother's before I came over because I get dirty. She hates that." She twisted the front of her shirt.

"You wanna play tag?" I asked, not sure if she'd like the idea. She smiled, smacked my arm, turned and flew down the porch stairs. She squealed as I followed her. I jetted past her, rounded an old stump to catch her on the arm, but she was faster than most kids and ducked out of my way.

Wuffers barked and chased me. I laughed as she nipped at my feet. Haelyn was just ahead of me. I ran faster to catch up. I was within two arms' length from her and gaining fast. Wuffers barked louder and nipped at my shirttail, pulling me away from Haelyn as I reached for the tag. "Wuff," I scolded, breathing heavy.

I slowed to take in just how far we'd run. Wuffers circled me, whining and yipping. Haelyn's head yanked over her shoulder, a puzzled look on her face. I walked toward her. Wuffers jumped at me.

I backed up. "What is your problem, Wuff?" A breeze washed over me and on it I caught a smell. I jerked my head in its direction, finally understanding what she was trying to say to me. I took a big whiff of the air and gagged. The odor was like stagnant water and muck and the smell of rotting animals. I had smelled that once when we discovered a deer carcass out hiking. There was also that other smell; the smell of magic. Creatures covered by the veil all had one common, unique odor. And I could smell it now, floating on the back of all the other nastiness. As my line of sight caught up with my nose, I saw Haelyn walking toward me. She was next to the source of the smell. The big, deep pond rippled as she passed.

My heart flopped in my chest. "Haelyn," I called. She stopped too close to the water. I started forward, but Wuff barked and leaned closer to me. "Wuff!" If she didn't let me past her, I wouldn't be able to get to Haelyn. "Haelyn! Come over here!" I waved my hand at her so she'd get my meaning. Haelyn turned and looked into the water.

"Hey," she said. "I think there's something in this pond. Come look." I knew there was something in the pond. And judging by the smell, it was something big enough to be a problem. Wuffers knew there was something in the pond and she was doing her best to keep me away from it.

"Come here, Haelyn! I want to show you something over here!" Wuffers turned and barked at her. Haelyn turned her head back to the pond and then bent down for a closer look. "No! Haelyn – ," I shouted, my hand stretching out to stop her, even though I stood twenty feet away.

The water rippled and a spiny hand shot from its surface. The skin covering a ropy set of muscles on an inhuman forearm glistened in a murky color of pond water. It latched on to Haelyn and yanked. Haelyn slipped forward onto her belly, her shoulders and chest splashing in the pond's edge. I ran as fast as I've ever ran, ignoring Wuffers's bark. I dove on top of Haelyn, wrapping my arms around her waist and pulled. She screamed and cried, "No! No! It's getting me!"

My stomach clenched in fear. I pulled harder. Wuffers barked and snarled, brushing up against me and diving for the arm that grabbed Haelyn. Haelyn and I slid further into the slime of the pond bank before the thing released Haelyn, its arm gripped between Wuffers's jaws. Wuffers shook her head, tearing at the thing's arm. I scrambled backward, yanking at Haelyn's shirt. It felt like I was moving like a snail through the mud. I couldn't get us far enough away fast enough.

The head of the Nehi burst from the pond's surface, spraying Haelyn and me with water. Wuffers was pushed away from the creature. She backed up against us, half blocking my view and barking like mad as the creature pulled itself out of the water to stand before us. Its green skin sparkled in the sun. Spreading back from its almost absent lips were jagged stripes of bright bluish green. It snarled through pointed teeth, its mouth jutting past the normal place people have mouths. It had only slits for a nose. It stared at us with black eyes rimmed in bright blood red. There was no white to its eyes.

It hissed around a mouthful of giant pointed teeth, snapping its jaws at Wuffers and gripping its bleeding arm. The stench of rotting meat rolled over me. Black spines sprouting with webbing between their bases rose from its head like a porcupine. The Nehi surged forward to grab at Haelyn's other arm, but Wuffers was a snarling barrier between us and the creature. Haelyn yanked her arm back as I pulled on her body. She would not quit screaming and it was starting to hurt my ears. Among the barking and screaming, the Nehi screeched back at us, the shrill cry piercing and other-worldly. Gray globs of mucus splatted wetly against my face, reeking of decay. I wanted to cry from the horror of the smell alone.

My ears throbbed and rang, sending a needle of pain right into my brain. I clapped my hands over my ears out of reaction. The creature lifted a leg, aimed and kicked Wuffers. My dog yelped and stumbled back, falling to the ground and whimpering in pain. The Nehi took two quick steps, reached down and grabbed at my arm. Where its spiny fingernails dug into my skin a pulsing pain like fire erupted. The smell of blood spiked the other mingling aromas of water, mud and rot and magic. I understood why Haelyn had been screaming as my own voice added to the chorus of Haelyn and the Nehi.

Wuffers's snarl broke the screeching of the Nehi. She was a dart of black fur. Her body slammed into the creature, clamping her white canines around the Nehi's leg, spines and all. Wuffers jerked her head back and forth, tearing into the thing's calf. The Nehi released its hold on me and Haelyn, its scream of pain ripping into the afternoon air. Gashes lined my arm under my shirt. The grey sweatshirt gaped in ribbons of material stained red. The blood poured heavier as I yanked on Haelyn to move us away from the pond beach.

I blinked away the blinding pain exploding across my eyes. Wuffers pulled on the water creature, fighting to get it away from us. The Nehi wrestled, twisting as its whole bony fishy body went down to the ground. It writhed and wriggled, swiping at Wuffers with its needle-like blackened nails.

I turned toward the house, breathed deeply, and screamed, "Mom!" The sound of the dragon within me echoed across the field. Wuffers yelped, long and loud. My gut twisted as I yanked my head toward my dog. The Nehi had Wuffers's head pinned against the bank, one hand against her head and the other against her shoulder. Wuffers jerked violently, snarling and snapping against the hands gripping her. The Nehi's head rose, her mouth widening impossibly. Its body lunged from the earth, up and up, her mouth opening wider and wider. I ran. The Nehi's mouth fell onto Wuffers neck. The yelp of pain was so unreal. Tears sprang to my eyes even as blood spurted up from Wuffers's neck and fell wet and warm on my face. I raised my muddy rain boot into the air and slammed it into the Nehi's head.

Black spines broke under my heel. The Nehi reared back, black and red eyes like the bits of wood at the bottom of a fire. Wuffers sagged to the ground. The Nehi stood from its crouched position over my dog. Its oversized webbed feet pushed it to its full height, a little smaller than Mama. Its teeth were stained red. My heart pounded in my chest. I stumbled back and fell. The creature's eyes brightened, its inhuman mouth stretching in a smile. There were three teeth broken, the fangs halved or quartered. Its slender tongue darted out of its gaping mouth as it hissed. The odor rolled over me as the speckled skin glistened in the afternoon sun. It took a step forward. Scale-coated arms reached for me.

Something caught its eyes. Its head jerked just before Mom's body landed with bare feet into its chest. The creature's body flew backward, its arms yanked away from the momentum of its race to the ground. It screeched then thudded, its head rebounding on the mucky earth. I ran toward Haelyn, pulling her away from the creature. The Nehi shook its head, regained composure and shoved, tossing Mom aside like a toy. Mom rolled away and pulled into a crouch. A growl ripped from her throat, sending a shivering tremor through the ground that reverberated through the soles of my feet. I wrapped my arms around Haelyn as she inhaled sharply.

"It's okay. It's just Mama. She's tough. She'll take care of the Nehi." As if reminded of our presence by the sound of my voice, the Nehi turned toward Haelyn and me. I backed up a step, shoving Haelyn behind me. In a blur Mom was standing in front of us.

"Get the fuck away from my daughter!" she said. Haelyn grabbed at the back of my gray sweatshirt. It pulled against my scratched arm, sending a wave of pain through me. Mom took two steps forward. Her clenched fist pulled back. The Nehi surged toward Mom, the spines on its head rising, mouth gaping around needle-like teeth as a snarl ripped from its mouth. Mom's voice echoed back in a dragon howl. Her fist smashed into the jaw of the creature. The creature flew away from Mom and landed with a thud. Its limp body jerked and spasmed, sparking with blue bits of lightning.

Mom shook her hands free of little blue sparks as she stomped toward the Nehi in bare feet. She reached for the thing, wrapped her hands around its neck and lifted it. She dragged it to the pond, pulling the blade from her thigh as she reached the water's edge. I could see the muscles of her arms as she worked to move the creature. She dropped the Nehi and turned to us. Her auburn hair swung around her face, her features were sharp and her eyes mismatched. "Look away, girls." There was no arguing with her. Haelyn and I turned, but Haelyn peeked over her shoulder as the sound of the knife sliced the air. I jerked her arm and she pulled her gaze away again.

There was a splash and I knew it was safe to turn around. Mom had already scooped Wuffers into her arms when I looked. When she walked toward the house, she passed Haelyn and me. Her gold eye was showing. Both of them spilled tears. One side of her mouth was twisted down. I was scared to death that Wuffers was dead.

"Get on up here, you two," she said as she passed. Her voice was jagged, like a piece of broken glass, her words stuttered as she held the whole weight of our wolador.

"Is Wuffers - ?" I swallowed past the bump in my throat.

"Not yet," she said. I rushed behind her, dragging Haelyn with me and cupping my right arm toward my stomach. Haelyn didn't say anything. Her eyes stayed big the whole walk back to the house. Only Mama grunted every now and then as she walked holding Wuffers.

Once we were inside the house, we followed Mama into the living room. "Aubry, run go get me clean sheets from the closet." I did run. This might be my fault that Wuffers was -. I cried as I ran back into the living room and laid the sheets onto the couch. Once Mama laid Wuffers as gentle as a baby onto the couch, she turned to me.

"Mama, I'm so sorry!" I sobbed. My stomach squeezed inside of me and my face burned under the tears spilling out of my eyes. My lungs heaved under the guilt of hurting Wuff. The room swam around me. "I didn't mean for it to happen. Wuff tried to stop me, but

Haelyn was getting hurt, Mama, and I couldn't leave her there. Please don't be angry with me!"

"Shh, shh, shh!" She pressed a finger over my mouth to stop my talking. "I am not angry with you, baby girl. You did good. Now, you're hurt. And so is Wuffers. And so is Haelyn. So, we're gonna have to get you all patched up, okay? Wuffers is hurt the worst. I need to fix her first. You and Haelyn go sit on the other couch and be quiet and patient until I can patch up Wuffers."

"You can fix her?"

"I'm going to try my best. Run get me my bag."

SIXTEEN ~ RORI – MAKING THE CALL

I heard Aubry's dragon voice from inside my bathroom, which was an inner room of the house. Abandoning the towels I was folding I ran, heck I probably flew, out of the house. If I had not been terrified for Aubry's safety I would have stopped short for the surprise of seeing a Nehi on this side of the lesser gate. First the hawk, then the dog, now the Nehi. Crawling fingers of fear prickled the skin on the backs of my arms as I cleaned and stitched the gaping wounds in Wuffers's neck.

Wuffers's breathing came soft and shallow. She hadn't even whined when I cleaned the wounds of the Nehi poison. Her eyes remained closed even through the stitching. Part way through, the little yunwi came out to join us. From the corner of my eye, I saw her climb right up into Aubry's lap and blend her hair to the wound on Aubry's arm. Haelyn watched the yunwi with fascination, fear still mingling on her face. The little yunwi growled at Haelyn once, pulled into Aubry's arm, away from Haelyn and stayed there.

After a few moments of stitching, I heard the soft pad of the yunwi's feet against the area rug. She pulled herself on to the couch next to Wuffers and toddled her way along the edge to Wuffers's chest. She sat down, her thick legs dangling over the edge of the couch. The white bandage on her thigh shone against her hair that turned black against the touch of Wuffers's fur. She looked at me with her big black, glittery eyes and smiled. She touched Wuffers's shoulder and began to sing.

Her sweet, high voice stretched away. The notes were slow and melodic. Then they picked up a quicker rhythm and lighter tone that painted pictures of spring and of things coming to life after the sleep of winter. I continued stitching but had to stop to wipe away tears that blurred my vision. The song was one of healing for Wuffers. It throbbed with magic. I could see it with my right eye, floating on the air around us, adding a gold shimmer to the sun-filled living room.

When her song ended, she continued to hum and kicked her legs softly over the edge of the couch. I finished the stitching and kissed Wuffers on the snout. She didn't stir, but her breathing sounded stronger. I bowed to the yunwi. "Thank you, Little One," I said. She put a hand to my face and smiled.

I turned to Aubry next. I wrapped my hands around her cheeks and looked deeply into her yellow-gold eyes. "I am so proud of you. You saved Wuffers's life, but your life is more important to me than even Wuffers. It was kind of crazy of you to go in after a Nehi to save your dog."

"Mama, I couldn't just watch it eat Wuffers." She hiccupped and tears ran fresh down her cheeks.

"I know, honey. I would have done the same thing, but - I don't want to lose you." I choked back sobs. This whole broken gate thing was becoming a big a deal. "You just gotta be careful, baby girl." I wrapped her in my arms. Her clothes were still wet and covered in mud and she reeked from where the Nehi had gotten its scent on her. I didn't care. I pressed my cheek into her wet curls and prayed she could soak in my strength to keep her safe. "Now, let's get a look at you."

I cleaned the gashes from the Nehi on both Aubry and Haelyn. Haelyn's short sleeve t-shirt was torn a bit on the sleeve and inner seam of the torso. And she was equally covered in mud and muck.

"It's okay," she said. "That's why I had these clothes on. Mom knows I play rough." Her eyes were still a little wide.

"Do you know what it was that got you?" I asked.

"I don't," she squeaked. "I just know it was freaky. And Aubry saved me from it." She looked at Aubry and smiled just a little. Her eyes stayed wide, though. Sort of manic. She sure enough saw the creature. So, was this a lost medicine woman? Her features screamed Native American, so I supposed it was possible. That would be an oh-so-much more better explanation than the cracked gate and weakening veil.

"Best you say some branches got a hold of you," I suggested. Her eyes snapped back to me. I was kneeled in front of her and had just finished wrapping the bandage around her arm.

"Mom wouldn't believe me if I told her anything else," she said. Whoa. So, she'd tried to tell her other things. And Mrs. Widow Edythe Turner had not believed the girl. Sounded about right. Anyone with a little magic was misunderstood. Why should Haelyn Turner be any different? So, perhaps this wasn't the weakening veil. A little piece of hope glimmered in me.

I patted her on the uninjured arm. "You can come talk to me any time you want, sweetheart," I whispered to her. She blinked at me and then smiled a little.

"Thank you, Mrs. Cantrell." She threw her arm around me. Startled, I let her hug my neck for a second before I wrapped an arm around her and patted her back.

After Haelyn got picked up and Aubry was tucked in, I made a phone call. The windows in the front room welcomed the dark of night. The moon hung on the eastern horizon, three-quarters full and cool blue. I pressed the phone to my ear and waited for it to ring. Wuffers still lay on the couch, her breathing shallow. Worms of worry wriggled in my stomach.

Josh answered after the first ring. "What's going on?" Josh asked. "What happened now?" Intuitive as always. Or maybe just scared given all the recent activity. "Is it the Demon Dog?" I paced in front of the window, watching the pond glitter in the moonlight. What I was going to do scared me more than a little.

"A Nehi broke through the water gate and attacked Aubry and a friend," I explained. "I need your help. Can you come over and stay with Aubry?" This was not the first time I'd relied on Josh as a babysitter while I performed Dragon-Bitten duties. "I mean, are you up for it? It's been a rough day," I said. This was probably not fair to ask for his help when he'd been on death's doorstep only hours ago. Was he even strong enough to drive here?

"Don't worry about me. How's our girl? Does she need healing?" I could hear him moving. Something on the other end of the line thumped. Josh grunted.

"Aubry's fine, but Wuff could use some magic. She's pretty bad tore up."

"She went after the Nehi?" Josh's voice rattled. It sounded like he was jogging.

"Yeah and Josh? I'm going to need to use the stone."

"What are you thinking?" he asked, quizzically.

"I need to call the Uktena."

SEVENTEEN ~ RORI - DRAGON WISDOM

Nehis don't scare me. I can take on a lesser dragon. Raven Mockers? No problem. Truth was I didn't get frightened of creatures. I was tougher than they were. But, calling on the Uktena? That scared the tar out of me.

I'd showered and draped myself in ceremonial white linens. I sat on the ottoman next to Wuffers and watched the local news in horror. "Has Halloween come early this year? Find out why some locals seem to think so." I pulled the comb through my hair while the commercials played, practicing breathing techniques to calm my stuttering heart. Wuffers was sleeping, her breath coming soft and slow. Her neck was covered in bandages I'd applied. I was sick with worry, not sure what the Nehi poison would do to her. Selfish as it was, I hoped Josh had the energy to heal her with the stone.

The door opened and closed and a repeated hush and thunk signaled Josh taking off his shoes. He whispered around the corner of the kitchen and living room, but before I could see him I could sense the power of the stone he carried.

Something deep in my gut said I was flirting with disaster by using the Ulunsuti twice in a single day. Something else in my heart said I had to do this if I wanted to keep the veil intact.

"Come on in," I told Josh. He tiptoed into the living room, his eyes wide as he looked me over. And then his gaze landed on Wuffers. He knelt by the couch, between the ottoman and my dog, placing the Ulunsuti stone in his lap. With his pointer finger, he stroked the space between Wuffers's nose, between her eyes and to her forehead. She exhaled deeply, a low breathy sound that was both full of pain and relief. My heart broke all over again for my dog. I put my hand on Josh's shoulder and he shivered.

I inhaled deeply, soaking in the scent of him. He always smelled delicious. Like he was made of the forest. He put a hand on my knee and electricity tingled up my thigh. I ignored it, but only with great effort. "What do you make of Wuffers?" I asked.

He stopped petting her and rested his hand on her shoulder, closed his eyes and hummed, low in his throat. The stream of energy between us pulsed across my body, into Josh where I gripped his shoulder and continued into my wolfdog. I could feel the stone feeding us magic. Wuffers's fur began to emanate a golden, glittery light, concentrated around the Nehi wound. After a moment, the buzzing energy faded and Josh released me and Wuffers.

"She will be fine. And soon. There is already magic on her and she needs no more help from me." He turned to me, head tilted. "Who did this healing for her?"

"Our little yunwi friend," I told him.

"Oh yeah?" Josh said, eyebrows rising. "You have a mighty ally in health and protection then."

"Maybe I should go wake her up for a blessing on me," I said, half smiling to myself, like it was a joke.

"Are you sure this is a good idea? I mean, twice in one day. Most Bitten don't handle the stone more than once in a lifetime. That's why there's a me." His blue eyes looked clear and his olive skin was blushed and healthy.

"You look good," I commented. Even his locks of dark, loose curls were vibrantly shiny. His mouth was framed in the gruffness of a few days' growth and the stubble made him more handsome in a rugged sort of way. The same longing I'd sated earlier burned under the surface of worry. Was it the stone or was it me? He grinned at me, leaned in and kissed me softly on the mouth. His lips were warm and comforting.

"Thanks, darlin'," he said, his voice a husky whisper. He backed away from me and looked me over. "This is a new look for you. Are you going for a virgin bride sacrifice sort of thing?" I rolled my eyes at him.

"It's required for meeting the Uktena," I said. "One must do everything one can to not offend the dragon, lest one would like to become dragon snacks." His face got really serious. Not the reaction I was looking for.

"I don't think you should do this. Why do you need to call her anyway?"

"I need help," I said and rose from the ottoman. I paced in front of the TV and was pleased to find it was proving my point. "See? Look." I pointed my comb at the news channel that had returned from commercial break. Josh turned his blue eyes from me to the newscaster and a small picture that expanded to fill the screen. The caption beneath it read, "Winged creature caught on camera."

"...where a young woman says while hiking she saw this. Acting quickly, the witness was able to snap a photo. Now, you maybe can't make out the details of this picture, but it would appear to be some form of humanoid, miniature winged creature, or so says the eye witness. The picture has circulated social media channels and now Waynesville and surrounding areas are under speculation for being the dwelling place... of fairies." She ended the sentence with that coy tone that said, 'Isn't that cute?'

The picture was a garbled mass of blurry greens with a center shape of gold. It was as the newscaster stated: humanoid, miniature and winged.

"That's a flyer," Josh said. He had changed seating and was watching from the couch opposite of Wuffers. His fists pushed into the cushion like he was about to launch himself toward the TV.

"This is why I have to talk to the dragon. I need to know how much damage was done to the water gate and I need to know if there's another way to heal the gates and the veil. And how to find the damn Hawk!" Frustration boiled up and spilled over. It was naturally fueled by the fear which had picked a pulse when the first gate had broken and steadily increased with the breaking of the second gate.

I paced in front of the window, glancing at the pond under the moonlight. My mind was made. I turned to Josh. He stood, stepped around the ottoman and pulled me into an embrace. His chest against my cheek flexed as he adjusted his arms around me. I pulled away a little to look up into his face. He bent and kissed my forehead then released me. My skin prickled in the chill of his arms' absence. And maybe nerves from what I was about to do.

"Don't get eaten," he said. I followed him back to the couch where he'd set the stone. After removing it from the cedar box, and then the deer hide, he held it in his hand where it glistened a vibrant white and stark red. "You'll need to feed it. And then once you do that the Uktena will come. You do know that calling her this way is not going to make her happy."

Basically, using the stone like this was like sending out a homing beacon for a competing Uktena to fight for land. When she arrived, she'd be rarin' to go and then she'd see me. I nodded once. There was no other way to call her. Not as an adult, already-Bitten Bitten who had venom in my veins from the Joining ceremony when I was twelve. He started to hand me the stone but I shook my head. "Wait until I get onto the porch. I might not make it to the door if I take it now." He grinned at me, but I was nothing but a quivering ball of nerves so I couldn't grin back.

Once we were on the porch, Josh tenderly lowered the stone into my waiting hands. I held it out in front of me, left hand holding bottom, right hand holding top. He kissed me one more time on the forehead and then quickly slipped back into the house, shutting the door on me and the waiting night. I took three slow, deep breaths before I descended the stairs and ventured out toward the pond.

The grass in the front yard was moist under my bare feet. The chill of the spring evening caressed my exposed skin. Tree frogs sang in the woods only yards from the pond. A whip-poor-will sounded off. The pond's surface flatly reflected the moon without hinting its deep secrets. No one could guess the small body of water surrounded by newly budding cattails could be a doorway to a mansion of underwater creatures. From this pond the Nehi could access the water gate, now cracked or broken, to their underwater village.

And from this pond I would access the Uktena's doorstep. Was all of this actually in this particular pond? No. Water is a source of magic and the creatures protected by the veil could access and use the magic in the water to travel where they willed. The network of water for them went beyond the connected rivers, streams and lakes. The Uktena was the ruler of the water realm and the place of banished creatures. That's why they called it the place where the Uktena lives.

Our Cherokee history and myths told of a hunter who'd obtained an Ulunsuti stone from an Uktena, and that was true enough, although the stone was lost since James Mooney had recorded our tales and history. It had been buried with the last priest to hold the stone and the gravesite had been forgotten. The history didn't include the tale of my heritage and the origin of the stone I held in my hand. And that was because we didn't want it written or spoken. The creatures of myth survived from our anonymity from the records James Mooney so thoroughly wrote. We knew that well enough from the first time Europeans stepped foot on this land.

People couldn't be trusted to care for non-magical animals. The slaughter of the bison was proof. As soon as settlers discovered yunwi and flyers and such, the population plummeted. They killed them from superstition, they killed them for sport, they killed them out of sheer fear of their existence. That is why the veil existed and that is why it had to stay in place.

I lowered myself to the pond bank, squishing in the mud and pressing my toes into the water's edge. I set the stone into my lap and pulled the knife from the sheath strapped to my thigh. The Ulunsuti stone vibrated as if it were eager for the feeding. The blade edge was sharp enough it didn't hurt when I drug it across the palm of my hand. The cut wasn't deep. It was just enough to let the blood flow.

I sheathed the knife while the blood collected in my hand then grasping the stone. I let the blood drip on its smooth surface.

And then, I waited.

I could have counted the breaths before the water began to boil. It bubbled in the center, sending waves washing over my feet. I backed away from the pond's edge and knelt in the muck. The bank began to move as dozens of critters, snakes, turtles, and lizards, crawled their way as fast as they could from the water and the alpha predator making its way to the surface. I fought back the instinct to follow them. This predator was bigger and badder and stronger than me and my survival instincts were kicking me right in the gut. The muscles of my arms and legs jerked as my body screamed to save my sorry ass, but I knelt right there in the mud and watched the horns break the water's surface as sheer terror reigned in my heart.

The Uktena was dreadfully beautiful. Her long, serpentine body was covered in scales that seemed to burn and spark as if a secret blue fire were kept in each one. Companion to her scales were red rings along her back the same vibrant scarlet as the stripe on the Ulunsuti stone. The dragon of water, banished to the hidden parts of the world, surged from the pond, making it seem more like a puddle. With its body still submerged in the water, the Uktena turned blazing golden eyes on me.

The Ulunsuti embedded in the forehead of the creature throbbed with light, mimicking the stone I held in my lap. The horns on either side of the stone in her head twisted up and away with deep grooves that spiraled with the twist of the horns. They were black as night. Black as the depths of the pools and caves she lived in. I cast my eyes to the ground as the serpent leaned in on me. She smelled of rivers in spring, of lightning and fresh rain. A piece of my soul wanted to give everything to stay in that smell, to run toward the Uktena, as if she would envelop me in a motherly embrace.

The other piece of me that was the same dragon as the serpent in front of me regarded the human side with impartial judgement. The human wanted what all humans wanted when they saw the Uktena – death. Sweet, beautiful surrender from all the nasty things we suffer in a frail form. The dragon's offer was seductive, but I couldn't be killed like a normal human. The Uktena had seen to that. She'd given me venom, twice over – once upon my birth into the Bitten line and then again upon Joining. Why did she do this? Because having the veil in place was as crucial to her survival as it was to the rest of the creatures. If people learned about a dragon, how soon would they capture and contain her, study her and eventually kill her or worse, use the power of the Ulunsuti for their purposes? It had been done by the Ani'Kutani and it could be done again.

I had something the Uktena didn't have. I had a human body. A way to blend. A disguise. I was a means to her survival. And how did we know this would absolutely be the case if the dragon were discovered? Because the Ulunsuti stone was an instrument to focus prophecy. The dragon knew the possible future.

The Uktena bent low and sniffed loudly. Her breath blew back the loose strands from my braid. Her breath was like the wind in a storm – sort of wild and dangerous. "You are not another Uktena. You are already Bitten. And you already have the jewel of my mother. And you do not run into my arms for death. So, why have you tricked me into your presence?" The voice of the serpent was something less physical and something far more painful as it echoed against the corners of my mind. The words were a translation of intention, rather than spoken language. Having a creature dump a message directly into my head hurt like the Dickens.

"I have only respect, Grandmother," I said ceremonially – and out loud. I couldn't chat with creatures with my mind. The only reason the Uktena could talk to me was because of our shared state of being dragon.

"Then tell me what you want and then let me take to the hunt again. There are a delicious number of Nehis on the loose and I'm still hungry." Great. I wondered what 'a delicious number' amounted to.

"Is the gate badly broken then?" I asked, raising my eyes to her scales, but not to her eyes or the stone.

"Cracked. Wounded and bleeding. That is two gates now, is it not?" She pulled herself from the water. It sloshed and lapped at the pond shore as she emerged. Her scales hushed through the mud and grass. Under the blue light of night and the blooming moon, her scales sparked and shined. I raised my eyes to catch a peek at her. She was so lovely. Her horns glimmered against the night sky, her golden eyes shining in the darkness. And blazing out with its own light was the Ulunsuti stone, vibrant and alive, feeding on the blood of the dragon herself, without the need of artificial sustenance like the stone in my lap that absorbed the blood from my hand.

"Yes, Grandmother. There is an enemy that is threatening the veil," I said.

"Oh yes. Such a delightful little diversion it's caused me. But, half-blood, don't you think you ought to get this under control? Before the veil breaks? I do sense a young one close by. A full-blood. Her sacrifice would cause you great heartache, would it not?"

Frustration was my name.

"Yes, Grandmother," I said, my teeth clenched together. "Can you see something, sense something that might help me find the enemy?" The hushing of her scales stopped. I dared to glance up, just a little. She was at the north side of the pond, maybe twenty feet from me. My ears whined. The hair on my arms and neck seized into an upright position. Ozone filled my nostrils. Crackling broke across the air. A tree near the dragon ignited in blue threads of lightning. I could feel her eyes on me.

"You need my help?" She whispered. "You need more than the blessing of my mother? More than the skills and power you've inherited? And that I, myself, have imparted on you through my precious venom?" I didn't dare move. I didn't dare speak. I wondered if she'd eat a Bitten. Had that happened before? I mean, if I screwed this whole thing up, couldn't she just make another Bitten?

The Uktena breathed in once, a crackle whipped through the air and then her presence loomed over me. "You really are a half-blood, aren't you?" she said. Was she cutting me down? "You might have been enough in a peace, but now...?" She let the question trail.

I'm not enough. I can't do it on my own. Huh. Well, there it was, wasn't it?

"You've got a point," I said. "I'm only half of this equation." I pushed myself up from the ground, holding the stone in my cut hand. "I understand now, Grandmother," I said to the Uktena. She peered down at me and then quick as a whip she coiled around me, not touching me, just surrounding me. I froze as the coils wrapped tighter and tighter, slithering over themselves to squeeze in on me. The Uktena reared back her head and hissed, showing off her sharp fangs. Lightning sparked, dancing over her flashing blue scales and emanating around us.

"If you eat me, who's going to fix the gates?" I asked, careful to not look her straight in the eyes. This wasn't going the way I wanted it to. I needed information on the Hawkman.

"Maybe I'll get someone new," she said. The top part of her body whipped around, squeezing in on me but still not touching. She really didn't have to touch me to kill me. With the electricity sparking in her scales, she could kill me right now.

"Let's face it, that'll take time. And you don't have the luxury of time." I raised my eyes to look her in the face. Her breath expanded her body and contracted it with each exhale. Her eyes locked onto me. At this distance I could see the pattern on them, a map of thin lines spread like cracked glass over the golden irises. I could also see the reflection in the stone and it was telling me everything I needed to know.

Images flashed across the surface. If she ate me, the veil would most certainly break. The sight of chaos was certain. I knelt to the ground and bowed my head. "Please. Can you tell me anything about the Hawkman that will help?"

By this time, I knew the message in the stone had not only passed across its surface, but also through the mind of the ancient dragon. A low grumble started somewhere in the coiled serpent around me, and then seemed to expand away to the horizon. "His banishment was meant to be permanent. His release was not without aid and his rise back to power will require assistance. He will need a human host and he will need another priest to conjure until he regains his power."

"So, he's possessed someone?" The dragon was silent while my wheels were turning. "Grandmother, how can I identify the Hawkman in his host body?"

"I cannot know this thing. My mother is the only Uktena who saw the Ani'Kutani priest when he joined with the Tlanuwa. She gave everything for your ancestor in order to stop the Hawkman. You must fight this enemy again. It is your duty and privilege."

My heart sank. Dead end. Still, maybe she knew another healing to the veil. "And what of the veil, Grandmother? Is there some other way to heal the veil if it breaks?" I looked up into her face. She didn't speak. Instead, the images on the Ulunsuti told the story. The third gate shattered. The veil broke. A knife was held to Aubry's neck. One with a white bone hilt and the etching of a hawk. I dropped my gaze, unable to watch any more. "Please, no more," I begged. Tears spilled from my eyes.

"You must stop the Ani'Kutani from breaking the third gate," she said.

"No. I can't. Remember? I'm just a half-baked version of the whole Bitten enchilada."

"What will you do then?" asked the dragon. Her body squeezed in on me. Ozone burned my nose. Danger, Will Robinson!

"I'm going to call my other half," I said. Her body was a mere inch from touching me. I was surrounded in a wall of mythical creature. I fingered the knife strapped to my thigh and counted to the seventh red ring on her back. That's where her heart was. I'd fight her to the death if I had to. Before I could pull the knife, her body ceased movement.

"That is a wise choice," she said, the sound of her voice in my mind echoed like the oncoming storm. I looked up into her face. Her tongue flicked past the oval space of her mouth and touched both points perfectly over my eyebrows. "Be strong," she said.

Energy washed through me. It was wild and cold, fragranced with water, like a thunderstorm in March. My breath hitched, stuck somewhere between my lungs and mouth. The Uktena flicked her tongue back into her mouth and watched me struggle to breathe. Spots swarmed my vision of golden eyes and flashing Ulunsuti stone. When the air found its way in and out again with a violent heave, she turned away from me. The pond welcomed her with barely a ripple.

Adrenaline whizzed through my veins. Stumbling, I rose from the ground, still working my lungs with the new energy that the Uktena had bestowed on me. I felt more alive, somehow lighter, and stronger. I dashed back to the house and climbed the stairs two at a time. Josh met me at the door, but I had no time for grateful embraces. He caught the stone I hastily dropped in his hands as I dodged past him. I yanked my phone off the kitchen counter. Josh closed the door behind me as I tapped the screen of my phone.

"Thank god you're okay. I watched from the window. I thought she was going to eat you." He was talking and walking toward me. When he got within an arm's reach he asked, "Who are you calling?" The relief from seeing me alive and whole turned to puzzlement. The Ulunsuti stone was still throbbing, still sending out waves of information and feeling.

"Can you put that thing away?" I asked, gripping my forehead to keep my brain from exploding. He looked down, surprised to see the stone still in his hand.

"Oh yeah, right," he said. He moved toward the living room and the containers to keep the stone safe. The phone rang twice before he picked up. A muzzy 'hello' growled through the speaker.

"Andy," I began, "I need you here."

EIGHTEEN ~ RORI – HALF MORE

When it came to Aubry, he couldn't argue. Andy was on the plane and here before the sun set the next day. And it wasn't quick enough. While he was flying across the country, I was planning our next move. And tending sick creatures, and ones that were not so sick.

"Alright, now, baby," I crooned. "Let's try out your legs."

Wuffers cut her orange eyes toward me, lifting her head and sniffing. That was a good sign. She sat up on her own and gingerly let herself down from the couch. As we made our circuit around the living room and dining area to the food bowls, Miney flew down the hall toward the living room. Miney was the yunwi. Aubry had decided to name her a short version of her favorite movie character.

Miney's hair was bubblegum pink and fading as she ran past the couches. She skidded around Wuffers, who groaned and growled all at the same time. It was one of those, 'I don't think I'm in the mood for this'. Or maybe, 'Watch out, you little brat.' Miney rounded the kitchen island. A cupboard opened. Noise clattered in to the living room. It sounded like Miney was trying to hide in the cupboard with pots and pans. Wuffers panted, ears pitched back.

"Aubry Anne," I said. "Come get Miney out of my kitchen!" Miney darted around the counter, stuck her tongue out at me, wiggled her fingers in her ears and then ran into the office. That creature had figured out what I'd said. Smart one.

Aubry slunk in, quieter than quiet. She pressed a finger to her mouth to signal me to silence. I winked at her and continued on my path with Wuffers. Wuffers took a small sip out of her water bowl, but never looked happier than when I helped her up onto the couch again. Aubry was searching through the living room for Miney, turning over couch pillows and sniffing the air.

I went into the kitchen and pretended to get a glass of water. I snuck a peek and saw Miney slip behind the monitor on the oak desk in the office next to the front door. When I caught Aubry's eyes, I jerked my head toward the office. A smile stretched across her face. Her eyebrows were cocked high as she fought a giggle.

She rounded the corner from where the living room met the entryway and then stood to the side of the office door. She raised her head and inhaled slow and steady, silently sniffing for her "prey". Her golden eyes lit up as she peered around the corner to the oak desk. She crept over the threshold, across the area rug, past the printer stand. The monitor on the desk was on. Miney had bumped the mouse and woken it. It still displayed my latest online research: information on the Cahokia Mounds and the Bird Man, though all the information was old news. I had shown Aubry last night, pointing out that the mummy, laid out on the white shells arranged in the shape of a bird, was the ancestor of our foremothers and the ancestor of our enemies, the Ani'Kutani priests. I was still piecing everything together, trying to get a handle on what was going on before anything else happened.

Miney hid behind the monitor, but she had not accounted for the long wisp of hair that stuck off her head and swooped over in a loop, nor her feet which poked out from under the monitor.

The office chair stood between Aubry and Miney's hiding place. She slipped past it, but bumped it. The wheel squeaked, Miney shouted, leapt over the monitor, knocking it onto the keyboard, hopped onto the chair and made for the door. Aubry's eyes locked onto Miney and with barely a move, she reached out and caught the little yunwi. They rolled onto the floor, Aubry giggling while Miney whined. Aubry pinned her to the ground and then tickled her sides.

Miney's laughter bubbled into the air, light and high and full of sunshine. The sound rolled through me and ignited giggles of my own. Wuffers raised her head and sniffed the air before laying her head back onto her pillow. Clearly, she couldn't be bothered.

Aubry let Miney up off the floor and hugged her. Miney purred and pressed her face into her shoulder.

Footsteps echoed up the stairs to the porch. I recognized them. Aubry turned to me. "Is somebody coming?" I could tell she recognized those footsteps too. I raised my eyebrows at her and looked at the door. The knob twisted, the door flew open. Sunshine spilled in around a human shape in the doorway.

Andy stepped over the threshold, dumping his bags by the door. Before he'd offloaded the overnight bag from his shoulder, I'd wrapped an arm around his neck.

"Thank god you're here," I said.

He choked on my hug. "Happy to see you too, sissy." I barely had time for a quick squeeze before Aubry and Miney were crawling – literally, crawling – onto Andy to say hello. Andy swooped Aubry up and when the little yunwi stretched her arms up for the same, Andy scooped her up as well, never even pausing. I was stunned Miney would be so warm to this new person. Was this a good thing? Would Miney be so trusting of all strangers or did she know that this was family of Aubry and so was safe?

"And who is this?" Andy asked Aubry as he let her slide to the floor. He turned wide, surprised eyes at me.

"This is Miney. She's my friend. I found her at school while we were hiking and brought her home because she was hurt. Look," Aubry said and touched Miney's leg near the bandaged cut.

"I see. So, Mama patched her up, huh?" Andy looked from Aubry to me. Miney put her hand on Andy's cheek, looking intently at his eyes. Andy's eyes went out of focus for a moment while his body swayed. He gently took Miney's hand away from his cheek and looked at her. "Not so loud, please," he said. His champagne skin turned pale and his shoulders slumped. Miney startled at his gentle admonishment. Like he'd spanked her but it took a moment for the embarrassment and hurt feelings to catch up. Her breath quickened like she would cry. "It's okay, hon', just tone it down a notch, okay?" Miney nodded, kicking her legs around Andy's waist. Andy let her down to the floor. When he straightened I could see the headache starting behind his eyes.

"I'll get you some ibuprofen," I said. He followed me into the kitchen while the girls trailed behind him, chatting away.

I reached for the medicine cabinet while Andy punctuated Aubry's story with the appropriate amounts of mm-hmms and ohs. I considered if it was time for Miney to return to the woods. We had taken her in to heal her. She was healed. The friendship growing between her and Aubry would make the leaving difficult if we continued to put it off. However, I wouldn't release her on her own. I would have to locate her family.

I added it to the list of things to mention to the Lady when we went to check on the third gate. I only hoped we wouldn't be too late.

NINETEEN ~ HAELYN – NO ANSWER

"You're doing it wrong," said Hawkman. His voice ratcheted through the clearing. It was cloudy and dreary out. The air was thick and muggy. The feather in my fingers was losing all its fine fibers from where I twisted it. I yawned. It was still early morning.

"I'm trying," I said. I was exhausted. We'd been doing this for more than an hour. "It's resisting me or something. It doesn't want to come through."

"Are you looking at it right," he asked.

"What do you mean?"

"Do you see it? Do you see its true nature? Are you seeing it in the right place?" He fired questions at me, pacing in the dirt in front of me.

"I'm doing what you told me to. I see the giant trees. I see the creature like you describe it. At first it started to come, but then it got stuck against something. Like the trees are holding it and won't let it go. And then, something new came into the picture."

"What? What new was in the picture?" I thought about it, rubbing my sweaty hand against the rough denim of my jeans.

"All I can see are snakes' eyes. Two pair. Golden colored." I didn't tell him they looked an awful lot like Aubry's eyes. "Now it's like it's hiding from the eyes." His eyes burned behind the emerald as he leaned over me. He gripped my chin between fingers that felt like a vice grip.

"Try. Harder," he spoke and jerked his fingers away from me. "We must have the Ganagi."

TWENTY ~ RORI - SPIRIT OF THE FOREST

We parked Andy's racer red rental car at the trailhead and headed into the trees. The forest around us was young with spring. Buds sprinkled the limbs of deciduous trees. Spindly trunks twisted up and spread out to form the canopy. Interspersed throughout the forest were evergreens, standing silent sentinel. Here and there, fallen logs covered in thick moss spawned the growth of new trees. The dark dirt path we hiked was wide enough for two people to stand side by side. It climbed and dipped steadily. Overhead the sky brooded with an even cover of gray that leaked through the green light of the forest. The air was still and thick with moisture that clung to my skin and clothes.

A storm was on its way and it set my nerves on edge.

Aubry and Miney were in between Andy and me. We stalked the trail more quietly than hares hiding in the brush. Other hikers, however, were a different story. As we approached the poplar grove, we could hear the stomping of a group of five up ahead, followed by another group of three. When they approached around a bend in the trail, the leader, a young Asian woman, startled at seeing the three of us (Miney hid herself) on the path without having heard us coming. We moved to the side and allowed the two groups to pass.

I rolled my shoulders back and away from my ears, fighting the tension that hung in the air, on my heart. I didn't like these people tromping around here. Something about the forest today was forbidding. I ground my teeth around the desire to yell at them to get out.

Two miles in from the trailhead, we climbed steeply over several sets of switchbacks. The trees grew closer here, hugging the sky over us like curious onlookers. One final bend turned us out into a small clearing. Smaller trees, dwarfed in the presence of the giants, skirted the gate trees at a safe distance, as if in reverence.

The twin poplars dominated the clearing, their trunks as wide as twenty regular trees. The lowest of the limbs sprouted from the trunks twenty feet from the ground. Bits of mistletoe clung to the mostly bare branches of the just wakening trees. They grew side by side, leaving enough space between them for two people to stand in. Bending toward each other, where their canopies spread into the dreary light of the cloudy morning, the branches tangled together like old friends holding hands.

A young couple stood in the clearing, snapping photos, murmuring at how awesome the trees were. We waited, pretending to rest, until they finished and left the clearing, leaving a trail of perfume, scented deodorant and cologne. There was another scent hanging on the forest air that caught my nose. Andy moved right up to the trunk of the left giant and patted the rough bark.

"Hello, gorgeous," he said. Then his head jerked toward me, his body jolted as his dual colored gaze fell onto me. "Whoa." He heaved like he'd been electrocuted and the shock stole his breath. Yanking his hand from the tree he leaned over and grabbed for his knees to support him.

"What is it?" The smell was maddening. There and not, strong and then gone.

"Something or someone has been here," he said as he worked on catching his breath. I strode over to the tree, smelling deeply. I growled around the inability to identify it. I ran my hands over the bark, little tingles of electricity sparked against my fingertips. "Can you feel it?"

"It just feels like my fingers are too cold," I told Andy. Andy pressed a hand to his temple. "What is it, Andy?"

"I can't tell. I just sense all this negative energy floating around." He squeezed his eyes tighter. "Man. My head." Poor Andy. This happened when he sensed magic and creatures' intentions. I walked over to him and patted his back, frowning at his discomfort.

Aubry tiptoed up to me and touched my sleeve, peering around me toward the trees. Miney was close to her, her head yanking in all directions to peer around the grove. I followed Aubry's gaze, seeking out the alien smell's source.

A guttural gurgle echoed across the forest air. No one would have heard. No normal person, anyway. Aubry's head jerked in the direction of the distant noise, her eyebrows raised, nose lifted to the air, golden eyes wide. The gate trees shuddered, their limbs creaking in a non-existent breeze. Aubry looked up, held out a hand and let a shower of blackened tree buds fall into her hand.

Every nerve in my body thrummed to life, opening up the full potential of dragon blood coursing through my veins and the extra boost of energy the Uktena had given me last night.

There was something achingly familiar about the noise in a wrong sort of way. Like an itch I couldn't reach, the memory evaded me. I stood and wrapped an arm around Aubry, my heart plucking a staccato bass.

"Let's get through the gate. I don't like having Aubry here with something I don't know lurking around." Andy pulled his body upright, pressed fingers into his forehead and nodded. He stood in front of the two trees, exhaling to pull himself together again. After considering them for a moment, he began to speak. His words fell incongruously with the tone of fear pulsing out of his mouth.

"You two are looking lovely today. Doing a fine job guarding everything." He surveyed the gate as he spoke. It was true. On the other side, at the moment, was the other side of the clearing. The barrier spell held, despite marks of something messing with the gate. I breathed a sigh of relief for that one piece of good news. Now we just had to keep it that way.

Andy perched his hands on his hips and half smiled up at them, though his eyes were rimmed red and black bags gathered underneath them. "You mind if we pass through?" A low groan and creak crawled over the still air, joined by a higher pitch of murmuring tree. The ground underneath us shook gently with the welcome the sentinels gave us. I clasped Aubry's hand, Miney clinging to her other one. With my right eye, I saw the air between the two trees shimmer in shades of rainbow iridescence. My head spun as the left eye fought to keep up with the disparate images being conveyed to my brain. I fought the wave of dizziness and nausea with practiced will. Andy bowed his head to the trees. "Thanks," he said.

Approaching with eyes peering through the slender stalks of ash trees, we slipped into the forest behind the gate. The giant twin poplars shivered as we passed. We had all been here a number of times, but it was still a breathtaking experience. Well, maybe Miney had never been here. Judging by her little gasp when we crossed over from what can be seen to what cannot, I guessed she hadn't.

No other human could travel here. Something else had tried to pass. Some other something to which I could not put a name. Questions flitted through my mind as I clung to Aubry even after we were safely through the portal. I knew it was safe here, but nothing felt safe. It was not until we were meandering over the darkened earth path cutting into the giant forest that I eased my grip on Aubry's shoulders and let her slip into her own footsteps.

If the forests in the Smoky Mountains are beautiful, this grove, where the heart of the forest beats was a heaven of trees. The woody residents towered over us, looking down with ancient eyes and ears of spreading limbs and unfurled leaves. Spring began here and then marched onto the surrounding forest. The loam of the earth was clean and fragrant. I inhaled deeply, letting the scent soak into my blood and awaken a wild need inside of me to just be. At the heart of the forest, all was as it should be. It was sanctuary for a person of magic. Except today, the guardian trees had wavered in fear. And so, I did too.

Leaf-filtered sunshine cast the sanctuary in a perpetual green glow and Aubry's gray fleece turned emerald. She did a cartwheel in the path before turning to smile at me. My smile was less genuine, restrained by worry. Aubry caught the scent of something and took off like a shot down a rabbit trail, Miney close on her heels.

A giant oak loitering next to the trail reached wide, sturdy arms into the forest air. Likely, I would have to wait for the Spirit of the Forest to find me, rather than me finding her. I shrugged at Worry and, crouching low, hoisted myself up to the first limb.

I walked along the heavy lower limb of the giant oak until it began to bend under my weight. When the leaves made a tiny whisper of noise from the shaking limb, I searched for the next branch up and jumped, hanging from the branch. I swung myself up onto the branch and straddled the limb. From this vantage point, I could see Aubry stalking a butterfly and Andy cooling his hands and neck in a nearby stream.

I swung my legs back and forth, the weight of my hiking boots pulling against my legs. The bark under my fingertips was rough, but the scratch of it somehow made me feel more alive.

I let the forest soak me in while I waited. Which ended up not taking as long as I expected.

"Rori Dragonblood," the voice echoed from below my perch. The man's face peered up at me, shining like a moon in a midnight sky. He smiled, his arms held behind his back and lost in the folds of roomy, light fabric. It had a hint of color to it. Maybe it was blue and maybe it was a little green. From where I sat, the colors didn't want to stay the same. The Nune regarded me with a flat gaze that did not question or wonder. Nunes annoyed me slightly. They were so... blah. Emotionless. In other words, boring.

They were really like errand boys for the Lady I came to see, although she had never summoned me before. I swung from the branch, landing solidly onto the branch below me. I stayed on tiptoe before diving off the tree limb, feet planting neatly in the leaf litter directly in front of the Nune. It was my goal in life to get a Nune to show emotional capacity. My eyebrows crept up to my hairline as I watched his face for a reaction. When I rose and dusted my hands off, he simply waved in a direction. His nondescript brownish blah hair absorbed the pale jade of the afternoon light.

"This way, Dragonblood," he intoned. He turned and adroitly walked away from me, intending for me to follow. I blew a gust of exasperation in his direction. Nunes are just weird.

I cupped my hand around my mouth and shouted, "C'mon y'all!" I suppose I could have hooted like an owl or something, but that wasn't really necessary. Aubry bound through a thicket, a crown of flowers atop her head. Miney was close behind with her own crown, which had caused the tuft of hair on the top of her head to change shades. Andy didn't arrive.

"Andy!" I shouted.

"The other Dragonblood has been joined by the Lady," the Nune said then turned in the path he made and continued forward. I frowned.

"Has been joined by?" Interesting choice of words. "Where did they join?" The Nune turned to look at me, a blank expression that I couldn't read.

"I do not understand," he said.

"Where are they?" I asked.

"You shall see soon," he replied.

"Why don't you just tell me?"

"The Lady did not ask it of me."

"So, you do only what she asks?"

He paused, blinked then replied, "Yes."

I thought I was on to something. "*Only* what she asks?"

He paused again. Blinked again. "Certain things, the Lady does not have to assign to be done."

"Are ya sure?"

His marble face stayed placid. "Mostly," he answered.

"Hmmm…" I said. "Sounds like you might be confused." My body had leaned forward as I watched his face for any sign of a reaction. His clothes fluttered in the soft breeze, a hush of leaves stirring the air around us, though he, himself remained motionless.

"The Lady will no longer wait," he said. "Let us go to her now." *Dang.* I was getting close on that last one. We followed the Nune down the path toward… wherever it was he was leading us. Toward wherever it was Andy had already arrived and been joined by the Lady.

I looked over my shoulder to Aubry. She had given Miney a piggy back. Awkward under the weight of the yunwi, she wobbled down the path. "Need some help, baby girl?" She shook her head, her little mouth quirking into a smile.

"I'm strong, Mama. I got this," she said. The yunwi twisted a strand of her hair with one of her free fingers and stared wide-eyed into the gaping tunnel of trees we moved toward. Birds chirped loud and strong around us, rattling the smaller limbs of bushes and skittering through fallen leaves. I even saw a couple of flyers amidst darting squirrels and hummingbirds.

As we climbed a small hill, the bird song faded. My instincts went on alert. The Nune continued forward, his light loose clothes undulating in the breeze. He was like a lemming. The Lady said go this way and so that is the way he was going, without any other thought process in play.

I slowed my pace and pulled Miney from Aubry's back, placing her down gently to the path. I pressed my finger to my lips and made sure they both understood. I made eye contact with Aubry and pointed to my ear and then my nose. She cast her golden gaze out into the trees, her ears perked. She lifted her nose to the next rush of wind coming at our faces as I did the same. The Nune meandered along the path unaware. A twisted part of me wanted to watch him keep stumbling into danger just to see what would happen.

When I heard the lumbering of heavy feet to the right of the path, I watched the Nune stop and simply stare into the trees. I grunted in disgust. I was going to have to save this worthless drone's life. Aubry crouched down and wrapped her arms around Miney in a protective embrace. "Stay here," I warned. I turned on my heel then turned back. "I mean it. Stay. Put." Aubry nodded, her eyes big. I could hear her heart racing like a rabbit. "It'll be okay, sweetpea. You're strong, remember? You got this." One corner of her mouth quirked in a nervous smile. I winked at her, and then turned back to the path ahead.

The roar of Udoqua rolled through the columns of trees. Sunshine splintered my eyesight in a sudden shaft of light as I ran. The outline of the massive beast lumbered through the trees to the right of the path. From what I could tell from my jolting perspective, it was moving fast. Fact: black bears can run thirty five miles per hour; Udoqua, their ancestor, having giant proportions of twice the size of a typical full grown male black bear can run a *lot* faster. I was even faster, having the boost of dragon venom in my DNA and in my bloodstream.

The Nune stood ahead of me, perfectly still on the path. I vaulted forward, aiming my body and outstretched arms toward the clueless Nune. Udoqua burst from the tree line as my shoulder caught the Nune under the shoulder blade. Wrapping an arm around him, I pushed him forward and out of the direct path of the giant bear. We landed in a heap in the dark, moist dirt. "You okay?" I growled into his ear. Before he could answer Udoqua snatched at my leg with his massive jaws. I screamed out loud as pain shot through the flesh on my ankle and calf. My body whipped off the Nune and went skittering over dirt, roots and leaf litter.

The pain in my ankle eased. I rolled and jumped to my feet, faltering on the injured one. Udoqua towered above me, his dark blue eyes flashing. He took two giant lunges forward, the hair on his body shaking with the movement. He looked down on me and roared, jaws inches from my face. I could handle intimidation but I was a little worn out of threats to my personal safety after the day I had yesterday. I turned my head as spittle flew from Udoqua's frothing mouth. I balled up my fist, pulled back and let it fly, feeling the surge of power like a lightning strike in a storm. Energy sizzled through my arm.

Udoqua grunted as my fist made contact with his roaring jaw. His head yanked to the side with my well-aimed punch. He sneezed around a sparking collection of blue energy. He reared back, standing on his two back feet. I looked up and up. This was a big bear. Standing like he was, he probably reached eight feet and some change. I readied myself as he roared.

I adjusted my stance. "Hey, I can do that too," I said. I reached deep in my gut, finding the dragon within me. When the roar split the forest air, it was big in a way that was incongruous with my body. Udoqua shuddered, turning his face to the side. He looked puzzled for sure, but not enough to back down.

Damn. I didn't want to fight him. He was an ancestor I had nothing but respect for. I had to show him who I was. I dropped myself into last night's meeting with the Uktena. What was it she'd done to me? I could feel the energy coiling around in my body but I didn't know what to do with it.

Udoqua lunged forward, pulled back his humongous paw and made to swing at me. I dodged, rolled and pulled into standing so fast my head swam. Udoqua was still looking at where I had been. Sheer confusion painted his face as his paw swiped through crackling blue air instead of making contact with my already bruised body.

So, that's what she'd done. Sweet. I danced from foot to foot.

Udoqua blinked, shook his head and looked around until his eyes landed on me. I grinned and jetted, leaving another trail of lightning and filling the forest path with the smell of ozone. Trees whirred past me, blurring together in a continuous loop of browns and greens. I circled the giant bear three times. Reddish fog emanated from the circuit I'd made. I exited the circle and stood back. There was a connection between me and the fog. I felt it like a string tying from my belly button and into the odd ring of cloud.

The fog crackled. Udoqua lunged toward me, but the reddish fog encompassing him cracked in sudden spark of lightning, smacking him on his nose. He reared back and wailed, shaking his head and rubbing his face with his paw. The connection tying me to the fog pulled. Udoqua roared then threw his body into another side of the fog, but again the storm zapped him like an electric fence. He tried once more with the same result and then exasperated, threw himself to the ground, panting and grunting.

"Calm yourself, big brother." The words resonated with dragon voice, my own natural tones bouncing inside the depth of the dragon that had joined with me. The Udoqua peered at me from the side of his face through the translucent fog. The intelligence in his eyes returned and I could see he was tracking now on who I was.

His ears flipped back as he looked around at the encompassing cloud of lightning. "Truce?" I asked. He laid his head on his forelegs and looked away from me. "That'll be just fine," I said. His head rose off of his forelegs, his nose waggling. "Do me a favor and let this Nune be for now. He needs to lead us to the Lady." The Udoqua nodded once, but not before his eyes snuck a peek at the Nune. Saliva dripped from his mouth as he worked on not looking at his quarry.

Experimentally, I focused on the invisible cord connecting me to the fog. I tried tugging at it. It crackled and sparked. Udoqua pulled his feet away from the back side of the encompassing wall. "Sorry 'bout that," I said. Frustration spread through my center. The Uktena hadn't instructed me on how to use this dang gift of hers. I tried not focusing on it, but that didn't do anything. "Go away," I told it, but it hung there, occasionally spitting blue lightning toward Big Brother who dodged it with nervous glances toward me. What was I supposed to do now?

Aubry walked up to me, Miney at her side, and took my hand. Her presence soothed me. "Mama, when did you learn to do that?" she asked.

"Last night," I told her. "The Uktena gave me another gift." And didn't tell me how to make it go away.

"It's really awesome," she said. She swung my hand back and forth, watching the fog hang around Big Brother. "Are you gonna make it stop now?" She looked up at me with her golden eyes. Well, hell. I sure wanted to.

I leaned down to her and spoke only loud enough so she could hear me and not the trapped, giant bear in the center of the artificial electricity storm. "Thing is. I'm not sure how."

"You don't?" she asked. I shook my head. "Is it kind of a magic?" I shrugged.

"I'm thinking so," I said.

"Oh. And Andy's the magic one," she said. She swung my arm some more, rubbing at her nose as she watched the fog. I looked on with her, wondering what the hell I was going to do. Aubry stopped swinging my hand and pulled it twice. "Mama, did you tell it 'thank you' for helping? Sometimes that's what Gram says to do."

"Uh, no. No, I didn't," I said. Could it be that easy?

"See if it works," she said. I looked down at her, feeling incompetent, but grateful.

"Alright," I said, shrugging. "Let's give it a shot." I focused on the fog again, but this time I marveled at how beautiful it was, how grateful I was that the Uktena had gifted it to me, and that I hadn't had to hurt Udoqua. And then after I had expressed my gratitude for it coming to my aid, I felt the connection loosen and dissolve. The fog dissipated with a last spark and crackle until it was gone. I smiled at Aubry.

"You did it, Mama," she said. "Good job." She held her hand up to me, which I smacked with my own then pumped my fist into the air.

"But, I couldn't have done it without you," I told her. "That was awesome advice."

"Thanks," she said. I high-fived her again. Big Brother approached us with slow, even paces, head lowered and ears twitching at our high-fives. The yunwi stared at the beast approaching us carefully. The giant bear looked at the yunwi, laid back his ears and growled. The yunwi trembled and snapped her eyes to the ground.

Pecking order established, I gestured to Aubry. The Udoqua sniffed in her direction. Aubry stretched her hand out in greeting to the beast. Her hand was so small in contrast to the size of him. Had I not known the absolute reverence that Udoqua had for the Bitten, I would have been terrified for my little girl.

Aubry giggled when his huge nose wiggled against her tiny hand. She pulled it away and wiped the moisture from the bear's nose on her jeans. She stepped a pace closer to him, her eyes alight as a smile stretched across her face then faltered as Udoqua pulled his massive head away slightly. She opened up her arms, raising them slowly and inched forward on her pink hiking boots. The giant bear looked away from her then at her then away as she got closer and closer. When she was close enough to brush his long, black fur she stopped and stood perfectly still. Air flowed in and out of my open mouth as my jaw hung slack at my little girl's bravery and heart.

At last the giant bear, having seen that Aubry was not giving in, tilted his massive head into her waiting arms. Aubry's shrill exhale wheezed into the air, muffled by the thick coat of Udoqua. The beast closed his eyes, his exhale whooshing big and relaxed into the afternoon forest air. Aubry nuzzled her auburn head into the bear's neck. The bear looked as though he had died and gone to heaven. His mouth twitched in a smile.

Because he'd chomped my leg, he gave us a lift, following the Nune like a carrot on a stick. I was guessing the Nune had a short life expectancy, judging by Udoqua's fixed stare. Not that it bothered the immortal. He simply went along, following the path his master had made for him. I kinda envied him. He had no worries in the world. No decisions to make. No emotions driving his actions.

We rolled along under the steady pace of the giant. All three of us fit atop the bear with room to spare. Aubry sat up front with a nervous Miney. Our trip was short, but I still wondered how Andy had gotten so far so quickly in the forest.

Abruptly, we stopped in the winding path. To the left was a small opening and nothing larger than a rabbit trail. "This is where you will find the Lady," intoned the Nune, gesturing toward the rabbit trail.

The Udoqua lowered himself to the ground, grunting with the effort. Aubry and Miney slid down the length of his side. I gingerly let myself down, using his fur like handholds to slow my descent. If he minded, he didn't say so. I touched my good foot to the ground first and hobbled on the throbbing gnawed-on one. His black fur shone in the green afternoon forest light. His eyes sparkled as Aubry approached and gave his neck another squeeze.

I would never have hugged Udoqua. She patted his brown muzzle as she pulled away, kissed the top of his massive nose and then whispered to him, "Can I see you again sometime?" The bear nodded not just once but several times. He nudged her belly with his nose, pressing his face against her body. She giggled and wrapped her arms around his snout. He lifted her a foot off the ground and bobbed her up and down in the air. She said, "WhoawhOawhoA," her voice bouncing with the bear's antics. He placed her back on the ground like a new mother places a newborn in its bassinette. Aubry bounded to my side and Udoqua rose to his feet again. He shuffled back and forth, somehow seeming brighter and lighter, maybe even bigger and more full of the magic that made him what he was. Miney was the last for bravery.

She shuffled forward, her eyes to the ground. Slowly, her thin, bright voice filled the air. The oaks and the ash looked down on her, silently listening to her little song. It amazed me how, though we could understand none of her words, we could see the picture she painted with her words and notes. The beast before us, towering so high looked upon the yunwi and listened intently to her song. In my mind, the yunwi bowed before Udoqua, a whole tribe of them listening to the bear sing. And then around the campfire the yunwi recited the songs that the bear had sung. They hunted in the forest and the bear appeared, leading them to the deer. The tribe of yunwi sang again, in praise to Udoqua for the songs and the meat to help them survive.

When the last notes of Miney's song, of her people's song, floated onto the humid air, Udoqua bowed deeply to the yunwi. Miney seemed lost at first, but then did her best to bow back, though she wobbled in the awkward stance of her uncertain feet. The honor that Udoqua had shown confirmed my suspicion that while yunwi are blessed to sing, this particular yunwi had a rare gift.

Udoqua rose, sniffed in my direction, dipping his head low in apology and then lumbered into the forest. Although, the Nune seemed unfettered by worry, he still seemed to have the good sense to get while the getting was good. He was nowhere to be seen.

After a painful scramble through the forest using the rabbit trail we arrived. My breath hitched and not because of the pain. I actually suffered a real twinge in my heart because of the beauty of the place. Every time I came here, the Lady found me in some place new. And every time, I was stunned at its magnificence. Aubry and Miney caught up to me. Aubry gasped.

A giant willow rose on the far bed of a creek that babbled, shallow, over rounded moss-covered stones. The waterfall to the right of us fell a short distance with a small rush of water from upstream over suspended rocks. Under the rock shelf, the creek water pooled, swirling before it found its way out. The water was completely transparent and under its invisible surface, rocks of every color glittered.

I searched the creek bank for Andy and at last saw him emerge from under the willow. "Hey sissy!" He seemed light, but there was a set to his dual-colored eyes that had me worried. The slight tension of his shoulders and the hand perched on his hip confirmed something was up. Not that I hadn't guessed that what with being summoned by the Lady.

I hobbled to a small foot bridge that looked as though it had grown there. The hand rails sprouted blooms of wisteria that hung heavy over the sides of the bridge, as though they wished to catch a glimpse of their reflection in the meandering creek beneath them. Bees hummed along the flowers, intermingled with an air creature featured on the news just a little more than a day ago. To my mundane eye, all I saw was a swarm of bees, but my golden eye could see the subtle things that set them apart. Their size was slightly bigger, their arms and legs were humanoid, and they had small faces beneath their large eyes.

Miney clapped her hands when she saw the little creatures. I smiled at her delight, until she snatched one off a wisteria bloom, turned it over in her hand and then chomped it in half. My smile faltered. I had no idea yunwi ate flyers. Aubry clutched her stomach and turned around until Miney was through with her snack, plugging her ears to block the unpleasant crunching sounds. Miney reached for another and Aubry placed a hand on hers. "No more," she said, her voice green with nausea. Miney's eyes welled, her mouth trembling. "No. More." Aubry said, making it final. Miney didn't cry out loud, but she sniveled as we passed over the bridge and came to the other side.

Andy met me there. He looked me over, his hands on his hips. "What happened to you?"

"Met Udoqua. He was hungry and didn't recognize me at first. You should have seen Aubry. It was amazing." Which reminded me. I turned to Aubry. "Aubry Anne. Whatever possessed you to hug that Udoqua?" She looked at me, puzzled, as if the answer were so obvious.

"He was sad. He was remembering when he used to be a person and that he had a daughter. He lost her." She turned back to Miney, who was looking longingly back at the bridge, buzzing with nymphs.

"How did you know his memories?" I asked.

"He told me," she said simply.

"How did he tell you?"

"Well, first I sensed it and then I asked him. In my mind. And he told me how his little girl died when she was my age. That's why he changed into a big bear. And it made him sad to see me. But it made him happy too. He's very old. Very, very old. And his sadness is so old and deep. So, I hugged him. 'Cause that's what you do when I'm sad and it makes me feel better." She smiled up at me.

"That was a very sweet and wise thing for you to do," I commended, wishing for the millionth time with a slow twist of an old knife that her father could see her. Andy shuffled up beside me while Miney reached an errant hand toward a passing flyer. Aubry yanked on her other hand to pull her away. Several other flyers darted above Miney, circled around Andy and me before drawing close to Aubry.

"Well," Andy began, "looks like someone is a little creature prodigy." Within seconds, a multitude of nymphs hung in the air around us. Miney fidgeted beside Aubry.

"Hello," Aubry said to them. At her greeting, the little bee-colored nymphs scattered. At least I thought it was her greeting, until another's presence tickled my awareness. Aubry hopped off my lap. Andy turned and planted his knees onto the forest floor. I mimicked my brother's pose, kneeling to the Lady. Aubry sank down and sat cross-legged beside us.

TWENTY-ONE ~ RORI - MAKE LIKE A TREE AND LEAF

The Spirit of the Forest; the Lady; Adohi; Ancestor. There were many names for her. She smelled of cedar and rain-drenched air and rivers and all things wild and growing free among the trees. She looked at Aubry with a light of fascination.

Her elongated, tan face hosted a set of wide green eyes with veins of purple and blue, rimmed with dark reddish brown. She had no hair, but a crown of trees like vines that crossed over each other, rising from her skull and covered in moss. She ran a delicate hand over the length of her bare stomach. What looked like tattoos ran down the length of her arms of vines, flowers, birds, nymphs, fish, rivers...

She stretched luxuriously, the fullness of her breasts thinning with outstretched arms. Leaves etched into her skin rose from their two dimensions and were birthed into life, falling to the forest floor. Her body creaked as she unfolded from her stretch.

"Aubry," her voice swelled like a river before a waterfall. My insides trembled at the Spirit's call to my daughter. And while I knew the honor it was for Aubry to be blessed with the attention of the Lady, part of me wanted to reach out, to pull Aubry close to me to protect her from whatever message would be given.

Aubry looked up at the Lady, uncertain in a way I had not seen with her before. Her lips pinched to one side, her head tilted, eyebrows furrowed and yet she made eye contact with Adohi unabashedly. "I can't hear you," she said finally. The Lady of the Forest laughed, big and warm and loud. She wrapped her image-laden arms over her bare midriff. The crown of tree limbs growing from her head sprang buds of white and pink flowers that bloomed in the span of a breath.

The flyers that had been placidly hovering around the wisteria on the bridge rushed to the Lady, drawing close to her face, bathing in her breath, in the humor that rolled from her mouth. Their wings shimmered and as they hovered around the Lady's face the movement of their flight left tracery lines in the air like glitter.

She shooed them away with a languid wave of her hand and stepped closer to Aubry. "That is because I am no creature." She extended a hand toward Aubry. The collection of images on her arms and legs shifted as if floating on water. A bird rose and took flight from the extended arm.

Aubry took the hand offered to her and rose from the ground. The lady wrapped a maternal arm around Aubry's shoulders as they walked a little ways toward the towering, sprawling willow, thick with sage green switches.

"So, what are you?" Aubry asked, looking up at the woman at her side.

"Well," she began. "I am like you in some ways. And like Brother in other ways."

"Why can I hear him and not you then?"

"Brother has gone the way of the creature, of the animal, but in doing so he has become a Spirit that goes on and on. He gave up his humanity to live in the forest."

"Because his heart hurt too much?"

"His reasons are his own." The Lady said this with a patience undercut with mild reprimand. "We are alike in that we are both Spirits."

Adohi lifted an arm toward the hanging switches of the willow, casting her gaze up into its branches. The tree moaned, an audible noise that stuttered through the glade, rattling the earth in tiny shivers of movement. She stepped the last steps toward the willow as switches intertwined themselves into a perfect swinging seat for two.

Aubry sat next to Adohi and looked up at her. They swung gently in the willow switch seat. "Do you know what your greatest strength is?" Adohi asked Aubry. Aubry's face was puzzled as she kicked her legs in the seat. She shook her head finally.

"I don't think I'm as strong as my mom," she said.

"Your strength is *your* strength and no one else's. And one day it will save you, as well as others." Adohi ran a hand down Aubry's auburn hair and when her hand touched, a flower sprung to life. Aubry reached up and touched one of the flowers and giggled.

Her legs kicked happily. "How'd you do that?"

"This," Adohi said, and as she spoke she reached both hands in front of her, cupping them. The images on her skin shifted and her hands filled with a multitude of butterflies of all different shapes and sizes. As they filled her hands they fluttered their wings and leapt into the air. Bright blue, black and gold, orange, pink, red, striped and dotted, the rainbow of butterfly wings floated on the air of the glade. "This is *my* greatest strength: to produce and to sustain life." Miney, who was sitting beside me, let out an 'ahhh...' of surprise and wonder.

Aubry stood from the willow seat, raised her arms in the air and turned in a slow circle in the hovering butterflies. Slowly the butterflies gathered around her, and lighted on her arms, her hair, her shirt. Her golden eyes stretched wide as she stood motionless at the collection of butterflies gathering around her. And then a large butterfly colored in greens and blues like the feathers of a peacock touched down on her nose. Her eyes crossed as she watched the insect land and then she burst out in laughter. As the noise erupted in the glade, the butterflies burst into the air away from Aubry. She rubbed at her nose. "That tickled," she said, still giggling. Aubry made her way back to us, sitting down between Andy and Miney.

Andy looked at me and smiled, but there was something really sad in the look on his face. Something that jarred inside of me and filled me with a sudden dread. I opened my mouth to ask him what the Lady had said to him, but Adohi's voice rose before mine.

"Rori Dragonblood," her voice echoed around the forest. I shifted my gaze back to her, coming into a kneeling position and bowing my head in deference. She had stood up from the swing in the willow switches. Her voice took on a different note. It was no longer kind and sweet, as it had been with Aubry. The weight of my responsibility tumbled back onto my shoulders. All my worry about the broken gates filled me up.

"There are shadows lurking in my forests. They threaten the creatures under protection of the veil for which you are responsible. Why have you not sought this shadow out and destroyed it?" Her tone was sweet but cut like a knife into my pride. I bristled then calmed myself before I said something regrettable.

"It is true I seek understanding of the breaking of the gates." Even in my own ears, my words grated out.

She looked down on me with her bright eyes, one green eyebrow rising. She shivered as new growth eased its way from the images on her skin. Vines began wrapping up her left arm. "There is great darkness ahead. Grave danger will come to all. Even this place," she gestured around her and a salamander slithered from her fingertips, down her arm and leapt to the earth. "Even me. I must hide myself away to prevent further darkness." Another creak resounded and she sighed, a mixture of pleasure and pain on her lips. She shifted and from her spine spread bark and the flesh of a tree.

"Hide? What is it that you're hiding from?" My nerves prickled and caught fire. There was worse ahead? Worse than a Nehi attacking my daughter? Worse than an unnamed sorcerer out there somewhere releasing ancient spirits from the place of dangerous creatures? "Please help me understand what's happening and how I can fix this." I pleaded, my pride turning to terror for my child.

Adohi turned to me, sudden sympathy coloring her face as she tilted her head to one side. "You cannot fix this on your own. You must rely on the strength of others to solve this."

"I won't needlessly put others in danger." A fierce anger rose inside of me. Flashes shot through my memory: Andy as a boy, hurt and scared as he clutched onto me, blood running down my face – not my blood but the blood of his assailant – even as Paul Burning's father slashed out and cut my gut open; Jameson's flat stare from where his body hung on the impaling length of a tree branch; Josh's pale face as his spirit hovered outside of his body; Aubry looking up at the Nehi as it advanced on her; Wuffers's shallow breathing around a jagged gash in her neck.

"Others will be in danger. It is not a matter of you putting them there. This is how it has always been. And yet you have always heaped the responsibility on you. This is not truth. This is your lie and a lie you must resolve in yourself." I blinked at her, the words slapping my pride with a sting. She turned from me as I puzzled her meaning, trying to make sense of it even as my insides screamed that Jameson would still be alive if I had done a better job at protecting him.

"Little one." The lady looked down on Miney with smiling eyes. "Your family will need you soon. Do not be afraid. Your voice is mighty." I considered her words even as Miney grabbed onto Aubry's hand, her glittering eyes peeking from under pressed brows. It was clear Miney thought of us as her family.

"Aubry," she said, yawing again, her eyes getting heavy. She backed a pace away as her feet widened and covered over with thick, heavy bark.

"Yes, ma'am?" asked Aubry.

"Be brave. Don't forget that you have strength and it is all your own."

"Brave for what?" I demanded, rising to my feet.

"Mmm... I need to sleep now." The vines on her arms had covered them and the bark rising from her feet had grown over the womanly curve of her hips.

"Please," I cried, "please, I need more information. A direction we should look. Something!" Cracking and snapping filled the forest air as a cedar sprang up around the woman whose speech made my heart race.

"Rori," she mumbled sleepily. My heart skipped a beat as I held my breath, waiting for a clue that would help me. "Your enemy is closer than you think."

I opened my mouth to ask what that meant: closer in location? Closer in relationships? A great groan of growing bark drowned out her words and her face covered in bark.

"Wait!" I cried out. "Wait, I need more information. What does that mean? Where should I look? Who should I consider suspect? Help me!" Nothing but more creaking and groaning as the cedar grew exponentially in front of our eyes. I took a step forward and fell to my knees, my eyes lifted to the branches bursting from the trunk that encapsulated the Lady of the Forest. Leaf buds appeared and shuddered into bloom and full foliage before my eyes. I raised my hands in supplication to her. One leaf shimmered among the collection of emerald leaves. It was gilded. I watched it break from the branch and swing heavily down from the tree and land with a slap into my outstretched hands.

I pulled it into me and looked at the leaf. Carved into the subtle gold sheen was the head of a bird, beak open as if crying out. When the image was emblazoned in my mind, the leaf crumbled and fell like dust to the forest floor.

TWENTY-TWO ~ RORI - FIRSTS

Andy sat with me the next afternoon on the big couch while we went over all the details of what was going on. He had his laptop perched on his thighs, legs extended and propped on the ottoman. Wuffers was lying on the floor beside me, which tickled me pink. She'd healed so much in just three days.

We had print outs scattered across the coffee table of information on artifacts from the Cahokia Mounds, including an article about a Birdman tablet that had been discovered then sold to an unknown buyer. That meant: dead end, but confirmation of the tablet we'd seen in Tom, the Ghost Hunter's episode in Georgia with the rotting deer carcass. A small spiral notebook sat on my lap. Notes were scrawled across the page.

We'd also been researching other religions and paranormal events of possession to find out how we could locate such a spiritual entity inhabiting a human. All my research was returning was how to identify if a person was possessed by a demon or negative energy or ghost or what have you. The verbiage depended on which line of spirituality I researched. The point was: person first, demon second. Not the other way around.

I rubbed my temples as I stared at my notes. Andy was clicking away at the laptop. Aubry was getting ready for her big sleepover at Haelyn's house. It was her first sleepover and she was extremely excited. Of course, Miney was not, because she had to stay here.

The clock was ticking and every moment that passed with the veil intact felt like borrowed time. I shifted my bandaged foot on the ottoman, repositioning the storage bag of ice so that it was a bit more comfortable. I am blessed with the ability to heal quickly, but having a bear twice the normal size of a black bear munch on my ankle took its toll.

Aubry ran into the room with her backpack slung over her purple sweatshirt and khaki pants. Her dark skin was so pretty against all that color. Her golden eyes shone and her curly auburn hair was pleated in a neat braid down to the middle of her back. She smiled, her round cheeks revealing her big adult teeth in the front and the baby ones on the side, one of which she'd lost a couple of days earlier.

"You ready to go, baby girl?" She nodded, nearly dancing from foot to foot.

"I'll take her," Andy said and stood up from the couch. He pulled his reading glasses from his face and set them in a pile of paperwork.

"You sure?"

"Yeah, it'll give us some uncle-niece bonding time, huh, hon'?" He pinched her cheeks as he passed her to get to his shoes.

"You good with that?" I asked her.

"Yes!" she said. "Can we drive the sporty car, Uncle Andy?"

"Oh, she's got a thing for the nice cars like her uncle," I groaned.

"Smart girl!" He high-fived her as he sat back on the couch and pulled on his immaculately clean sneakers. I compared them to my sneakers: old, covered in mud and wearing through at the toe.

"Come over here," I waved Aubry over to my perch on the couch. I wrapped her up and told her, "Be good. Mind your manners. Don't forget to brush your teeth tonight before you go to bed. I'm only a phone call away. You call me if you want to come home for any reason at all, okay?"

"Okay, Mama." She hugged my neck. I inhaled her scent and stroked her hair.

"I love you so much," I said into her ear.

"I love you too," she said.

As she left I couldn't help but feel worried. The nagging sensation ate at my gut as they walked out the door. I guess it was my first sleepover for her too.

TWENTY-THREE ~ AUBRY - SLEEPOVER

"Aubry," Edythe said to me. "This is Devon. Devon, this is Aubry." I didn't like him. Everything about him made my skin crawl, but the worst was his eyes. There were flashes of fire behind his green irises. I didn't know what that was, but I could feel this other something that I didn't like. I decided to stay away from him and not talk to him unless I had to.

I nodded in his direction as his mother introduced us. Devon nodded back, one corner of his mouth quirking up. He licked his lips and grinned widely, his green eyes growing. He was a teenager and stood a head above his mom. Edythe looked at her son and fidgeted with the rings on her fingers. She reached down and adjusted the red tablecloth on the dining table and fussed with the place mat. Haelyn took my arm and pulled on me. Edythe and Devon whipped out of sight.

"Haelyn, dinner is ready," Edythe called behind us. "Let your friend put her backpack away and then come back down."

"Yes, ma'am," Haelyn said without turning. We ran through the big open entryway, past the formal living room and up the wide set of stairs. I stopped at the bottom of them and adjusted the backpack. It felt really heavy. I looked around at the house that Haelyn lived in. My house was cozy and nice. This house was old and kinda creepy. After we climbed the first flight we climbed again until we were staring at a door smaller than the others. Haelyn looked at me and smiled. "This is my room. It's the attic," she explained.

"Cool," I said. "You get to sleep in the attic?"

"You do too," she said. "Tonight anyway. Wanna check it out?"

"Yeah."

Haelyn pushed on the door, but it wouldn't give. She shoved her shoulder into it, grunting until it rasped open with a pop. The room was tall in the middle and slanted down at both sides. It was bigger than I thought it would be. Haelyn's bed was small and covered with an old quilt and a few stuffed animals. The walls were painted green on one side and the others were wood, like the outside. Haelyn had some toys in a chest and some coming out of her open closet door. Other than the few toys around, her room was pretty clean.

Once we got inside, I let my backpack slide to the floor, glad to have the weight off my shoulders. When my backpack said 'oomph', I turned around. Haelyn was saying something about the stuffed animals on her bed. The zipper on my backpack wiggled and then Miney's head popped out of the hole. I waved her down before Haelyn turned back around. I grabbed my hands behind my back and side stepped in front of the backpack to make sure Miney couldn't be seen.

"Did you bring an animal or anything?" she asked. *I guess I did,* I thought.

"No." I shook my head, not knowing exactly why I was lying to Haelyn. She'd seen Miney before. Something about Devon and the house made me want to keep her a secret.

"Oh. Well, okay. You ready for dinner?"

I nodded.

"'Kay," she said. She walked past me and through the door. I let her go out and listened to her take some steps down the stairs before I turned to Miney.

"Miney! Why'd you come? What happens if you get seen by Devon or Mrs. Turner?" I asked her. She poked her head out, looked behind at the wall and colored herself like the wood behind her. "You have to stay in here," I told her. She looked up at me with her wide sparkly black eyes and nodded then sat down again in my backpack on top of my clean clothes. I sighed and zipped up the backpack. Haelyn poked her head around the door.

"You comin'?"

"Sorry," I said. "I forgot to put something in my backpack." I stood up and went out of the room, pulling her door shut and praying that her mom or big brother didn't get nosy and that Miney didn't get curious. "Okay, I'm ready." She looked at me like I was weird, but went down the stairs any way, and into the dining room for dinner.

TWENTY-FOUR ~ RORI - RESCUE

Andy and I decided we needed a break while we mulled over the facts and the possibilities. So, we headed into town for ice cream. My mind buzzed with information on the Cahokia Mounds. The civilization had performed some major human sacrifice when they buried the bodily remains of the Hawkman after he married his spirit with the giant Hawk. So, whatever magic they'd worked on him had kept his spirit alive inside the host for centuries.

Now that he was out, the ancient Hawkman Ani'Kutani was out, he was breaking gates and releasing monsters. And that was threatening the integrity of the veil. Since he was masquerading as a normal person, I hadn't a clue how to find him. We'd gone to where the trouble was and found no person there mucking with the gates. Clearly, the ancient Ani'Kutani was working his magic from a distance.

We passed people in the parking lot of the Waynesville Plaza and I looked at them all to see if something was identifiably another entity living within them. No such luck. The sun dipped low in the horizon and clouds capped the tree-laden hills. There was a mild breeze. I smelled rain on its way.

Andy walked ahead of me in the same stony silence we'd been in all afternoon reading through religious websites and hunting down information on the mounds. The ice cream shop was situated in the open parking lot across from a strip mall. They had a drive-through, but I wanted to sit and enjoy the warm waffle cone and cold ice cream in all its freshness. Hopefully, the sugar would spark some idea on what I needed to do next.

I pulled the glass door open. The doorbell jingled. The blue and red walls of Jack the Dipper Ice Cream parlor were vibrant and new. I inhaled the waffle cone scent deeply, my shoulders rising and falling as I exhaled exuberantly.

Andy shuffled up to the counter to peer through the glass at the rainbow of flavors. I danced to the counter beside him. "I feel guilty," said Andy as he fixed his gaze on the rocky road.

"Yeah, let's not tell Aubry we came," I suggested. "It'll be our gloriously sweet secret."

A teenage girl came to the counter, sporting a baseball cap and tie-dye shirt with the Jack the Dipper logo. Her long golden brown hair fell down her back in a perfect plait. She was skinny and when she smiled and said "hello" her mouth glinted in silver. "Rocky road," said Andy to the girl, pointing to the ice cream of his choice. "Two scoops. In a waffle cone dipped in chocolate. Drizzled with hot fudge. Please. Oh. And pile on some whipped cream and a cherry. It's a cheat day." He winked at the girl who blushed fabulously before she started scooping ice cream out of the freezer. He turned to me and rubbed his hands together, his eyes bright. "Yum," he added.

"Here you go," drawled the girl, smiling to show the collection of metal in her mouth. She handed Andy his ice cream over the counter and turned to me. Andy slurped at his two scoops and purred. I salivated. "How 'bout you?" the girl asked.

"I want a plain waffle cone, please. And then I'll take the strawberries and cheesecake and a scoop of plain chocolate on top of that."

After we paid for our ice cream we parked ourselves at one of the small brown tables. Ice Cream Girl passed shy glances toward Andy, pretending to swipe down a table near us. When the teenager had strutted away to stalk the stretch of tile behind the counter and stare, I interrupted Andy's religious experience with his dessert to chat with him.

"So, we know what, exactly? Finding a demon is next to impossible?"

He slurped a couple of times, saying 'Mmm' in a way that indicated he had a thought but needed to swallow before he spoke. I licked my scoop of chocolate. The ice cream froze my tongue momentarily before warming again. I bit into the scoop and rolled it around my mouth. It numbed my tongue and gums and as it melted, the sweet chocolate rolled down my throat in thick waves.

"Well, not exactly. I was thinking about it on the drive here. I think there may be a way."

I paused mid bite. "What?" I asked, leaning forward.

"Well," he said around a mouthful of whipped cream and hot fudge. He wiped his lips with a napkin and continued. "You know how Aubry could hear Udoqua because as the Lady put it, he'd gone the way of the creature?" I didn't like the sound of this.

"Yeah," I drawled, cautious.

He propped an elbow onto the table, as if the ice cream cone had gotten heavy and he needed assistance. I took a bite of my ice cream. Soft, sweet and chilled mixed with crunchy and warm. He looked at me seriously with wide sea-green eyes - we were wearing our contacts. "Well, Aubry's not the only one that can hear creatures. What if I try meditating on the spirit, see if I can pick something up on the universe's airwaves?" I took a bite while he was talking.

"Have you done anything like that before?" I asked around a mouthful.

"Not per se, but when I work with creatures, I enter a sort of meditation to connect with them and understand what's going on. I've never tried it without being right next to a creature. But, it's worth a shot, don't you think?"

"Okay, what happens when you meditate with creatures?" I asked, worry niggling at my stomach and mixing unpleasantly with the ice cream.

"Well, usually, I'm just seeing the wound, sensing the intentions. Sometimes I feel the pain or their mood. If this is successful, I could understand what the Hawkman's goal is and maybe get a hint at where he is. That's what I'd be focusing on."

"Do they know you're looking at them? Do they sense you in return?" I asked. He opened his mouth to respond. My phone rang. "Hold that thought," I told him.

"Hello?" I said into my phone.

"Rori." It was Mom. I looked at Andy nervously. I had been counting on her leaving me alone since our disagreement.

"What's up?"

"Chief Mack called me. A woman was just taken to the hospital and claims an animal attacked her. I went down to the ER to take a look at her wounds to decipher the kind of animal."

I hung my head, knowing what she had to say next couldn't be good. "Not another one."

"It was a lesser dragon. She had a hard time explaining how the 'animal' managed to melt off the whole of her calf. At least she was smart enough to turn and run."

"Shit," I said. The crack in the veil was getting large enough people were seeing things while getting attacked from the creatures it was releasing. The veil could not break. It must not. Healing it again would be impossible. I swallowed around my fear. The history of the gate's construction sent a wave of panic coursing through me. Andy looked up. He swallowed and half rose. His chair squealed against the hardwood.

"Is Aubry okay?" His eyes were bright, the ice cream clutched in his hands forgotten.

"Is that Andy?" Mom asked. I closed my eyes and bowed my head with the phone still pressed to my ear. Damn. Andy was still staring at me, clearly ready to toss aside his cone and run out the door.

"Yes, Mom, that's Andy." Andy's open mouth closed in a snap and he hurled himself back to his chair.

"I think I've lost my appetite," he said and looked at his ice cream accusingly.

"You didn't tell me your brother was in town," she hissed.

"So?" I said, feeling a little like a highschooler. "What's it matter if Andy is in town to visit me?" There was a quiet stretch and then Mom sighed.

"You need to get out to Lake Junaluska. This is more your sort of thing. I'm getting too old for this." Her voice was tired and rattled a little.

"Who got burned?" I asked, my anger itching inside of me like poison ivy.

"Patricia Dott."

"You mean, like Mrs. Dott? Like fourth grade teacher Mrs. Dott? As in Aubry's teacher?"

"The very same." Her voice cut through the phone. "And listen to me," she urged, the venom slipping into her voice and sawing through the air waves and into my smart phone. "Leave. Andy. Out of this."

"Mom, really?" I said. "Why is it always like this with you?" Andy shoved away from the table and carefully, mournfully, dropped his ice cream cone into the garbage. He frowned when he sat back down, crossing his arms over his fleece-clad chest and kicking out his leg in a lazy recline.

"Just listen to me!" she growled, the dragon voice full in her tone.

"I'm not getting bullied by you, Mom."

"Rori, I have –" I hung up on her. Bitterness swirled in my mouth. I stood and tossed my uneaten ice cream into the hole in the side counter for the garbage can. We had to get the dragon back to her home. The more critters outside of the protection of the gates the more strain was on the veil.

"Well," Andy said. His eyebrows rose as he regarded his manicured fingers. His legs wiggled the wooden chair. "What fun adventure are we about to set out on?"

Lake Junaluska was northeast of Waynesville. Darkness and storm clouds gobbled up the day and left the Dotts' residence in a dreary gray-blotted blackness. My eyesight, amped up with the dragon venom, could see pretty well. Andy, not so much. I grabbed the mag light from the trunk of my SUV, glad we'd taken my car and not the rental sports car.

I inhaled deeply while Andy closed his eyes, drifting on intuition. The world of blackness came alive through smell. The oncoming rain perfumed the air and hung with bloated anticipation. The lake on which the residence sat rippled on the night breeze. Lake water lapped gently against the muddy, reed-strewn shore. A peppering of coyote added to the medley, along with skunk, squirrel, opossum, and hibernating snakes, getting restless in their dens. Under the aroma of pine, bitter and green, and the loam of leaf litter and soil drifted a smoky rank of charred earth.

Andy peered over at me as I removed my contact and flicked it in the rock drive of Aubry's teacher's house. The house sat at the end of the drive, the porch light on, the carport empty.

The little house, perched on the tree-covered property, was a log cabin of sorts. It was modest with four walls, a front porch and paned windows. I set off toward it and wished I hadn't hung up on Mom; she maybe had more information on where Mrs. Dott had been when she'd encountered the lesser dragon. I was going by smell alone here.

Raised flower beds surrounded the house. Little green shoots cast in the shadow of night were just peeking above the darker shadow of the soil. The porch was tidy and sported a swinging bench that would look out over the lake and sunrise in the morning, and as it was now, the occasional glimpse of the moon through a chink in the gathering storm.

Andy stepped in front of me, the crescent moon catching his face in its soft glow. He tripped in a hole in the ground and fell into me. I caught him in a firm grip around his slender shoulders and pushed him back upright. He wobbled as he untangled his feet and pointed, running his other hand through the thickness of his shadowed auburn hair. I followed his outstretched arm.

I wobbled, nausea gripping me before I took control of my body with a cleansing breath. The trees on the other side of the lake were illuminated in sickly green only seen by my right eye. "Well, there's our guy." I turned to Andy. He had his right eye covered with his right hand.

His left eye, my right eye; that's how the vision got split between us. I guess it wasn't the hole that had made him trip. "Ready?"

"Yeah," he said, "sure."

"Can you run?"

"In the dark?"

"We'll walk fast."

And we did, arriving at the place next to the lake that was a perfect nest for a lesser dragon. The close crop of overgrown brush glowed where the dragon had coated his new home in a layer of acid, turning the vegetation into a dome like glowing paper Mache.

"Ew..." said Andy. He was right: it smelled horrid. Like putrefying garbage. My nose wrinkled and I fought back a growl. My guts clenched around disgust. These lesser dragons were like coyotes were to wolves. Sort of natural enemies to the Uktena and we Bitten.

"Alright, we haven't got all night. Let's get this done. You want to call it out?" I asked.

"Yeah. This'll be good practice." He plopped down in a pile of leaf litter, his legs folding underneath him. His back was straight, his breath fogging ever so slightly in the cool evening. His eyes closed, his breath slowed as he fell into a trance. I stood by, shifting from one tennis shoe to the next and looking at my surroundings. We were just inside the forest and the trees were widely distributed. I could maneuver pretty easily here. I ran a shoe over the dirt and leaf litter and readied myself for the work ahead. My knife was strapped to my leg, but that would take some pretty close quarters. Plus, I wasn't out to kill the creature.

A big branch poked out of a collection of shrubs. That would work nicely. Andy was still meditating, or whatever it is he did to get in touch with creatures. I walked over to the shrub and my potential cudgel. Wrapping my hands around the thick end, I yanked on it and was surprised when it didn't pull from the vegetation. "Mmph." I pulled again, but it was stubborn. My hands clapped over my hip bones as my heartbeat and breath slowed to normal.

Determined that a branch would not get the best of me, I repositioned and put all my muscles into it. Earth tore and the branch creaked in defiance, but in the end I won. "Ha ha!" I shouted just as Andy called out.

"Rori!" I turned, my shoes scuffing through dirt and acorn shells. A spray of neon green shot toward me. I pulled the five foot branch in front of me, but it wasn't *that* thick. Scorching pain splashed across my forearm. I screamed, the sound thrumming with dragon voice. The neon substance bubbled on my skin. Lucky for me, my skin was more like hide. I wasn't impervious, but it didn't eat away my muscle like it did Mrs. Dott. Not that I felt very sorry for her. What with not calling me when a bully punched my poor daughter in the face and gave her a shiner she'd worn for days.

"Dammit Andy!" I wiped away the lesser dragon's venom on my pants. That was stupid. My pants sizzled and left a gaping hole to reveal my upper thigh. "A little warning would have been nice."

"Well, what the hell were you doing over there?" The dragon stretched its many wings, throwing back its head, its slender jaws opening wide and letting out a shriek.

"Andy, back up!" He scrabbled in the dirt and leaves, leaning against a nearby oak for support. The dragon turned, its wings rippled fluorescent orange, blue and green. Its legless green body, armored in spiked and undulating hide, turned in Andy's direction. It was no longer than a large water moccasin, although much wider and much more deadly.

I pulled the branch back over my shoulder and let it fly. I screamed against the acid burn pulling on the skin of my forearm. Okay, maybe I felt a little bad for Mrs. Dott. The branch found its target. The dragon squealed, a high pitch noise like the letting out of helium from a balloon. A track of green shot through the forest, over the nest.

"God, Rori," Andy panted, "she's pregnant."

"Of *course* she is," I muttered. "So, what are you saying?"

"I'm saying, be careful." His voice was jagged with feeling.

"Andy," I began, readying myself for the green body hurtling itself my way. "It burned a woman's leg off. How 'bout my safety and well-being?"

"Rori, we're part dragon. For god's sake, *she's pregnant*!"

"How the fuck do you expect me to be careful with an acid-spewing dragon? Furthermore,"

EEEeeeee!!! The dragon screeched, eyes black as night fixed on me, white fangs glinting. I grunted as I swung and knocked it off course. Andy made a hissing noise of anxiety.

"Furthermore," I continued, breathing hard, "it's *full* dragon."

"Oh, just. Just don't hurt her!" Andy suggested helpfully.

"Andy. Umph." The dragon head-butted me in the gut, bypassing the carefully aimed blow from my claymore-like tree branch. I thanked all my lucky stars lesser dragons didn't have horns like the Uktena. Air evaded me as I went to a knee. Spots flowered in the periphery of my vision, which had tunneled. The dragon rose up on its collection of wings which undulated in a perpetual wave of movement. It leaned back, its body dulled from neon green to gray while its cheeks burned bright neon green.

"Shit. Rori, move!"

The sputter of acid bursting from the dragon's mouth sizzled through the clearing. Air whooshed into my deprived lungs as my abdomen finally relaxed. I rolled, hoping I was rolling in the right direction. Rocks dug into my knees where I landed. The ground next to me crackled, sparking and smoking before muddying into a dull green. The dragon tossed its slender snout into the air, screeching in frustration.

"Little fucker." I rubbed my stomach where its solid skull had rammed me. The branch in my hand ground into the skin of my hand as I yanked it in an uppercut toward the dragon. Aim found target. The dragon lurched into the air, knocking against a high branch in a nearby oak and slamming into the dirt. The dragon lay unmoving, draped over a collection of roots from a cedar, save for a gentle rise and fall of its chest.

Andy rushed to the dragon while I caught my breath. "She's okay still. You just knocked her out."

"I'm fine too. Thanks for asking," I said. He didn't even look back at me. So much for brotherly love.

Wrangling a lesser dragon heavy with eggs and dripping acid into the back of the SUV was hard enough. And that was after carrying it back to the car, followed by another grueling hike out to the lesser gate. I had the thing strapped to my back using a jimmy-rigged combination of bungee cords and Andy's fleece sweatshirt.

I lowered my body weight to the ground, breathing hard. My tank top was soaked with sweat despite the chill of the night air. The dragon's mouth touched my elbow one last time. I hissed at the sore spot. "Damn it."

Andy dropped beside me and began untying the dragon from my shoulders. I twisted and shifted until the weight of it slid to the ground. Turning, I regarded the unconscious creature. She really was beautiful.

Andy scooped her up with his fleece still wrapped around her and headed to the gate. The crack we had healed once was larger. It sparked and fizzled, leaking a greenish mist that steamed up into the cloudy night sky.

"At least it's not raining," I said. Andy umphed an agreement, working hard to carry our rescue back to its home.

Passing through the gate is like trying to walk through a thin sheet of gelatin. It gave, but it resisted at first. Andy placed the dragon gently down in a nearby crop of bare, scrubby bushes. Rolling the creature off the fleece, he then draped it over the nearby bush and stood. He dusted his hands off on his jeans and winced.

"Let me see," I said. He showed me his arm where the dragon's mouth had touched the bare skin. A dime size hole gaped into his flesh. His skin hadn't ever formed the Kevlar-like quality like mine. Whether that was because he hadn't been bitten by the Uktena, or whether it was because he was a male, we would never know. I mushed my mouth around, thought about the ice cream I left behind and after gathering it, I spat into the wound. Andy jumped.

"Ack! Warn a person before you do that. That's just nasty." His lip curled back in disgust.

"Don't be a baby. Look, it's already getting better. Probably 'cause we're on this side of the veil." The wound sizzled, filling in with overlapping and freshly pink layers of flesh before it gathered at the top of the wound and formed new skin. The round patch shone brightly in contrast to the slightly tinted other parts of his arm that had been exposed to sunshine. "There. All better."

"Yuck," he said, wiping off the extra saliva on his green polo.

"Oh, come on." I marched back toward the gate. I pushed myself through the barrier, feeling it give way more easily because of the crack. Turning around I reached a hand in for Andy and found him staring at me through the slightly shining substance separating the rest of the world.

Andy simply stared at me. No, he was staring through me. Shivers raced up my spine and spilled down my arms, the night freezing cold in a moment. Thunder cracked, breaking a night of stillness. I knew what that look meant. I slipped back into the Place Where the Uktena Lives, wrapped my arms gently around him, braced myself and waited. He wasn't breathing, but I didn't dare startle him. His mouth hung open, his mismatched eyes wide and out of focus.

Silence stretched out for much longer than I liked. Something shifted and darted in the shadows past Andy. He still wasn't breathing. I'd never seen him slip into an intuition trance for this long. A shadow among the bracken made a low whooping noise, just audible to my sensitive ears. "Shit. Andy," I whispered quietly. If I shook him out of it, he'd be thrown into a seizure.

A new shadow appeared to my left, catching on my periphery before it slipped away. Andy was turning blue. His slack face stared without seeing. Growls rippled in the air. The earth trembled beneath me. My feet and legs vibrated. Air whistled in and out of my lungs, double-time.

The gate was two feet away. Behind us the darkness reigned. Rocks shifted somewhere. The ground shuddered with a thud. Another thud. The shadows in the bracken to our left and right scrabbled and ran, darting through the empty space where we stood, and into scrub-covered hills over my left shoulder. Andy began to sway, probably due to the lack of oxygen.

The darkness swelled. Two red lights of eyes split open and peered down. I craned my neck to look at it. Something underneath the red eyes glinted. The eyes grew larger as the monstrous head of the giant creature leaned close to us. It sniffed. The air around us whooshed away and into the monstrous four-slitted nose of the giant. Followed by a rush of warm air blowing in the opposite direction. My hair flew first forward and then back in the exhale of the creature. I retched on the odor. The gruff hacking beginnings of a snarl hiccupped on the night air.

My eyes watered as I trembled. Even for my extreme strength, I was no match for this guy. The giant smacked his jaws, long exposed teeth clacking together. That didn't bode well.

Silence hung for a second that stretched away as my heart stuttered and Andy wobbled. A great groaning broke on the air as the giant reared back on two of its four legs. Andy teetered backward. The animal, all shadows, shining eye lights and glistening teeth lunged forward.

"Sorry, bro." I squeezed him tight and dove. The gelatinous barrier of the gate gave way. Andy spasmed, but god, he breathed. I couldn't have been happier to hear any other sound in the world. Our bodies smacked onto hard ground. Andy's teeth cracked together. Scrambling to my knees, I rolled his shaking body onto his side.

Thump!

The sound resounded through the open field. I looked back at the gate to see the head of the horned creature, twice the size of a buffalo head, at least the size of a big ass elephant's head, hurtling toward the shimmering sparking oval gate made by the tree limb.

Blam!

The creature's head rammed against the gate. Sparks blew from the crack, lighting the night sky in electric blue. The crack widened, a huge chunk falling to the dead grass beneath it. Andy's jerking body finally relaxed. I put my hand on his back, reassured at the air moving in and out in a steady rhythm.

The giant behind the gate had retreated and was lost to the shadows. I breathed a sigh of relief as Andy sat up. "Are you okay?"

"I think so. We gotta go, though." My phone rang. I took it out and swiped the screen to answer.

"You took him there didn't you?" My mom shouted before I had time to say anything.

"Yeah, Mom. Contrary to your belief, Andy is as much a Bitten as you and I are." Annoyance gave over to anger. "You know, what is your problem, anyway? Why are like this to him?" Andy reached a hand toward me, waving away my frustration. Like it was okay that Mom kept him away from what he was. It was not okay.

"Is he okay?" she asked, her voice shrill. "You took him behind the gate, didn't you? I could feel it. How is he acting now?"

"I'm sorry, what? It sounds as if you care." I said. Andy was waving at me now, a little more frantically. I ignored him, because this business with Mom wasn't done yet.

"Answer my question, Rori Anne."

"Yes, he's okay. Mostly." A fluttery sigh of relief, hitched with a gut-felt sob.

"Give him the phone. I want to talk to him." Andy looked put off, but pressed the phone to his ear.

"Mom, listen, we don't really have time for a heart to heart." I leaned in closer to hear what she had to say.

"How do you feel? What did you see?"

"Yeah, I'm fine." Apathy leaked from his voice. I heard him not answer the latter question. "We really have to go, though, Mom."

"I know, I know. It's just. All this time, I was so afraid..."

"Of what?" Andy asked. "Afraid your gay son also had gifts? That the dragon venom really did get passed to a boy? Have you ever paid attention? Don't you get it? You can ignore it all you want. I am what I am. Nothing you do or don't do is going to change that."

"No, no. I know you have gifts. I know you have power. You're an intuitive with the creatures. But, no other male has ever been born in the line of the Bitten. Our ancestry is shared, Andy." Andy paused, the phone clapped to his ear. The realization passed over his face. First shock. Then hurt. Then anger.

"So," he began, "you thought if I developed my power, I would turn into an Ani'Kutani. Like I was really some murderous freak instead of your son." His voice broke on the last two words. He hung his head, pinching the bridge of his nose, as the phone buzzed in silence on the other end. She had nothing to say to that. My arms trembled as a red haze of anger burned away in me. I reached over and pulled the phone gently away from him. He let it slide from his fingers as a sob ratcheted out of his guts. I hung up on my mom without another word.

I stared at the blank phone screen, unable to comprehend how a mother, being one myself, could care so little for their child. To fear them because of their difference rather than embracing them, encouraging them, growing them.

That was our job as parents. That was what we did. I wrapped an arm around Andy as a realization struck me. I questioned my own parenting. Was I doing everything I could to encourage Aubry to be who she was? Or was I trying to fit her into my mold. Chagrin flooded through me.

"I have to be better for Aubry. I have to let her be her," I said out loud. Andy's head yanked up, his breath wheezing in as he stopped crying. His golden and sea-green eyes were swollen and red.

He grabbed at my shoulders. "Something's happened. I think the third gate just broke."

"Why? What did you see?" I asked. A dose of adrenaline dumped into my bloodstream.

"I think Lady Adohi just showed me the gate being broken. And then, I don't know. It was like an incoming call I couldn't answer. Someone was reaching out to me."

"You mean, like how Aubry asked Udoqua about his daughter?" It was like I'd slapped him.

"We've got to get to Aubry," he said.

TWENTY-FIVE ~ AUBRY - FIRE IN THE SKY

Haelyn was screaming. Wind ripped through my braid and blinded my eyes. Tears beaded up and flew across my temples and into the air. If I could breathe at all I know I'd be hyperventilating. As it was, I fought the wind flying at me to catch just a little to fill my lungs. Rain pelted us. Claws dug into my back and I momentarily jerked toward the ground. I cried out in pain as a new scorching cut opened the skin of my back.

Lights passed underneath us, of houses and cars and street lights. I wanted to call out to the lights. To the people who were around the lights. "Help me!" Even as I screamed, I knew they wouldn't hear me. I was way up here, and they were way down there. We moved through the air in the claws of the flying flame so fast we were hardly in the air at all before we jolted downward.

The hawk cried out, a sound that scraped against my eardrums. An open patch of earth grew bigger. The claws released us. I yelped, but a puddle of mud broke my fall with a squish. I looked back up to the thing that used to be Devon.

We had eaten dinner. Everyone was nervous at the table. Devon hadn't touched his food and yet he looked hungry. I had asked to call my mom. I wanted to go home. Devon had knocked the phone from Edythe's hands as she handed it to me. And then the fire had glowed in his eyes and his skin had steamed and smoked. I had reached out with my mind, like I did with Udoqua. Andy was like me, so I fought to call him, but I was so afraid I couldn't connect the same way I had with Big Brother.

"Spoiling dessert, little one?" he'd said. "But, I had so many plans." First, Devon had been there and then the flame had erupted from within, consuming his body and then there was nothing but the Hawk left. Edythe had screamed over and over until the flame hawk had reached a hand toward her, spoken a word and then her squeals strangled, her face had reddened, purpled and then she'd finally stopped, and slumped in the chair. Something had scratched at the front door. "Go get the door, Haelyn." She had shaken her head at first, tears spilling down her face. I couldn't understand what was happening.

"Please. Don't," she'd said in a voice I could hardly hear. A low growling moan had reverberated through the front door. It was eerie and awful and made all the hairs on my arms and legs stand straight up. Darkness had bubbled and spilled through the door. Darkness you could see and darkness you could feel.

"Open it, now," he had shouted. She jumped in her seat and even though she looked like she'd rather do anything else, she got up, unlocked the door and let the Ganagi right into her house. And that's when the hawk had grabbed Haelyn and me, yanking us out of the house and off the firm earth.

Now, overhead the fire hawk crackled and sparked, the light illuminating a small patch of the clearing in an angry red glow. It cried out, flapped and darted back the way we'd come.

Haelyn crawled up next to me, covered in mud, and grabbed at my hand. Her eyes were focused away from me, wide and shining through a splatter of mud. Her mouth hung open. She was scared to death, I guessed from the flight of the fire hawk. Or maybe because her brother had turned into the fire hawk. Or that there was a new monster in her house.

I went to wrap my arm around her shoulders, but she shook my hand then pointed. The ground shuddered. My breath caught in my throat. Eyes the color of burning embers rose above the bushes, then the trees. I screamed. The giant creature thudded toward us. I could see in the darkness and wished I couldn't. Teeth glinted in a lipless smile that was anything but happy. Four nostrils breathed in the air, the sound ripping through the quiet of the night. Nothing else living was within a mile of where we were. I could smell that. I could hear that. And I knew that meant this creature was a predator.

I reached out through my other sense. The creature's thoughts jumbled into themselves, a whirring of colors and instincts. And a need that pulsed red and aching. *Hungry.*

TWENTY-SIX ~ RORI - THE SMELL OF MAGIC

I've never seen Andy run so fast. He was keeping up in front of me, over the rock-strewn Boogerman Trail. My bones jolted with each pounding step into the uneven ground. But my body couldn't out-rattle my nerves, which were alive with panic.

We practically flew into the parked SUV. Andy panted in the passenger seat. The engine revved, the lights flashed on. Rocks flew, pinging against the red paint that I didn't give two shits about at the moment. Andy strapped himself in as I pulled the gear into drive and pulled away from the trailhead. The road twisted and curved in the circle of light cast in front of us by the brights. When Andy didn't sound like he was going to slip into an asthma fit, I demanded: "Talk."

"Lady Adohi popped into my mind. She told me to see. And then a monster-ish, dark creature approached the third gate. It scratched at the gate over and over until finally, a big crack split across it." He grabbed hold of his chest. I fought back the intense need to dissolve into a puddle of useless tears.

"We're too late," I said, my stomach clenched up against itself. Andy didn't speak. A steady mist had started up and fell outside, pattering onto the exterior of the car. I turned the wipers on. Road dust mixed with the rainwater and smeared across the windshield.

It took way too long to get to the northeast side of Waynesville under cover of a steadily growing downpour. After our run and the drive, a good forty-five minutes had passed, which felt more like an eternity. We pulled into the Turners' neighborhood. I slammed on my brakes as a dog darted in front of the SUV. "Shit!"

"That dog was huge!" Andy said. Once my heart stopped beating in my throat, I drove toward Edythe's house. The oncoming lights of a fast-moving van blinded me momentarily before I turned into the Turners' driveway.

When we got to the front door I checked my cell phone, realizing how late it was. The digital screen read 00:28. I wondered how crazy she was going to think we were. I knocked on the door, peering through the small yellow window with texture on it like the bottoms of mason jars. Through it a light shone. Reassured, I waited. When no one came to the door I knocked again. I rolled my shoulders to ease the tension building between my shoulder blades.

"This isn't right," Andy said behind me. He pushed past me and threw open the door. It was unlocked. He rushed into the entryway and into the living room, me on his heels.

He stopped abruptly. I ran into his back. I backed up a bit and then peered over Andy's shoulder. A teenage boy I assumed was Haelyn's older brother, Devon stood with his back to us in the middle of a thrashed living room. The scent of animal soaked the air.

A lamp lay on the floor, a victim in the melee. The shade on it revealed the raw bulb and cast the floor of the room in a small circle of bright light that ended by Devon's feet. The twenty foot ceiling was lost to shadow.

The material on the ugly floral sofa peeled away from the cushion beneath where it had been ripped apart. Bits of yellow cushion littered the hardwood. A jagged semicircle of missing oak coffee table gaped on its corner with a collection of splinters jutting out. The entertainment stand bore a wild set of scratch marks and blood spatters.

"What the hell happened here?" I rushed toward Devon, but Andy threw his arm up. I halted against the steel barrier of his arm, my left foot that was in mid-stride flying forward then yanking back. I said, "Oomph," at the sudden impact.

"Where are they?" Andy asked. He didn't move his arm. He stood in a ready stance, his head lowered and looking at Devon through serious eyebrows. The fun-loving, sarcastic brother I loved vanished in the sudden tension straining his voice. I smelled the air again, unable to quit sampling the flavor. Old and musty, it clung to my nose and mouth.

Devon turned toward us, one small pivot at a time. His plain gray t-shirt and ratty jeans were smeared in dark red. His hands were coated and his face smattered in scarlet splotches. His green eyes stretched wide as he looked around the room. His chest rose and fell in rapid succession, his breath a steady sawing of air, his pale face slack in a look of horror. As he moved aside, a pool of blood stretched behind him.

Blood, but no bodies. Every hair on my body sprang up, a current of electric fear bringing them upright.

"Where's Aubry?" My voice whispered in raw notes as panic coursed through me, leaving me numb. Devon shuffled a small step toward us. His mouth opened, his hand lifting toward me as if he were about to speak. I pushed Andy aside. He gave, stepping out of the way for me. "Where's my daughter? Aubry!" I shouted into the darkened high ceilings. No one came. No one shouted back.

Devon breathed in, his voice stuttered out. No words, just a sound. A small confused sound of a teenage boy. And then, his eyes rolled back in his head and he slumped to the floor. His head smacked into the hardwood. His body rolled slightly, his face softened so much that it seemed impossible he could be responsible for… whatever happened here tonight.

My eyes were on fire. My heart rattled in a husk empty of anything except for a shrill fear. Andy turned to me, grabbing onto my shoulders, his mismatched eyes round with fear. "Go look," he commanded.

I nodded and tears fell from my eyes, surprising me. Was I crying? My legs wobbled uncontrollably as I lunged past Devon's inert body, stepping over chunks of sofa stuffing and splintered wood from the destroyed coffee table.

"Aubry!" I screamed, my shout threaded with dragon voice. Behind me, Andy's voice rose.

"Hello, this Andy Ferrish. Yes, I'm at Edythe Turner's residence. I'm not sure what's happened here, but there's a big pool of blood and the teenager here passed out when we confronted him." A pause. "There also might be some missing persons. We're still looking. Yes. Thank you."

My legs felt like lead as I climbed the stairs. On the second floor a bedroom door hung crooked on broken hinges. I pushed it aside and peered in. "Aubry?" But the room was most definitely Devon's, with a dark blue comforter, laundry scattered on the floor and posters of metal bands pinned to the walls. The room was quiet, and there was no smell of Aubry.

The second room I found on the same floor was clearly the master. The bedspread looked like spring had vomited on it and all along the headboard were pillows of varying shapes and colors to coordinate with the floral bedspread. I called for Aubry again and sniffed the air, nearly sneezing on the thick scent of perfume that drenched the room.

The third floor held just one attic bedroom. The door was squeezed into the frame so much that I pushed a shoulder into it to open it. Haelyn's odor greeted me across the stale air of the closed room. The twin bed stretched on the far wall held a collection of stuffed animals. There were a few toys scattered on the floor and a closet hung open to my right. As I stepped into the room my leg brushed something. A backpack sat propped against the pale blue walls. It was Aubry's backpack. Aubry was nowhere to be seen.

I crossed the room in two strides and pulled open the closet door. Shadows leaked out, but no Aubry. No Haelyn. Underneath the bed was devoid of anything but lost socks, a pair of old converse shoes and a Barbie doll.

Those were the only places in the cramped bedroom a little girl could hide.

Her scent was there. Old, but still hanging. There was something else too. An odor even more prevalent than Aubry's. I inhaled deeply as I turned a circle in the room, making sure I wasn't missing anything. The backpack caught my eye. It was a vivid collection of bright yellow, spring green and pink. The zipper moved. I rushed toward it and yanked it the rest of the way open.

For a moment, I expected to find Aubry staring back at me, as stupid as the idea was. I wanted her safe so bad the laws of physics didn't have to apply to hope. So, I was shocked to see Miney's glittering black eyes regarding me with worry pulling at her face. She immediately climbed into my arms. I wrapped them around her, the softness of her fur almost comforting. Her heartbeat pitter-pattered unevenly against my chest as she shivered. I held her for a moment. She had Aubry's scent on her, which nearly drove me mad. It wasn't my daughter I was holding, it was a creature.

Knowing the police were on the way, I rushed Miney downstairs and deposited her into the back of the SUV. "Stay here and stay out of sight," I told her. She nodded and allowed her fur to blend into the cream leather of the seat.

I went back into the house and Andy and I dragged Devon to the dining room and tied him to a chair using bungee cords we found in one of Edythe's kitchen drawers. "I searched everywhere down here," Andy told me. I paced the floor while Devon slumped, strapped to the dining room chair.

Andy threw himself into a chair at the dining room table, splay-legged, brows pressed into fingertips. "When I walked in…" Andy trailed off, he curled his fingers on his outstretched arms as though he were grasping for answers. "Something was here." I looked at Devon. I wanted to strangle him until the truth choked out and he told me what he knew about the girls' disappearance. I couldn't trust that my strength wouldn't overwhelm me. And killing him would put me no closer to my Aubry.

"What do you mean?"

"It reeks of magic in here," Andy said, finally. "Old magic."

"You can smell magic?"

"It's not a smell. It's not a seeing thing either. It's a … I dunno," he threw up his hands, "it's a something else that I can't put words to." He shrugged his shoulder, rubbing a hand across the back of his neck. There was a smear of blood staining the sleeve of his gray Henley from when we'd moved Devon. "Rori, I think the Hawkman was here. And Devon had to have seen it all. He could give us a clue." He rubbed his golden eye with the heel of his hand.

"Is the sense still here?" He looked up at me and shook his head.

"No. It's gone now." He went back to rubbing his eye. "Except…"

"What?" I asked.

"There's a lingering sense in the smell. You do smell that, right?"

"Yeah, and I can't put my finger on what it is."

"It's like fading chaos." He whirled his hands in the air dramatically. "If I compared it to color, it would be all bright yellows, murky blacks and twisting reds. And it sort of beats, like to a rhythm, but this one… it's all outta whack. Totally arrhythmic." His eyes lost focus as he searched for a way to explain a sensation to which I could not relate. Nonetheless, I could understand the sense of chaos he explained. I didn't have that other sense he was talking about, but the smell reeked of raw animal instinct, sick with anger and bloodlust.

I heard wheels on gravel and jetted to the door. When I pulled it open, the Chief took a long look at me. "Sorry to see you answering this door and not Edythe Turner," he said, his voice a deep rumble. Two officers flanked the Chief. I pulled the door wide and gestured them inside.

His smooth, long gait moved him effortlessly over the threshold, the click of his cowboy boots resounding off the high ceiling of the entryway. He brushed a long-fingered hand over gray mustaches and goatee, a thumb hooked into a belt loop as he kicked his right boot out, leaning on his left leg. He surveyed the mess of the living room, his dark, small eyes passing over the wreckage and finally flicking to Devon, bungee-corded to the dining room chair. He raised a dark gray, bushy eyebrow and aimed his gaze at me.

"We thought it'd be best. In case he tried to run," I explained, plowing through the squirmy feeling in my gut that told me that had been a stupid thing to think. He made a nonverbal grunt and looked over to Andy who sat straight in his seat and looked back, unpestered with the aching need I felt to cower. I shook myself internally. There are few people in this world that make me nervous. Waynesville's Chief of Police, Mack, did.

Mack Hayes turned back to me. "So," he said. That was my cue to tell him what happened. So, I did, minus all the parts of Andy sensing magic. "Alright," Mack began, his voice reminded me of taking a shot of bourbon; smooth and with a lot of kick. "Let's wake this little guy up and see what he's got to say." He cast a lazy glance at the blonde officer.

"Yes, sir," the officer said and headed out the door. When he returned he wore blue medical gloves and pinched a small white package. He approached Devon, ripped the top off the package, holding it away from him. He held Devon's head in one hand and passed the package under his nose with the other. Devon jerked his head away, his green eyes flying open. His breath immediately sped up to near hyperventilating.

The blonde officer stalked around to the kitchen, looking around and then finally locating the trash under the sink. He slipped off the gloves and tossed them in with the used smelling salts. Devon's breathing slowed, but I could hear his rabbit-like heart beat from where I stood as he stared wide-eyed at the Chief and two officers. The Chief took three long strides and situated himself in front of Devon.

He looked down at him, his gray head cocked to one side, thumbs hooked into belt loops. "Son," he said. "Name's Mack. Yours?"

Devon blinked. Swallowed. Then spoke. "De-Devon, sir," he said.

"Devon. What's goin' on here tonight?"

"I - ," he began, "He took the girls away somewhere. And then, he came back..." He looked out into the living room where the pool of blood was. Tears poured down his cheeks. "My mom," his voice cracked. "There was –" He doubled over. A splash echoed and then the smell of vomit filled the air. He coughed and spat. I wrinkled my nose at the odor. It smelled acrid and carried the stench of old blood.

When he raised his head he huffed and rolled his head in a circle to loosen his shoulders. His face and neck glistened with sweat. A trickle of blood ran down his lip from his nose. When he caught his breath, he looked at me, a plea in his eyes. "There was – " he doubled over again and puked. He growled between heaves. "Please," he heaved, "please help me." He jerked his head up long enough for me to look straight into his eyes. A flash of fire crossed over them so quickly I could have imagined it. Then he bent over and puked. Blood spattered the floor as he fought to catch his breath.

"Get the ambulance on the line," the Chief ordered.

"That's it?" I asked. "He pukes a little and you're just going to call an ambulance? What if he's puking because his guilt is making him sick?"

"Mrs. Cantrell, I can understand your dismay, but you best feel lucky I'm not questioning you." He leveled me with a serious gaze. I stared at him, my mouth hanging open. Was he serious? "You did call me, from this house, after you so-called found this boy near a pool of blood in his own house. What exactly were you doing here, anyway?"

I inhaled the sharp air, scented by blood and old magic and vomit, firing up an anger that chomped away at my innards and begged to be let loose. He didn't have a clue. Didn't have any idea what it was like to be a widowed mother with a child gone missing. How dare he.

"Let's not get yer engine revved," he said, holding his hands up in placation. I snapped my jaws shut on a perfectly good explanation of what exactly I was doing here. "I know your daughter's missing. And that she was here last time you saw her. Just let me make it abundantly clear to you." He paused. Rolled his tongue between his teeth. As if that would keep him from saying too much. "That is very much a reason to detain you."

I looked at him, feeling my lips curl up into the crook of my nose, my teeth bared. My arms had gone rigid and my stomach shivered with nerves. I kept my mouth clenched tight on any response I ached to give him. I was rewarded with a tear slipping from my eye and almost screamed at the insanity of the emotion; the helplessness that threatened to gobble me whole.

"That's fabulous." I heard Andy's voice and was surprised that it was right in my ear. When had he stood up from his perch in the dining chair? When had he approached and taken a stance right next to me? "So, tell me, Chief, what exactly are you doing to find Aubry, Haelyn and Mrs. Turner? You've got a pretty long list of people gone missing. You really think detaining the mother of one of the missing children is going to help you find them?"

I snuck a peek at him from the corner of my eye. He held the Chief's gaze like a pit bull with prey between its jaws. The Chief's jaw moved first to the left and then to the right. His nostrils flared as he contemplated what to do next. He wasn't at all threatened by my brother's thoughts on his job. I could see it: he was considering how much time he was wasting and whether he was making decisions that would bring people currently in danger back to safety. That was the rub for him. So, in all, a well-intentioned man, but still, a man that threatened to stand between me and finding my daughter.

He raised a gnarled finger and pointed it to Andy, squinting one eye as he spoke. "He still goes to the hospital. Sorry son, that's my duty. Can't be takin' someone in that's pukin' up blood, for Christ's sake." We heard the whirl of the sirens shortly after.

I stood with my back to the living room. I couldn't look anymore. The smell of blood made me want to run screaming. So, I dashed outside while the Chief spoke to the paramedics, pointing to the ground where Devon had puked and describing his ills. Other paramedics had untied him, loaded him on to a gurney and cuffed him there. He remained still and pale through the entire process. I worried he was really sick and not the person responsible for three missing people. And then I worried he was. I ached to hear what he knew. Everything in me screamed with doubt while I watched from the porch as the paramedics carried him out of the house unconscious.

"We're calling in the search party to scout the immediate area," Mack told me. Relief swept over me. Josh would be searching for Aubry. Josh would be here soon. The thought filled me with a hope that I clung to, wrapping emotional arms around it and squeezing. Josh, the man who had the best record on the team for tracking and finding lost persons. The rain fell just on the other side of the eve I stood under. And I thought, *I hope Aubry is in the rain somewhere. I hope she is cold and shivering.* Because the alternative made my blood freeze.

Andy and I stood next to each other as the two officers and Chief conferred, alternated with speaking on their radios strapped to their shoulders. When my phone rang the clock read 01:30. I had expected to see his face in person, but instead Josh's picture appeared on the screen. I swiped the phone with my thumb, my hope crashing into my stomach like molten lead.

"Josh?"

TWENTY-SEVEN ~ RORI - THE SEARCH

"Rori," Josh whispered. "There's a wolf outside my trailer."

"Why aren't you here?" I blurted, unable to contain the raw terror pumping through me for my daughter. "Didn't you get the call? Aubry's missing. Haelyn's missing. Edythe Turner is missing. There's blood inside Edythe's house. It reeks of magic and the one person who might have had a clue, or is maybe even the one responsible, just got carted off to the hospital! I need you here. Now, dammit! I need you!" Those last three words sent me over. I crumpled to the porch, the boards biting into my knees, feeling utterly weak and powerless.

Andy knelt beside me, his eyes confused, the question on his face.

"I know, Rori. I know. I am here for you. Please believe that. I think this wolf has something to do with Aubry's disappearance. It's not your run-of-the-mill, native red wolf."

"What?"

"It's stalking around outside my house. And sniffing." The questions pulled me from my sinking despair and sent me into problem-solving mode. I snuffled for a moment, shoved away the tears streaming down my cheeks.

"What's it sniffing for?" As soon as the words came out of my mouth the answer struck me. Andy leaned in to hear the other side of the conversation better.

"Well, I'm guessing it's not for my fifty inch plasma," he joked, his voice wavering with nerves. There was only one thing Josh had that a creature would be interested in.

"Why's everybody want that fucking stone?" I pressed my fingers into my forehead. I recalled the Lesser's conversation with me and how she had been surprised I didn't know... something. Something feathered across my consciousness so quickly that I couldn't grasp hold of it. I sighed when the thought flitted out of reach. My brain. Stress isn't conducive to problem-solving.

"Rori, we have to keep the stone safe," Andy interjected. Crawling anxiety tickled through me.

"Your vision?" I asked him. On the other end of the line, Josh asked if that was Andy.

"Yes. Come on. Let's go save your boyfriend." Andy stood up and offered a hand.

"Sit tight. We'll be there as soon as we can." I told Josh.

"Right. I'll go toss a stick and see if it wants to fetch," he joked, but I could hear the rising fear in his voice.

I took Andy's offered hand as I ended the call. Outside the protection of the eve the rain picked up, filling the air with percussive cacophony and a cold wind scented in water. More vehicles were pulling up. People were gathering, carrying flashlights and radios under black umbrellas, which made the group look like one misshapen hunched raven. Mack had unfolded a map and was pointing to it under the blaze of a mag light. Porch lights down the street lit one at a time as officers knocked on the doors and inquired about what they might know.

Andy moved down the steps, darting to the SUV. On numb legs, I wobbled over to Mack. "I have a lead," I shouted through the drumming of the rain. He nodded, his gray mustaches hiding his pinched mouth.

"Call me when you find out more," he shouted back and pulled a card from an inside pocket of his black duster coat. It was a nice one. The kind that defied the rain. I took the card and shoved it in my sweatshirt pocket, nodded then dashed to the SUV. I was soaked by the time I crawled into the driver's seat.

I started the car and turned the heat to high after I saw Andy shivering in nothing but his soaked Henley. Miney was curled into his lap. As I pulled out he told me, "She's scared to death. I think she knows something about what happened." I looked him up and down.

"Creature mind meld thing? Do you have a constant migraine with her around?"

"It's a bit uncomfortable, but I think I'm getting used to it, because of her." He looked down at Miney. She reached out a pudgy hand and touched his cheek. He stroked the hair on the top of her head.

"So, she saw what happened?" I turned onto the highway, honking my horn at some jackass that wouldn't move to the left lane and let me in from the onramp. He honked back. I revved the engine, switched lanes, sped up to him, turned on my cab light and flipped him the bird over a horrified Andy. Then I jetted past him. Andy was gripping the oh-shit handle and Miney, eyes wide.

"Shit, Rori. It won't do Josh any good if you get us killed on the way to his house."

"Whatever! Tell me what happened with Devon already and quit being a queen."

"I'll stop being a queen when you stop being an insensitive bitch!"

"Oh that's nice. I'm the bitch."

"Um. Yeah!" He was right. I was being a bitch. I ground my teeth and punched the steering wheel.

"Fine! I'm sorry. I'm sorry, okay?"

"You're not the only one worried, Rori."

"I know."

"I'm here and I'm helping."

"I know."

"Just because you're stressed out doesn't mean you can commit vehicular homicide."

"I know!" I shouted.

"Then slow the fuck down!" I looked down at the speedometer and let off the gas. The needle slipped from over one hundred to seventy-five. The wipers couldn't keep up.

"Sorry," I muttered. I gave him a minute before pushing him to talk about what he knew, even though waiting made me twitch in frustration. He didn't need a prompt.

"Listening to her, it's all a jumble of images and colors. If you think like a toddler, they kind of make sense." He stroked Miney's hair swoop, absently styling it into submission. She looked up at him, her big, sparkling eyes shining. Then he frowned. "The Hawkman was there. It had to be him. Also, Miney saw him as a flame. A bird-shaped flame."

Miney looked up at me. She scrambled to her feet in Andy's lap. "Watch it, little one." Miney spread her thick, hair-covered arms out and flapped them.

"Tia-wu-da!" Her little voice climbed as she repeated the word over and over, flapping her arms. "Tia-wu-da A-s-ga-ya!" Her inflection was different than when I heard Cherokee spoken, but the two words were clear: Hawkman.

"Yes, Hawkman," Andy said to Miney. He stroked her hair as she settled back into his lap then looked at me. I snatched a glance at his somber face before returning my eyes to the rain-washed road. He had more bad news. "And now he has his very own pet Ganagi." He stopped talking while my insides twisted.

"The dog we almost ran over…"

"Must have been the Ganagi," Andy confirmed, mentally catching up with me at the same time. "And that must be what broke the gate trying to get free to follow the call of his master."

"So, that's what's at Josh's," I said.

"The Ganagi's at Josh's house? You didn't tell me that!"

"I just figured it out!" The speedometer crept back up to one hundred.

"A Ganagi is looking for the stone?"

"Well, it's not looking for his fifty inch plasma!" I let the information sink in. "Why would the Hawkman send the Ganagi for the Ulunsuti stone? Why not just get it himself?"

"You're forgetting he wouldn't be able to sense its presence. He needs something to sniff it out."

I swerved around a pick-up truck in the fast lane, narrowly missing a sedan in the slow lane. We hydroplaned through the darkness of the stormy night as I pulled back into the fast lane.

"What else did she see?"

"The Hawkman sacrificed Edythe as a host to the Ganagi." Andy swallowed hard. "It was gruesome. Miney covered her eyes for a lot of it." I shivered.

I could imagine the slow process of the hide clamping into Edythe's skin, melding with her muscle, contorting her bones. No wonder there was so much blood. She was being slowly consumed by the wolf skin. Right now, as the wolf held her close inside its clutches, she'd be screaming without a sound to be freed. Her mind would be ripping into a thousand pieces. Alive but without a hope of ever living again after the torture the demon wolf would inflict on her, body and soul. I hadn't liked the woman, but I wouldn't wish it on my worst enemy.

"Wait, wait," I said, our conversation catching up to me. "The Hawkman has to have something sniff out the stone for him."

"Yes. They don't have heightened senses from the Uktena like we do. Er – you do. Their magic is strictly in casting spells," Andy said.

"So that's why the Raven Mocker tried to steal the stone. He made her and then sent her to find the stone."

"The Ganagi cannot get a hold of the stone. That will make him way more powerful."

I maneuvered around a black van parked to the side of the rock road. "More powerful, to do what?" I asked, thinking of my daughter, stolen away somewhere, in the presence of a hawk-shaped flame who was the ancient enemy and father of my foremother. She had rebelled against him and his sick religious, power-hungry ways against the Cahokians and the creatures of myth. He had thrown her in with the Uktena they'd captured, but the Uktena saw a way out and instead of eating her, had given her a nibble that changed my ancestry up to this very day.

And when it was all said and done, the Ani'Kutani was banished and stripped of power by his own daughter. That had to leave an undying need for revenge.

TWENTY-EIGHT ~ RORI - THE DEMON WOLF

We parked the SUV down the road with Miney inside. She obediently blended her hair into the passenger seat. I wasn't going to make the same mistake of bowling right into a dangerous situation like I had with the Lesser.

Andy and I exited the SUV. The rain slowed to a soft patter under the cover of darkness. Clouds overhead rolled out, giants skidding past stars and a bright moon. Spring showers are always so unpredictable. Andy ducked into the fringe of forest skirting Josh's property with me on his heels. Our feet whispered over the leaf litter through the newly budding oaks and ash. The forest here was more open with lots of space between the trunks. The view opened up to me, but it would also be open to the Ganagi, if it was even watching for anything.

The smell on the air filled me with information. Birds, rabbits, raccoon, all the normal smells were old. The animals had retreated to a safe distance from the Ganagi. And a good thing, since it would be consuming as much flesh as possible to sustain the host. To keep Edythe alive through the torture. Sure enough, I smelled blood. I picked up my pace and followed my nose through the muddy bracken. Shadows edged away from the moonlight, shy in the darkness.

Crouching, I touched the shredded corpse of a coyote. The animal was still warm. Animal tracks led away from the dining area. A typical tracker would never be able to identify the strange stretched humanoid hand and foot marks in the muddy earth.

The smell of rot grew the closer we got to Josh's trailer. Rot and blood. Andy drew me close to his perch behind an oak. He pointed toward the white trailer peeking through the trees. The mass of twisted animal hide appeared in my mundane eye like nothing more than an empty wolf skin. The right eye saw the creature as it really was. Wolf skin crawled up the elongated arms of Edythe, the skin torn and exposing pink muscle underneath. The jagged stretch of hide concealed the face, but I could see strands of Edythe's brownish hair escaping under the seam of hide at the jaw line. And matted in every part of the hide was blood.

The wolf ambled along, overlong human legs making the gait awkward. Humans as hosts anatomically made for an odd combination with the animal form. Edythe's delicate wrists would be pounding into the ground. Even being fed by dark magic and copious amounts of flesh to fuel the demon could not overcome entirely the frailty of her natural proportions. The Ganagi stumbled as it made its way over the rock driveway. Something in its mouth glinted against moonlight escaping the blankets of a passing rain cloud. My skin caught fire as panic seared my senses.

"It has the stone," I breathed. I burst from behind the oak, dragon venom exploding through my circulatory system, and ran through the columns of trees. The Ganagi swiveled its massive, distorted head at me. Bloodshot emerald human eyes stared back at me from the surrounding gray and mottled hide. The hair on my neck sprang to attention. It snarled past a bloody mouth, teeth turned to long and jagged canines, jaw jutting past the normal position of a human, and gripping the white and red Ulunsuti stone.

My legs launched me through the spindly trunks of poplars and ash. The light mist slicked across my skin. I soaked it in, drawing on the element the Uktena was rooted in. My eyesight snapped into brighter focus. My breath came slow and steady. The creature darted to the far side of a clearing, twenty feet away. "Andy, little help here."

"Working on it!" I didn't dare turn to look at Andy. I ran around the clearing to the opposite side of the wolf to hem it in. Wobbling on what were probably broken wrists, the Edythe-devoured hide turned to me.

"You're not getting away with that stone," I said. Its hackles rose and the voice that was half shadow and half twisted Edythe snarled around the stone.

I stepped into the circle of light cast by the full moon through a gap in the clouds. The clearing was all blues and shadow. I focused my right eye on the Ganagi, turning my head slightly to reduce the double image vying for reconciliation.

The Ganagi stepped forward. The stone's energy wafted toward me. A thrill of power went skittering along my nerves. A fiery pain awakened in my gut and shoulder blades. My mundane eye flickered between the real image and the mundane, like a radio station coming into the range of its tower: first static then music. Electricity danced along that other network inside my body. My muscles twitched in reaction. Biting back a berserker laugh, I bolted toward the Ganagi, pulling back my fist, preparing for the first blow.

My feet passed over the ground like wind through the trees. The leaf litter rustled and then the face of the Ganagi zoomed in to my vision. The left eye switched to a full on position with my proximity to the stone. I added a little juice from the electricity pulsing through me as I swung. Edythe's brown hair jerked from under the jagged and bloody hide seam. Edythe's emerald eyes widened as her head, the wolf's head, yanked upward and away. The stone flew out of its mouth, glittering, beautiful, and thunked to the ground near a fallen log sprouting gray mushrooms.

The creature stumbled but did not fall. It righted itself, shook its head and snapped a haunted Edythe gaze at me. Andy cried out. I darted a glance at him while I crouched in the ready position. Kneeling at the clearing's edge, Andy wrapped his fingers around his stylish auburn hair, eyes squeezed tight. "Andy!"

"Edythe. She's still in there. She -," his voice strangled for a moment with a gut-wrenching scream that seemed to echo Edythe's pain, "- can *feel* everything." If Andy knew what she was feeling, that meant he was feeling it too.

"Andy, let it go!"

"No, I can help!" His forehead was beaded with sweat. Edythe's voice leaked out of the contorted mouth. First the moan took on a quality of a whimper and then grew until the cry choked out very human and in more suffering than I'd ever heard a person bear. Edythe's stretched and sinew-exposed arms bent until the head lowered to the ground as the screams ripped out of a raw throat. The night could not absorb such a sound, and it keened away, born on the wind in haunting notes.

The hide undulated over Edythe's body then squeezed down around her middle. A sickening series of crunches reverberated across the clearing. Edythe's retching cries were swallowed by the darkness of a howl that sounded as if it were formed of hell's shadows.

Andy lurched forward, his hands clawing into the wet muck of the forest floor. His forearms bunched, the muscles standing out even in the darkness of night. "Let her go, goddammit." His eyes sprang open. The Ganagi swiveled its head in Andy's direction. It dove toward him. Andy sprang to his feet, hands formed in an odd gesture, as if he was prying open an imaginary object. He screamed in a titan effort. I ran, meaning to cut off the Ganagi's path. I let the jittery energy of electricity build inside the palms of my hands. My tennis shoes slipped in the muddied earth. The wind caught my hair. Andy's face came into focus, his brows pinched, his mouth wide as he screamed, his eyes mismatched and steely. The Ganagi and I raced toward Andy. I was close enough to smell the rank odor. Close enough to make out the small teeth at the edge of the hide gripping into Edythe's flesh.

"Andy!" Half a step too late, the Ganagi beat me. I made one last ditch effort as the Ganagi lurched toward my brother. Jumping, I reached out and touched the hide, my hands tingling with jagged blue sparks. In the same moment, Andy's hands yanked away from each other, his muscled arms straining against the invisible object.

Electricity exploded under the hide, shooting out little flames and sparks where the teeth of the Ganagi hide embedded into Edythe's body. Simultaneously, the Ganagi and Edythe burst away from each other. The head of the hide jerked up into the air, while Edythe's ruined face fell toward the ground. Andy was screaming like the berserker I had always thought was only in me. The hide pulled away, the skin still attached to Edythe spraying away in chunks of bloodied paleness.

Her limp, stretched form lay on the ground, steaming and naked of both clothing and skin. The Ganagi slumped to the forest floor, looking so much like a simple pelt of an animal it was hard to believe it was a demon. Edythe did not move. Andy, sweating and heaving in the night air, ran toward her, skidding to a stop in the mud. He rolled her over, cradling her neck tenderly, as if she did not look so unbearably monstrous.

Her face was unrecognizable, except for her eyes, glinting emerald, full of terror and staring blindly up into a gentle rain that picked up rhythm. Andy put a hand to her white neck. After a moment, his head sunk to his chest. His hand moved from her neck to her eyes and when he moved his hand away the eyes were closed. How had things gotten so out of control? I punched my leg in frustration.

I pushed myself from the mud and teetered through the clearing, my legs wobbly from the discharge of electricity. The Ulunsuti stone lay untouched. Its stark, milky white shone in the falling rain, the red stripe pulsing from dull to vivid. I turned my head to one side as I approached it. It had done this before. I plucked through my memories, trying to recall.

I stood near it, contemplating whether it was wise to pick it up, wondering what sort of reaction I would have to handling it. I imagined sprouting wings and flying was probably possible. Perhaps with it, I could easily find Aubry and bring her back to safety.

And then I wondered where Josh was. Why he hadn't come out here. Why he hadn't arrived to warn us.

I turned my head to speak my worry to Andy. My view swiveled, taking in the clearing, the naked trees, the night, the light rain. A black and gray shape lurched at me from the ground. I ducked. The Ganagi sailed over me, nothing but animated hide flying on the air like a sick magic carpet. It dropped to the ground. I dove toward the stone. The Ganagi snatched it up in a two-dimensional fold where the mouth would be. I grabbed for it, missed and fell to the ground. "No!"

The Ganagi flew through the trees, rising above the canopy, the Ulunsuti stone winking against the darkness of the hide.

TWENTY-NINE ~ AUBRY - MONSTER

It was confused at first. I followed its thoughts as they jumped around searching for us, its thinking like clouds of shifting color. First red then a mottled gray and brown then a mucky green. It was really frustrated and hungry.

I guessed it was because we were so drenched in mud that our smell was hidden. The monster stomped around the clearing, huffing and snuffling. The horns on its head rose into the night, twisted bone structures like wicked swords. Its hide was covered in long, shaggy fur and it stomped around on hooved feet.

We were tucked into a dip in a mound of dirt. The nearby lake lapped against the muddy shore. Haelyn clung to my arm as we sat, staring out into the open space occupied by the giant creature. Rain pelted down on us. I pulled my sweatshirt hood up over my head. Haelyn shivered. She was only wearing a t-shirt that looked like it used to be Devon's.

I tried to soothe the monster with my thoughts. I closed my eyes and focused my energy, like Nana had taught me, and let the feeling of calm flow out. Haelyn jerked my arm, her breath so loud I was sure the creature would hear us before it smelled us out. The giant sneezed loudly, sniffed then jerked its massive head toward us.

"Run!" I yanked out of the crouched position, grabbed Haelyn's hand and ran. The thudding of the creature chasing us thundered under our feet. Haelyn screamed. The creature roared, a stuttering howl that hurt my sensitive ears. I looked behind me long enough to see the creature, head down, horns facing forward and growing in speed and size. I yanked my gaze forward. Haelyn stumbled. I pulled her up before she could fall and continued running.

The lake that stretched away ahead of us glittered darkly under the pelting rain. We neared the muddy bank. My tennis shoes slipped. My stomach jumped into my throat as I fell to the ground. My teeth clacked with the force of my fall, my elbows aching with the sudden impact.

Haelyn screamed. The monster charged, shaggy hair flying. It reared its head and bellowed. I cried out, pulling myself clumsily to the water's edge, hoping, praying. My heart hammered away. Air evaded me and I gasped for breath. I sobbed. Haelyn clawed at my arm as she screamed, her words lost to me.

"Help!" I shouted and felt the cool water splash around my searching hand.

THIRTY ~ RORI - MEDICINE MAN

If I could fly, I would. I punched the mud and growled as the Ganagi swept out of sight. My stomach squeezed around frustration as tears slipped from my eyes. "Aubry!" I cried out, dragon voice shredding the night air. My daughter. Sobbing, I pushed myself up from the mud.

A rustle in the leaves caught my attention. My gaze jerked to a nearby crop of undergrowth. Raw with emotion, I lurched toward it. Still sobbing, I grabbed at the source of the noise. Thorns brushed across my skin. My hand folded around the neck of something. Material scraped across my mud-crusted fingernails. I hauled at the noise-maker, grunting with effort.

The man scrabbled awkwardly as his body cleared a fallen log. His arms flailed. "Wait! Don't kill me! I can help." I dragged him to the middle of the clearing then straddled him from where he lay face up on his back. Pinning his arms with my knees, I folded my arms onto my legs and peered at my captive.

"Why would I need your help?" I flicked the man's forehead. He flinched behind a set of thick glasses. There were still tears on my face. Edythe's body lay contorted and bloody only several paces from me and the man. The stench of rot hung on the air. A gaping wound of panic bled into my soul and with it anger and sorrow and hopelessness. "Who the fuck are you and why the fuck are you here?"

Andy pushed himself up from the forest floor and teetered over to us, stopping when his muddied sneakers brushed against the man's hair. He looked down at the man, his face unreadable. The man peered up at him then back to me. He wiggled against my weight without moving anything. I'm like a solid rock. His mouth trembled in a collection of thick, dark whiskers. There was something familiar about him. "Whoa," he breathed. "Just whoa. I'm not trying to hurt you."

I laughed, the sound ripping away from me in a sudden snarl of humorless mirth. I turned slightly and poked at the man's t-shirt clad chubby belly. "That's a joke, right?"

"Hey," he said.

Andy knelt so quickly his movement blurred. Gently, he placed a hand on the man's forehead and closed his eyes. Shaggy's breath hitched as he whimpered. When Andy opened his eyes again I could have sworn they were both sea-green. He looked down at the man. "How long have you been following Haelyn Turner?"

My breath quickened. I leaned forward, my heart pumping blood and venom through my veins. Was he helping the Hawkman? My knees dug into the man's arms. He hissed, shaking his head back and forth, his scraggly mess of dark hair whipping over his forehead. His small eyes were as wide as they could get behind the thick rims of his glasses. "You've got it wrong. It's not the girl I'm following."

"Oh yeah? Maybe it was the grown woman then?" I gestured over to Edythe's dead body.

"I'm a ghost hunter," he shouted, grinding his teeth against the pain where I was pinning his shoulders. "I was chasing that creature thing. Not the girl. Ow. But the girl. She's caught up in this."

I blinked and looked at the man again. I bent my face closer to him. "Tom? As in ghost hunter, Tom?" He nodded and hissed. My brain fought to make sense of someone I watched on the web being in my presence. "I guess our meeting was bound to happen at some point," I finally said. I eased up on the pressure under my knees, but didn't get up. He had information I needed. Before I could launch into a list of questions, he interrupted my thought process.

"Listen, you've gotta go help whoever's in that trailer. I swear, I'll stay here. I mean you no harm. I'm afraid the guy's hurt." Shit. Josh.

My eyes yanked up to Andy, fear banging away inside my chest where a heart used to live. Andy's stony concern met my sheer panic. I pushed myself from the man at the same time Andy stood. I held out a hand to the man and yanked him to his feet, his face startled with the ease at which I pulled his weight. "You're coming with us. I'm not letting one more person get away that might know something."

"Fine by me," Tom said. He walked over to where he'd been crouched in the bushes and pulled a flip flop out of the bramble, replacing it on his foot. Andy and I turned and began jogging, leaving the man to lumber along behind us.

My innards knotted around the anticipation of what I would see as I climbed the porch stairs. The screen hung crooked on the lower hinges, the top torn from the frame. I kicked the obstacle out of my way. Everything in me both wanted to rush into Josh's house and simultaneously beat a hasty retreat. I played tug of war with my fear, my legs jerked as I fought to push myself to the front door. The green lawn carpet of the covered porch crunched under my muddied black and white tennis shoes. My lungs heaved and burned. One step after another, as I drew closer to the trailer door, my body rebelled to cross the threshold.

Tom's ragged breathing filled the covered porch. He entered, but stood in the corner, grabbing his knees and wheezing. Something warm surrounded my shoulders. I jumped and looked up to see Andy looking down at me. Against his soaked Henley, his mismatched eyes shone brightly. It could have been the tears making them sparkly. His mouth was a firm, flat line. He squeezed my shoulders.

He let go of me and stepped to the threshold. The door was open. From where I stood, I saw him peer into the trailer. His eyes widened. My knees buckled, but before I could fall I lurched forward. I ducked under his arm that gripped the doorway. "No, Rori!" His grasping finger scraped my bare upper arm as I moved past him and into Josh's living room.

My body gave in and I crumpled to the brown berber.

The carpet fibers bit into my palms. My eyes were glued to Josh, sprawled on the floor, an open flannel robe framed his torn torso. The carpet turned black beneath him. His arms flung to his sides, one leg was bent at the knee while the other stuck straight out. His face looked away from me and his dark curls smashed together in parts that gleamed with wet blood. The smell of his life leaking onto the living room floor stabbed at my senses, burning my nostrils, tearing at my eyes. I was scared for Josh, but in the background, whirring in my mind were the hands of a clock ticking out the time that the veil held and Aubry was lost to me.

Andy knelt beside me, examining Josh with his practiced doctor gaze. I didn't have the stone this time to attempt infusing him with strength enough to come back. This was going to have to be all traditional western medicine.

"I need a couple of clean towels," Andy said, moving aside the ripped shards of flannel from Josh's neck and pressing his fingers in to count the pulse. I turned and jetted out, my legs moving me automatically to the little linen closet in the hallway. I grabbed the two lonely towels in the gaping cupboard and ran back to Andy.

My thoughts gnashed at each other. Josh was on the verge of death. Death, whose face I'd stared into too many times. The years of abstaining from a relationship with Josh had not kept me from any pain at his loss. I still ached as Death loomed, a stranger I could not control, could not bully into compliance.

I tried not to think about how much blood was on the floor as I knelt beside Josh. "Is he still…" I let the question trail.

"He's hanging on," Andy said. "Do me a favor, sis, and call 9-1-1." He moved with precise speed, placing the towels carefully over the wounds on Josh's belly. My phone was out and I had dialed emergency before I knew what I'd done. There was an anesthetic sense to my movements.

The Ganagi had the stone, which was bad, according to Andy. Andy, whom I'd had to defend as a child from an abduction. Whom I'd failed to protect entirely. Whom I'd avenged. And nearly died myself. Mom had saved me. Barely. I'd nearly die again for my daughter if I were given the chance. *God, give me the chance and I'll happily die to keep her safe. Keep her safe, God, Goddess, Udoqua, Lady in the Forest, Uktena, SOMEBODY!* I pelted out prayers to all the greater and lesser gods and goddesses I could think of, knowing full well, the responsibility for Aubry's safety was solely mine. And I was failing her. As I failed Josh. As I failed Jameson.

The answers to the operator's questions tumbled from my mouth like ice cubes from a fridge dispenser. Numb, I rattled out Josh's address and described his wounds.

When she hung up with me, I clambered over to Josh. He wasn't moving, his eyes stayed shut, but there was the slightest hush of air hissing past his lips. I brushed his hair away from his olive skin. My heart flitted around inside me as hope rose again. "Come on, Josh.

Don't leave me and I promise I'll make it worthwhile." Andy walked over to the front door and flipped on the porch light then twisted the knob to a nearby table lamp. I blinked in the sudden light.

Josh's nose was broken. Dried blood collected under his swollen nostrils. One of his eyes was puffed up and a bruise blossomed on the left side of his mouth. A cut above his eyebrow had bled into his long eyelashes. All this was nothing compared to the gaping diagonal lines crossing his torso in a collection of bloody gashes, now under the cover of forest green and yellow towels. There was so much blood. A person couldn't survive the loss of so much blood, could they?

His flannel robe lay in pieces next to his left arm. Blood oozed from puncture wounds where the Ganagi had bitten him on the shoulder and neck. I stayed glued to the spot next to him, watching his breath barely whispering past his lips, anxious that his lungs would keep working, willing his heart to keep pumping. The sirens whined as the emergency vehicles made their way closer to us, closer to saving Josh.

They knew him, of course, since he was a volunteer search and rescue leader. It took a whole five minutes for them to arrive. Fifteen guys piled into the living room, shoving Andy and I aside and getting to work, shouting orders at each other, calling out stats. I could barely breathe from the crush of uniformed bodies in the small space of Josh's trailer. They inserted an IV, took his pulse and blood pressure. He was in a collar, strapped to the backboard and being carted out the wider back door before I had time to wonder if he'd be okay in their care.

In the flurry of activity, one of the middle-aged firemen peppered Andy and I with a litany of questions. We told him what we knew, meaning, we told him we had come to see him about the search and rescue of Aubry and found him in this state, and then they were gone. He was gone.

And yet, as the sirens whirred into the distant hush of spring rain, I was relieved he was gone so I could get back to worrying about Aubry and the veil.

THIRTY-ONE ~ AUBRY - ALLY

The monster's shaggy head swooped down, glinting teeth pulled apart in an impossibly wide gesture that would gobble each of us in a single bite.

The water shifted against my hand. I closed my eyes and waited to die. A yowl punctured the air. The stuttering yelp of the giant creature made my eyes yank open. Moving like shadow, a smaller shape darted around our attacker. Neon green eyes shone in the darkness. The snarling whale-like growl of the Velith vied with the screams of the shaggy giant.

The giant lowered its head then jerked a twisted horn upward. The Velith darted away first then fast as lightening, swiped at the oversized, four-slitted nose of the beast. It yelped in pain, shaking its head and backing away from the Velith. The underwater panther snarled and swiped again, driving the giant back. Smack, smack, smack. Over and over, the Velith darted and attacked.

The Velith cornered the beast against a boulder and a collection of trees. She lunged at the monster, black fur shimmering. The giant reared up on its back legs, frustration screaming through the muddy yellows of its thoughts. The underwater panther dove toward the exposed belly of the beast. Her mouth stretched open, white canines glinting. Driving the canines in like daggers, she thrust her head forward, claws grabbing at dark hide. The giant's eyes rolled up in fear. The force of the Velith's attack knocked the creature backward and to the side. The ground shuddered under its fall. On its back, the hooved feet of the giant kicked wildly but the Velith could not be removed. A heavy slurping filled the air while the giant thrashed.

THIRTY-TWO ~ RORI - HUNTER

I stood in the covered porch area looking out at the night with a numbness growing inside me. Tom was standing out in Josh's yard, an instrument held in his hand that connected to a set of large earphones clapped around his hairy head. "Whoa," he whispered, leaning closer to the instrument. "What the hell is this?" I shuffled over the green "grass" carpet and down the cement stairs, holding the screen aside for Andy.

Once in the yard, we looked out into the forest, our gaze unable to keep from wandering to the location of Edythe Turner's body. "What's our next move, sis?"

"Hey, guys," Tom said, turning toward us, but not breaking his fixed gaze on the black instrument clutched in his hands. I thought for a moment, trying to decide where to go to look for Aubry. Where would the Hawkman have taken the girls, and to what purpose? I shuddered at the thought, a new terror seeping into my veins. "Guys. You guys! You gotta look at this."

Tom flip-flopped closer toward us. Shadowed lumps of acorns crunched under his clumsy feet. The sound of grinding shells scraped against my ears. The world tilted.

"I think I'm going to puke," Andy said. I turned toward him. He was on his knees on the ground. My phone rang in my pocket.

"Hey, are y'all okay?" Tom said. I looked at him. He was tall, I thought. And then I realized I was looking up at him while the world around me rocked like a see-saw. I pulled my phone out. It was Mom. I tried to swipe at the screen, but my fingers wouldn't obey. The periphery of my vision blurred. My head exploded. At least, that's what it felt like. I clenched my teeth against a growling scream of sheer agony. Andy's voice ripped the night air. I dropped the phone as I clapped my fingers around my head to keep it together.

The pain climbed a rapid crescendo and when I wished for death, it happened. The world went black.

A soft humming roused me. A smell like fresh flowers brushed across my senses. Something tickled against my face. I cracked my eyes. Lightning flashes of pain seared across my brain. Flyers flitted around my face, filling the night with a luminescent glow of oranges and yellows and greens. Their wings buzzed, pushing air into my face. Their little faces peered at me though many-faceted, insect-like eyes.

I breathed their scent deeply. Energy rushed through my lungs, transferring to my blood. I pushed myself off the ground, the pain in my head had decreased to a dull throb. One more breath, deep and full. The light hanging around the flyers seeped into my muscles. I sighed in relief as the last of the pain eased away.

I closed my eyes in relief. The image of Lady Adohi rose against the blackness of subconsciousness. The vision in my mind cleared, revealing a piercing gaze of hazel, green, and purple-veined eyes. Her body was covered in tattoo images of flyers, which lifted from the two dimensions on her skin into life. They sprang from her, darting away into my mind's periphery. Darkness encompassed the Lady. In reality I could still hear the buzzing of flyer wings. They were acting as a link to Lady Adohi.

She sighed deeply. Her gaze yanked away from me, looking into some other reality. She looked back at me. "Rori and Andy of the Uktena's Blood," she addressed. She pulled her arms into her bare body. "See!" Her voice clanged like a bell. Fear replaced her look of compassion as she looked to her left. My vision swiveled.

Darkness remained. I breathed once. Twice. A bone rattling thud resounded around me. Muffled crackling grew into ear-splitting creaks. A crack broke open in front of my vision. I stepped back. No. Lady Adohi stepped back. She pressed her hands against the inside of the tree, on either side of the growing crack. The images on her bare, tanned arms shifted, vines leaping up and filling the gap until darkness reigned again.

A knife slashed through the vines. Two hands grasped at the space the knife made and pulled. Red shadows seeped into the small space. It swirled and shifted as the gap in the tree grew. Lady Adohi opened her hands, green pods coming to life from sketch-like traces. She blew on them. They sprang open at a four-seam cross section at the top. A fine white cloud of tiny spores ejected from the pods. They swiftly formed a line and were sucked toward the hands still pulling apart the Lady's protective layer of vines. As the spores lit onto the skin of the attacker, blisters formed and then exploded in a gruesome spray of blood and pus. Screaming agony echoed into the crack. The hands yanked away.

The vines quickly filled in, but a new smoke was leaking through. The Lady coughed, wheezed. She reached out her hands, but the vines growing from her tattoos cracked and fell to dust before they came to fruition. The crack came apart. Adohi breathed in the fresh air.

A man's face swam up out of the darkness. His black hair swept across a tanned face covered in a thin beard. My breath caught. My breath? The Lady's breath? They were indistinguishable in this place. The man raised a knife of jagged stone with a hand covered in smoking wounds. His mouth parted open, brows furrowed, a snarl twisting his face. Dark eyes glinted.

The knife burned a sickly orangish red as he infused it with his dark magic. Smoke trailed the knife as it bore down. My chest exploded in sudden pain. Bare, tattooed arms rose in my view. The vision filled with reds and pinks. The arms shuddered. The tattoos raced over the skin, springing up a multitude of vines, leaves, butterflies, frogs, flyers, flowers burst into the blackness in a rainbow of shadowed colors. The man slashed at the life fleeing the Lady's body. Flyers, cut and bleeding, screeched and fell away. The arms in my vision dropped. The animals and vegetation that had sprung to life withered and died in the blink of an eye.

Gasping, I fell forward to the muddy ground. The flyers around me screamed, a sound like the whistling of a kettle, rising in an unbearable cacophony. I clapped my hands to my ears. They keened away, their lights burning so brightly the details of their wings and tiny faces were lost in the glow. In front of me, Tom had fallen to his knees. He peered through his thick glasses at the tiny creatures, mouth gaping.

And then, they rose into the sky and burst away from us, leaving a trail of multicolored light in their wake. All around us the forest groaned. The trees shimmied, shivered, drooped. My guts twisted. Andy crawled up to me. We heaved, leaning against each other. Tears fell from my eyes. Andy's sobs burst into the air. I wrapped an arm around his shoulders.

"That was insane. What just happened?" Tom crawled over to us.

"Lady Adohi, the living spirit of the forest was just murdered by an Ani'Kutani."

"An Ani'Kutani who is supposed to be dead," Andy said, his words hitching on sorrow and disgust. He pushed himself from the ground. He wiped the tears from his eyes and offered me a hand. I took it gratefully. He yanked. I flew skyward, catching air before I lurched to the ground. "Sorry. I guess I don't know my own strength."

He looked at me apologetically. Our faces mirrored shared surprise. Simultaneously, we pointed at each other. "Your eyes."

Tom stood and dusted off his board shorts. The large earphones were strapped around his neck. He looked between us and shrugged. I looked into Andy's eyes, no longer two different colors, but one. They were both gold with sea-green rims. I looked around me now, with my new eyes. There was nothing magic to see at the moment, but when I thought about it, I had seen all the flyers without the split vision.

I looked over to Tom. "Tom, what did you just see?" Tom was looking at his black box, shaking it then banging on it with a meaty hand. He looked up at me.

"Wouldn't I like to know." He shuffled closer to me. "What were those things? They were like... faeries. Or nymphs. Or something." I jerked my gaze to Andy.

"It's broken. That's how he was able to kill her." My world teetered. Crashing waves of sorrow and panic battered me. Tears slipped and slid down my face. Sobs ripped from me as I stuttered: "No. No, no, no."

Andy had his forehead clapped in his hand. "There has to be another way. There just has to be."

"I won't do it," I said. On the heels of my defiance was the fear for the world I'd sacrifice to save my child. In my mind's eyes, creatures were hunted and slaughtered.

"Won't do what?" Tom asked, looking between me and Andy. "I don't get it."

"The veil is broken," I explained, barely able to make my voice utter the words. "Centuries ago, when Europeans started taking over America, our ancestor made a sacrifice to cast a spell big enough to hide the creatures of myth and magic."

"Whoa. You mean there's like a lot of different creatures?" I could see the excitement on his face and wanted to smack him. "And I could see the faerie things because someone took down this veil?" I nodded numbly.

"And if I can see it, so will everyone else." I nodded again. "Oh that's not good. People don't know how to deal with the paranormal." There was a war going on in Tom. He scowled. "Man. My whole life is focused on finding and exposing the paranormal. But, I really didn't think there was a lot to expose. Ya know? Like, in my heart even I wondered if what I saw was real. But, now I can actually see them and so can everyone else. That's a bum deal." He sighed heavily. "Alright, what do we do to fix it?"

I turned my face from him as the shivering fear took me over. "Like I said, it requires a sacrifice." I waited for Tom to play mental catch up.

"Well, what sort of sacrifice?" he asked. I looked at Andy. His shoulders were slumped in defeat.

"My daughter," I stated flatly. "An innocent and a dragon-born."

"Seriously? You're telling me your ancestor killed her own daughter?"

"Go turn on a radio, Tom. Why don't you listen in on the news for half a minute."

"What? Uh. Okay," he said and to my surprise, began fidgeting with a second black box strapped across his body. Fuzz echoed across the night. Tom's head was trained on the portable radio.

"When did you get that?" I asked.

"Hm?" he asked and looked up for a second before looking back at the radio at the clip of a female voice finding its way through the static. "Oh. While everyone was working on the dude in the trailer, I went to my van and grabbed a few things."

"You usually have a radio with you?" I asked.

"Well yeah," he said. "Sometimes the ghosts like to talk through the static. I don't usually have it turned to an actual station though."

"You thought something about this situation suggested a ghost?" I asked.

"Hey, man. I don't have a clue what's going on here. This is some crazy stuff." He sort of laughed then looked at me, and his laugh strangled to a stop. He looked back at his radio, clearly trying to avoid eye contact with me. "Oh. Here we go."

"-throughout the town. Police are admonishing people to stay indoors and lock their windows and doors tonight until the source of the strange activity is located. Again, people. We have confirmed reports of several strange encounters tonight. At the PetSmart in Waynesville, a woman found what she describes as a giant spider – a height of three feet and a width of approximately four feet – habitating near the birds and amphibians. The creature was shot and killed by a police officer that responded to the call. Witnesses say it was unlike anything they'd ever seen."

"They killed a dreamcatcher," Andy said, wrapping an arm over his stomach and perching a hand to his hip.

"What's a dreamcatcher?" Tom asked, his excitement uncontained.

"Sh!" I said.

"Also, there's been a sighting of a giant dog creature. Some report this as the urban legend of the demon dog of Valle Crucis. The creature has not yet been caught. And then near Junaluska, people have called into the show tonight to tell us of a flying bonfire. I have had three calls and they all sound like the same phenomenon. The last caller said the flame was flying west toward Cataloochee." Andy and I locked eyes with each other.

"Hawkman," we said at the same time.

"What?" Tom asked. "What's a hawkman?"

"We gotta go." Wherever the Hawkman was had to be where Aubry was. I didn't know how to heal the veil without the sacrifice that'd been performed by my ancestor. All I knew was I had to get to Aubry. I had to save her. And yet, I had to save the creatures too. It was my duty. The thought of the dreamcatcher, a peaceful creature, being shot and killed sent spasms through me. What other creatures were being tortured and killed and captured?

Andy sidled up to me. "Aubry first. Creatures after." I looked up at him and nodded around grinding my teeth.

"Right," I said. "We'll figure something else out. Something. We have to." The desperation was obvious in my voice, even to me. Andy gripped my arm, his face a mask of determination. I nodded and turned from him. I started walking then began to jog toward the road.

That was precisely when Mack Hayes' shiny black police car pulled into the drive, catching me in the headlights like a scared jackrabbit.

THIRTY-THREE ~ RORI - ATTITUDE ADJUSTMENT

I hung my head as Mack climbed out of the driver's side of the cop car and strutted to me. Pressing my fingers into my forehead I waited for it. Edythe Turner's body was fifty feet from us in the woods, torn and mangled. There was no way a person could have done to her what had happened. Would they see it that way? Were they listening to the radio? I was sure they would know about the creatures by now. Right?

On the other hand, Andy and I were at the scene of the crime at Edythe's house when Mack had arrived and now we were here with Edythe's corpse. It didn't look good. And I just didn't have time for it.

Mack looked us up and down and I realized for the first time what a mess we were. Andy and I were both covered in mud. I had an acid burn hole on the right leg of my workout pants and several smaller ones on the shoulder of my red t-shirt. My hair was wet with rain and a quick glance at my forearms revealed speckles of blood.

Andy's Henley was torn and muddied. Where he'd rolled up the sleeves, dirt spattered his skin. He retained dark circles under his eyes and he had a touch of Josh's blood on his shirt and his knees from where he had been trying to help him.

And then there was Tom, covered with equipment, from the radio strapped over his bulging belly and the earphones slung around his neck and the camera hanging on his chest. "You didn't call, so I thought I'd wander over," Mack said. He looked Tom up and down. It was still only March and the man wore board shorts and a t-shirt and barely hanging on to his furry feet were a pair of cheap flip-flops.

Another police car pulled up and the two cops that had been with him earlier jumped out of the car, looking far less casual than Mack.

The blonde cop stood ten feet away from us, flashing his mag light around in the dark of Josh's front yard. The brunette listened to his radio then walked away to answer the person on the other end. I opened my mouth to speak, but the blonde cop spoke first. "We passed the van on the way in. Did y'all go look in on it yet?"

Andy and I looked at each other. Tom piped up, "The van's mine." He raised his hand, as if addressing the class. This gesture seemed to signal to the cops and before the man could say another word, two guns were drawn and approaching. I side-stepped out of the way.

"Put your hands in the air!" Blonde shouted. He pointed the gun at the ground, but it was still drawn.

"Listen, he's not a bad guy, guys. He's a ghost hunter," I explained. "He's been following the strange activity here." Mack hadn't moved. He stood, thumbs tucked into his pockets, cowboy hat dripping rain, one boot kicked out and leaning heavily on his right leg. The silence spread as Mack eyed the overweight geek with a piercing gaze.

"Van's yours, is it?" He asked, ignoring me. Mack shifted, readjusting his weight. "Let's go take a look at it then."

Andy and I followed along as Mack led the way down the rock road in the darkness of early morning. Tom followed us and bringing up the rear were the two cops. "Listen, the van's for my work. I'm not a creeper. It's like the lady says." Mack ignored him.

On the side of the rock road ahead was parked the black van we had passed on our way in. Mack went to the back of it, flicked a hand in the direction of the double doors and said, "Open it up, son." Tom shoved a pudgy hand into his pocket and withdrew a set of keys. The two cops edged closer.

Tom was talking while he unlocked the van. "I don't follow people." He paused from sorting through the keys and looked up at the Chief of Police. "I follow the paranormal."

"Open. Up. The damn. Door." Mack's North Carolina drawl enunciated the words and coated them in sorghum. He stood with his hands on his scrawny hip bones, his duster pulled away from the plain black button-up underneath. He stared into the mud first then into the heavens, as if calling upon God's grace to bless him with a measure of patience only a higher power could provide.

The ghost-hunting Californianite's gaze whipped back to the collection of keys in his hands. He fumbled through them, pulling out a singular selection and mashing it into the chrome door handle.

There was a mechanical snick and then a long creak. Both cops pulled mag lights and flashed them into the van. Digital lights gleamed back in small dots of unperturbed indifference.

Tom shuffled forward. "Uh…" he began. He showed his empty hands to both cops as he moved into the van. "Let me just…" Climbing up, he reached and pushed on several lights mounted on the ceiling. They reminded me of buttons on game shows that people punched to signal they had the right answer. Illuminated in the blue glow of the push-button lights a collection of cameras, monitors and microphones looked back. On a small corkboard above dual monitors and a keyboard tray were pinned pictures of local legends and reported hauntings. I climbed inside the van, sat in the chair, and looked at his collection.

Littering the van wall were images of the white lady of the French Broad River, the vampire panther, and the dismal swamp. My eyes fell onto a crudely sketched rendering of the demon dog of Valle Crucis. Mack leaned into the van, exploring it with his eyes. He pulled at his hat as his eyes fell away, his mouth pressed into a thin line between his thick mustaches and stubbly chin. Looking up at his accompanying officers, he waved away their drawn weapons.

I leaned back in the chair, my gaze absently wandering over the pictures, until it lit on one in particular. "What's so special about this house?" I pointed to the picture. Mack turned his head back. Andy climbed up into the van and crouched down beside me. The photo was shiny and new, as if he'd snapped it recently. Even the foliage matched their current spring state.

"I got a call from a friend in the area," Tom explained. He rubbed a hand over the back of his neck. "He said some neighbors of his said they'd seen some things they couldn't explain. He wanted me to come check it out." He shrugged. "So, I figured, why the hell not? Ya know? North Carolina has tons of stuff I haven't investigated yet. Seemed worth the trip."

"And, uh…" Mack yanked at his hat again, shuffled from one boot to the other, propped a hand on his belted hip. He peered over at Tom through raised caterpillar gray eyebrows. "Did you find anything?"

"Tonight. Yes. Tonight I did." Andy and I straightened. Tom's small eyes widened behind his bottle-thick glasses.

"Where did it go?" I asked.

"What did you see?" Andy asked at the same time. Tom was breathing heavy now, looking between me and Andy and Mack Hayes. Mack's incredulity shot to me and Andy. I could feel his stare, but ignored it. I only had eyes for Tom.

"The girl you thought I was following. It took her." I gripped Andy's shoulder.

"Just her. Just Haelyn." Hope geysered inside and instantly guilt swept over me. Aubry had escaped. She was hiding somewhere. She had gotten away from the Hawkman.

"No, he had a second girl." A guttural, animalistic whimper escaped from my mouth. My body fell forward onto Andy's shoulder. Andy wrapped an arm around me. Tears streamed down my face. Tom's voice was muffled through tears and Andy's embrace. "I've been watching for a couple of days. I videotaped some of it. It's in there," he was saying. "A few hours ago, I saw the flame shoot out of the backyard of that house," I opened my eyes and looked at Tom. He was pointing to the picture and addressing Mack, who grinned like he was placating a fool. "Scared the shit out of me. It was carrying two little girls. You could see them because of the house light and the flame itself. Ya know?"

Mack nodded. "Sure."

"So then it took off –"

"Let me guess. It went west." My voice scraped out of my throat as I rose from the chair. Andy jumped from the van and held out a hand to me. I took it as I climbed down onto the rock road. Mack Hayes looked at me as if I'd sprouted horns.

"That's right. Almost due west. Maybe slightly north."

Andy and I looked at each other. His face was grim. His eyes shadowed with unrest and his earlier oxygen-deprived prophetic fit. "The first broken gate," we said to each other. I turned away from the van, away from Tom the Ghost Hunter, away from Mack Hayes and Josh's trailer and the horrible mangled corpse of Edythe Turner. Andy was in step beside me as we walked away.

"Alright, now, hold on a second." Mack said. I didn't have a second. I continued walking. "Now, hold on."

His voice rose. "Where the hell do you think you're headed to?"

"Somewhere you can't follow."

"Young lady, you get back here." I stopped in the middle of the road and turned back to Mack Hayes. The two cops looked confused. So did poor Chief Mack.

"My daughter has been abducted. I'm going to get her. End of story."

"Why don't you let us do our job, Ms. Cantrell."

"It's *Mrs.* Cantrell. You remember that." I advanced on him. Anger welled up in me. "You remember I'm a widower and raising a daughter that I nearly lost. I'm not going to lose her like I lost Jameson."

"And you think you can do that all by yourself?" Mack said, his tone sarcastic. He hit a nerve. My insides crumpled. I couldn't do it alone. I didn't even know if once I found Aubry I could save her. I knew I couldn't save her and save the nation of creatures whom I was born to protect. My insides tore in opposite directions at the vying needs in me. Protect my daughter. Protect the veil. I couldn't do both. I would fail one way or another.

"She's not going to do it alone," Andy said. He stood next to me, arms folded across his chest.

"Oh good," Mack said. "A woman and a fag go a-rescuing. That's sweet." He chuckled. Well, he started to chuckle. Andy reached for me and missed. I was gone. My body flew through the air. Mack slammed against the open van door. The van shook with the impact. The air fled Mack's body as my arm pinned him in. Through the red buzz of anger I heard the officers pull their weapons from the holsters. I pressed my body into Mack's. If they were going to shoot, they'd have to take the chance of harming their precious Chief of Police. And they wouldn't do that. My breasts pushed against Mack's chest as I leaned my mouth next to his ear. My heart thrummed, heavy and steady through me and into Mack where I held him firmly by his shoulders. He wiggled, unable to move. I bit back a manic laugh.

Flashes of my eight-year-old form lurching through the air to my brother's assailant raced through my mind. I didn't want to kill Mack and I wasn't going to let him stop us either. He looked into my eyes and slowly raised his hands in a gesture of surrender. I could feel Tom near us backing away. Two guns were pointed at me. Andy was behind the cops.

"That's right, Chief. A woman and a gay man are going to do what you *can't*. I bet that just chaps your hide, doesn't it?" I said. Mack looked at me without emotion.

"Rori," he said, a warning in a voice wavering in tired pain, "Put me down. And let's talk about this."

"There's nothing to talk about. I'm going to get my daughter. You're going to Junaluska Regional Hospital to guard Devon until you get some answers out of him."

"If you don't put me down, I'm going to have to arrest you for assaulting an officer of the law."

"If you arrest me, my daughter will die. And so will Haelyn Turner. Like her mother."

Well, shit.

"What do you know about Edythe Turner?" Mack asked. I gritted my teeth. Stupid. If I hadn't said anything, they would have moved on and I could have disposed of Edythe's body later. She'd be a missing person from now to eternity.

"Tom," I said without turning from Mack. "Tell the Chief of Police why you're here."

Rocks shuffled under Tom's flip-flopped feet. "After the flame left, it came back to the house. I heard screaming inside. And then this huge – thing – came out of the house. I've never seen anything like it. It was like an empty wolf hide. So, I followed it and it led me here. It went into that guy's house. And then I saw these two pull up, so I got out of the van and followed them."

"But the wolf hide wasn't empty, was it?" I asked Tom. Mack's jaw twitched where he ground his teeth together.

"I'm done with this damn nonsense – " Mack began.

"Let him answer," I whispered into Mack's ear, still pressing myself into him, still holding him to the van door. He shifted and growled. He smelled like soap and unscented laundry detergent. Clean, brisk. His breath smelled of black coffee.

"I really wish you'd put me down," he whispered back.

"I don't know what you'll do, and I can't risk my daughter's safety."

"You're already doing that."

"I'll put you down if you'll listen."

"What's your back-up move, sweetheart?" He didn't think I had one. I tried not to laugh and failed.

"You know all those crazy local myths you've been chalking up to people's overactive imaginations?" Mack looked at me like I was truly a dangerous criminal, really unsure if his safety was compromised. "How would you like to find out they're all true?"

THIRTY-FOUR ~ AUBRY - HAELYN'S MYSTERY

When the Velith was done eating it sauntered over to me, gliding over the ground with its six legs. The giant creature lay still under the moonlight, a mountain of fur and empty flesh. Haelyn and I had found a nearby fallen tree to sit on. The Velith locked eyes with Haelyn and growled. I looked behind me. What was it about her that all the creatures hated?

She's my friend, I told the underwater panther. She looked back to me, her neon green eyes softening. She bent down and butted her head into my chest, nearly knocking me over the log. I smiled, running a hand over the silky dense fur. A purr rolled through the creature, rumbling into me.

Haelyn reached a hand toward the Velith. The panther pulled away and hissed, exposing its long, sharp fangs. Haelyn jerked her hand away and yelped. I stepped forward and scratched at the panther's cheeks with both hands. It turned toward me again, settling into the attention, eyes drooping.

Thank you for saving us, I told her. Creatures don't think in full sentences. They think in emotions and smells and flashes of images. And they all think a little differently. The Velith's thoughts were calm and organized. Unlike the giant thing that had attacked us whose thoughts had been a jumble of instincts. Her aura was blue now and with it came pictures of me inside my mom. Someone had almost killed me then. And the Velith had stopped them. I saw the man's face in my mind's eye.

Startled I looked behind me at Haelyn and saw the man's face in hers.

THIRTY-FIVE ~ HAELYN - BLOOD OF MY BLOOD

She knew. My heart skipped around and fear squeezed cold fingers around my neck. I backed away from her.

"You're Ani'Kutani," Aubry said, turning with the underwater panther behind her.

"What?" I pretended to not know what she was talking about.

"The Hawkman. The one that's inside Devon is our ancestor. He's bad." When she said bad, she stretched it out. I nodded.

"Very bad," I said.

"What does he want with us? Why did he bring us here?" she asked. The underwater panther nudged her arm. Aubry absently patted at the creature's ebony head. The long tail behind him flicked slowly back and forth. I could feel the power rolling off of it. It was full of blood. Full. If I were to kill that creature, I could be so strong. So could Devon. And the stronger Devon got, the easier he could kill Aubry. And Aubry was my friend. I squirmed at the guilt inside me.

"You need to send it away," I nodded toward the Velith.

"Why?" she asked, still patting at the creature's giant head. It purred, nudging up against her ribs.

"Because Devon," I explained, "he'll use him."

"She's a she," she said it nice.

"He'll use *her* then."

She tilted her head to one side. "What do you mean?"

I opened my mouth to explain, but the sound of fire filled the air. Aubry and I jerked our eyes to the sky to see the flame flying down toward us. I darted over to Aubry. "Listen, Aubry, you have to run away."

"Not without you," she said. The Velith looked at the oncoming flame and hissed. Rounding us, it stood between us and the Hawkman as he descended. As soon as he touched the earth, Devon emerged from the flames, the fire sucking inside of my brother's body.

His eyes were sunken above dark circles. His cheeks were hollow, his lips dry and smudged at the corner with something dark. He was so skinny. The Hawkman was eating away at my brother. I wasn't even sure there was anything left of my brother in the husk of a teenager the fire consumed.

Devon stopped a few paces in front of us, his ember eyes burning as he regarded the underwater panther with the same hunger I felt. I shuffled a step away from Aubry, my body wanting to go to Devon, for him to teach me something new. I could already feel the darkness waiting for me, feel a chant building in my throat. His gaze caught mine and a corner of his stained mouth jerked to a half smile. Ashamed at his realization of my eagerness, I took a step closer to Aubry. My body shivered and not from the cold.

"You've done awfully well tonight, Granddaughter. First your Bitten friend and now a Velith." Aubry's golden gaze bored into me.

"Haelyn?" Her voice shivered. Her hand paused on the Velith's back. The night sky erupted in rain. The rain filled the air with a cold snappish smell. My feet squished in the muddy lake bank as I shuffled, unable to decide what to do.

"I didn't mean to," I squeaked. "He made me. He told me he'd kill my brother and mom."

"He killed your mom anyway," she said. The Velith turned toward me, a growl rumbling from deep in its blood-filled belly. Under the cover of night, the panther was almost indistinguishable, save for its bright neon green eyes.

"No. He just used her for the Ganagi." I felt the lie in my words.

"Haelyn," Aubry said softly, "Nobody can survive wearing the Ganagi. It breaks down their body. They just can't get better from it." Tears fell down my cheeks, mixing with the rain pelting me, soaking my t-shirt.

"That's not true," Devon said in a sing-song voice, crossing his arms over a stained gray t-shirt.

"It is too true." Aubry's voice sounded stubborn.

"Not. And while I'd love for you to see that proven, I've decided to change plans." The flame burst out of Devon's body. He began to chant, the voice of his old self, deep and thrumming, filled the rain-drenched air while the voice of the hawk keened away.

The Velith snarled through its elongated canines, overly long whiskers dripping rain. Its neon eyes were nearly lost in a grin of warning. Its barbed tail whipped back and forth, its six legs bunching in a muscular crouch.

Power rolled off the Velith in waves. My heart hammered at the feel of it. I reached for the feather I'd tucked into the side my jeans. My feet shuffled away from the Velith and from Aubry.

The Hawkman's chant rose. The Velith's head bent and slowly, but surely its slender, black body came to rest on his six legs. We hadn't killed anything this big or this magical before. The fire turned to me as the chant came to a halt. Grinning among the flames was the odd mish-mash of features. A black beak protruded over a mouth of sharpened teeth. His eyes were pits of blackness that stretched wide. The edge of the flame feathered away from the coal-colored center. His feet were a combination of man and the claws of the hawk. And nowhere in the Hawkman was my brother's presence. It was as if in this form he gave up the teenage body.

Flames rose and wavered from the top of his head as he glared at me. I looked away from the horror of his face. "Take the Velith," he commanded. His clawed and feathered hands reached inside himself and pulled out a butcher knife. It was one from my mom's kitchen. My mom. I wondered if what Aubry said was true. Was she really dead? She couldn't come back from the Ganagi?

My hands shook. Hawkman tossed the knife. It splattered into the wet, muddy ground. The Velith mewled a wobbly sound of frustration. It clawed at the earth, but otherwise stayed pinned with the Hawkman's magic. I walked toward the knife.

"The copper will heal your mother, Haelyn. And Devon. I have it pinned for you. All you have to do is kill it.

You've done it before. This is easy," coaxed the Hawkman. It was true. I had done it before. I bent and gripped the plastic knife handle. I left the feather in my unoccupied hand and turned toward the Velith and Aubry.

Aubry's golden eyes yanked toward me. "What are you doing?" I walked toward the underwater panther. The Hawkman's eyes bored into my back. I was within five steps of the Velith, its aura of panic throbbing reds and blacks. It shook its head, growling and hissing against the control over it. I was hungry for it. Hungry to push the knife into the throat of the panther and feel its life force sucking into me. Feel the magic inside me well up. And then. To be able to fix Devon. To fix my mom.

My eyes were fixed on the underwater panther. I raised the knife. Aubry's movement caught my eyes. She jumped up, using the panther as a boost, her braid flinging into the rain. She landed in front of the panther and leaned against it. "You are not going to hurt this creature," she said. I raised the knife. Aubry held out her hand, shaking her head back and forth. "I won't let you." Tears welled up in her eyes. "Don't make me hurt you, Haelyn." The panther's fear called to me. A sort of tugging on my insides. I took one more step, glanced behind me at the hawk flame.

I lifted the knife and slammed it into the ground. The mud gave way with a gritty slurp. The knife stuck into the earth. Aubry stuck her chin up. One side of my mouth rose. She smiled at me. A bright smile of relief.

Her gaze yanked away from me. I rose, adjusting my feet to turn. A blinding pain exploded through the side of my head. And then nothing.

THIRTY-SIX ~ AUBRY - ANCESTOR

He struck my friend. Even though she was Ani'Kutani, and I knew she'd really wanted to kill the underwater panther and take all the energy from its blood, she hadn't.

"Leave her alone!" I shouted. And now I stood. The only person between the death of my friend and the most awesome creature I'd ever met. I'd called to her and she'd come to my aid. Like Miney had. They came to me to protect me, and then what did I do? Just hurt them?

No.

Mama said I was strong. Grammy said I was smart. Andy said I was kind. I wasn't like Mama. Not all of me. I was just me. Just me. That could be enough, couldn't it?

I closed my eyes as the rain fell around me. It splatted against the top of my head and nose and forehead. My hands caught the drops and my skin soaked it up as I called on dragon venom that was written in my blood.

The fire of the Hawkman crackled and I knew without looking, he was getting closer to me. I was so afraid of him. The Velith mewled behind me. Her thoughts flitted though me. *Run away! Don't look back.* I quieted my thoughts, like Grammy taught me when we were drawing energy.

The face of Adohi popped into my mind. What was it she had said? I let my thoughts drift, even though I knew the Hawkman could kill me at any time. My greatest strength. She'd told me my greatest strength would save me and others someday. I didn't know what my greatest strength was. And the Hawkman was close. I thought if I opened my eyes, his face would be right in mine. He was a nasty soul. All reds and blacks and muddy oranges. He wanted more than anything to kill me. To suck up the blood of my ancestor. To finally have the revenge against his daughter for her rebellion.

And then, I realized... I was hearing him.

My eyes sprang open. "You've gone the way of the creature. Like Big Brother." The gaping black eyes stared. His wings of flame thrust downward. The rain didn't touch him. I listened. He was confused by what I said. It didn't matter. He was going to kill me anyway.

"No, you're not." I told him. The mouth under the beak opened, and a stench rolled over me.

"I see," he said. He tapped a clawed finger to where a head might be if it weren't all flames. "You hear me."

I shook my head slowly. "That's not all."

He lunged for me. The sound of fire ripped through the rain drops. A clawed hand shot toward me. I raised my hands, flung them toward the fiery hawk. Glowing blue rainwater slicked from my fingertips and sliced through the air like missiles. My fingers spread out as my blue rain dug into the wings of the hawk. "Stop!" My voice climbed, not just a shout; it vibrated with dragon voice.

Lines of eerie blue stretched from my fingertips to the hawk's wings – ten points of light shiny in the darkness. They vibrated with the touch of dragon voice, spreading blue down the hawk's wings as if syrup were pouring over the flames. Hawkman wriggled against my shield, but he couldn't move. The substance had already encased his entire body. Under the clearish blue coating the flames still danced.

His blackened eyes flickered to green. I faltered at the sudden appearance of Devon's face. The blue shield flashed. The fire extinguished. The Hawk disappeared and Devon fell to the ground hard, landing on his knees.

Haelyn stirred next to me. I peeked. She still lay on the ground, but her head rolled to the side, to see her brother. Devon's head slumped to his chest. His hands hung sadly in front of him. "Devon?" I asked. The blue light died. He was breathing. His hair smoking in the rain. I couldn't see his face.

Haelyn's breath quickened. "Devon, are you okay?" she asked, her voice raw as she struggled to a crawling position in the black mud.

I tiptoed up to him. "Devon?" His body swayed like he would fall. I reached out a hand. His hand shot up and gripped my wrist. I squealed in surprise, pulling on my arm, but his grip was unbreakable. His head slowly rose, the mop of sandy hair hanging in his blackened eyes.

"Nope. Wrong again."

I screamed. The dragon voice this time reverberated through the swampy clearing like a fog horn on a beach. He reached his free hand out, fingers extended. The knife Haelyn had stuck in the ground shot toward him. It whizzed through the air and slapped into his hand. I jerked away. He brought the knife up. Haelyn's scream echoed mine. I squeezed my eyelids shut and waited for the cut.

It didn't come.

I yanked my eyes open. Devon's face went slack as a gurgle escaped his mouth. The grip on my wrist loosened. The knife fell to the ground. My feet squelched through the mud as I shuffled back. Blood spurted from Devon's neck from a thin line against his pale skin. He choked again and then fell hard into the mud.

Behind me, the underwater panther fled, big paws padding across the ground until she slipped into the water.

Haelyn wailed, wrapping her thin arms around her brother's shoulders. The emerald returned to his eyes as a shadow the size of a giant hawk burst into the air above him. Smoky red eyes peered down at me as the dark wings flapped in the rainy night sky. It cried, an ear-splitting sound that somehow sounded unreal. Un-here. Then it shot up into the air, and flew away. Flew into the darkness of the gated place where the monsters live. Probably to find some other host to inhabit.

I turned to Haelyn. She held Devon's limp body on her tattered jeans. Her hands were coated red. The rain slowed. Her short hair hung around her heart-shaped face. She had a hand on his neck, but the blood had already pumped past her small fingers and pooled underneath them. She wept.

Haelyn had killed her own brother. For me.

An awful horror squeezed my belly. She killed him. She'd used her magic to slit his throat before he could kill me. Now, it was over.

I shuffled over, patted her back. I could find Mom now and get us home. We could find Mrs. Turner. And Devon... My heart broke in a thousand tiny pieces as I looked at Devon's bruised and stained face. Vacant emerald eyes stared back at me, mouth hanging in surprise. We couldn't do anything for him now.

"It was the only way," Haelyn whispered through a series of hiccups. "I had to kill the Hawkman's host or he would never go away. He told me so."

"Haelyn –"

"He was going to kill you," she explained, the words rushing out of her. "He was going to use your blood to make him inseparable from Devon. The things he made me do..." Haelyn looked down in to her brother's face. No, past his face. Past everything. "He made me make friends with you!" Her head whipped up to me, her dark eyes stretched so far they looked as though they would pop out of her face. "And I did it. I did it. I wanted to know what the power was like. I killed things, Aubry. I killed. I killed." She rocked, squeezing Devon's shoulders, looking out into her past. I opened my mouth to sooth her, to say something comforting, but the squishy feeling inside wouldn't go away, and it stole my words. Instead someone else spoke.

"I can't believe you killed him." A man's voice echoed around the muddy clearing. He laughed. The form of a sweatshirt and jeans and boots walked into the range of our vision. "Wow. Well, you sure saved my skin there, darlin'." He paused, kicked out a leg, shook his head, crossed his arms and chuckled past a set of crooked teeth.

From the shadows a new horror crawled out. Limping along, the hide of a Ganagi pulled itself near the stranger. The shining Ulunsuti stone in its mouth glinted in the darkness.

THIRTY-SEVEN ~ RORI - THE WOMAN, THE FAG AND A BEAR

"We'll let you do your job," I told Mack. "Come on, let's go 'a-hunting' together." I lowered Mack to the ground. He straightened his button-up shirt, his whiskers bristling under a scowl. I held out my hand. He eyed me, clearly deciding what to do with me.

"Hold on," he said. "Where is Edythe Turner?"

"In the trees, that direction." I pointed.

"Bo and Jesse. Go check it out." Guns were holstered as the two cops shuffled away. Soon we heard the buzz of Mack's radio. He pulled it off the hook on his belt. "Go ahead."

"There's a body here. It's completely mangled. I've never seen anything like it. It looks like she's been stretched out. I can't even say for sure it's Edythe Turner."

"Very well. Call in the coroner and we'll see if we can ID on dentals." He hooked the radio back to his belt and looked at me. "I ought to arrest you," he said. "What the hell happened here?"

I thought about that. How in the world would I explain all this to someone who didn't even believe in the world I lived? "Listen, there's a lot going on here you're just not going to understand. Edythe was murdered by a demon of sorts." I thought I was translating fairly well. He stared at me like I was a lunatic. "Don't look at me like that. Have you been listening to the radio at all tonight?"

"I concede there are some strange things happening tonight," he said.

"Look. The only thing you really need to know is that Aubry and Haelyn are at Cataloochee and we need to get there before our chances run out to save them." I didn't say anything about the veil and not knowing if I could save Aubry from that fate. Mack's jaws ground from one side to another. He pointed a finger at me.

"I don't trust you. And I don't trust all this shit happening around here. I don't like it. It's unnatural. Like that woman earlier tonight." He paused and looked up at the heavens. "God, she looked like she'd taken a dunk in acid." He pulled his hat off and scratched at his gray head. He replaced his hat and looked around at the lightening sky. "Well, hell. I guess so long as you're in my sight, I'll follow your lead." I nodded curtly and turned from Mack, intending to head toward the car. The clouds still flitted fitfully overhead. The moon had set. A breeze ebbed and flowed, the bare vegetation grabbing at it with meager claws. I crunched along the rock road, Mack's boots grinding along behind me.

A rustle in the undergrowth off the road caught my ears. My head whipped around. A bear lumbered from the forest. Mack pulled his gun on the giant black bear. He cocked and squeezed the trigger. The bear shimmered, shifted and dodged the bullet. I knocked the gun from Mack's hands as Big Brother's image grew watery then materialized into a man, a bear skin drawn around bare shoulders.

Mack stared.

I bowed my head. Never had I seen the Cherokee of legend, the one that had left the tribe to become a bear, to teach the Cherokee the way to hunt, appear in human form. It looked as if it pained him. His blue eyes were full of sorrow, dark skin radiant, black hair pulled into braids that spilled over his muscular pectorals. He opened his mouth to speak, but nothing came out. He cleared his throat, a sound that rumbled like the bear's at first then grew to a man-sized growl.

"Your daughter's voice cries out with the dragon," he said to me. My mouth gaped.

I lurched forward, unable to control myself. Andy jogged toward me. Udoqua looked him over then nodded his head in his direction.

"It is good you are here." Andy nodded back, less respectively and more stunned. Flip-flops flapped up behind us. Big Brother regarded Tom the ghost hunter and Mack with an indifferent air. "Just you two. It is too dangerous for these men."

I turned my head to Mack, smug smile plastered across my face. "Hear that? It's too dangerous for you, but not the woman and the fag." Mack was staring open-mouthed at the man that had just been a bear. He glanced at me then back to Udoqua. When Udoqua simply stared back, Mack turned to me.

"I'm losin' my goddamn mind," Mack said.

"This is the part where you say you're sorry for being a bigot," Andy said. Mack cleared his throat, still shooting glances back to Big Brother.

"Well, go on then and follow him if it'll get you to Aubry and Haelyn." He halfway raised his hands into the air, shaking his head in a defeated gesture.

"Come," Big Brother said and then stepped back into the forest. Andy and I followed him. We were just in the bracken when a squeal caught us up short. The three of us turned our gaze. Miney jogged through the undergrowth, skipping over logs, dodging around trees. She reached us within seconds, wrapping her arms around Andy's leg. She looked up at him with her starry eyes. "Dee-dee!" He reached down and let her climb into his arms.

"Alright, we're ready," Andy said.

THIRTY-EIGHT ~ AUBRY - PATERNITY

The sky turned a heavy gray as the rain stopped. Morning was coming, but the newness it brought wasn't the kind to make me smile. Instead of Wuffers's kisses to wake me, the rot of the mangled and possessed animal hide wafted on the morning's breeze. Eyeless gaps looked up at this new stranger. We all looked at this new man.

Haelyn's broken heart was written on her face. The dark-haired man made his slow way through the mud toward Haelyn. He held out his hands as if in surrender then he lowered himself into a crouch near her. His hands were covered in black-rimmed pits of angry red.

His baggy olive green sweatshirt was stained and ripped. He looked down at Haelyn with dark eyes filled with tears. The color dancing around his body shone a bloated, crimson red. Haelyn shuffled away, but the man reached out to her. In one movement, he scooped her up into his arms. Devon's body slid from Haelyn's lap and splatted in the mud.

"Hush, now," he told her as her struggle against this stranger's grasp turned to fighting. "Haelyn, Haelyn. Stop!" She stilled at the sound of her name, her breath wheezing. "I'm sorry. I didn't mean to yell."

She just stared at him. Her lips were parted, her eyes wide. "Please don't hurt me."

"No. I would never hurt you." He shifted in his awkward half-kneeling position in the mud, adjusting Haelyn's weight in the crooks of his arms so that she was sitting on his one knee. "Can't you tell who I am, Doll?" His voice drawled. She shrunk away from the sweet name he called her. She stared, searching his face for an answer. "I'm your daddy."

"Paul Burning," I whispered the name my mother had uttered in the worst of moods, when she didn't think I was watching or listening. I knew the name of my father's killer. "You." My hand rose slowly from my side, like it had a mind of its own. "You're the one who killed my dad." His head swung to me, eyes unwilling to break from the lock on his daughter's face. His aura shifted and swayed, burning bright red and undercut with black. He rose, setting Haelyn to the ground gently.

"So." He stepped toward me, his movements rocking him side to side, like weights hung from his shoulders. Haelyn looked at him then at me and back again. "You are the spawn of the devil herself." I pulled away from his approach. His smile spread, stretching his cheeks into grooved corners that framed a crooked set of yellow teeth.

"You better not be talking about my mom." My hands clenched at my sides. I shivered. Maybe because in the early morning hours it was cold and my sweatshirt was soaked in rainwater. Maybe because I was angry. Maybe because I was scared.

"I most certainly am. I'm just surprised Haelyn wasn't wiped out already like she did to her mama." Haelyn's mouth stretched open. She looked at me with the question on her face.

"He's lying, Haelyn. My mom wouldn't just kill somebody. It was the Hawkman who killed her with the Ganagi."

"No, Haelyn, your mama, Cynthia Burning has been dead for nearly as long as you've been alive. Edythe Turner was your mom's sister. This one," Paul Burning pointed carelessly to the corpse of Haelyn's brother. "He was Edythe's child. Your cousin."

"Don't talk about him like that," Haelyn walked over to me and grabbed my hand.

It didn't matter to her what the man had called him. Devon was her brother. He'd been overtaken and tortured and now he was dead. She leaned into me, silent tears slipping down her cheeks.

Paul Burning shuffled up to us. "Are you siding with them?"

She didn't turn. Didn't look at this new enemy. I could feel his presence hanging there, impatient, ready to move, ready to act, but torn at his daughter's sorrow and refusal. "Honey, he was just your cousin. I had to release the Hawkman. Don't you see? Without him, the Bitten would have known immediately who it was." She yanked her dark gaze up to him.

"You did this?" He took a step back. Haelyn's hand tightened around mine. "You made Devon be taken over by that thing?"

"I didn't know," he said. "It was the only way I could be with you again."

"It made him so sick! The thing in him tortured him. And I had to kill him. Because he was going to kill Aubry."

Her face was a hard mask. Paul Burning lifted his hands. "Baby girl, it had to be that way. I'm sorry it took your cousin –"

"Brother," Haelyn shouted, squeezing my hand so it hurt. She took a step toward Paul Burning.

"Okay, Okay." He gestured with his open hands face-forward in a slow-down movement. "Your brother. But, honey, be reasonable. Don't you want to have someone around that understands you? That understands the hunger?" Haelyn's hand loosened. She didn't look at her father. He stepped closer. I shied away from his nearness. "Someone that can help you with the magic? Things are going to get better for us now. I can help. Because I'm your daddy." He shuffled closer to Haelyn. She looked up at him.

"My dad died a long time ago. In an oil rig accident."

"No. No, I'm your dad." He kneeled down next to her. "Edythe's husband, your uncle is the one that died in an oil rig accident. I'm still alive."

"I don't care. You killed Devon. Go away." She pushed on his chest. He tottered, his face falling first then turning to a snarl.

"No. I am not going away. You're going to learn to love me. 'Cause I'm your daddy." He grabbed her by both arms, lifting her into the air and shaking her.

"Hey, stop it! Leave her alone," I shouted. Paul Burning stretched a hand toward the Ganagi that had all but melted into the mud. With a flick of his fingers the Ulunsuti stone whizzed through the air toward him. He caught it like a baseball then pocketed it with a quick movement.

"And you." He snatched at my arm. I might be strong, like my mom, but I could not fight the power he had over me. Something other than his own energy pulsed around him, coiling around his arms and chest and legs. As if his anger called it out. "I've got a little surprise for your mama. Let's go meet her, hmmm?" He yanked on our arms, pulling us through the mud toward a set of spiny trees. The image between them shimmered back with tall, giant evergreens, not the swamp we were in.

I pulled on him with all my might. My senses tingled with danger. But, I had fought all night to keep safe. I was tired and hungry and dirty. So when his hand didn't give, I followed him through the gate and into the Heart of the Forest.

THIRTY-NINE ~ RORI - THE HEART OF THE FOREST

Big Brother turned and was once again a giant bear. His black coat shimmered with a fine layer of tiny rain drops. Andy stumbled as he followed through the lightening forest. I grabbed on to him to keep him from falling face first into the mud. He pressed his fingers into his eyebrows. "He's talking to me. In my head. I've never made out words before him. It's loud."

"What's he saying?" I asked, my heart trilling.

"I think I'm going to throw up," Andy said. Miney slipped from his grip. She climbed down, but stayed close. He tripped on nothing, slumped over and true to his word, puked into the mud. I rubbed his back until his stomach was empty. The Udoqua paused and regarded us over his shoulder. When Andy finally stood straight again, wiping at the corners of his mouth, Big Brother sneezed loudly.

"I'm so sorry," Andy said, waving his hands in the air. "I'm not used to people's voices clattering around with my own thoughts." He paused, regarding the bear whose nose twitched as his massive form swayed from side to side. "Okay, we gotta hurry, sis."

"What's going on?" I asked and moved at the same time, gripping Andy around the middle to help support him.

"He's trying to help Aubry. He knows where they are now."

"Where?"

"Come on," he urged and kept moving. "He's going to take us." The bear turned to us. Andy didn't hesitate. He wrapped an arm around the bear's neck, Miney darted forward and grabbed on to Andy's leg.

I followed Andy's lead and wrapped my arm around the other side of Udoqua's neck. The coarse outer fur gave way to the soft undercoat. The bear's breath huffed through its throat, which rattled into my shaky limbs. He smelled of the forest, like pine and loamy earth and air saturated with dew. The animal musk of the bear hung around him, but then there was that something else that evaded my ability to identify. It was something sweet, something cloying that made my mouth water and my gut churn with a sudden hunger. I had never been this close to the ancient ancestor before and now I wondered if he kept his distance for good reason.

"You smell delicious," I told the bear. His dark eyes darted to me and a growl rumbled through his body.

"He says to focus on the task at hand and not be distracted by the taste of magic," Andy told me, his eyes sort of glazing over as he relayed the message.

"That's magic? That's what it smells like?"

"You can smell it too?" Andy looked at me stunned. "So, it's not just our vision."

"But, I can't hear Udoqua." I said.

Andy looked at me over the ears of the bear, his mouth quirked to one side. "Hm... guess that just makes me extra special." I stuck my tongue out at him. That was fine. I didn't want the gift of hearing creatures. That sounded like more of a curse than a blessing.

We walked toward a set of pine trees springing up in a collection of blackberry bushes. Udoqua skirted the prickly growth to a side that opened up to the pair of gate trees. Except no gate shimmered in the space between the dark evergreen trunks. What the veil spell did was to hide the places where gates lived. This was to keep the normal folk from wandering into other lands where dangerous creatures were. Or conversely, to keep the fantastic creatures safe from harm by the normal people.

The gap between the trees opened up to a completely different scene than the forest around us. Stretching away into the semi-darkness and fading stars loomed the giant old growth of evergreen and pine and trees for which we no longer had names. I gripped onto Udoqua's fur more tightly as we headed into the gate. His warm scent covered me and I basked in the glow of forest and tree and root. The smell of earth wafted up from him in heady waves of purest nature. If I could live in that smell, I would.

The bear stepped forward. His muscles moved under the loose hide in rolling waves. I could almost feel the fibers of the muscles bunching and stretching. My feet found their way to the gate like butterfly wings on a breeze.

Passing through was another thing.

The moment my tennis shoe passed the threshold a horrid nausea gripped my insides and shook them like a dog with a bone. The loveliness that was the bear's scent was lost to me in an awful warning that throbbed through my very being. Once over, my arm slipped from around the giant bear's neck and I stumbled forward to the ground. Pine needles bit at the palms of my hands and the aroma wafted up to my burning, sensitive nose.

"What the hell?" I said, holding onto the world so it would quit rocking. Andy was copying me, only he was draped over a nearby tree root.

He panted for a minute before attempting speech. "Big Brother says it's because the Lady is no longer. She was the Heart's gatekeeper. She knew the Bitten were friends of her home and so she had always allowed safe passage. Now that she is passed, the forest is attempting to protect itself. Especially after the attack by the Ani'Kutani. Udoqua is the only reason we were let in."

"Well, I'm so glad the forest is feeling gracious toward Brother Bear." I said, wondering what might have happened if we'd attempted entry without him.

Udoqua turned toward us, stomped both feet in the muddy ground, his fur shaking out the collection of rain drops. A growl ripped from his throat, dry and vibrating, deep and, above all, full of urgency. Andy didn't need to translate. I stumbled away from the ancient being. As I turned away from him and looked at the sunrise peeking over the rocky trail, I saw the beast lumber back through the gate.

"Where is he going? He's not coming with us?" I asked Andy.

"This is the help he's giving." Andy shrugged and reached down to pick Miney up. It's not that I wasn't grateful, I just thought maybe an ancient spirit of beast and forest could be helpful, depending on what was in store for us.

I grabbed Andy's free hand. Aubry was here somewhere. Close, presumably, for the bear to have brought us here. Anxiety gnawed at my gut while my head swam with exhaustion. The forest was so quiet. So sad.

"They're mourning the Lady," Andy said, as if reading my mind.

"I still can't believe it. I can't believe she's gone."

"And Paul Burning is alive in her place."

"He's been the one behind this the whole time." My memory ratcheted back to Tom's show in the house in Georgia. Springing up in my mind's eye were the images of the sacrificial deer, the fire and the broken Hawkman tablet. "He released the Hawkman."

Andy nodded, his eyes growing then narrowing as he peered down the path stretching away under an archway of giant pine and cedar. The sky lightened by the second.

"Then murdered the Lady of the Forest," I added. Of course, he had sought out the most powerful being he could find, kill and then be fueled by the magic. He needed the fuel for one more act. An act that would both restore the broken veil and put him in power over the Dragon Bitten. My mind traced away at possible futures which held a gaping place where Aubry was, and a world in which Paul Burning had possession of the Ulunsuti stone fueled by the blood of the Bitten, which was infused with the Uktena's venom.

Palpitations stole away my breath. I clutched at my chest as the pain sliced up to my collarbone and through my shoulder blade. Andy squeezed my hand. "Rori, take a deep, slow breath." I obeyed, fighting the panic that left me panting and seeing stars in my periphery. "Look at me, sis." Andy looked back at me with warm golden eyes. "I know it's scary, but we're going to get through this, okay?"

"Will Aubry?" My voice rattled out the question. He kept his mouth closed for a moment, as if considering what to say. Then, slowly he nodded.

"I don't know," he finally said and his voice cracked. "But, she definitely won't be if we don't hurry." I took two more calming breaths, not to ease the worry, but to calm my body enough to move forward.

"Okay, I think I'm okay now." Andy released my hand and looked down the path.

"Straight ahead," he said. The trail ahead bent north and out of sight. I marched forward, Andy at my side, a grim look of determination forcing the corners of his mouth down. Miney clung to his neck, her eyes wide and sparkling in the gray and green light of the forest. There were no critters around. The hair on the nape of my neck sprang up at the eerie quiet draping the morning like a thick, wet blanket.

The trail narrowed and we were abruptly scrambling through bramble growing at the feet of the giants. Vines scratched at my bare arms. I winced, pulled the plant from where it had found purchase in my golden skin and moved on. A bend in the small path turned us more south then bent back east. I rounded the corner to the sound of tinkling water. The clearing opened up in front of me. Dark dirt littered with acorn shells and old pine needles housed a large fallen cedar log. Over the smell of water and soil and pine, a cloying sweetness grabbed at my nose. I knew that smell.

Scanning the clearing for the wearer of the overwhelming scent, I saw her. My Aubry.

I stumbled forward. "Aubry!" Tears fled my eyes. She was alive. She still wore the little purple sweatshirt and jeans from yesterday. Her face and clothes were covered in mud. She looked at me through smudges of dirt.

"Mama!" I took two steps toward her when a voice cut through me and stalled my forward momentum.

"Rori Cantrell. It's been a while. Glad you could make it."

My head swiveled to the right. Haelyn stood in tattered and dirty hand-me-down clothes covered in blood next to a man I'd thought dead for the last nine years. Hatred sprang through me like fire catching to lighter fluid. A snarl ripped out of my mouth through gritted teeth. An aching need to plunge a knife in my enemy's throat made my fingers twitch at my sides.

Paul Burning stared back at me, clad in jeans and an olive green sweatshirt. His skin was dark with exposure to the sun. Paul kicked a heavy boot in the dirt and propped a hand on one hip. A sly smile crept across his face.

"I see you're surprised to see me. It wasn't easy getting in here." He gestured around the heart of the forest.

"You released the Hawkman. And broke the veil," I stated. "You killed the Lady of the Forest." All over Waynesville there were sure to be creatures dying. Startled by their appearance people would react to the strange unknown with violence. My insides quivered. An entire population of creatures would be snuffed out. And to fix it?

"Well, I can't take all the credit," he said, the smile plastering his face made one corner of his nose quirk. "I had some help." He gestured to Haelyn. "And this." He pulled the Ulunsuti stone from his jeans pocket and tossed it up and down in the air before replacing it. "Let me introduce you. This is Haelyn, my daughter. I'd love to introduce you to my wife, but she died nine years ago. Because of you." He jabbed a calloused finger in the air in my direction, sly smile turning to a sneer.

"And then you attacked me with the Ganagi, killing my husband and yourself." My bones turned to ice, my muscles lapping up the burst of venom in my veins, fueling me through the exhaustion. But more than anger, a tickling excitement thrilled through me at the thought of killing my husband's killer. I'd been denied the opportunity because he had killed himself. Or so I had thought. "And now you're standing here, and I'm guessing up to no good babysitting these two girls." Haelyn looked at me, her eyes wide as if she were surprised at the extension of my protection over her. Ani'Kutani or not, she was still a little girl.

"Soon to be one little girl." His eyes darted toward my daughter. Aubry pulled her legs into her chest and wrapped her arms around them. Her body shook slightly as her wide golden eyes darted around the clearing. Then her head slowed, her face lifted to a breeze rustling through the trees. Her hunched shoulders loosened, falling away from her ears. A light smile touched her mouth. It took a moment before I understood.

Andy stood behind me and lightly touched my back. I looked over my shoulder and gave an imperceptible nod. Paul Burning moved toward Aubry in two long strides. I jumped forward across the clearing, but not in time. Paul held my daughter, her back against him, the same jagged knife to her throat that had killed the Lady of the Forest. I growled, the dragon's voice erupting from me and filling the clearing with my obvious hatred. Haelyn's cry competed with my voice. "No, please, don't hurt her!"

"Baby girl, I have to now. The veil is broken. If we leave it that way all those creatures we use to fuel our magic will get killed." Aubry's small face was unburdened by fear. Her mouth was set, her eyes soft.

"That's right," she said. "You have to kill me. The veil has to be healed." She turned to me. I could barely see her through the haze of tears. "Mama, I think that's what the Lady meant. This is my unique power. This is what I'm meant to do."

"No," I muttered. "That can't be. I'll keep it from happening. I'll protect you."

"But, remember what she said, Mama?" Paul kept on holding the knife to her throat, a crooked grin on his face, knowing he'd won, knowing Aubry was right. "She said it's not your fault and you have to let people help make things right. You have to let me do this," she said. She leaned forward against the blade, hissing as blood trickled from the cut. I screamed.

Haelyn did too. "Don't hurt her!" she shouted. "She saved my life. She's my friend." As she spoke the air in the little clearing sucked in on itself, growing still and quiet. Her hair slowly began to rise around her ears. The knife pressing into Aubry's throat moved away from her neck. Paul's forearm muscles bulged with effort. My heart eased only a little. Aubry looked patiently resigned at her friend.

"You have to let this happen, Haelyn," she said. Was that true? Was it right?

"I have to know," I said to stall and wracking my brain to find another way out of a situation to which I could see no other choice, "how'd you do it? How'd you survive the Ganagi?"

"It wasn't fucking easy," he said. Aubry swallowed around the knife at her neck. A new trickle of blood ran down her olive skin and into the neckline of her sweatshirt. My insides quivered. Paul shifted, resituating his grip on Aubry's upper arm, relaxing his fight against the magic his daughter was putting on his hand to restrain the knife. "I prepared myself. Before I took the Ganagi on. Why do you think my body wasn't mangled?

Yes, I saw you look at me, thinking I was dead. I saw your husband impaled on the tree." He laughed while barbed wire squeezed around the tender bits of my heart meant for Jameson alone. My jaw clenched against the image Paul painted in my memory's eye.

"If I hadn't been out of it from the spell, I would have danced on the hood of your car." Hatred rolled through me.

"And what was the cost of the spell? What was the sacrifice?" All Ani'Kutani magic operated on sucking away life. There was only one source powerful enough for that kind of magic. Only one living entity that could grant a boost so big as to resurrect the dead. Paul faltered, grinding his jumbled teeth as a dullness settled in his black eyes. "I guess I should say, 'who was the sacrifice'?"

His grip loosened on the knife. He glanced at Haelyn, licked his lips, frowned. "It had to have been a child," I continued, seeing how it rattled him. "An infant, I'd guess. And one of your own." Haelyn's quizzical gaze on her father turned to shock.

"You killed my brother or sister?" Her mouth fell open, her dark eyes startled to saucers in her paling face. Paul refused to look at his daughter.

"She was dying, baby. Born with half a heart. And you poor mama got a bad infection of the blood from birthing you two. The doctors couldn't help them." He was shaking when he said it. He adjusted Aubry in his arms, shifting from foot to foot. The nimbus of the Lady's life he'd absorbed through the murder throbbed around him, made him jumpy with energy. He was like a drug addict going through a high. Had he been jonesing for a fix when he'd murdered his wife and daughter?

"She?" Haelyn whispered. "A sister." She looked at her father, her eyebrows squeezed together over her dark eyes. "So, you killed her? How old was she? What was her name?"

"She was your twin." I nearly fell over. Andy gasped. I felt our connection tighten at the thought of losing each other. Paul rocked again, looked away from Haelyn as he muttered her name, like a confession only a crazy person could utter without remorse. "We named her Vivi – Vivianna. She was a beautiful baby. Full of energy."

Haelyn's face fell to the dirt. I could see the thoughts flooding her young mind. "I had a twin. And you killed her. Killed her so that you could kill more people. You killed a little baby. You left me alone with my aunt and she was mean to me. You took everything! And then you left me! For years. And I never knew. I never knew why I didn't belong and why all of the creatures hated me. And it wasn't even my fault. Then you came back and released that thing on my brother!" Andy and I inhaled. It had been Devon.

"Devon was the Hawkman," Andy hissed at me. Haelyn had been living with a demon for weeks. Tears streamed down Haelyn's face as she screamed. "Do you even care what that was like?" She swiped at her face and smoothed her features. Then she raised a hand and gestured in the air at her father.

"No -," he shouted then hurtled through the air. His body crashed into a giant pine and crumpled to the dark forest floor. Aubry was yanked by the momentum of Haelyn's push on her father and skidded across the clearing. Before Aubry had time to push herself up Andy and I rushed in for her. I scooped her up, relief washing over me at the feel of her warm and alive body in my arms again. Andy stood in front of us like a shield.

Paul growled. "Haelyn Burning!" He gripped the knife as he yelled her name.

"That's not my last name. You left me. You killed my twin and my brother! You aren't my dad." She stood with her feet in a wide stance, her fists clenched at her sides, her chin to her chest as she stared at the man that claimed his parentage on her. She refused it.

"You're my child and you'll do as I say." He took a step toward her.

"No."

"Yes, you will!" he shouted at her. "Get your friend from them and bring her to me."

"No. I won't. And you can't make me."

"You idiot! You stupid little girl! Don't you see she has to die now? Only her blood will heal the veil. And I can teach you. I can teach you to use your power. It can be so wonderful. The feeling of their life force inside of you. It's like no other sensation." He was looking up and away, lost in the feel of stolen life. His aura was a throbbing mass of black. The sickness of his addiction to killing leaked out into the clearing, choking me. Haelyn held up her hands, coated in dried blood.

"I don't want any more power." Her face streamed with tears, her body shaking. "My brother was with that demon I had to kill. I am not helping you! I will stop you!"

"Baby girl, this is all for you. This is so we don't have to live under their thumb." He jabbed a finger in my direction. "They're what's wrong with our lives. If it weren't for them, your Mama would still be here. Your sister would still be here. Your cousin would still be here. Besides. He wasn't even your brother." He said the words, but the need written in his eyes was the ruler of his intention.

"He was my brother! He loved me more than you ever did!"

Paul shook his head, lips lost in a grimace. "Haelyn. You don't know what you're saying. You're sticking up for these people and they'll do nothing but put a knife in your throat, first chance they get."

"That's not true! Aubry saved me. Mrs. Cantrell is nice to me."

"Honey, that woman killed your mother."

"You're a liar!" Aubry shouted. "Mama wouldn't do that."

"She did do that. By keeping me from the Velith, she forced her death. I could have saved her. She's a murderer."

"You're the only murderer here," Haelyn accused.

"You'll remember you love me. You just need some time. I'm the only one that can take care of you and give you a life you deserve." He shuffled a few steps away then pressed his hand into the pine and muttered something. A green nimbus surrounded him as the tree cracked and groaned. The noise split through the air, the dying tree crying out as its life source sucked away into the Ani'Kutani. The pine twisted, splintering in the middle and showering Paul in a spray of bark and sap. He flinched as splinters hit his face, but rose to his full height as he stared at Haelyn. She stared back in defiance, her hands back at her sides and clenched around the blood of her cousin.

The tree shook, casting the ground below in a rain of pinecones and needles. I covered Aubry's face with my own. Andy turned, grabbing on to me in an embrace that protected Aubry in a cocoon. Miney clung to Andy's leg. Broken pieces of the tree pelted my head and back. Twigs fell onto us and then a heavier branch smacked into my exposed back, the impact erupting with a burning sensation across the skin.

Andy yelped as his embrace lurched away from Aubry and me. I stumbled forward and looked up in time to see Andy thrown into a boulder at the edge of the clearing closest to where we had entered. "Andy!" He lay on the ground, his face in the dirt.

My grip on Aubry slackened and I tightened my muscles around her. "I'm not letting you go, baby girl." I scrambled over to Andy, shaking his shoulder to wake him. "Andy!" His head rose, his breath quickening. He pushed himself up from the ground as the tree rained pine and bark on us. Andy stood next to me, stumbling back against the boulder as he watched Paul Burning.

Paul's face was a mask of pleasure, cast in a jittery, eerie green as he stretched his hand toward my daughter, his other hand gripping the dying tree. The giant evergreen groaned, twisting and bending over the lake. A crack louder than the closest thunder resounded through the clearing. Aubry clapped her hands over her ears. Andy wrapped an arm around me and Aubry. Miney gripped onto Andy's leg. The tree, broken in half, fell away from the Ani'Kutani.

Birds in the distance sent out a cry of distress. The smash of the tree exploded across the forest. Paul grunted, his teeth bared, and yanked on the invisible hold he had on Aubry. Our grip was not enough. Not even with the two people that loved her more than anything in the world. It still wasn't enough. We grasped desperately as the pull intensified. "No, no, no, no!" Andy shouted. And just like that, she was out of my safety again. She reached for me as she flew from my arms. Her face resigned. My stomach fell into itself. Miney chased after Aubry. Andy reached out for her, but she was already halfway across the clearing.

Paul's arm wrapped around Aubry's shoulders as he raised the knife. He giggled, showing his crooked teeth. The swirling mass of energy around him wobbled around his body. It was overkill. She was small, my daughter. It would not take so much pressure to kill her. Paul's biceps and forearms flexed around his grip on the blade's handle.

"Mama!" The knife came down. I cried out. I even closed my eyes for a moment. Not wanting to see the blow that killed my daughter and healed the veil. The blow delivered by the same man that killed my husband. When I opened my eyes again, Miney was standing in front of Paul, her arms outspread. She screamed. The note resounded like an opera singer crying for help. All things fell silent as the noise stretched away on the gray morning light. I cringed at the volume. But the note was not for mourning. This was a magic older than the Ani'Kutani's power and it had stopped the momentum of the knife.

Paul's face crumpled. Bits of the amassing energy flew away from him.

"Keep it up, Miney!" I shouted. The auras of the lives he'd taken wisped away from him like smoke caught in the wind. Miney was sending the energy away, draining Paul of his power. Within moments, all the green energy of the tree and some of the golden white energy of the Lady had dissipated. He screamed in frustration as the knife fell from his grip.

Aubry shoved his arm off her shoulders and ran to the little yunwi. Dropping to her knees, she reached for the creature. Miney stopped screaming, reaching her arms out for the embrace Aubry offered.

Haelyn ran toward Aubry, her eyes darting between her and her father. She was steps away when Paul lurched to his feet, heaving great lungfuls of air. He shook his head and groaned, gripping his head with his free hand. "You little shit," he shouted. Stumbling, he dashed toward Aubry and Miney. Both Ani'Kutani raced for my daughter.

Aubry turned from the embrace she had on the yunwi, protecting Miney behind her back. Paul's eyes were locked onto Aubry, a snarl ripping from the horrible look of empty hunger and hatred. He raised the knife, falling to his knees to get himself closer. I pushed off to run to her. There was no way I would get to her in time. Aubry stared at him, brows drawn together, teeth clenched. Paul skidded toward her. Finally within range, his arm arced toward Aubry. Aubry bared her chest, closed her eyes, arms open to receive the death blow. Haelyn dove. A sickening crunch pierced the air.

Haelyn gasped around the knife in her chest as she looked into her father's eyes. "Haelyn." Paul's voice cracked around the name. The two syllables trembled with disappointment, with chagrin, with grief.

Haelyn swallowed, gurgled, her breath hitched. Paul pulled the knife from her tiny chest. Her eyes yanked wide open momentarily and she cried in pain. Paul set the knife on the ground, cupped Haelyn's head in his big hand and lowered his daughter gently to the forest floor. Blood poured out of the open wound, soaking the old gray t-shirt in scarlet. Aubry scooped up Miney and scrambled to me.

Paul leaned over his daughter. Tears pouring from his eyes, he uttered, "Why'd you do that?"

"She –" Haelyn gulped, her eyes rolling around, her breath shallow. "She's good. My friend. I wanted to be good. Like her."

"Not like me," Paul said. I could almost feel the dawning of truth breaking over Paul's soul. The regret of years of wrong choices glinted in his dark eyes as he saw the sacrifice his daughter made, her right choice. She chose to save a life instead of taking it.

His face crumpled in on itself. Tears poured down his cheeks, splattering Haelyn's tattered t-shirt that blossomed red with her blood. Rustling in the trees behind us, made me turn. Udoqua strode into the clearing. He lifted his nose to the air. Aubry jumped up and ran to him. She threw her arms around his neck.

"Help her!" The giant bear tenderly lay his massive head against hers. Momentarily, my child was lost from sight behind the creature we called Big Brother. Then he straightened and Aubry backed away. The bear lumbered toward Paul and Haelyn. Two steps and then the bear shimmered and in its place stood a man.

On his shoulders hung his bearskin, a mantle of black and glistening fur. His legs were clad in leather pants, but his muscled chest and abs were bare. His face was a perfect mask of solemnity and sorrow.

He whispered over the ground and knelt next to Paul and the dying Haelyn. Her eyes shifted toward him and grew large. Her mouth hung open and lungs heaved shallow and quick. But he was not looking at Haelyn. He locked blue eyes with Paul Burning. Paul shook, rocking slowly as he cradled his daughter's head in his hand.

Andy sat in the dirt with Miney in his lap. A gash lined his forehead. "Andy, you're hurt," I told him. Half of his face was hidden behind a sheet of blood. He pressed a hand to his forehead and pulled back to find his fingertips red. He wiped it on his jeans then pulled his gray sweatshirt off, carefully folded it into a small rectangle, and pressed it to the wound.

"It's a vascular area. It'll be fine." Big Brother turned at the sound of Andy's voice.

"You are Healer," he said and pointed to Andy.

Andy's eyes went wide. "Well –" he stuttered, "Yes, I am a doctor."

"No," Big Brother cut the air between them with the word. "You hear the heart. The soul. You are Healer. Come." He motioned Andy over. Andy looked at me with eyes as big as plates. He stood, sweatshirt still pressed to the wound on his head, and walked over to Big Brother. Once he had settled next to the trio, Big Brother looked back into Paul Burning's eyes.

"Give us the stone," he said. Paul's jaw clenched. "Or she will die and I will curse you to walk the land with me and know your regret for eternity." Big Brother's words growled with the voice of the bear. Paul reached into his jeans pocket and pulled out the Ulunsuti stone. He handed it to Big Brother, who took it ceremoniously with one hand cupping and the other hand covering. Udoqua bowed his head over the stone. The shrill of the Ulunsuti's call fluttered through me. I grabbed onto Aubry to distract myself from my lust for the stone.

Andy looked down at Haelyn, laid aside his sweatshirt and knelt over her. Haelyn's breath hitched twice, the thump of her heart slowing until it stopped.

A rushing noise like being caught in a wind tunnel filled the little opening. Everyone in the clearing lifted their heads, turning this way and that to understand the source of the noise. The world shimmied around us. Trees vibrated and groaned. The call of the underwater panther warbled from far off, joined by the sound of flyers' song, yunwi and dreamcatchers and giants. Their voices lifted to the air as the veil re-wove itself with the sacrifice of this Ani'Kutani girl, descendant of the same bloodline as the Bitten.

"She's gone," Andy said without looking up. And there it was. A lovely golden aura hovering just above her body. Her lips were pale, her body still.

"You feel this," Big Brother said and pressed a fist to his muscled chest, "In here."

Andy looked up at him, his mouth quirked to one side. "Yes," he confirmed.

"This is magic that you feel. Life is magic. Her magic is fading, but it is not gone yet. What do you feel of him?" He gestured to Paul.

Andy turned to Burning, his lips sneered. "Darkness."

"Under the darkness," Big Brother said. Andy looked at Big Brother, studying his eyes and face. Then he turned back to Paul who stared at his dead daughter.

"Fear, regret, self-loathing..."

"Under," Big Brother emphasized the word with patience. Andy took a deep breath and closed his eyes, letting the air flow back out of his lungs. He was quiet for a long moment.

"Love," Andy said finally. "I sense his love and pride for his daughter. Love for his wife. He is amazed at Haelyn's courage."

"There is the magic you will use." Big Brother smiled slightly at him. He turned to Paul. "Do you want your daughter to live?" Paul's silence broke and sobs burst from his mouth.

"I'll do anything." Big Brother nodded solemnly, looking at Paul down the length of his straight nose.

"So be it. Clasp the stone." Paul put a hand on top of the stone. "Now, Healer, you must transfer his love to her and call her magic back to her." Andy looked at Big Brother. I could see the question on his face: "how?", but he never spoke it. He simply looked at Big Brother, seeking the answer in the ancient one's gaze. Then, as if he had plucked it from Big Brother's brain, he nodded.

Placing a hand on Paul's shoulder and the other on Haelyn's chest, Andy bowed his head. Big Brother placed his empty hand onto Andy's shoulder. Andy's breath caught, his shoulders hunching up. That was the power of the stone coursing through him. I recalled the feeling, the sheer delight of the magic made available from the venom in every fiber of my being. I twitched at the thought.

"Mama, what's wrong?" Aubry asked.

"The stone is powerful. It calls to my blood."

"That's what that is?" she asked.

"You feel it?"

"Mm-hmm… it sorta tickles."

Andy's breath came heavily in and out. His nostrils flared and lips pressed together. The golden aura from Lady Adohi's life Paul had absorbed shone around him and mingled with a rose red. The colors shifted around each other, first slowly then gaining speed into a vortex of twirling light. Andy pressed his eyes shut tighter. Paul gasped, leaning to one side, nearly falling over. His skin paled to gray, his eyes rolling back in his head.

"I love you, Haelyn," He looked down at his daughter, her face still, her breath absent.

"Keep going," Big Brother urged. Andy, eyes still closed, had the face of a man deadlifting three times his weight.

Paul's shoulders slumped. He looked down at his daughter as his breath quickened. Pain crossed his face. He closed his eyes to it then opened them again with a grunt of effort as he looked at his progeny. His eyes were full of an aching determination.

Paul bowed his head, fighting to not pant. He still held her head. The light and colors twisted up his body, first leaving his stomach and coalescing around his heart, shoulders and head. They bent over, like a surreal slinky falling to the next step. "You be good, hon'. Be good like I couldn't be."

As the light leaked into Haelyn's body, it left Paul. He threw his head back and grunted. I could only imagine the pain he was in. He slumped over, his body falling with a thud to the ground. Gray and weak, a hole in his chest opened like a rose blooming in summer. His blood blotted the olive green shirt, a puddle forming under him. He wheezed and gurgled. A trickle of blood snaked out of the corner of his mouth and dripped onto the ground. He looked at Haelyn from where he lay in the mud, fighting for every last breath. The golden aura floating above

Haelyn descended, touching onto her chest then slowly absorbing into her heart where the knife had plunged.

When the orb was gone, Haelyn gasped. And with one last wet breath, Paul looked on his daughter and smiled.

FORTY ~ RORI - LOST AND FOUND

We were all covered in varying degrees of filth, composed of blood and mud. Andy still had the stone and a shimmering rainbow pulsed around his body. Big Brother had left, his work complete. He had saved the life of a child. In another life, he'd failed. In this one he succeeded. Aubry and Haelyn led us to the lesser gate where they'd entered the heart of the forest. The swampy area of the broken gate squelched under our shoes.

I caught my breath as we nearly stumbled over Devon's body. I wrapped Haelyn into the side of my body, using it as a shield to her view. She didn't need to see him like this again. I squeezed her, wondering about the toll this whole thing would take on her soul. She wrapped her arms around my waist and sobbed into me.

We marched past the corpse of the giant creature. Its skin was drawn back away from exposed teeth. Its eyes stared without seeing. I bit back the questions. There would be time for telling later.

Miney was cradled in Andy's arms. Sunlight cut through the still air and jammed into my tired eyes. When we came to a stop at the gate, I swayed with exhaustion. My body ached, my eyes burned, my spirit was heavy. But that was all bearable with the feel of my daughter's hand clasped firmly in mine.

"One last thing to do, girls." I told them. With Haelyn on my left and Aubry on my right, they peered up to me. "There are two missing critters. And we can't heal the gate until they're back inside."

The remaining shards still clinging to the arched tree limbs forming the gate glimmered in the morning light. On the other side, Tom stood next to my mom with wide eyes. Andy shuffled, Miney still held in his arms as he looked out toward the lake to our right instead of at Mom. She darted a glance toward her son then hung her head, her shoulders rolling forward. I didn't want her here, but I wasn't too proud to get her help to fix all this.

I turned away from that situation and knelt next to the girls. "You've been through so much already. Do you think you can be brave one more time?" Aubry nodded. Haelyn looked away from me and out into the sky, blue and boiling with white and gray storm clouds. Sunshine grew then eased and grew again. Haelyn held black bags under tired eyes. The reflection of the clouds and sky skittered across her dark eyes.

She looked down at me from where I squatted in the mud. "One more time?" she asked, her eyebrows pinched. Tears gathered and spilled down her round, dirt-smudged cheeks. I nodded. "And then, I don't want to ever use magic again."

"I'll never make you," I promised.

"Okay. I'll do it." I rose and reached toward Tom and Mom. "The tablet, please." Tom looked pretty worse for the wear. His curly mop of dark hair fell around his thick glasses as he reached in the pocket of his board shorts. His flip-flop covered feet were crusted in dirt and mud which licked up his shins and stained his shirt. He pulled the pieces of the birdman tablet from his pocket and shuffled forward, extending a closed fist to me. I shook my head.

"No, Haelyn must do this. She's the only one strong enough." I didn't say why. I didn't say that by killing her cousin, Devon, and releasing the Hawkman she'd imbued herself with blood magic. And not just blood. Blood of both a relative and blood that'd been infused with the power of an ancient spirit. Nobody needed to hear that. She looked up at me, worry written in her drawn eyebrows and thin frown. I nodded to her. "You can do this. We're all here for you."

Andy lowered Miney to the ground and stood next to Haelyn as she opened her hand to Tom. Mom stood to the right of Tom. We circled the threshold of the broken gate. Aubry clasped my hand while Miney trotted over and took Aubry's hand. I placed a hand onto Haelyn's shoulder, while Andy took the opposite one then reached for Mom's hand. She hesitated.

"You don't get a choice." Andy's voice cut through the morning air. "Your opinion counts for shit right now, and probably forever." His breath hitched around anger as he grabbed at her hand. She ground her teeth and lowered her head. Next to her, Tom fidgeted.

"So, should I, like, step away, er..."

"You're a part of this, friend. And I'll let you in on a little secret." He looked at me, mouth gaping. "Everyone has magic to one degree or another. You see the creatures even through the veil, though not always clearly. So, I'm guessing your magic is stronger than others'." He still stood there, just staring. "Grab a hand, man." He startled and reached for mom's hand. Turning, he nearly jumped as he looked down at Miney, who lifted a hand to Tom, gazing at him with sparkling black eyes. Slowly, he extended his hand.

"Haelyn," Mom said. "Take the two pieces in either hand and hold it up for the Hawk to find." Haelyn fumbled with the broken tablet, the pieces pinched in her small hands. "Okay, people. Focus all of your thought, all your attention on the Hawkman and call him back."

Andy and I had a hand each rested on Haelyn's small shoulders. She brought the tablet up, the pieces facing each other where the crack had split it apart. Her breath slowed, her eyes half closing. Her tattered t-shirt, ripped and stained, hung around her small body. She swayed to some unheard song. The rhythm picked its way through the circle and soon we all joined in.

Haelyn's tiny voice grew from tentative to a steely soprano as she chanted, "Hawkman, Hawkman, Hawkman…" Her arms shivered. Her breath caught. "He's here!"

"It's okay," I said. "We're all here." Haelyn's arms dropped several inches. Her eyes were seas of fear.

"Haelyn," Aubry said from across the circle. "It's going to be okay. Keep going." Flames burst into the air of the clearing. Tom stumbled back, screaming out. Mom kept him safely in his position in the circle. The flame shivered. Blue-fringed orange fire raised unreal wings. The Hawkman cried out, a sound like the darkest spaces of Hell in the voice of a hawk's cry. Haelyn shivered, crying out, tears spilling down her stained cheeks.

The Hawkman billowed, growing in size. Heat brushed my face with searing fingers.

"I can't do this!" Haelyn cried.

"Yes, you can!" Aubry shouted. She raised her hand, mine following with it. Gesturing toward the Hawkman, I felt the power gather around her. The hair along my arms sprang to attention.

"What are you doing?" My mom shouted past the roar of the flame.

Without breaking her gaze on the monster in front of her, Aubry answered: "Helping." And then the power left her tiny body with the percussion of a bass being strummed with the amp turned to full blast. Vibrations jolted the center of my torso. My ears popped on the sound of it then rang in an insistent whine. The Hawkman's twisted man and bird face snarled in Aubry's direction. It flapped its fiery wings as if to raise itself and launch toward my daughter, but went nowhere. It flung its head left then right, thrashing against the invisible hold Aubry had on him.

Haelyn looked past me at Aubry, at the determination glinting in her golden eyes. Could so much fierceness live in a nine-year-old? In a sweet thing like my daughter? Haelyn raised her hands again, the shiver still echoing into my clasp on her shoulder.

I looked at the Hawkman. There was something I could do to help. Inhaling deeply, I opened my mouth and roared with dragon voice. The demon in the center of our circle cringed. Mom caught my eye before turning to the flame in the center. Gripping Andy's and Tom's hands she inhaled and let the dragon roar fly from her mouth. Andy's eyes were half lidded and I knew he'd already been working his own magic on the Hawkman, coaxing it into the tablet.

Miney's voice joined the dragon roars, her high notes picking out a tune that rang in a sharp staccato. It tripped along, growing in intensity, gathering speed and force. The Hawkman shrank, the blue flames extinguished. It inched toward Haelyn, fighting every centimeter. Haelyn raised the broken tablet high. The pieces etched with the image of the Hawkman sparked and smoked as the dark entity that had been released, flame by flame, was sucked into the stone.

Haelyn screamed as the flames surrounded her outstretched arms.

"It's burning her!" Tom shouted. There was nothing we could do about it. The thing had to be done. I roared louder. Aubry's power intensified. Miney's song rose. The flame shrank into the tablet. Haelyn didn't let it drop. She held the pieces even as fire licked up her arms, the skin on her hands sizzling and bubbling.

With a deafening screech the head of the Hawkman sank into the pieces of stone. As the last flame extinguished the tablet snapped together. Haelyn let it go, screaming in agony as her arms smoked like charred wood. It thunked into the ground, smoking for a moment before extinguishing, looking more like something you'd find in a museum than an ancient talisman holding so much evil.

Haelyn trembled. Andy ran to her, scooping her up before sitting down with her on a nearby log. The stink of burning flesh wafted over the broken gate. Andy wrapped Haelyn up in an encompassing embrace. "Aubry, y'all call back the demon dog. I'll tend to Haelyn." Aubry nodded.

We closed the small circle with Mom's hand finding mine. Aubry barely closed her eyes when the sound of thudding feet echoed across the plain. Aubry smiled. The demon dog came into view. He ran full speed toward the gate, tongue lolling out of a mouth filled with wickedly sharp teeth. I suspected it was smiling, but under the ember-colored eyes, the stretched mouth looked more menacing than friendly.

"Tom and Grandma," Aubry said, "you should move." They quickly obliged, Tom's flip-flops sounding off as the demon dog bounded through the gate. A deep rumble of a growl echoed across the field and into the gate. The ground shook with the noise. Tom jumped.

"Oh my god, your daughter," he screamed. He started toward her, but Mom held him back.

"Chill out," she said, "and watch." She pointed. The demon dog of Valle Crucis came to a screeching halt in front of Aubry, leaning down to level its head to her. Its short stub of a tail wagged. Aubry giggled as it nudged into her belly. She rubbed the nose of the giant animal with her tiny hand. Its breath blew Aubry's matted hair up in gusts.

"Good dog," she told him and laid her head on his nose. Her eyes closed as she rubbed absently at his gray skin. The dog's eyes followed suit as he lowered his massive body to the ground.

Tom stared at the spectacle with an open mouth. "Whoa. That's just... unreal." He nudged at his thick glasses with a knuckle and went on staring.

"Looks like it's just you and me now," I told Mom. "Time to heal the gate." She nodded. The lump in her throat was almost visible. The woman who'd birthed and raised us then doubted her own child's love and humanity had nothing to say. She looked up into my face. Her bottle-dark hair had gray peeking out at the roots. The skin around her chin and neck was wrinkled. Her golden eyes were tired and cast in purplish fatigue. I wondered if she'd cried.

"I'm just sorry –"

"Stop right there." I held a hand up then lowered all but my index finger. "You don't talk to me about this. You talk to the son you thought was a monster. You work it out with him." I stabbed the finger toward Andy. Mom lowered her head again, a huff of a sigh taking the place of so many words I wouldn't allow her to say to me. "Let's heal the gate. Then you can work on healing the broken relationship with your child. If you can get past your issues."

"I never thought he was a monster," she said. "I only knew the potential."

"No, you only knew one side of the potential. You never considered what he truly is."

"You're right. I didn't."

"I'm glad you realize that. Because tonight, I couldn't have gotten Aubry back without Andy." I looked over at him, his aura still pulsing with rainbows of light from holding the Ulunsuti stone. He held Haelyn's burned hands, the darkened skin getting lighter in shades by the moment. I nudged a chin in his direction. "Look. Look at your son. Does that look like something a monster would do?"

Mom looked over at him from where she'd been fixated on the muddy ground. The sunshine was hanging above the horizon. The air was warming, the breeze carrying away the moisture from the rain the night before. Her mouth fell slightly. "How's he doing that?"

"That's his magic: healing. You should have seen what he did an hour ago." I crossed my arms feeling smug at the amount of evidence I had of Andy's un-monsterishness. She inhaled deeply, letting it flow back out. Haelyn watched Andy intently as the magic he worked by drawing on the Ulunsuti stone healed her. When Andy at last opened his eyes, his body swaying, Haelyn held up her arms as the new skin glistened in the morning sunlight. A smile spread across her face. She turned to Andy, grinning. He grinned back, looking like he'd fall over in exhaustion any second. Haelyn threw her arms around his neck and squeezed. His chuckle rolled out of him. He wrapped his arms around Haelyn and hugged her.

"You did real good. You didn't give up even when you were in pain." She disentangled herself from him, but kept her arms on his shoulders and looked into his eyes for long seconds.

Finally, she spoke. "You're a good person." She smiled then slid from his lap. Startled, he watched her move away. His face crumpled as tears slid from his newly changed eyes. He wiped at his cheeks as his shoulders fell. Mom stood in front of me, tears streaming down her face. Andy's gaze lifted and fell onto Mom. He sat straighter, defiantly. After a moment Mom broke her gaze.

"Let's get this done so we can all go home and sleep. It's been a long night." Her voice was clotted with emotion. She turned toward the gate, her back to Andy, and held out a hand for me. I couldn't know if things would get better between them, but I knew it would get better for Andy. It already had. He was a good person. He'd keep growing and fighting for happiness, despite everything that'd been thrown his way. Or maybe because of everything that'd been thrown his way.

As I grasped Mom's hand in mine and let the venom in my veins course through me I looked out past the broken gate, past the long night and into a new day.

FORTY-ONE ~ RORI - THE END AND THE BEGINNING

December flew upon us faster than I could keep up with. The Christmas lists the girls had given me were longer than I could afford, but it left me room to pick and choose so there were surprises. Today was shopping day and Andy was in town to help and celebrate the holiday. Shopping. His favorite thing. I was sure it was a talent. He was at least as good at shopping as he was at healing.

"Alright, girls!" I yelled. "Time to load up and get to school!" Wuffers's bark broke from the back of the house and giggles floated through the hall and into the living room. Little feet clattered to a crescendo and the girls burst into the living room with Wuffers in hot pursuit, Miney on her back. Miney stroked Wuffers's ears and slid off her back then wrapped her arms around the wolfdog. Wuffers laid her head against the yunwi, her tail wagging then shook free and trotted over to me. I put her food down on the linoleum floor and fluffed her lopsided ears back and forth before she lowered her head to her chow.

Haelyn and Aubry took turns hugging Miney. I handed the girls their backpacks. Aubry was bundled in jeans and a nice sweater Andy had bought her. Haelyn had put on tights, thick boots, a cord skirt and sweater, also picked out by Andy. It turned out she loved clothes and fashion as much as Andy. He had a blast shopping with the girls. I hardly had to buy them clothes.

"Ready to go girls?" I asked them.

"Yes, ma'am." Haelyn nodded. Her recent haircut was cute as snot. She liked it short around her ears and since she'd been with us, we'd been able to get her healthy and her hair shone black and silky. The little pink barrette pulled the long front away from her face. She smiled up at me then grabbed my legs. "I love you." I patted her head, smoothed my hand over her silky hair then grabbed her back.

"I love you too, sweetness." Aubry tackled us.

"I love both of you!" I kissed them both on the cheeks, growling as I did it until they giggled and pulled away. "Andy, we doin' this or what?"

"Coming!" he yelled and trotted out from the guest room, pristinely dressed in nice jeans, a blue striped dress shirt and solid sweater combo. He looked at me with his newly matching eyes. After the veil had been broken and then rehealed by Haelyn's death and rebirth, our eyes had healed as well. His were sea-green with gold radiating from the middle and mine were gold with a sea-green inner ring. And we were both able to see beyond the veil with both eyes.

Andy picked up Miney and gave her a squeeze. "You be a good girl today, okay?" Miney nodded and hugged Andy's neck. He put her down and regarded the girls, who were both waiting patiently by the door. "Looking good girls." Haelyn smiled big at him.

"Thank you," they said in unison. I don't know how we ever lived without Haelyn. Sure the transition had been rough at first. She had been traumatized beyond what any child had been through. Her magic had changed too. She was more like a Bitten. Her death had ended her power as an Ani'Kutani. It was sort of like a reboot.

Both the girls had lots to recover from. Some days they were sad and quiet. Other days, it was as if nothing had happened. We worked through it all, taking time to talk or time to be quiet, whichever needed to happen the most.

As for the short period of time that the veil had been broken: some people in the area had some new mysteries to fuel urban legends for the next century. Tom Bradley, the ghost hunter didn't have enough film, even for the hour or so that the veil had been turned off. He was happy as a clam when we'd seen him after finding Aubry and Haelyn. I offered him the spare bedroom for when he was back in town. I knew he wouldn't find much with the veil being healed, but he was a good guy and deserved a perk for pointing us in the right direction to look for Aubry.

Paul Burning was the name of homicidal legends, for the torture and murders of Edythe and Devon Turner. They were calling it a homicide suicide. It was another new mystery for the locals as well. He was supposed to have already been dead. So, now the rumor circulating was that he still wasn't really dead.

I pushed my feet into my sneakers and pulled on my coat. The girls trundled out of the house, backpacks strapped over their winter coats. Andy slipped through the door. I was just about to leave when Josh stumbled out of my bedroom. Bleary eyed, he flopped up to me on bare feet, his bare chest exposed to the chill wafting through the door. The scars across his torso were wicked and still raised and red. It made him look like a badass, which he kinda was.

"Hey, sleepy-head," I said. He knuckled his blue eyes and grumbled. The waves on his head were a messy tangle. He glowed with health again. I opened my arms up and he fell onto me.

"Sorry I slept in," he mumbled into my ear. Shivers ran down my neck where his breath brushed my skin. "I love you. You know that?"

"I do," I said, soaking in the heat from his body. He'd given up the stone. Handed it to a relative that was a bit more skilled in the art of protecting themselves. He stayed here sometimes. And we went about the business of being a couple tentatively. The girls liked him and he was good with them. Kind and caring. I still had an achy hole in my heart for Jameson's love. It would never totally go away, but I had grown a new space for Josh. And it was all his.

"Have fun shopping," he said and pulled away to kiss me on top of the head. I kissed his collarbone, his neck and then his mouth met mine. The sudden fire in my belly made me forget about the girls waiting in the car to go to school.

"Ahem." Andy's voice brought me back to reality. "Yeah," he started. "Hunky guy without your shirt on, go back to bed so my sister can stay on task today, would ya?" Josh chuckled at him.

"Yes, sir." He saluted and made an about-face. I watched him walk away, sneaking a peek at his fine backside, before I closed the door to the house and locked the deadbolt.

It was a new day. I stood on the porch and breathed deeply. The sky was clear blue, a few clouds flitting overhead. The forests of the Smoky Mountains rose under the sentinel watch of the snow-capped peaks. I knew amidst the trees creatures were getting along with life.

"You ready, sis?" Andy looked up at me where he paused halfway down the stairs.

"I am," I said. "I am ready."